T0395546

Praise for *No God in Durango*

"Robert Gleason's *NO GOD IN DURANGO* is a blistering ride across Mexico that mixes history, real-life characters, and a shattering tale of greed, corruption, and the machinations of war. Best of all, it's also a fascinating, devastating look at the one of the most daunting nihilist philosophers—Friedrich Nietzsche. Get ready for a no-holds-barred adventure like no other."

—James Rollins, #1 *New York Times* bestseling author of *Kingdom of Bones*

"What are a philosopher like Fredrich Neitzche and a historical figure like Otto von Bismark doing in a thriller, let alone one about Mexico? Well, I have five words for you: YOU HAVE TO FIND OUT! This is historical thriller writing at its absolute best, a knock-your-socks off ride down a path so twisted and so ferociously dangerous that, if you're anything like me, you will leap from page to page, jumping off one cliff after another as you go. This is a roaring river of thrills of a read."

—Whitley Strieber, the #1 *New York Times* bestselling author of *Communion* and *The Grays*

"From the first page, you are plunged into a swirling, turbulent, fast-flowing river of plots and plots within plots, of characters from history and characters spawned in a vivid imagination, of ideas and action and words, a torrent of words, from wisecracks to the wisdom of the ages, words about high falutin' ideals and low, base instincts, about the meaning of God and the best way to build an artillery piece… and so much more. It's a book you'll read quickly, because that's how the prose and plot and characters rush at you. And it's a book to think about afterward because there may be no god in Durango, but Gleason's characters go looking for him, if only to make sure that he's dead."

—William Martin, *New York Times* bestselling author of *The Lincoln Letter* and *December '41*.

"Surprised doesn't adequately describe my reaction to *No God in Durango.* More like "stunned." The characters are vivid, the action outrageous, but it's also fun and fast-moving. And lurking under the prose, I could see some serious scholarship. Using the historical characters to move the plot along provides plenty of surprises, but also provokes some deeper thoughts. The nonfiction Afterword was inspired."

—Larry Bond, *New York Times* bestelling author of *Red Phoenix* and *Cold Choices*

"As a novelist, Robert Gleason always leads his readers to a place beyond their expectations. But this time, with *No God In Durango*, Gleason has outdone himself. This irresistible novel spins world history into a viper-like coil that strikes with fangs of fury. The venom is brilliant writing, unforgettable images, ingenious dialogue, and wild bursts of violence. The author brings together Mexico's president, Germany's chancellor, a former Confederate general, a brilliant philosopher, various tycoons, a famous journalist and even the fugitive bank robber, Frank James. Where are they meeting? Durango's finest brothel, of course. What are they planning? A violent takeover of one of the world's richest gold mines, and that's just for starters. Driven by their lusts for power and lucre, these ruthless schemers intend to annihilate any force that attempts to stand in their way. Only one man has the guts and killing skills to shut down this international cartel: The author's famous antihero—The Outlaw, Torn Slater. Of course, Torn Slater will enlist the aid of the Wild West's most dangerous gun slingers: Wyatt Earp, Doc Holiday, Bat Masterson, and Belle Starr."

—Mike Blakely, Spur Award-winning author of *Short Grass Song*

"Amazing narrative command. Everything is strong: storytelling and characterization as well as pace and tempo. Technicolor and wide screen combined, remarkably researched, Jackson Cain has written both a thriller and a western."

—Richard Wheeler, winner of Western Writers' Lifetime Achievement Award and five other major awards

"This is the Wild West—as vividly recreated as has ever been done on the page or screen. Characters, action, detail, atmosphere, all are superbly rendered, giving the reader a breathtaking, can't-stop-now experience. Hits with the force of a Winchester '73 bullet and the kick of a wild horse. Very highly recommended!"

—Ralph Peters, *New York Times* bestselling author of *Judgement at Appomattox* and winner of three Boyd Awards and the Hammett Prize

"I'm beyond impressed. Every sentence is beautifully crafted and rich with authority and authenticity."

—Lucia St. Clair-Robson, winner of two Spur Awards

"William Johnstone and Louis L'Amour, there's a new gunslinger in town, and his name is Jackson Cain. More authentic than dirt and sagebrush, tougher than the James-Younger brothers and Custer's Seventh Cavalry combined, Cain book packs all the punch of a 100-caliber Gatling Gun and all the momentum than a downhill, runaway express train. Jackson Cain is the genuine article."

—David Hagberg, *New York Times* bestselling author of *Flash Points* and winner of five major book awards

"Forget about William Johnstone and Zane Grey, Longarm and Louis L'Amour, Jackson Cain can out-write them all. From Porfirio Diaz to Otto von Bismarck and Friedrich Nietzsche, from Belle Starr and Frank James to Wyatt Earp, Bat Masterson and Doc Holliday, *No God in Durango* has it all. Jackson Cain brings together a legendary cast of characters in unforgettable settings. His shootouts, high-stakes poker games, prison breaks and train heists hit home with pulse-pounding action and blood-curdling thrills. Never has the Wild West been wilder, more authentically rendered or its tales more entertainingly told!"

—Ward Larsen, *USA Today* bestselling author of *Assassin's Run* and winner of six major book awards

No God in Durango

An Outlaw Torn Slater Western

Jackson Cain

kensingtonbooks.com

KENSINGTON BOOKS are published by

Kensington Publishing Corp.
900 Third Avenue, 26th Floor
New York, NY 10022

ISBN-13: 978-1-4967-6243-6
ISBN-13: 978-0-7860-4630-0 (ebook)

The authorized representative in the EU for product safety and compliance
is eucomply OU, Parnu mnt 139b-14, Apt 123
Tallinn, Berlin 11317, hello@eucompliancepartner.com

152578809

"I am no man; I am dynamite."
—Friedrich Nietzsche, *Ecce Homo,* 1. "Why I Am a Destiny"

"I preach not contentedness, but more power; not peace, but war; not virtue, but efficiency. The weak and defective must go to the wall: that is the first principle....And we must help them go."

—Friedrich Nietzsche, *The Anti-Christ*, Section 2

"A good and healthy aristocracy must acquiesce, with a good conscience, in the sacrifice of a legion of individuals, who, for its benefit, must be reduced to slaves and tools. The masses have no right to exist on their own account: their sole excuse for living lies in their usefulness as a sort of superstructure or scaffolding, upon which a more select race of beings may be elevated."

—Friedrich Nietzsche, *Beyond Good and Evil*, Section 258

"Compassion drains strength....Suffering is made contagious by compassion....Compassion preserves whatever is ripe for destruction....It gives life itself a gloomy and dubious aspect. Humankind has ventured to call compassion a virtue....Compassion is the modus operandi of nihilism. Let me repeat: this depressing and contagious instinct stands against all those instincts which work for the preservation and enhancement of life: in the role of protector of the miserable, compassion is a prime agent of decadence—compassion persuades to extinction...."

—Friedrich Nietzsche, *The Antichrist*, Section 7

"Man should be educated for war, and women for the recreation of the warrior; all else is folly....You are going to women? Do not forget the whip."

— Friedrich Nietzsche, *Thus Spake Zarathustra:* Part I, Chapter 18, "On Little Old and Young Women"

"[T]here will be wars the likes of which have never been seen...."

—Friedrich Nietzsche, *Ecce Homo*

"...the arid desert, beyond all faith, where Nietzsche in his madness was staked...."

—Malcolm Braly, *False Starts: A Memoir of San Quentin and Other Prisons*

PART I

Bismarck hated that miserable pissoir of a nation known as Méjico. He thought the whole damn place ought to be cemented over.

CHAPTER 1

Torn Slater slowly leaned forward in bed and propped himself up against the five large satin pillows behind him. Esmeralda Emeliana Escobar—the most beautiful woman in all of Durango—was sitting beside him. Obsessed with his wanted poster, she was struggling fitfully to read it to him. Slater not only detested the poster, he was sick of hearing her read it out loud, and he'd finally torn up all her old ones. Those dodgers had been in Spanish, but she'd somehow located one in English, which she now read haltingly and badly. Grabbing a mezcal bottle off the bedside table, he helped himself to a long pull out of the neck.

He needed it.

He no longer cared how beautiful she was. It didn't matter to him that she had long luscious ebony hair, creamy-white skin, and a figure that made a pope want to blow out six stained-glass Vatican windows with a sawed-off, eight-gauge, double-barrel Greener. The damn *mujer* [woman] was driving him muy loco.

Tipping the bottle up, he took a hard strong pull and, to his dismay, instead of a long drink, he heard a rasping gurgle and found himself sucking air out of it. Staring into the bottle's opening, he found himself eyeball-to-eyeball with the mezcal worm. How *many* of those damn things had he stared at, shaken and then prized out of a bottle's neck and eaten?

A thousand?

Ten thousand?

He had no idea.

God, he needed another bottle of mezcal.

Still reading the damned wanted poster, Esmeralda was going on and on about its physical descriptions of Slater.

"Hey, amigo, can you help me with some of the words?"

She shoved the poster under his nose, grabbed him by the back of his head and forced him to read that part of the poster describing his...*scars.*

**BACK HEAVILY SCARIFIED WITH THE WIDE
WHITE STRIPES OF YUMA AND
SONORA PRISONS.
REST OF BODY—A MAZE OF MULTIPLE
BULLET AND KNIFE SCARS,
INCLUDING DIAGONAL
BAYONET SCAR TRAVERSING TORSO FROM
LEFT GROIN TO RIGHT ARMPIT.
PUCKERED BULLET
HOLE ENTERING BELOW LEFT
CLAVICLE, EXITING
ABOVE SHOULDER BLADES**

When Esmeralda was like this, there was nothing Slater could do but play along—and for some inexplicable reason, he found it difficult to say no to her. So he read it to her, but now she was less interested in the words than the physical stigmata themselves, scars that had disfigured his hard-used body for so many years now. As he read, she sensuously rubbed "the wide white stripes of Yuma and Sonora Prisons" adorning his back. She languidly luxuriated over "the diagonal bayonet scar traversing torso from left groin to right armpit." A red, mean, bitch of a scar, Slater had to admit it was disturbing. He sometimes glimpsed it in a hotel mirror, and it startled even him. The "puckered bullet hole entering below left clavicle, exiting above shoulder blades" also fascinated Esmeralda. Even now, she was pausing to kiss it.

"Here, amigo," Esmeralda said to him, pointing to the words on the poster, "read what it says here, por favor."

Slater read numbly in a monotone:

WANTED FOR TRAIN
ROBBERY, BANK ROBBERY,
HIJACKING OF ARMS AND TROOP SHIPMENTS,
ESCAPE FROM YUMA AND SONORA PRISONS
AND MANY COUNTS OF
MURDER–MOST–FOUL.

"That is muy malo," she said. Very bad.

"It ain't good," Slater conceded.

"And this picture here of you," she said, "it is very mean, very ugly. You look way better than that."

Slater did not know what to say to that one.

"And here—the re-ward"—Esmeralda placed the accent on the first syllable—"is $20,000. That is 80,000 pesos, no?"

Slater allowed that it was.

"Ey, that is muchos dineros." Her smile was now dazzling. "You must be a very important man that the governments of two countries will pay so much money for you."

Again, he had no idea how to respond, so he said nothing and looked away.

"But here is the part that bothers me, amigo. Here, read it, por favor."

Slater read aloud.

OUTLAW TORN SLATER:
WANTED IN 13 STATES AND
TERRITORIES AS WELL
AS THE STATES OF SONORA AND CHIHUAHUA

$20,000 REWARD
WANTED: DEAD

"Amigo, they say here that you are wanted in both America and madre Méjico. It says you are worth $20,000. But then they say you are 'wanted dead.' Does that mean that the two governments won't pay any dinero for you if you're brought in...*alive*?"

"Apparently," Slater had to admit.

"You must be muy important that they fear you so much," Esmeralda said, again rubbing the scars on his belly and chest.

Hija de la gran puta, Muerta, [daughter of the great whore, Death] the outlaw silently cursed. What Slater needed was another bottle of mezcal, eight hours' sleep, and then to get free of both Esmeralda and Durango.

But to do that he'd need to find someplace else, where he'd be safe from the law. Was it possible there was another city, town, country, world—someplace, somewhere, somehow—where he wasn't wanted? It didn't seem likely. Outlaw Torn Slater was wanted...*everywhere.* So far, the closest he'd come to some reasonable facsimile of safety was right here in Durango at El Placio de Plaser de Esmeralda. Otherwise known as "Esmeralda's Place of Pleasure." Durango was capital of the State of Durango and the most corrupt city in all of Méjico, which, being the most corrupt nation in the western hemisphere, was no small feat. If Slater could not purchase protection here in Durango, he could not purchase it anywhere. So far, he was relatively safe in this city, and he had to admit, Esmeralda was no small part of that protection package. He'd been inexplicably close to her sister—a nun, no less—and, once, after she'd gotten him out of a very bad jam, he'd promised her that he would track down her sister, Esmeralda, and help her. One thing led to another, and before he knew it, Esmeralda claimed to have fallen in love with the outlaw—something Slater seriously doubted.

Still, she had given him a place to lay low and was providing him with more protection—and even affection—than he was used to.

But he didn't know how much longer he could take it.

Raising his voice, he thundered to nobody in particular, "Anyone got another bottle of mezcal? How else am I supposed to wash down this goddamn worm?"

"I'll find you one," Esmeralda said.

Esmeralda was starting to get out of bed, when one of her women employees hammered furiously on the bedroom door, then burst into the room. Dressed in a short white dress, she was stammering:

"Senorita, Senor Slater, we got six Sinaloan hombres malos trying to drag our mujers out of one of the rooms. You got to stop them."

Esmeralda turned and stared at Slater, deadly serious. The men were threatening her women, meaning her livelihood, and in Esmeralda's world, money trumped everything else, every time, all the time.

Torn Slater was the one who was now climbing out of bed.

He had business to take care of.

Part of him felt as if he'd been saved by the bell.

CHAPTER 2

Friedrich Nietzsche—professor, philosopher, and distinguished litterateur—sat, barefoot, on his bed in his white cotton nightshirt. He wasn't pleased to be staying in a Durango brothel.

Nietzsche didn't care how superior it was to the other Durango hotels, which was what Porfirio Diaz's majordomo had boasted to him. Nor did Nietzsche appreciate it when the man told him he "could have any puta in the casa free and gratis—a gift from our esteemed generalissimo!" What kind of a man did that idiot think he was?

The thought of his offer made Nietzsche's blood boil.

But, on the other hand, why should Durango be different? Everything about this horrendous country boiled his blood until it bubbled in his veins like seething, smoking, molten lava.

Nor was Diaz the only man Nietzsche was pissed at. His friend and mentor—the great, globally celebrated composer, Richard Wagner—had talked him into visiting Méjico, practically coercing him into making the voyage; and in retrospect, Wagner's hounding him to make the trip was something he might never forgive him for. That high-pressure campaign was causing Nietzsche to reconsider his entire relationship with the legendary artiste.

Nietzsche was sorry he'd ever heard of Méjico. Investigating all those haciendas had easily been the worst experience of his life.

* * *

The ship had docked two months ago, and he had disembarked in Veracruz. He was then unceremoniously taken on a Cook's tour of a dozen of Méjico's largest and most lucrative agricultural and mining operations. Each one contained hundreds of thousands of acres of sugar, cotton, sisal—otherwise known as hemp—crops with highly profitable export potential, as well as mountainous quantities of valuable gold, silver, and copper ore.

Nietzsche had quickly recognized that Diaz was so focused on piling up export revenue that he was blindly oblivious to the nutritional needs of his people. In Méjico, 90 percent of arable land was in the hands of foreign plutocrats, and their plantations produced almost no corn or beans or wheat or rice. Méjicano merchants had to import those foodstuffs at vertiginously high prices and then pass those costs onto Méjico's famished and impecunious citizenry.

But it wasn't just the cynicism of Diaz's economic strategy that infuriated Nietzsche, it was Diaz's treatment of his workers. In Méjico, workers—in fact, 90 percent of the population—weren't workers at all but de facto slaves. Diaz constantly replenished and expanded his stock of forced laborers by brutally abducting all the drunks, criminals, or impoverished slum-dwellers that his huge armies of bounty hunters could lay their hands on. It was all done very efficiently. Their victims were too indigent, ignorant, or illiterate to hire lawyers and protest. And since Diaz's hacendados kept their peons incommunicado and incognito, friends and relatives never knew where their loved ones were imprisoned.

But every hell has some antechamber even more terrifying—a compartment of horrors more hideous than anything else that underworld has to offer. In Méjico, Nietzsche thought that country's slave-labor mines had clear claim to that noxious honor. They indubitably served as Méjico's bottommost pit—a nethermost circle of hell that Dante in his most diabolic nightmares could never have conjured up.

In his whole life, Friedrich Wilhelm Nietzsche had never imagined—let alone seen—men and women living and laboring under such vile conditions. Méjico was a world in which floggings were continuous, rapes routine, and starvation pandemic. During the two months in which he'd visited those haciendas, he had never seen a peon smile—let alone laugh or sing or dance. They appeared to the young man as misery incarnate.

* * *

Nietzsche swung his legs off the bed and began getting dressed. Today, he would be meeting the Iron Chancellor, Otto Eduard Leopold von Bismarck, at breakfast for the first time. He'd already dropped his reports off with the chancellor's executive assistant, whom he now understood was deathly ill with dysentery. His heart went out to the man, but he also hoped he'd gotten his reports to the chancellor before he'd become stricken. Nietzsche was curious how the great man would respond to his observations and analysis. He fervently hoped that Bismarck would read his dispatches, agree, and say:

"Friedrich, let's leave this godforsaken place *now*—on the first thing displacing water. I want to get the hell out of Méjico, mucho pronto, and never look back."

Gott im Himmel, how Nietzsche hated Méjico.

Almost as much as he now hated Richard Wagner. What in hell's name had ever possessed that august composer to tell him he had to go to Méjico, that it was "the opportunity of a lifetime" and that it would "change your life forever"? He had even said, "Its climate will improve your health."

He couldn't believe Wagner—the man whom Nietzsche had previously admired more than any other individual in the world—had sweet-talked and browbeaten him into this horrific descent into hell's abyss.

He swore on his father's grave he'd make Wagner suffer—just as he, Friedrich Wilhelm Nietzsche, was suffering at this very moment.

He'd thought Wagner was his friend.

He swore he'd make the man pay, if it was the last thing he'd ever do.

CHAPTER 3

Outlaw Torn Slater left his room in a hurry—with Esmeralda hounding him every step of the way. The brothel madam had not even allowed him time to get dressed. Walking up the hallway, he was still buttoning up his shirt and pants, strapping and buckling his gun belt around his waist, inserting a blackjack and a second .44 into his waistband, slipping a throwing knife up one shirt sleeve, an over-and-under .38-caliber derringer under the other. He didn't have time to check his loads or double-check the back sheath for his Arkansas toothpick.

From down the hall and around the corner, he could hear the screaming and screeching of putas and the banging of beds and chairs on floors and walls. If these Sinaloa pimps were in the business of kidnapping putas, they weren't very good at it. The whores sounded like they were putting up one hell of a fight.

Turning the corner, Slater saw the room where the men and prostitutes were fighting. The door was open. He walked up to it and sneaked a quick look inside. He counted six men in charro attire—short tight black jackets with matching pants, boots, and narrow-brimmed chaluba hats, white shirts and currata wrist quirts. At least two men were pummeling the putas with their fists. One bandito had dragged a mujer onto a bed; another had his victim jammed up against a wall, her dress down around her knees, as they clumsily attempted to rape them. One of them was braining a puta with his pistol butt. The whore went down in mid-yell like she'd been shot, not slugged.

The banditos outnumbered Slater six to one, which weren't great odds, and he did not want to give them time to use the women as shields. Since this was a situation that would never see the inside of a courtroom, there was no point in nuanced subtleties or fine distinctions. Cocking both his Colts, he entered the room...guns blazing.

He dropped all six men with seven rounds in less than five seconds, all seven shots coalescing into one protracted blast. The room, still ringing with the echoing roar of seven rapidly fired gunshots, was filled with whitish black-powder smoke. The smell and taste of the air was acridly sulfurous. Through the haze he could make out the men—all of them trapped in the repulsive repose of awkward, ugly, untimely...*death.* One man lay belly down over a chair, the top half of his head blown away. Another was propped up, back against the wall, clutching a massive bleeding-sucking-pulsating hole in his throat, his lips mouthing mute curses, the light in his eyes fading, dimming, then vanishing entirely, after which all the curses ceased. His chin fell heavily, angularly against his right clavicle. Another man was sprawled on the floor, face up, his twitching arms and legs at full spread-eagle, surrounded by a rapidly expanding pool of his own blood. A fourth had been trying to escape Slater's fusillade through the window, when he caught a round in the chest. Walking up to it and looking out, Slater saw him lying face down in the street. The four-story fall had broken his neck, and his head was now skewed at a grotesque angle. In his back was an exit hole almost big enough for Robert E. Lee to march the Army of Virginia through. Bandits number five and six had been the erstwhile rapists, their boots and shirts still on, their pants down around their knees. Well, their raping days were over. They had died instantly in mid-ravishment—one next to the wall, the other still on the now blood-befouled bed.

Well, that's one form of coitus interruptus, Slater thought bleakly.

CHAPTER 4

Otto von Bismarck, the chancellor of Germany, had only spent a week in Méjico, but that was enough for him to utterly loathe it. He especially hated Durango and, most of all, he detested his present living quarters. He didn't care if the place possessed "the most luxurious accommodations in 'the State and City of Durango,'" as Diaz's majordomo had informed him.

Bismarck was still living in a brothel-casino.

Wasn't Bismarck the man who, in 1870, had steamrolled over the French Army, had captured their leader, Napoleon III, at Sedan, had laid siege to Paris, conquered that country, and then annexed Alsace-Lorraine? In fact, he'd done far more than that. During the war, he had, through sheer force of personal will, united all thirty-nine disparate, intransigent, quarreling German states into a single cohesive nation. During the last fifteen years, he had even performed a genuine economic miracle. He had transformed his newly created, utterly agrarian homeland into the most overwhelmingly industrialized powerhouse in all the world, rivaled only by the United States of America.

He wasn't called the Iron Chancellor for nothing.

So what was he doing in a hellhole like Durango, Mexico, staying in a casa de puta, where the finest cuisine was rawhide-tough steak with sides of frijoles-and-tortillas—all of it smothered in scorchingly hot chili peppers, washed down with copious quantities of beer and tequila?

And why was he serenaded to sleep at night by the ululations of fornicating whores and their rutting, howling hombres?

Why was Bismarck sleeping in...*a fucking bordello?*

Because he had allowed his emperor, Wilhelm I, to talk him into this preposterous trip on behalf of Alfred Krupp—owner of the biggest arms and steel works on the continent—where he, assisted by Otto von Bismarck, was to put together "the biggest arms deal in history."

Bismarck could still remember that night at the palace when Kaiser Wilhelm had plied him with Napoleon "Year of the Comet" cognac, Chateau Lafite champagne, and St. Petersburg's best Beluga caviar. Wilhelm had then offered Bismarck the most glorious gift of his career in government: He promised him an arms package that would make the Reich's military pre-eminent throughout Europe for the rest of the century and it would not cost the Reichstag and the German voters a single solitary Reichsmark.

* * *

"The Kruppwerk has struck a spectacular arms deal with Mexico," the Kaiser had drunkenly enthused. "Those odious Méjicano imbeciles are so backward, they are only one generation away from sacrificing their sons on pyramid altars and hurling their virginal daughters into blazing volcanoes. They're only two generations out of the trees! They know nothing about sophisticated arms transactions. Alfred Krupp assures me he can charge them…anything. He will make so much money off that moron, Diaz, that he will be able to charge an exorbitant percentage of our future arms bills against Diaz's. I've seen his contracts with Diaz and run through the numbers with the old man, and they really work. It's the deal of a lifetime for him—and for Germany."

"Und was ist der Fang?" Bismarck asked. What's the catch?

"Diaz insists that the deal has to be made el Presidente to el Presidente—between Generalissimo Diaz and our own Grand Chancellor."

The Kaiser quickly refilled Bismarck's cognac glass to the brim and topped off his own beer stein.

* * *

How had he ever allowed himself to be railroaded? Bismarck prided himself on his ability to pull the wool over the Kaiser's eyes, bluff him when necessary, but to always bend the emperor to his own iron will.

So what had happened?

Sitting up in bed, he stared at the notebooks strewn across it. The Kaiser had sent a young man named Friedrich Nietzsche ahead of them to explore economic opportunities in Mexico, and he'd surveyed some potentially lucrative hacienda deals on Wilhelm's behalf. Germany could conceivably walk away with millions of acres of prime farmland, which were also covered with mountains rich in invaluable mineral deposits—iron, copper, coal, silver, even gold. Diaz even offered the services of his mestizo workers, men and women who in Méjico were known as peons.

"Free, gratis, no remuneration necessary," Diaz had told Krupp.

Bismarck didn't completely grasp the labor situation here in Méjico, but Diaz had assured Krupp that Méjico's hacendados did not have to pay their laborers a single peso. Bismarck had no reason to doubt him, but, frankly, he did not see how businessmen in Méjico could get away with paying their employees...*nada.*

He assumed that the Méjicano strongman would explain all that when he met him later this morning.

Bismarck stared at the papers in front of him. Such transactions bored him to tears. One good thing was that the young man who had written these reports was an amazingly good writer. Bismarck himself was much lauded for his own literary ability and could recognize writing talent in others.

Friedrich Wilhelm Nietzsche really knew how to turn a phrase.

CHAPTER 5

Two of the whores—now covered with bandito blood—were slipping out from under the inert bodies of their rapists. Relieved to be alive and rescued, they were grinning and laughing giddily.

They were not alone in their elation. All six of them, in fact, were delirious with gratitude and relief. They swarmed Slater, sobbing, hugging and kissing him. Cries of "Eres mucho hombre" [You are much man] and "muy macho" filled the room along with rousing choruses of "Muchas gracias! Muchas gracias! Muchas gracias! Muchas gracias!" In fact, three of them were trying to force him into one of the two beds right there in front of God and everyone—with the bodies of six men, bleeding out on the bedroom floor, and not even cold. They were unbuckling his belt, unbuttoning his shirt, yanking off his boots, pulling down his pants and trying to kiss him all at the same time.

Slater hadn't gotten a look at them before but now saw that they were surprisingly good-looking—and young. They all had long, lush tresses, black and shiny as obsidian. Their eyes were moist, demure yet lascivious. And most of all imploring—thankful that he'd saved them from a fate worse than death and overwhelmed by the ecstasy of their sudden, unexpected salvation.

Now all six were all over him like water moccasins, coiling themselves around a drowning man.

At that very moment, however, Esmeralda, the establishment's proprietress, burst through the door, thundering at the top of her lungs:

"I leave you alone for five minutes, and you're in bed with every puta *in la casa entera*?" [in the whole house]

Dragging the putas off Slater one by one, however, she could not help but notice the desperate urgency of his need.

"On the other hand, this could be an instructive, teachable moment for all of you," she said, nervously clearing her throat.

At which point, Esmeralda Emeliana Escobar threw herself on top of the outlaw with heedless, reckless, unthinking...*abandon.*

And the other six mujers leaped on top of them both, laughing happily and giggling giddily.

CHAPTER 6

The screams down the hall had seriously upset Friedrich Nietzsche, but the rapid sequence of gunshots had almost scared him out of his wits. They were then followed by more unnerving screeches and shrieks, which were then followed by a chorus of sobbing howls that sounded more ecstatic than horrific. Lord only knew what caused those inhuman, ungodly wails.

Whatever the case, Nietzsche knew he had to do something. People could be wounded and exsanguinating, nor would it be the first time he'd witnessed such atrocities. His mind wandered back to his days in the German military…

* * *

…Friedrich Nietzsche had served in the German Army in 1867 during Bismarck's struggle to unite the Northern German States. Serving in an equestrian artillery regiment near Naumburg, twenty-three-year-old Friedrich had sustained a serious chest wound early on and had missed most of that war. In 1870, however, he had joined up again—this time serving as a hospital orderly. He'd witnessed the effects of war, up close and personal, in those wards. Furthermore, he knew how to treat gunshot wounds. He knew, for example, that if he could simply get tourniquets on the victims' shot-up limbs, the chances of them not bleeding to death mounted exponentially. He knew when to treat people propped up and when to treat them lying down. Nietzsche had ministered to countless hemorrhaging German soldiers.

* * *

One thing Nietzsche knew for sure: He had to do...*something.* His honor demanded it. He had to go down the hall immediately. Still barefoot and in his nightshirt, he left his room and jogged down the hall. The shrill screams had now morphed into ululating howls and growling moans, and he increased his pace.

When he reached the room, the door was closed, but the unearthly groans and shrieks combined with the stench of gun smoke left no doubt in Nietzsche's mind that something horrifying was occurring on the other side of that door.

Turning the knob, he stealthily eased the door open.

The first thing that caught his eye was the five deceased banditos. Nietzsche had seen dead men many times, and these five were now definitively dead, deader than dead, as dead as they would ever be. No respecter of propriety, Death had taken all of them as it found them—without warning and with shocking suddenness. Indifferent to appearances or personal dignity, Death did not care about the unsightliness of the men's posthumous remains. Several lay on the floor; one was propped up against a wall; another was bent over a chair; two were flopped on a bed.

But then—almost against his will—his eyes fixed on another sight. There, on one bloodied bed, in front of God, the devil, and the bleeding-out, murdered hombres, one naked, spread-eagled man, flat on his back, was being sexually assaulted by what appeared to be seven lust-crazed harpies. One was straddling him, her head thrown back, her eyes rolled all the way into the back of her head till only the whites showed. She was muttering low, slow curses. The only one he could divine was "*hijo de la grand puta, Muerta*" [son of the old whore, Death] All the while, her body convulsed and shook with the paroxysms of unconstrained desire.

Then there were the other six women. They were on the supine man like hyenas on a kill, plundering every part of him that they could.

Thankfully, the man appeared to have passed out.

Having partaken of an eclectic education, Friedrich Nietzsche had once perused the Sir Richard Burton translation of *One Thousand and One Arabian Nights,* which had tintinnabulated with erotic extravaganzas of every size, shape, gender and dimension. He'd also read the ancient Hindu text called

The Kama Sutra, in which every form and combination of sexual connection known to God and el Diabolo were alleged to appear. Nothing, however, in any of those two works combined could top what was appearing to him right now, right before his eyes on that bed. It was as if every sex act in *One Thousand and One Arabian Nights* and *The Kama Sutra* was being perpetrated right there before Nietzsche's eyes, all at the same time, on that single man by the seven deranged women on that solitary brothel bed.

Well, Nietzsche was supposed to do something, but what? The murdered men were past praying for. They needed a priest, not his medical attention. As for the women and the man on that bed—

Suddenly, the man seemed to come to. Turning his head, he caught Nietzsche's eye—Nietzsche, who stood there unarmed, without shoes or slippers, and in his nightshirt. The man's gaze was neither forbidding nor unfriendly, but, still, nonetheless, the young man found himself looking into the hardest, flattest, blackest eyes he'd ever seen in his entire life.

Nietzsche then noticed that the man still held on to both cocked pistols in his large outflung fists.

Nietzsche could only shake his head in shock and dismay. He still could not credit what he was seeing.

Why was he in Méjico?

What he was witnessing was more than his wits could process. It was beyond anything he'd ever heard of. He would try to forget what he'd seen. It transcended wickedness and depredation and depravity. It was transgression beyond transgression beyond transgression.

Here, in Méjico, Nietzsche was encountering sin of an entirely different order.

Turning around, he headed back to his room as quickly as he could move his legs.

CHAPTER 7

One man did not attempt to investigate the gunshots and screams. That man was Otto von Bismarck, Iron Chancellor and Father of the New German State. He was a man made of sterner stuff.

Or so he had once thought.

Poring over Friedrich Nietzsche's prolific reports on the slave-labor mines and plantation-hellholes of Méjico, he was shocked to the point of stupefaction. Those Sinaloan pimps could have fired an 88mm howitzer next to his desk and he wouldn't have heard it. Nietzsche's reports electrified—even terrified—him. His descriptions of Méjicano slavery were worse than anything Bismarck had ever read. The country pretended slavery didn't exist. Mexico claimed to have outlawed slavery in 1829, but that law was a joke. The slave drivers concealed their ownership of the peons behind such euphemisms as "forced service," "contract labor," and "debt peonage." And since the hacendados owned the judges—the entire legal system, for that matter—the law looked the other way, even when the overseers beat and worked their peons to death.

Bismarck had never heard of anything like the horrors of Diaz's forced-labor hacendado system. The owners often worked their chattels to death out of sheer spite.

* * *

Nor was escape a viable option. If they ran off, the populace invariably informed on them for the price on their heads or out of fear that, if they did not inform on the escaped slaves, they could be accused later on of abetting the escape.

In that case they would be summarily incarcerated in prison mines or forced-labor plantations.

Nor was living off the land an option for runaway slaves. Mexico was too destitute, food too scarce. Observers reported that the escapados were almost invariably caught, after which they faced unendurable floggings and starvation rations. Consequently, only the most recklessly brave or desperately foolhardy attempted escape.

Chastisement of slaves was universal. The goal was to—always, continually—force more labor out of them. Their overseers called out individual slaves and ordered daily whippings, which they call "cleanups." The slaves, who were, thus, singled out, received them during the morning and evening roll call. They were also administered during the day, usually after the overseers accused a slave of not working hard enough. The overseers had the prisoners beaten with canes or with knotted hemp ropes, soaked in brine.

The owners habitually starved their peons. Chronic hunger tended to fatigue the slaves, making them more malleable. The overseers also believed hunger forced their slaves to work harder in the hope of obtaining additional rations—or out of the fear that their rations might be cut even further. And, of course, the less money the owners spent feeding the slaves, the more profit they realized.

* * *

Bismarck had studied the American Civil War and was familiar with that country's slavery system. He knew that the South had treated its slaves cruelly—especially after 1840. At that time, the English—and then the New England's manufacturers—had perfected their steam-driven spinning mills. Cotton could then be fabricated, quickly, in industrial quantities and transported in steamships worldwide. The price of raw cotton soared. Southern plantation owners bought every slave that could show a pulse, draw a breath, and perambulate, then worked them mercilessly, wringing every red cent imaginable out of them, flogging those whom they even suspected of indolence.

Still, the Southerners did not routinely beat, starve, and work their chattel to death in the same way the Méjicano overseers did. The South's slaves were worth too much money and were too expensive to replace. Méjicano slaves, on the other hand, were worth almost nothing. If one died, the slaveowners could replace him or her for next to...*nada.* They had the entire population of Méjico from which they could conscript their peons. They simply had bounty hunters dragoon criminals, drunks, the helplessly destitute, or the merely unlucky into slavery. As slaves, they were kept incommunicado and incognito, so relatives could not find them. The slaves themselves were too poor and illiterate to mount legal defenses. The hacendados owned both their laborers and the magistrates, who, therefore, asked no pesky questions.

The Méjicano slaveowners usually enslaved the families together—not out of any altruism. They'd found that the husbands were less likely to run away if it meant leaving their families behind to fend for themselves and suffer retribution for the man's escape. The owners viewed the wives and children not as cherished family members but...*hostages to fortune.*

Such was Diaz's Méjico.

Such was the country the Kaiser and Alfred Krupp had decided to arm to the teeth with the most advanced, most lethal ordnance in human history.

Over my dead body, Bismarck thought angrily.

Which could become a reality quicker than he'd previously thought, if he didn't watch his step and cover his tracks. He and Nietzsche were on their own down here. It had occurred to Bismarck, more than once, that the two of them might not survive this expedition. What had started out as a very ingenious swindle of a Méjicano tyrant could well result in their own agonizing demise. What would stop Diaz from installing them in one of his slave-labor hell-mines or one of his hacienda infernos? Diaz could crush them like insects any time he chose and tell the Kaiser they had died in surgery, under rockslides or fornicating in one of Méjico's innumerable hard-trade sporting houses. He could tell the Kaiser any stupid story he wanted and who would refute it back here in Méjico?

No one.

They had to play along with the maniac, biding their time until they could escape.

Bismarck hated that miserable pissoir of a nation known as Méjico. He thought the whole goddamn place ought to be cemented over. He wanted to go back to Germany so bad he could taste it.

CHAPTER 8

The screams and the gunshots hadn't bothered Frank James one bit. For one thing, he'd been sleeping on the other side of the massive brothel/gambling hall, and anyway, after a lifetime of war and guerilla conflicts, Frank James was inured to gunfire. Also he was in Durango. Gunshots rang through the city every hour of the day and night. Violence here was ubiquitously incessant—in the blood, a way of life.

What had tormented Frank's sleep wasn't gunshots or putas' screams but nightmares. Ever since Bob Ford had shot his brother in the back—while Jess was standing on a chair and adjusting a framed picture—he hadn't had a decent night's sleep. And down here in Durango, he needed his sleep. He couldn't afford to be fatigued. He needed all his wits. So he'd taken laudanum the night before.

He had another reason to drug himself. He was joining that fanatic General Joseph "Jo" Shelby and that lunatic adjutant of his, the newspaper editor, John Newman Edwards. The three of them were to strategize their evening dinner with Porfirio Diaz. That meeting would determine how they lived out the rest of their lives—wealthy as Croesus, owning and running vast Méjicano haciendas; or as hunted desperados, perpetually on the run—either dead or doing time.

Frank wished Edwards wasn't with them. Edwards had written countless articles extolling Frank and Jess as "heroes of the Lost Confederate Cause" and had made Frank and his brother the two most famous, most notorious, most hunted men in America. He'd shouted at Edwards many times that "fame for an outlaw is just a complicated way of committing suicide," but Edwards wouldn't listen. He'd just say to Frank:

"Why can't you be more like Jess? Jess loves the fame, the notoriety, being the center of national—hell, global!—attention. Frank, you know what Jess did the other day? He wrote Governor Crittenden and told him he'd had enough of the governor's attacks, of him offering rewards for the capture of you two, dead or alive. He told the governor that now he, Jesse James, was coming after him. He'd wreck a train, if he had to, to catch him. That he was 'cutting out Crittenden's heart, carving it up into strips, then smoking and eating it like country-cured bacon.'"

Edwards had a point about Jess. His brother loved the attention, begged Edwards for more headlines, more newspaper and magazine pieces, more controversy, more rage, more praise, praise, praise. Jesse's ego was unappeasable, and Jess could not stop telling Edwards how much he loved everything the man wrote.

In the end, Frank believed Edwards's inflammatory articles and Jesse's omnivorous vanity got him killed.

He felt himself dozing off. Again, he was dreaming of Missouri, this time of his childhood.

* * *

He dreamed of his father's distant death in the California goldfields, where he claimed he was going to make the family "richer than God." All that that gold-mining had gotten the old man was...dead. Furthermore, his death only seemed to make their mother, Zerelda, who, on her best days, had an uncontrollable temper, even angrier. After the memorial service and the church supper, as soon as they reached home, their mother took the horsewhip down from the hall hook and thrashed Jess and himself within an inch of their lives for no reason either of them could ever ascertain. He could not say whom his mother whipped worse that evening—himself, Jess, or the slaves—but that night after the memorial service, Frank was especially sorry for the slaves. They hadn't even been at the service. They had done nothing wrong. Nor had he or Jess.

When Zerelda was in one of her rages, they were all just something between the dark and the light.

Something to...whip.

Damn, she was one vicious bitch.

After that evening, the floggings would become routine. Hardly a day or night went by when she wasn't reaching for the horsewhip and flogging her sons like rented mules.

Maybe, Frank wondered idly, it was Ma and her horsewhip or those peach switches of hers that turned Jess so goddamn mean.

* * *

Slowly, as Frank awoke from his violent revery, his mind drifted to Shakespeare, who, Frank believed, always had the last word on everything. From Frank's point of view, the Sweet Swan of Avon was the world's premier poet of tragedy and death. Frank believed *Hamlet* was the wisest work he'd ever read, but *Macbeth* often seemed to hit closer to home, when it came to summing up his and Jesse's savagely murderous lives.

And the butcher's bill was now coming due. Part of it was paid when their gang was shot to pieces outside of Northfield. He and Jess escaped on horseback, and Cole Younger survived to face life in prison. But then, just a few months ago, Bob Ford murdered Jess, and now he, Frank, was down here stuck in that hell on earth called Méjico. He knew in his soul he should just get it over with, save the gods the trouble of arranging his despicable end, do the world a favor, and blow his own brains out. Macbeth contemplated the same inescapable fate under very similar circumstances. The accuracy with which Shakespeare elucidated the truth of Frank's life froze Frank James to his core. As Macbeth had said about a similar cold-blooded killing-for-profit that Macbeth was about to undertake:

> **If it were done when 'tis done, then 'twere well**
> **It were done quickly: if the assassination**
> **Could trammel up the consequence…**
> **that but this blow**
> **Might be the be–all and the end–all here,**
> **But here, upon this bank and shoal of time,**
> **We'd jump the life to come. But in these cases**
> **We still have judgment here; that we but teach**
> **Bloody instructions, which, being taught, return**

To plague the inventor: this even–handed justice
Commends the ingredients of our poison'd chalice
To our own lips.

However, like Macbeth and Hamlet before him, Frank lacked the nerve. He couldn't do the Dutch. He couldn't count the number of times he'd put a Colt to his temple. Still, he'd never done it. He hadn't had the nerve to pull the trigger—still didn't have it—and lacked that faith that he'd "jump the life to come."

CHAPTER 9

Friedrich Nietzsche put down his journal. He'd just finished entering his depiction of what he'd seen in that room. More visual details were coming back to him. One of the whores had been kissing the man passionately—almost furiously—when another puta pulled her away. Before the other woman could take her place, Nietzsche had seen the man open his eyes. Glancing around the room, the man's gaze had met his. The man's look was utterly expressionless.

That was Nietzsche's problem.

He did not know how to describe those orbs. Once in the Great Sonoran Desert, he had come upon a diamondback resting on a boulder. Its wedge-shaped head was levitating languidly above its coiled body, its tongue flicking in and out of its body, its rattles buzzing. Most of all, however, what had gotten to Nietzsche had been its eyes—eyes like the stranger's, except instead of ebony orbs, the diamondback's were dominated by amber-yellow, vertically distended pupils. Otherwise, they connoted the same qualities as the man's: They were completely inhuman, almost in-animal. He was staring into eyes that had diced at the foot of the cross, prevailed in countless gladiatorial matches in Rome's arena and slogged the long trek home from every war ever since—from Tours to Agincourt to Waterloo to Antietam, eyes that knew they had nothing left to lose and nothing left to love.

Ever since coming to Méjico, Nietzsche had heard stories of the legendary gringo bandito known as "Outlaw Torn Slater." He was told the man was wanted in all of Méjico and thirteen American states and territories "for every crime known to God, el Diabolo, and man." He'd seen wanted posters describing his physical characteristics—including the bullet and bayonet scars on his face and torso.

It was said he "wore the wide white stripes of Yuma and Sonora Prisons on his back."

When Nietzsche had pointed to the wanted poster and suggested to one of his companions that Slater seemed to have gone through a lot, his compadre responded:

"He is a man not unacquainted with violence."

Indeed.

Nietzsche had never seen a photo of Slater and did not know if any existed, but he'd seen his unflattering likeness drawn on countless wanted posters ever since. The words on the poster read:

80,000 pesos
Se buscan meurtos

In other words: "Wanted Dead."

Slater was so dangerous that bringing him in alive in the United States was no longer a remunerative option.

Nor did Diaz want Outlaw Torn Slater living, breathing, and languishing in prison. Diaz now wanted Slater belly-down over a saddle. Bringing him back alive was worth...*nada.*

Slater was arguably the most dangerous man Nietzsche had ever heard of.

He also knew in his soul that Slater was the man who'd killed those six bandito pimps who'd been trying to kidnap the whores, and that, afterward, Slater had fornicated with every one of the women.

All at once.

What kind of man was this Outlaw Torn Slater? He was like no man Nietzsche had ever heard of.

He wondered if he would meet him again.

PART II

"We'd have been bigger than Halley's Comet, richer than the Golconda and more famous than... *God!*"

—James Sutherland

CHAPTER 1

Decked out in a gray linen, knee-length duster and a black, flat-crowned, broad-brimmed Plainsman hat, Slater was wearing his traveling clothes. For good reason. He'd stayed too long at the dance and was getting ready to leave Durango.

Standing on one of the cantina balconies, he surveyed the huge, sprawling room below—perhaps for the last time. Leaning over the black iron railing, he studied the scores of gaming tables covered with green baize, listened absently to the slap of the pasteboards, the patter of the dealers, clad in white shirts with black elbow garters, calling out—"*rey y la reina*" [queen and a king], "*deuce en un tres*" [two on a three], "*repartidor's juego*" [dealer's game] and "*la apertura es de cinco pesos*" [the ante's five pesos]. Taking in the clicking and ratcheting roulette wheels, he casually noted the rattle of the dice, the profanity and the shouts of joy, the banter and supplications of the whores, all the smells too...beer, tequila, tobacco and the cloying scent of the putas' perfume. He also studied the women in their too-tight clothes, their black net stockings and ebony, heeled boots, the wide sashaying swing of their hips as they hustled drinks from table to table, occasionally putting down a tray to escort a customer into one of the curtained-off bolt-holes along the walls or leading him onto the steps and toward the upstairs cribs. Six stories of rooms surrounded the gambling hall on all sides. Whores—whose upper bodies draped over the railings above—ogled the action below, sometimes shouting and gesticulating to individual customers and inviting them to meet them upstairs.

It was Slater's kind of place—he had to admit it.

The mariachi band was excellent. Slater especially liked the music, and he'd miss it, if he left Durango that night. In a corner, the musicians played all the great Méjicano songs—"Dormir Contigo," "Te Desean," "Corrido," "La Incondicional," "Terco Corazón," "Mio," "El Son de la Negra," "La Cárcel de Cananea," "Algo Tienes," "Vive el Verano," and "Te Amo." The band included a trumpet, an accordion, a violin, a high-pitched, round-backed vihuela guitar and its big, bulky, bass counterpart, a guitarrón. It was currently playing "La Paloma," which a mujer was singing. A song of farewell, Slater liked it very much. That his life was one of constant farewells was a fact not lost on him. The gambling hall boasted a sizable dance floor, and since Durango's main fort was just outside of the city, a quarter of the clientele were soldiers in gray uniforms. A dozen or more cavalry officers were sporting brown, roweled riding boots, which clinked on the wood floor when they walked and more loudly when they danced. The other half of the dancers were civilians. White cotton shirts and faded Levis were popular among the civilian men, white cotton dresses among the women. Since El Placio de Plaser de Esmeralda was an upscale establishment, even the putas dressed in white.

Fluent in Spanish, Slater understood the lyrics and absently took them in:

Cuando salí de la Durango,
¡Válgame Dios!
Nadie me ha visto salir
Si no fuí yo.

Y una linda Guachinanga
Allá voy yo,
Que se vino trás de mi,
Que si, señor.

Si a tu ventana llega
Una paloma,
Trátala con cariño
Que es mi persona.

Cuéntala tus amores,
Bien de mi vida,
Corónala de flores
Que es cosa mía.

Ay, chinita que sí,
Ay, que darme tu amor
Ay, que vente conmigo,
Chinita, a donde vivo yo.

The singer then warbled the ballad in English for the big-spending, hard-living gringos in the crowd, who were currently down Méjico way, debauching their bodies, squandering their money, and losing their souls in Durango's most lecherously treacherous fleshpots:

Tonight, as the moon rises silver above the sea,
I long for the harbor where you wait for me,
Do you, for I know you sorrow when we're apart,
I wish I could send a messenger from my heart.

Then you may find a dove waiting at your window,
Singing a song of love to you at your window,
Let it come in and there as it flies above you,
Know that its heart is mine and it sings I love you.

Let your sorrow take wings,
Let your heart ever sing love,
As you cherish the memory of our love,
That a dove may bring.

Then you may find a dove waiting at your window,
Singing a song of love to you at your window,
Let it come in and there as it flies above you,
Know that its heart is mine and it sings I love you.

Slater slowly surveyed the customers at the gaming tables. They were mostly men, the only women being the ever-smiling, ever-attractive, ever-enticing putas. Men clearly did not bring their wives and fiancées to places like El Placio de Plaser de Esmeralda.

The staircases connecting the balcony bedrooms with the floor below teemed with hombres and whores. Again, Slater looked to the balconies and studied the countless putas, leaning out over the black iron railings, occasionally draping a black-stockinged leg and high-heeled boot over the railing. It occurred to Slater that he'd never seen so much commodious decolletage and so many disconcerting derrieres in his life.

Slater's eyes then returned to the floor below. The putas down there were flirting with the gamblers, sitting on the laps of the biggest winners. They were attractive, but the mujers, hovering over the balconies, were the more beautiful and far more expensive. So when the really big winners tired of gambling, they'd turn over their hands, grab their winnings, then look upward and survey the ladies overhead. Right now, the winner at a stud poker table was nodding toward his puta de noche—one with particularly commanding cleavage—and waving her down to the floor for a closer look. Standing straight up, the senorita cocked her index finger and thumb as if they were a pistola, then fired them at him. She ambled over to the staircase and headed downstairs to meet her newest compadre.

Slater's eyes returned to the green baize-covered table in the far corner. Iced buckets of champagne, bottles of Madeira, and brandy were in front of and alongside these high rollers as well as plates full of caviar and pâté. The men all smoked cigars and their women thin black cigarillos.

Slater could not believe the sheer temerity of those assembled at the largest of these corner tables. Méjico's supreme ruler and generalissimo, Porfirio Diaz himself, was meeting with James Sutherland and the only two non-puta women seated at the tables—the ever-delectable, everlastingly desirable, Anglo-American business mogul turned robber baroness, Judith McKillian, and the indescribably wealthy, inconceivably cruel yet irresistibly beautiful La Senorita Dolorosa, the de facto ruler of both Chihuahua and Sinaloa. That the four of them were meeting in public was in itself audacious, but that they were joined by General Joseph O. Shelby, formerly of the Confederate States of America; the newspaper publisher John Newman Edwards; and the notorious outlaw Frank James was beyond belief. Glancing around, Slater quickly observed that almost two dozen federales backed up by bodyguards dressed as civilians were deployed nearby. So, at least, Diaz and his entourage were well protected.

Removing a silver mescal flask from the inside pocket of his knee-length gray linen duster, Torn Slater helped himself to a long drink.

What the hell were Diaz and that bunch planning?

Slater studied them more closely. Diaz and Shelby wore military uniforms. Frank James was solemn as boiled owl in a dark frock coat, a white shirt, and a black Stetson. Around his throat was a large looping bow tie of the finest Pongee silk. Black as India ink, it contrasted starkly against his ivory-white shirt. Its two loops, large and floppy, were perpendicular to the tie's loose ends, which were maybe eight inches in length. They hung down his chest, long and dangling.

The women were dressed in riding gear—long-sleeved ruffled blouses, jodhpurs stuffed into black, thigh-high, brilliantly burnished riding boots, heeled with gleaming silver rowels. Riding crops were looped to their wrists. Slater had never seen the McKillian woman without a wrist quirt of some sort. Today, the Senorita favored black attire, McKillian gray. The Senorita wore her long ebony tresses flung casually over her right shoulder and was hatless. McKillian's thick, lustrous auburn hair hung all the way down to her waist. Atop her head she sported a slate-gray deerstalker cap.

The man next to her, James Sutherland, one of the richest men on earth, was dressed in charro attire—tight trousers and a short snug jacket, both black as anthracite, matching riding boots and a felt sombrero of the same hue with a small flat brim and a steeple crown. He was gripping a teak cigarette holder and cigarette between his teeth and kept a monocle over his right eye.

They certainly didn't need money. Diaz, Sutherland and the two women were among the wealthiest magnates in the western hemisphere—and almost undoubtedly the most blatantly brutal. The Senorita had reputedly resurrected the torture chambers of the Spanish Inquisition, brought back its iniquitous inquisitors and then sentenced her more inept inamoratos to its racks, strappados, and iron maidens. She was even more infamous throughout México for having constructed a replica of the Aztec Pyramid of the Sun in one of her more lavish haciendas. She was rumored to have forced faux-Aztec priests to rip the hearts out of her spurned paramours atop that heretical temple. Her legions of lovers reportedly lived in abject quaking terror of her ungovernable temper and unimaginable wrath.

He gestured to Marita Morales, one of the nearby putas. Stunningly beautiful, she was the most financially successful whore in Durango and a friend of his. She came over to him.

"Grab a tray and wait on that table over there." He pointed to Diaz's and the Senorita's table. "Hang around. Try to hear what they're saying."

"Desde luego," she said. Of course.

CHAPTER 2

Judith McKillian sat at the big corner table with Generalissimo Porfirio Diaz and his chief financial patron, the governor of both Chihuahua and Sonora—the incomprehensibly rich and unfathomably wicked Senorita Dolorosa. On the other side of the Senorita sat McKillian's friend and sometimes business partner, the English billionaire James Sutherland. To his right was seated the notorious bank- and train-robber Frank James and two of his cronies—whose names she could not remember.

McKillian also could not remember ever being this bored before. The sensation, for her, was a true agony—like shooting pain, tooth-chattering chills, a skyrocketing fever or quaking terror. She actually believed her personal brand of ennui was worse than any of those afflictions. It seemed to crawl up and down her body like an army of huge, hairy...*tarantulas.*

Over the years, she'd developed a technique for coping with such boredom. She forced herself to study her surroundings in excruciating, nerve-racking detail, and so now she focused on the brothel-gambling hell with rapt attention. She counted the numbers of tables, doxies, musicians, card players, dice shooters, roulette gamblers and poker players. She studied the musicians—currently playing "La Golondrina," which, ordinarily, she might have enjoyed. She watched the ladies bent over the balconies and selling their bodies.

None of it did any good.

Still boredom tortured her hideously.

She decided to focus on couture, starting with Diaz. He was wearing a tan generalissimo's uniform, the front weighted down by at least a half a ton of meretricious medals, over a third of them French. As always, he favored a downward sweeping, coal-black bandito mustache, a tan campaign hat, the right side folded up and affixed to the crown.

Then there was the eternally stylish Senorita. Like herself, she was attired in riding garb. She wore her shiny obsidian-black hair long. Her wide-set flaring cheekbones framed eyes black and brutal as the grave, but which glinted with mean merriment when she was happy or erotically aroused.

It was said that the men in her life suffered the tortures of the damned and that their horrifically tortured remains were inevitably and ignominiously fed to the Senorita's prized swine.

Frank James was decked out in a black frock coat, matching hand-laced bow tie and a Stetson. Under the coat, he wore a white ruffled shirt. He was clean-shaven and, in contrast to his frightening reputation, he had surprisingly kind eyes.

Then there were his two associates—John Newman Edwards, newspaper publisher/editor/reporter and former adjutant to General Jo Shelby, seated to Edwards's right. Both men wore gray Confederate officers' uniforms, beribboned and bemedaled. She wanted to inform them that war had ended seventeen years ago and that they'd lost, but her contempt for them was so immense she did not bother. McKillian viewed such hopeless screwups as infra dignitatem.

Unfortunately, the detailed survey of her surroundings did her no good. Her tedium had not subsided—not for a second.

In this case, the cause of her distress was glaringly apparent. The people she was sitting with were driving her to distraction. She despised almost everything about them, but most of all she detested their monotonous conversation. All these morons talked about was M-O-N-E-Y—otherwise known as…

Filthy lucre, greenbacks, currency, dough, dollars, pesos, hard cash, bucks, greenbacks, banknotes, legal tender, long green, funds, assets, loot, coinage, silver-and-gold, capital, spare change, specie, beads-and-wampum.

Clearly, riches—and the pursuit thereof—were the only thing on her companions' minds, and they had no idea how eternally dull it made them.

McKillian had money and viewed it as no big deal. Furthermore, she didn't rob banks or enslave people to acquire it. She came into her nine-figure fortune the old-fashioned way.

She married it.

Oh, did she ever.

Her late husband was none other than Howard J. Sandover, the Wall Street magnate who had, among other things, cornered the world market on bat guano. She recalled his interminable disquisitions on the history, theory and practice of the guano industry....

* * *

In 1802, Howard used to endlessly explain to her, the German explorer, Alexander von Humboldt, while investigating the guano deposits on Callao Island off the coast of Peru, discovered the effectiveness of guano in fabricating fertilizer. He proclaimed its marvelous fertilizing properties to the world with evangelical passion. Howard quickly became Humboldt's most devoted disciple, raced to seize every guano island he could find, then mined that nitrogen-rich excrement for all it was worth. He quickly cornered the world bat- and bird-shit market and acquired a fortune far beyond all reckoning or measure.

Later, he likewise took over most of Chile's bat guano caves and potassium nitrate mining operations. He then moved into manufacturing the fertilizer himself and quickly became the planet's most powerful "fertilizer king."

* * *

By the time McKillian took up with him, he was near eighty. Sexually deprived for most of his life, he was now making up for lost time.

With Judith McKillian—at the time an exorbitantly expensive courtesan.

She could barely stand to kiss the old geezer, let alone have sex with him, and he was incredibly demanding in his proclivities and passions. Also his heart was so debilitated that he courted death with every dalliance. So in exchange for her amatory favors, she demanded and received a major rewriting of his will. In order to facilitate and later to intensify their liaisons, he'd begun taking highly ill-advised—in fact, downright dangerous—risks. He'd even started to inject himself with homeopathic doses of...*strychnine.* An astonishingly efficacious—but notoriously lethal—erectile stimulant, the old man could not perform without it.

Sensing a possible financial opportunity, McKillian took over the strychnine injections herself. She added a few innovations of her own, however. She began lashing his arms and legs to the four bedposts, giving him a few licks from her riding crop—which aroused him to no end—and then loading the hypodermic with an extra drop or two of the pernicious nerve agent, Crotalus atrox—or diamondback—venom. After tying off the brachial artery, which was situated in the anterior section of the bicep, she would insert the needle directly into that conduit and push the plunger home.

Then give the old man the ride of his life.

Or of his demise.

Meaning, one time, after recklessly expanding his dose of the viciously virulent neurotoxins, she fucked him...*to death.*

After which his $600 million fortune in batshit and saltpeter mines was 100 percent hers.

Her eyes continued to wander around the big room. Clearly, she needed something to relieve her monotony. She hadn't been laid in over two weeks. Maybe a good-looking gentleman and a roll in one of those upstairs cathouse bunks would lift her increasingly irate spirits.

She continued to study the room, searching for an appropriate target.

No, no, no, no, no, she thought as she mentally rejected man after man after man.

Then, out of the blue, there he was standing fifty paces away. All dressed up in a gray Méjicano capitan's uniform stood a tall, gorgeous, well-built cavalry officer with a nice smile and ramrod-straight posture.

After making very hard eye contact, she waved him over.

He nervously approached her table.

CHAPTER 3

Torn Slater continued surveying the whorehouse-gambling hell below. He could not imagine what Diaz was doing with such a strange assortment of people. Tycoons, yes, but a Civil War general, a bank robber, a journalist? Why?

Slater found the McKillian woman's behavior particularly puzzling. She seemed to be scanning the people around the room, as if in search of something or someone. Suddenly, she backed up her chair from the table, stood, stared into the eyes of a Méjicano federale capitan and waved him over. She was pointing at a champagne bottle, chilling in an ice bucket, and shouting. He crossed the room, walked up to her and proceeded to pop the bottle's cork. Pouring a drink, he handed her the glass. Taking it, she threw the drink in his gape-jawed face, slapped him twice—with each hand, hard, getting her back into each blow. Then grabbing his arm, she pulled the officer, who was frantically rubbing his blood-red cheeks, toward the stairs, dragging him to the upstairs bawdy-house rooms. He—haltingly, reluctantly—followed her.

What the hell was going on?

Was she going to bed a federale officer in a puta's crib?

Apparently, the people at her table shared none of Slater's confusion. They stood up, roared their approval vociferously. He could hear their thunderous screams across the loud, crowded gambling hall, clear as day:

"BRAVO!"

"OLÉ!"

"WELL DONE!"

"OUTSTANDING!"
"GOOD JOB!"
"FORTISSIMO!"

Her companions then filled their own glasses with champagne, raised them in toast toward the brothel boudoir, toward which McKillian was still brutally pushing and pulling el capitan. Offering her more raucous salutations, Diaz and his entourage greedily gulped their drinks, then slammed the glasses down on the table and, once again, laughed heartily before sitting down.

Searching the stairs with his eyes, Slater located Judith McKillian and the hapless capitan on the sixth-floor landing. She was dragging him by the arm toward a room. Opening the door, she started to yank him inside, only to have him hesitate and pull back. Stepping onto the walkway, she leaned back, then, spinning around, slashed her riding crop across his left cheek as hard as she knew how, getting every ounce of her body weight behind the swing. El capitan stumbled backward, his eyes tearing profusely. Choking back sobs, he furiously massaged his crimson-welted cheek with both hands.

This time when Judith McKillian grabbed him by the arm and pulled him into the room, he hung his head sheepishly and did not resist.

CHAPTER 4

Frank James, General Joseph Shelby and John Newman Edwards stared at Porfirio Diaz and his three friends, confused. Judith McKillian had just summarily summoned a young cavalry capitan over to their table and then dragged him off up a flight of stairs. They were now disporting themselves in one of the upstairs bedrooms.

The tension at the table was palpable.

"I hope Senora McKillian wasn't too abrupt," James Sutherland said to no one in particular. He always spoke with a patrician smirk and a supercilious upper-class English accent. "Ever since her esteemed husband passed away, she hasn't been quite herself. In fact, she's been rather erratic."

"The atmosphere here's conducive to erratic behavior," Edwards drawled indolently with a sonorous Southern accent.

"I personally find the atmosphere in this august emporium quite...*stimulating*," the Senorita said, smiling brightly.

"Still, a brothel-gambling hell is a rather dubious place to meet and discuss business," Edwards said. "Is there any particular reason you chose this place to meet?"

"The Senorita and I like to occasionally go out among our people," Diaz said.

"We like rubbing shoulders with the hoi polloi," the Senorita said. "It's important for us to occasionally see how the other, lesser half of Méjico magnifico lives."

"How admirable," Shelby said, confused at his hosts' bizarre behavior but determined to keep the mood amiable.

"And I am honored," Edwards said, "to meet with you all here—or anywhere." He, too, was trying to keep the conversation pleasant.

"The honor is ours," the Senorita said. "I cannot tell you the number of nights that General Shelby and Senor Edwards have regaled us with stirring tales of yours and your brother, Jesse's, war against the United States government. Your exploits are most impressive."

"Yours," Sutherland said, "is a true David versus Goliath saga."

"I'm sure," the Senorita said, "if we had had you fighting alongside us in our Méjicano–Americano war almost forty years ago, the outcome would have been far more agreeable for our side."

Frank James thought he detected a veiled disdain in the Senorita's voice and in her imperious smile. Still, he nodded politely and said nothing.

"The outcome would have been far more advantageous for us," Diaz said agreeably. "You are a most accomplished warrior. I have heard those same stories and have read of your daring adventures in our country's papers as well. You are much-feared by the American railroad-banking systems—even your political system."

"Is it true," the Senorita asked, "that your late brother threatened to castrate the governor of Missouri 'like a goddamned steer'—I believe, was the way he phrased it—'in order to rid future generations of his demented descendants'?"

"I loved my brother," Frank James said, "but he was intemperate and imprudent. Such remarks drove the governor to put an irresistible price on Jesse's head. In the end, those threats cost my brother his life."

"You sound critical of Jesse," Edwards said irascibly.

"I am merely suggesting," Frank said, "that Jesse was not always wise."

"I've read that Bob Ford collected the governor's blood bounty," Diaz said, "after he killed your sainted brother."

"Every last goddamned dime," Edwards said between gritted teeth.

"Still," the Senorita said, "you and your brother did an amazing job. You put the fear of God into your country's railroad and banking industries."

"And the nation's express companies," Edwards said.

"Those are the firms which are charged with and responsible for all the financial shipments in the US," General Shelby explained. "What Frank and Jess accomplished was truly a wonder."

"Then a compliment on your machismo," the Senorita said, raising a glass.

They all toasted Frank and Jesse James's depredations.

"You have all but brought much of America's financial system to its knees," James Sutherland said, nodding appreciatively.

Again, Frank nodded respectfully.

"But now you come to our earthly paradise, Méjico glorioso," Diaz observed. "May I ask, what brings you here?"

"Other than the exquisite pleasure of our most invigorating companionship," the Senorita added, smiling delightfully.

Frank James glanced warily at the waitresses and putas surrounding their table. Looking at Diaz, he said:

"This table isn't all that discreet, Generalissimo."

"Never fear, my friend," Diaz said. "These ladies speak no English."

"They hardly speak Spanish," Sutherland said.

"Most of them still struggle with Nahuatl," the Senorita said, Nahuatl being Méjico's predominant indigenous language and the ancient tongue of the Aztecs.

Frank James leaned forward and said in hushed tones, "Our problem is that we've become too successful, too famous in the old US of A. Our unflattering likenesses are in all the papers, periodicals and rotogravures."

"And on post office walls," Edwards said.

"The federal government is hell-bent on hunting us down, then trying and hanging us," Frank James said, "and they are indomitable. We can't stand up to them much longer."

"They defeated the entire Confederacy," General Shelby said, "back in the days when we had two million men under arms. What can a few surviving rebels all by themselves accomplish?"

"How did you and your brother," the Senorita asked, "inspire so much governmental fear and hate?"

"A lot of that money we stole was federal loans," Frank James said, "sent to federal banks to keep them afloat."

"The Federal Banking Act of 1866 required Washington to provide its federal banks with 'liquidity,'" Edwards said by way of explanation, "which means they send them enough money to keep them in business."

"Funds to which I and my late brother most ungraciously helped ourselves," Frank said, leaning back, a subtle smile spreading across his mustached mouth, "a small indiscretion which the government of the United States seems unwilling to forget or forgive."

"And now you believe we could be of some assistance?" Diaz asked. "How...por favor?"

"Your country could provide us with a safe haven," Frank said, leaning forward, fixing Diaz with a serious stare, "with a base of operations from which we could launch our assaults on our former country's banks and trains."

"A safe haven to which they could then return," Edwards added, "after such...*business transactions.*"

"Highly lucrative...*transactions,*" General Shelby said.

"With *our* considerable bounty," Frank said. He emphasized the word *our.*

"By *our* you are suggesting we would share in the profits as well?" the Senorita asked with an amicable smile.

"You would get the lion's share of the bounty," Frank said.

"I am moved by your philanthropic generosity," Diaz said, "but I can't help wondering what I have done to deserve such unsought-after largesse."

"We want to compensate you," Frank said, "for any animosity our government might feel toward you when you ignore our country's extradition demands."

"And that bounty would be worth the wrath of the US government, because—?" the Senorita asked.

"Since Grant federalized the banks," Frank James said, "prodigious payroll shipments are now made by rail, and since we now have compatriots in Washington's Treasury Department, who are still loyal to the Confederate cause, we can get all the dates, times, trains and schedules."

"Moreover," Edwards said, "our assaults would not be crude holdups but precisely executed military operations, during which we would loot those money trains piecemeal. Afterward, we will discreetly smuggle those money bags across your border and into your country's coffers."

Leaning back, Diaz treated them to his gaudiest smile. "You are too kind. I do not deserve so much beneficence."

"It is not completely undeserved," General Shelby said. "I told my friends here about certain discussions I had a few years ago with your former emperor, Maximilian, and how he said he would provide myself and certain allies with fertile lands, start-up capital, free labor, enough for us to establish our own version of 'the Confederate States,' not in America but in Méjico."

"How magnanimous of Maximilian," the Senorita said.

"We do have one additional proviso," Shelby said, "which will realize your grandest hopes and most fervent dreams—a proposition that you will find most...*enthralling*."

"We are all ears," the Senorita said, treating their guest to a smile as resplendent as the sun, blazing in a cloudless sky over the vast expanses of the Great Sonoran Desert at dawn.

PART III

"You're saying our employers are a little...*rapacious?*" Nietzsche asked Bismarck.

CHAPTER 1

Judith McKillian scrupulously studied her reflection in the bedroom wall mirror. She had to admit she looked magnificent. Her luscious mane of flame-red hair was abundantly flung over her shoulder, rather than down her back. The effect was deliberate. She did not like it when her titian-hued tresses obscured her derriere, and she was pleased with the cut of her jodhpurs. She liked her riding breeches taut with her pant legs—tightly, immaculately—tucked into jet-black riding boots, heeled with sterling silver Chihuahua rowels, boots and spurs both polished to a high gloss. That her equally tight gray silk blouse was missing two top buttons only made her haute couture appear all the more daring.

Of el capitan, she was less confident.

Situated behind her, sitting up on the bed in his tan dress uniform, his Remington revolver was still strapped to his hip, and his flat-brimmed steeple-crowned cavalry officer's hat fixed firmly on his head. She could glimpse him surreptitiously in the mirror and saw that his eyes were locked unblinkingly on her backside.

Allowing herself a small vicious smile, McKillian spun around, feigning blind rage, and began savagely whipping her boot tops.

"Are you un idioto completo," she shouted in Spanish. A complete idiot. "Did you really think a woman of my inestimable refinement and indubitable breeding would sully her self-esteem and stainless reputation by bedding a low-born, unwashed soldado such as yourself?"

Removing his hat, he placed it over his heart. Rising from the bed and bowing, he said:

"A thousand pardons, Senorita. I clearly misconstrued your willingness to accompany me into this boudoir as a desire to engage in more intimate activities. I was clearly mistaken. But may I ask: Why am I here? You wanted to do what?"

"I wanted to find out," the Senorita said, "how you bean-eating, tequila-chugging Méjicano morons live. I wanted to see if the hombres down here had anything below their belts besides rancid frijoles and explosive diarrhea. I wanted to see if there were any men in this godforsaken hellhole of a country or if you'd all turned desert oysters."

"Desert oysters?" he asked. "I do not understand the expression?"

"It's what they call in Texas fried longhorn testicles, stupido."

"I still don't get it."

"Meaning, were you born cojoneless or did your mamacitas castrate all of you hombres putos at birth?"

He stared at her, speechless, his eyes blinking rapidly.

"You still don't get it, do you?" she asked.

He stared back at her in abject, gape-jawed silence.

"Do I have to do your thinking for you," Judith McKillian roared, "as well as your fornicating?"

"You mean you really do want to—?" he asked.

"Madre de dios!" Judith McKillian shrieked. "Are all the hombres in Méjico as dumb and impotent as you?"

"Es verdad," he admitted shyly. It's true.

"Then I suppose I'm going to have to undress you too."

McKillian turned to her right, as if to walk away, but then, wheeling around, hit him off the pivot on the hinge of the jaw with a hard roundhouse right. His knees sagged, and the light dimmed in his eyes. Throwing a shoulder into his left side, she bulldozed him onto the bed.

Turning around, she straddled his legs and began dexterously removing his spurs, pulling the big brown military boots off his feet with swift, practiced precision.

"Senorita?" he asked in blank astonishment, finally coming to. "What are you—?"

"Do you expect to romper me with your boots and pants on? Don't they teach you cocksucking cabrones anything down here?"

"Muchas disculpas," he said with a whimper. Many apologies.

Grabbing both boots off the bed, she flung them against the wall as hard as she knew how.

Judith McKillian then began unbuckling his military belt.

CHAPTER 2

Friedrich Nietzsche, dressed in a white planter's suit and a matching Panama hat, stood outside Bismarck's door. He had only met him twice since arriving in Durango, and he was in awe of him.

Still, he rapped sharply on the door—three times.

"Come in," he heard Bismarck shout.

Nietzsche entered. He found the great man in a spacious hotel room with five large windows and a panoramic view of downtown Durango. An enormous square bed with four bedposts and a red satin canopy stood in the corner. Alongside it was a chest of drawers, a rolltop desk and leather-padded armchair. By the far wall was a sitting area with four chairs, a sofa and an assortment of coffee and end tables. All the furniture was made of hand-carved mahogany. Nietzsche counted two wall closets. By Durango standards, Bismarck's room was the height of luxury.

Not that the Iron Chancellor was in any way impressed. He sat there on the bed, impassive, barefoot, in a white shirt and shorts. He looked groggy and exhausted, as if he'd just gotten up.

"Hand me my trousers and suitcoat," Bismarck said sleepily. They were hung on the door.

Nietzsche had heard that Bismarck's two servants and executive assistant were down with dysentery. The chancellor was no longer a young man and completely on his own. Nietzsche realized Bismarck would need all the help the younger man could offer.

Nietzsche quickly fetched the pair of white cotton trousers as well as a matching suitcoat. He handed them to Bismarck, who put them on.

"Shirt," the chancellor said. "It's in the closet."

Nietzsche found a freshly ironed white silk shirt, hanging up.

"Shoes?"

My God, Nietzsche thought. *He isn't used to dressing himself.*

Returning to the closet, Nietzsche found them on the floor and picked them up.

At last, the great man was dressed.

Bismarck then asked Nietzsche for a cup of coffee. "Pour one for yourself," he added, gesturing toward a coffee service on a nearby end table.

Pouring them each a cup, Nietzsche sat on the sofa.

"Well, you've been here two months," Bismarck observed brusquely. "I've read your reports on Diaz's haciendas and mining operations that you've visited. What is your private, off-the-record assessment of them—and of Diaz's Méjico?"

"In Europe," Nietzsche said, "we deride this country as 'Barbarous Méjico.' The characterization is not misplaced."

"Meaning?"

"I think someone should burn this place down to bedrock," Nietzsche said, "and sow its fields with salt."

"You find nothing redeeming about this country?" Bismarck asked.

"Méjico's all right if you believe in the basic principle of tenth-century feudalism," Nietzsche said. "If you think national economies should be totally based on forced labor. If you see nothing wrong with enslaving, torturing and working to death 90 percent of a country's population."

"And our attitude toward Diaz should be what?" Bismarck asked. "How should you and I treat him and his backers?"

"We should walk softly, speak cautiously and treat these people with tremendous trepidation," Nietzsche said, his eyes fixed intently on Bismarck, his hands on his knees, leaning forward.

"Your reasons?"

"Chancellor, if I've learned one thing here, it is that Diaz and his friends are not lightweight people, that their ruthlessness knows no limits and that we are five thousand miles from home. They could tell Kaiser Wilhelm that we fell off our horses, ate a bad tortilla, burst an appendix or died of cholera. No one in this country would say otherwise. No one in this country would gainsay their lies. Meanwhile, Diaz and his friends would never miss a night's sleep. They enslave people by the millions, never think twice and are beyond cruelty. They see nothing wrong in their crimes."

"Our government would protest."

"Méjico is too far away. Their complaints would fall on deaf ears here."

"We could cancel our trade agreements."

"We have no substantive trade agreements to cancel."

"Which is why we are here."

Nietzsche said nothing.

"You really think Diaz, the Senorita and their friends are capable of murdering us?" Bismarck asked.

For the first time since he'd arrived in Méjico, Friedrich Nietzsche threw back his head and howled hilariously—laughing like a loon and braying like a mule.

"So you think," Bismarck said, "that these people might very well kill us if we cross them?"

"These people would shoot stars if they saw them fall."

"You mean they have no respect for human life?"

"They are more than a little bit in love with bloody death."

Bismarck considered Nietzsche's statement a long moment.

"But Diaz wants us to ship advanced technology to Méjico," Bismarck pointed out. "He's approached all the nations of Europe as well as the United States. His overtures are paying off. Steamships dock here on a regular basis. He's laying track, buying trains and stringing telegraph lines all over this country. He's boring mines and building factories. He's dragging Méjico kicking and screaming into the modern world."

"Most of that is financed by American plutocrats," Nietzsche said, "not by us. We have no leverage here—yet."

"You also said in your reports that he's pathologically greedy," Bismarck said.

"He'd take pennies off a dead man's eyes and put back lead slugs," Nietzsche said.

"How about his colleagues—James Sutherland, Judith McKillian, the so-called Senorita. They are spectacularly rich. Money can't be all that important to them. They certainly no longer need to flaunt it. Yet you say their avarice, like that of Diaz, is all-consuming."

"They'd suck blood from bats," Nietzsche said evenly.

"And your recommendation is?"

"Lie like rug-dealers," Nietzsche said. "Tell them anything they want to hear, then get the hell out of Méjico and back to Germany on the first available boat."

"And that is your considered opinion?"

"Read my reports."

"I have read them," Bismarck said, shaking his head sadly, "and, sadly, unfortunately, I…*concur.*"

CHAPTER 3

"And now, General Shelby," Generalissimo Diaz asked, "may I ask, what brings you to our earthly paradise, *Méjico carinoso*?" [loving Méjico]

"I have men spread out across the entire southern United States," General Jo Shelby explained, looking Diaz and each of his friends squarely in the eye, one at a time. "I'm talking about men like Frank and Edwards here, men with iron in their cojones, fire in their blood and rifle barrels for spines: men who don't kiss ass but kick it—and, if so ordered, kill it. I am here to offer you their services."

"In exchange for what, mi general?" The Senorita pronounced it "hen-er-al."

"Méjico's previous emperor," Shelby said, "Maximilian, personally promised me millions of acres of land, free peons to work it, even start-up capital. I'm hoping you will make good on Maximilian's promise—in exchange for services rendered."

"Maximilian is dead," Sutherland pointed out.

"He was declared a traitor to the Méjicano cause," the Senorita explained, "and to Revolucion."

"We shot that Austrian archduke *hideputa* [son of a whore] against a wall," Diaz said, "like the common thief he was."

"I know," Shelby said.

"So why on earth would Porfirio honor Maximilian's worthless promise?" the Senorita asked. Her tone was intimidating, but her smile was luminescent, even seductive. Still, despite her great beauty, Shelby found it difficult to look her in the eye. Most men found it difficult to meet her gaze.

"Because we will make you the same promise and proposition that we made Maximilian," General Shelby said.

"And that was?" Diaz asked.

"To make you all richer than God," Shelby said.

Edwards raised his glass. *"Al dinero, a la guerra y a la muerto!"* To money, to war and to death.

Standing, they all lifted their glasses and repeated the toast so thunderously that it echoed and reverberated throughout every cubic inch of the colossal casino. People everywhere turned to stare at their table—dumbstruck, their eyes bulging, their hands trembling over their mouths. That the most malevolent people in all of Méjico were suddenly so merry was, for most people, a source of... *terror.*

"And we are to do what to deserve your unwarranted magnanimity?" Diaz asked.

"We will invade that part of your former native land," Shelby said, "now known as 'the Arizona Territory,' conquer and occupy it on behalf of you and your friends, Generalissimo, and hold it for you as long as you wish."

"Most notably," John Newman Edwards said, "we will commandeer and run for you a certain piece of heaven on earth known as Rancho de Cielo. Its mines and croplands make it the most profitable 900,000 acres of real estate in all of North America and its prodigious proceeds will belong to you and to you alone."

"Yes," Diaz said, "I have heard the stories of its immense riches, but is it really that valuable?"

"Katherine Ryan, her mines and refineries are solely responsible for 70 percent of Arizona's silver, gold, copper and lead production. Her agricultural holdings produce two-thirds of the territory's corn and cotton. She owns 90 percent of the area's cattle. She is, arguably, the wealthiest woman west of the Mississippi. Own her Rancho de Cielo, and you own the territory. We can give it to you, signed, sealed, legally contracted for."

"With the t's crossed and i's dotted?" the Senorita asked.

"We will dot them for you," Edwards said, "with dollar signs."

"Rancho de Cielo will be yours to do with as you see fit," General Shelby said.

"And the government in Washington will allow your operation to succeed because?" Diaz asked.

"Because they are too busy chasing that Chiricahua war chief, Geronimo," Edwards said, "all over Méjico to do anything about it."

"So you will also provide Geronimo with shelter, supplies and concealment," General Shelby said, "forcing the American cavalry to chase him forever and ever, obsessed with him eternally, never catching him, thereby leaving us alone to do as we please."

"And by the time they get around to noticing us," Shelby said, "we will have legal papers, all signed and notarized, transferring El Rancho de Cielo to us."

"Which means," Edwards said, "that you will own El Rancho de Cielo and all of its riches lock, stock with both barrels smoking."

"By the time the US government is aware of what we've done," Edwards said, "the entire legal transaction will be a fait accompli, every word in our documents and deeds vetted by lawyers. The paperwork will be contractually...*bulletproof*."

Diaz and his friends joined in Shelby's booming, knee-slapping hilarity.

"And when the former owners complain?" James Sutherland asked.

"Who said they'll be around to complain?" Edwards asked.

Again, their laughter roared and soared.

"Compadres," the Senorita said, "we *do* think alike."

"My friends," Diaz asked Shelby, "I feel as if you and I are brothers-verdad, under the skin, joined at the hip in our mother's womb. Do you feel the same way? Are you sure you are not Méjicanos?"

Again, they all raised their glasses in toast, their guffaws exploding, shaking the room and convulsing everyone around them.

CHAPTER 4

When el capitan came to, he was stark-naked and spread-eagled on the bed. He had a goose egg on the side of his temple, where the McKillian woman had, in the course of his most recent beating, brained him with the leaded buttstock of her riding crop. As his vision slowly began to focus and the pounding in his head subsided to a dull roar, he saw that McKillian was standing over him, methodically thrashing her right boot-top with her horsewhip.

"Did it ever occur to you that your offer of that champagne bottle," McKillian said, "was an insult? Did you really think that a woman of my taste and discernment could ever consider drinking and conversing, let alone copulating, with someone as plebian as yourself?"

He attempted to respond but realized he had a sock stuffed in his mouth and halfway down his throat.

When he tried to extricate it, he found that he couldn't move his arms.

Or his legs.

His wrists were tightly lashed with rawhide thongs to the four bedposts.

His vision was now clear enough that he could see that his ankles were bound to the bedposts as well.

El capitan was starting to worry.

He feared that the riding crop's butt had cracked his skull.

He feared what the rest of the crop was going to do to him… all over again.

He didn't have long to wait.

"That's the problem with you muy macho Méjicano hombres," Judith McKillian said. "You think women are your rightful prey, disposable pleasures, with whom you can have your wanton way, use, abuse and then cavalierly discard. Isn't that right?"

Completely gagged, he could only bleat and burp.

"I'll take that as a yes, a confession of guilt," McKillian said. "Now, I'm not a priest. I can't offer absolution. I can, however, assist you in a good, heartfelt, sincerely offered act of contrition. I think in the Catholic faith it is called La Via Dolorosa—the Path of Pain. I know this little lesson in humility will smart, leave you sadder and probably no wiser. Still, we must try. What is life worth, if we don't attempt to help our fellow mortals, our esteemed brothers and sisters, through this pilgrim's progress, this veil of tears?"

Raising her brown hippopotamus-hide crop high above her head, she brought it down with a whistling hiss across his ass.

The scream that tore out of his lungs was instantly muffled by the stocking shoved halfway down his esophagus.

His eyes flooded with tears, and muted sobs racked his spasming body.

"No, Capitan, I can see you have evil in your heart, wicked thoughts in your head, that you are a sinner in the hands of an angry god—or should I say...*goddess?* For, in point of fact, whether you know it or not, I am she—that immortal deity and that you have been looking for me, high and low these many years, in truth, your entire benighted life, and now, guess what? *You have found me.* I am here, standing, gloriously, over you—all the pain and trouble, joy and sorrow, all the hidden fears and clandestine yearnings you have sought to suppress but have always, forever, secretly desired." Giving the man her widest, most luminescent smile, Judith McKillian leaned down and whispered in his ear, all the while, softly stroking his cheek:

"Welcome to my world, puto."

She then, with both hands, laid the crop across his backside as if she were the legendary rail-driving John Henry, hammering the last spike into the First Transcontinental Railroad.

His choking howls seemed to go on forever, but, at last, eventually, like all things mortal, they subsided, rasped and rattled, then slowly died away.

"God, that feels good!" Judith McKillian roared, throwing her head back, smiling sublimely, her eyes staring upward, as if fixed on the heavens, as if gratefully thanking some monstrously malign, infinitely malevolent...*god.*

Raising the whip high overhead, she began to thrash the convulsing, blubbering cavalry officer with a hard heart, hooded eyes and ruthless resolute fury.

CHAPTER 5

"We have no problem providing you with enough acreage and peon labor," Diaz said, "to allow you a most lucrative retirement. What sort of crops do you wish to farm?"

"What sort of crops do well here in Méjico?" Edwards asked.

"Sugar is the most profitable, I am told," Sutherland said. "They have splendid marshlands down in Chiapas, which are perfect for sugarcane. I own several plantations down there myself."

"If you can fight off the crocodiles," the Senorita said.

"Jess and I grew up raising hemp," Frank said, "what you call sisal down here. It's used to make rope, twine, carpets, bags, hats. It's a great export crop. There's nothing I don't know about growing sisal."

"Excelente!" Diaz said, giving them his most expansive, mustachioed smile.

"How many acres and how many peons," Frank asked, "were you thinking about giving us in exchange for all that hard Yankee currency?"

"I was thinking more about square miles," Diaz said, "several thousand square miles and at least ten thousand laborers—free laborers, of course—to work so much land."

"At the very least," Sutherland added.

"Since the peons raise their own foodstuffs, make their own clothes and build their own housing," the Senorita pointed out, "you don't have to pay for their room and board. They really do cost...*nada*."

"Nor do you have to worry about them succumbing from all that hard labor under the Méjicano sun," Sutherland said.

"You can work them just as hard as you want," the Senorita said.

"Why's that?" Frank asked. He was now more than a little nervous. He was starting to think that he might not want to know the answer.

"Unlike all that labor you Confederates used before the War of Northern Aggression," the Senorita said, "peons do come free. And since we don't have to pay for them, you don't have to purchase your peons from us."

"Where do you obtain them?" Jess asked.

"We simply conscript our Méjicanos," Diaz said. "I thought you knew. Everyone down here does."

"Which Méjicanos?" Frank asked.

"Any and all Méjicanos," Diaz said. "We conscript them wherever we find them."

"Sometimes we have to hit them over the head," the Senorita said, "but that is no matter. The important thing is that we don't have to pay them."

"You're right that we had to purchase the slaves we worked," General Shelby said, "and they were goddamned expensive."

"That makes no business sense at all," Diaz said, shaking his head. "To this day, I've never understood why you paid for your peons."

"Because we aren't allowed to enslave white Americans," Frank explained.

"If you'd won your war, you could have," Diaz suggested. "The Confederate Army could have enslaved all those northern bleeding-heart abolitionists—who, before the war, hounded you so mercilessly—and then put them to work in your cotton fields."

"I like the sound of that," General Shelby said. "I'd love nothing more than to get old U. S. Grant down here, picking cotton and chopping sugarcane."

"And trembling under the overseer's lash," Edwards added.

"Oh, you will love it down here," the Senorita said, smiling brightly, munificently. "Are you sure you aren't part Méjicano?"

CHAPTER 6

Judith McKillian caught a glimpse of herself in the bedroom wall mirror. She paused to admire her skin-tight slate-gray jodhpurs, stuffed into her ebony riding boots, and her glittering rowels. She likewise delighted in her blazing-red waist-length tresses and her wickedly glinting, emerald eyes. In her own considered opinion she looked...*goddamned good.*

She wished she could be more complimentary of her hard-used riding crop, still looped to her wrist.

It was not to be.

That poor thing looked beaten half to death.

She could not even tuck it back under her arm. It was dripping and drenched with too much gore. Instead of grayish brown, the hippopotamus-hide quirt was now a brilliant, glistening crimson. In fact, blood drops were cascading off of it and dropping onto the floor.

She had to admit that she'd kind of lost it for a while. She'd flogged many people many times, but usually they were servants or inept lovers or men with certain kinks. And she'd always been in control of her emotions.

Not this time.

Definitely not this time.

When she started flailing on the trussed-up, densely gagged man, spread-eagled and prone on the bed, she just let herself go; in the end, she couldn't stop. Even as he gagged and coughed, whimpered and groaned, she continued flogging him. She'd had to watch where she placed the strokes. Certain portions of his body she'd whipped so many times that they were now gory crevices, so she took aim at fresher, less abused parts of his body.

She did not want those untouched parts of his corpus to feel left out.

In the end, she'd flogged every square inch of el capitan. The result was that his corpus was now a maze of crimson whip welts punctuated by bloody slashes, and he was no longer conscious.

In fact, he barely seemed to be breathing.

McKillian wondered if he was suffocating on the gag. Chuckling and chortling softly to herself, she pulled on the gag, which was now crammed deeply into his throat. She decided it might not do to have him succumb in their bedroom, so she finally yanked it out of his throat and mouth. She'd then stick her head out the door and see if one of the adjacent rooms was empty. If so, she'd abandon him in one of those boudoirs.

She grabbed his gun belt up off the floor. Slipping it over her left shoulder, she walked out the door and confirmed that both rooms were empty.

She went back into her own room and stared at the prone, bloody and comatose man. Untying his ankles, she wrestled him off the bed and stood him up.

"Now, you have to help me, ducks," McKillian said to el capitan as she attempted to walk him out of the room. Maneuvering him out into the hall, which was thankfully empty, she muscled him toward the room to her right.

To her horror, he couldn't walk—not even a single step. Furthermore, he was over six feet, a good two hundred pounds and far too heavy for her to pick up and carry.

When he began keeling over, like a felled redwood, it was all she could do to brace him against the balcony's black iron railing.

CHAPTER 7

Slater stared at the puta standing next to him in blank astonishment, shaking his head.

He was so incredulous that he made her repeat Shelby's proposition to Diaz and his friends a second time. After she finished, Slater still could not stop shaking his head and still did not respond to her intelligence.

"So what do you think?" she finally asked.

"That Diaz and his friends didn't take my warning to heart."

"Es verdad," that is true, the puta said. "And as I recall, you once told them to leave your friends in el norte alone."

"Yes, I did."

"But the general now says that they're planning a full frontal assault on El Rancho de Cielo," the puta said, "and eventually on the entire American Southwest. I believe that Diaz intends for that general to supply them with weapons."

"Which means that I'm going down there to talk to those sons of bitches," Slater said.

"There are too many of them," Rosario said, "especially when you add in all of Diaz's bodyguards."

"Then I'll have to cut them down to size," Slater said.

"But what can you possibly say to them," Rosario said, her face and voice skeptical, "to make them change their minds?"

"I can make it clear to them in words that the deaf can hear and the blind can see. I'll make it just as plain as the balls on a tall dog, as obvious as a fart in Sunday church, that if they fuck with me, I'll feed them their cojones for breakfast. So you tell Raphael, Armando and Ortega to cover me from this balcony, in case Diaz's men start to throw down."

"That is not smart, Senor Slater. They have a federale army down there, surrounding Diaz and his gringo friends. They will shoot you where you stand. Raphael, Armando and Ortega can't stop them."

"Not if I gun them first."

"Don't you understand. There are too many of them."

"Not for a man of my machismo."

She treated Slater to a raw burst of contemptuous laughter.

"What's so funny?"

"I was just thinking: If you want to die, you should do it in my bedroom. I'll fuck you to death. You'll be just as dead, but your dying would be more fun."

"Yes, it would be."

Slater allowed her a small but affectionate smile.

"What kind of weapons do you have?"

"Two single-action Army Colts."

"That is not enough."

"It's gotten me this far."

"But now you are about to take on over almost two dozen professional killers with two pissy belt guns," the puta said, her face strained and sad. "That is not enough. Even worse, it is not very smart. In fact, it is muy loco y mucho stupido."

"Es verdad. I'd have brought a Gatling," Slater said to her as an afterthought, as he headed toward the stairs, "but it tears the shit out of my holster."

CHAPTER 8

Friedrich Nietzsche and Otto von Bismarck were crossing the casino floor toward Diaz and his friends, seated at the big corner table. They were about a hundred paces from them.

"What kind of people are these?" Bismarck asked.

"Devils," Nietzsche said.

They paused to study Diaz and his companions.

"Do you still think we are in danger?" Bismarck asked.

Nietzsche snorted derisively.

"But I am the chancellor of Germany," Bismarck said indignantly. "They wouldn't dare lay hands on me."

"A chancellor," Nietzsche said, "whose assistants and bodyguards are all sick unto death with—and probably expiring from—Montezuma's revenge. Even now, they are vomiting and excreting their brains and lives out of every orifice and pore in their bodies. A chancellor, whose only ally in this godforsaken land, is a young failing philosopher, namely me, with a long medical history of chronic dyspepsia, severe depression and every kind of debilitating decrepitude known to God and man."

"What have we gotten ourselves into?" Bismarck asked him.

"We are trapped in a garden grown rank and gross in nature," Nietzsche said grimly.

"You're quoting *Hamlet*," Bismarck said, "and he was referring to Denmark, not this 'madre Méjico,' as the people in this benighted land call their country."

"Same thing," Nietzsche said.

They continued to stare at Diaz and his friend in contemplative silence.

"You still want to arm these people with the best weapons technology der Vaterland has to offer?" Nietzsche asked, breaking the silence.

"I never did," Bismarck said. "Alfred Krupp, the great global arms merchant, did."

"And we are to do what?" Nietzsche asked.

"He says he needs us to close the deal," Bismarck said.

"How do you see our role here?" Nietzsche asked.

"I now believe Diaz views us as staked goats," Bismarck said.

"I wonder what our emperor, Kaiser Wilhelm, would say if he were here and saw all this," Nietzsche said.

"He'd probably demand that Diaz double his weapons order, and then tell Krupp to triple their asking price," Bismarck said.

"You're saying our employers are a little...*rapacious?*" Nietzsche asked Bismarck.

"Do you think Diaz and his friends have a monopoly on blind ambition and violent avarice?" Bismarck asked.

"I suppose not."

"For Alfred Krupp and our esteemed Kaiser," Bismarck said, "the accumulation of riches is not everything, it is the only thing."

The Reich chancellor took a Reichsmark out of his pocket and showed it to Nietzsche. It had the national emblem of an eagle on it with its wings fully extended.

"See that bird," Bismarck said. "Let's say it was the proverbial golden goose from Aesop's fable instead of a golden eagle. The two men that sent us here, they wouldn't just kill it. They'd sodomize it first, then eat it. Then afterward, they'd finish off everything that was left—beak, feathers, talons, all. And this coin here? They would squeeze it till that eagle screamed like a banshee, clawed out its own eyes and pissed blood. So yes, they will do business with Diaz and those people there. They see this arms sale as the deal of a lifetime, and they're putting our lives in peril in order to close it."

Bismarck and Nietzsche continued watching the people at the table.

CHAPTER 9

Diaz, the Senorita and Sutherland stared at Shelby and his friends a long moment, frankly dubious.

"You overestimate me. I know the newspapers wrote about Jess and me as if we were Genghis Khan and Attila the Hun, but I'm not and we aren't."

"I think you're uno mucho hombre," the Senorita said, "y muy macho."

"General Shelby," Diaz finally said, "if you think you, Edwards and the inestimable Frank James will be powerful enough to take on the entire American Army, you're no tiene sano, as we say down here. You are not sane."

"You tried taking on the entire US of A before," the Senorita said. "I believe you called it 'the War of Northern Aggression.'"

"You remember how that one went," Sutherland said in his most pompously patronizing English accent.

"This time we will start small," Edwards said. "With a raid on one very wealthy American hacienda."

"One packed to the rafters with opulent silver and copper mines," Shelby said, "as well as illimitable tracts of cotton and unending acreage of cornfields and bean fields."

"Even if you seize it," Diaz said, "what will stop Washington from sending the United States Army to take it back?"

"Generalissimo," Shelby said, addressing Diaz by the title he knew he most preferred, "Edwards and I, these last fifteen years, have been recruiting a clandestine army of unreconstructed rebels—Texans mostly—who are still loyal to the Lost Confederate Cause. We have transported many of them to

Sonora already. They are waiting there for your orders. They will recross that border and attack El Rancho de Cielo. We need you, however, to supply us with any heavy ordnance you can spare. We will need some big guns if we are to storm and seize that hacienda."

"And we would do this *why?*" the Senorita asked.

"Forty years ago," General Shelby said, "our President James Polk invaded Méjico and stole 50 percent of your beloved country. I remember it well, because I served in that expeditionary force. It is only fair that you should now take it back."

"Not if I can have any say in the matter."

The people seated at the table, looked up at the speaker. Outlaw Torn Slater was standing before them in a long gray duster and a black Plainsman hat.

"Senor Slater," Porfirio Diaz said in his most floridly unctuous English. Treating them to a broad, beaming smile, he rose to his feet and bowed extravagantly at the waist. "I have missed you so much. It is wonderful to see you again. I cannot speak for my friends and partners—Senor Sutherland, the ever-delightful Judith McKillian, who has temporarily left our table, and the ever-delectable Senorita Dolorosa—but I'm sure they feel the same."

The Senorita, for her part, stared ambivalently at Slater, at a loss for words, torn somewhere between pathological rage and abject...*terror.*

"I sent you a message," Slater said, "that if I ever heard about you or any of your friends crossing that border line and coming after friends of mine, there'd be hell to pay and blood on the floor. Well, that bill's come due."

"But we are all down here, in Durango, in madre Méjico," Diaz said mellifluously. "We wish you and your friends no harm."

"You wish to invade Arizona, seize Rancho de Cielo," Slater said, "and then reclaim the entire territory."

"So you overheard our little tête-à-tête," Diaz said, looking disappointed. "That is not very polite—eavesdropping on your close amigos. But then perhaps you would like to participate in our endeavor. The spoils of this little war will be considerable. I always have employment opportunities for a man with your...*singular skills.* Perhaps you have a question or two about the job's requirements and your prospective...*remuneration.*"

"My only question is which of you hideputas do I gun first," Slater said.

"How about starting with those hombres there," Diaz said, pointing to a group of six bodyguards in tan federale uniforms that had seemingly materialized out of nowhere and were now on his left. Diaz then pointed to six more bodyguards dressed in civilian attire but with pistols in shoulder harnesses under their suitcoats. They were standing on his right. Their hands were resting on their sidearms. "I must warn you. These men are all my bodyguards, and they are all excellent shots."

"Whatever you say," Slater said pleasantly.

He flung the left half of the lightweight duster over his shoulder. An 8-gauge double-barrel Greener—sawed-off at the breech and with half of the stock removed so that it had a pistol grip—hung from his left shoulder on a thong. Slater swung it up from his side. His left hand was already clasping the cut-down buttstock, his right reaching for the breech. Slater was still raising it up, belly-high, when it thundered—Nietzsche would later recall—like a Wagnerian Gotterdammerung, recoiling high over Slater's head, and the six men on Diaz's left exploded into scarlet spume and bloody fog.

Tossing the other portion of the duster over his right shoulder, Slater quickly grabbed a second double-barreled 8-gauge, hanging at his right side from a similar leather thong. Slater's right hand was already grabbing it by its pistol grip, his left hand on its breech. The Greener blazed and roared like a hellmouth opened wide, and the second group of federales vaporized into a crimson spindrift and carmine mist. A split second later, the brace of .44 Army Colts in cross-draw holsters were in Slater's fists.

He emptied them into ten more federales in less than twelve seconds.

Catching a peripheral blur on his right, Slater snaked the under-and-over .38-caliber Remington derringer out of his left sleeve and shot a charging federale, coming at him from that direction, in the forehead. Dropping to his right knee, Slater fired the other low-angle round up and under the chin of the uniformed attacker coming up on his left.

When he suddenly saw, ten feet in front of him, a captain of the guard, with a bona fide horse pistol, a no-shit .44-caliber Walker Colt pointed between his eyes—so big it was designed for saddle holsters and meant to replace cavalry carbines. The man held it, two-handed, and was cocking it with a double-click that seemed to Slater loud enough to wake the dead.

"You got me, amigo," Slater said, placing his hands behind his head. "I surrender. I know when I'm licked."

"En el piso," el capitan shouted. On the floor.

"I'm on it, boss," Slater said, still on one knee.

"You rattlesnakes aren't so tough," the captain said in English, "not after I pull your fangs."

Suddenly, Slater's right hand whipped out from behind his head with a thirteen-inch Arkansas toothpick clutched in his grip, and in one smooth, single motion, he hurled it, full force, as hard as he knew how. Striking the captain squarely in the throat, the blade exited his nape a full four inches. The man's eyes rolled back. Dropping the Colt, he collapsed to his knees and fell sideways onto the floor.

Simultaneously, bandito rifle shots were ringing out along the overhead balconies, and random federales were dropping like puppets unstrung, red blood blossoming and billowing out of their chests and foreheads.

Diaz and his associates were already cowering under the table.

CHAPTER 10

On the sixth-story balcony, high above Diaz and his friends, Judith McKillian—blindly furious and oblivious to the gunplay below—was cursing her naked, trussed-up, semi-conscious capitan, who was still backed up against the railing but wobbling badly. He was also an unsightly mess, his naked body covered with hundreds of bleeding, deeply gouged, crisscrossing whip welts.

"I've had enough of you Méjicano castratos," McKillian shouted at el capitan and at her friends down below at the top of her lungs. "You can eat my shit—you miserable hombre-capon—and fucking die!"

El capitan's gun belt was hung over her shoulder. Yanking his Colt Dragoon revolver out of the holster and leveling it at him with both hands, McKillian fired five .44-caliber point-blank rounds in rapid succession into his chest and stomach. The big gun jumped in her fists with each shot.

Breaking the rail loose from the walkway as he fell, el capitan toppled over the sixth-floor balcony railing and flipped a full 180 degrees on the way down. Consequently, his body landed belly down onto Diaz's table with a deafening blast, like an 88mm cannonball from outer space. He shattered the big table like bone china. Their ice buckets had been filled with champagne and sauvignon blanc, and bottles of Napoleon cognac and the vintage cru classe 1818 Chateau Lafite Rothchild Bordeaux together with their dishes of black caviar, camembert cheese, pâté de foie gras and the cut-up flat loaves of pan de la campagne had sat on the table. Those that el capitan did not land on shot straight up into the air when his body hit, crashing at last on the floor and breaking the table's contents into hundreds of pieces. The splintered remains of all that glass were strewn around the floor along with the wreckage of the table, on top of which lay the severely flogged and shot-up body of the naked man, who was now dying before their very eyes, his body spread-eagled over a widening, pulsating pool of his blood. Less than a foot from and perpendicular to the dying capitan lay the captain of the guard, whom Slater had knifed and who—his jugular vein and carotid artery completely severed—was hemorrhaging mightily, the staghorn-handled Arkansas toothpick still protruding from the throat.

But McKillian's victim hadn't finished dying. His body shuddered convulsively and then settled, the breath whooshing out of his lungs, the light fading from his eyes, and yet he was—somehow, impossibly, miraculously—still alive. His mouth was moving silently, and his eyes looked alert. He seemed to be aware of his surroundings. The Senorita, who, with catlike reflexes, had two-handedly grabbed a falling magnum of Dom Perignon out of the air, quickly took a pull out of the bottle's neck—then another and another. Emptying the remaining few ounces onto el capitan's remains, she offered the dying man a farewell toast.

"Vaya con Dios y diabolo." Go with God and the devil.

All the while, Diaz, Sutherland and the Senorita were cheering Judith McKillian excitedly.

"Good show!" Sutherland thundered.

"Excellent job with that whip, Judith dear," the Senorita yelled.

"Extraordinary marksmanship!" Diaz roared.

"Magnifico!" Sutherland exclaimed.

Judith McKillian, meanwhile, was already descending the brothel stairs, her mocking laughter ringing the rafters, the big Colt Dragoon still smoking in her fist.

No one in El Palacio de Placer de Esmeralda could take their eyes off of her. Queen Victoria could not have commanded greater terror and trepidation.

When Judith McKillian reached the cathouse-casino's main floor, she threw her head back and howled uproariously:

"Goddamn, I feel good!"

CHAPTER 11

Appalled at the carnage Judith McKillian had just visited on El Palacio de Placer de Esmeralda but still grimly curious, Nietzsche and Bismarck walked toward Diaz's table for a closer look. Over their right shoulders, they quickly spotted Judith McKillian, bounding down the steps like a mountain goat, three and four at a time. Reaching the casino floor, she swaggered up to her friends.

"I am so sick of this ludicrous land," McKillian shouted to no one in particular. "Where do I have to go to find a real man? Patagonia? Tierra dela Fuego? Katmandu? I certainly can't find one *here*, not in this eternal, infernal plague pit, not in this lamentable lunatic asylum of a nation, the one you detestable degenerates call...*madre Méjico!*"

Stepping over the knifed federale, she walked up to el capitan and bent at the waist in order to more closely admire her whip-scarred handiwork. He lay supine atop the smashed table, the broken fragments of which were now scattered randomly, his arms and legs spread out before her. He was, nonetheless, incomprehensibly...*breathing.* Suddenly, his eyes locked on McKillian's in dumbstruck disbelief.

Rearing back, McKillian drove the toe of her heavy black riding boot resoundingly and repeatedly into his crotch, its rowel spinning and jangling with every kick, el capitan's unclothed and bloody, whip-scarred body convulsing in agony. All the while, McKillian cursed the groaning man in the foulest, most barbarous language imaginable—in both English and Spanish. Calming down, she finally announced sternly to her friends:

"I don't want this *pedazo podrido de excrement* [piece of rotten excrement] anyplace near me!"

"What did he do to so displease you, my dear?" the Senorita asked genially, placing a placating hand on McKillian's shoulder.

"He failed me in the most shocking, most appalling and most damnable way imaginable," McKillian said with a snort, removing her deerstalker cap, throwing it off to the side and flinging her long flame-hued hair over her left shoulder.

"And which way is that?" the Senorita asked, still smiling affably.

"Between the sheets!" McKillian thundered.

She carefully replaced the captain's Dragoon .44 Colt in the holster still hanging from her shoulder.

"I understand, my dear," the Senorita said. "Completely. Let me help you educate this uncouth, unmanly...*blackguard*."

The Senorita reared back and drove her own right ebony riding boot into the capitan's groin so hard Nietzsche and Bismarck thought they heard his pelvis crack.

By now, however, el capitan's body was thankfully inert.

"I'm not sure *I* understand," Diaz said with a look of great perplexity. "My dear, Judith, did you *really* have to shoot him...*five* times? Isn't that a bit...*excessive?*"

"He had only himself to blame," McKillian explained, genuinely indignant, personally insulted. "He disappointed me most severely, and I am the last woman in the world any man wants to disappoint."

CHAPTER 12

"I'll say she is," Bismarck whispered to Nietzsche.

For a long moment, Bismarck and Nietzsche watched Diaz and his friends from a discreet distance in silent horror.

"I've read that great beauty," Nietzsche finally asked, "is invariably bloodthirsty. Is that true?"

"In Méjico, it seems to be," Bismarck answered, nodding.

Again, they quietly observed Diaz and his guests.

Again, Nietzsche could not take the silence.

Turning to Bismarck, he noted:

"The Kaiser is out of his mind if he expects us to help him sell Krupp's cannons and those other high-powered weapons to these barbarians."

"If Diaz can help bankroll Germany's defense program," Bismarck said, "our emperor would sell him half the firstborn of our Fatherland. In his world view, our nation's military security transcends everything else."

"How does Alfred Krupp view such transactions?" Nietzsche asked.

"His only categorical imperatives," Bismarck said, "are his company's bottom line and his own personal bank balance."

"Are you suggesting that Alfred Krupp has no moral compass?" Nietzsche asked. "That the profit motive is his only polestar?"

"Let me put it this way," Bismarck said. "Alfred Krupp sells such weapons to our fiercest enemy—Russia—and tries to sell them to our other most dangerous foe, France. And they seek to destroy us. Méjico is no threat at all, so why should he see anything wrong with arming Diaz to the teeth? After all, Diaz's lunatic land is five thousand miles away from us—across an entire Atlantic Ocean. Méjico could not menace Germany if she tried. So the Kaiser views Méjico and Diaz and his colleagues solely as a source of revenue—nothing more."

"That Diaz murders and enslaves his entire population is of no consequence?" Nietzsche asked.

"None."

"Then if Krupp and the Kaiser lived in Christ's time," Nietzsche said, "they'd be backing Caesar and his centurions, not our Savior, right?"

Bismarck detonated with sarcastic laughter. It took him a long time to catch his breath afterward, but he was finally able to say:

"Thank you, young Friedrich. I needed that. I haven't had one good laugh since leaving Germany. Yes, Caesar and his centurions would understand Krupp and our emperor perfectly. That *is* precisely how Wilhelm thinks. He was born two thousand years too late. He should have been a Roman, and, yes, he lives for war. War is his primum mobile. The happiest time of all was fighting Napoleon in his youth. He would have also made an excellent centurion."

"I don't understand."

"You're a student of Latin, right?"

"Yes."

"Then you'll remember what Kaiser means in that ancient tongue—Caesar. Where did you think the word came from? The Romans."

"Perhaps, but the emperor still hasn't met Diaz and his friends. He doesn't understand the depths of their depravity."

"So don't be too hard on him," Bismarck said. "I looked on these people the same way—until I met them."

"Then what do we do?"

"We walk soft," Bismarck said, "and make no sudden moves. And never forget we are strangers in their very strange land. They are as lethal and relentless a threat to us as they were to el capitan."

Nietzsche and Bismarck turned to stare at the people seated at the table.

CHAPTER 13

Another man was vociferously approaching Diaz's table.

"Well, I've had just enough of you and your insane outbursts," the man yelled, shouldering his way through the surrounding crowd. He was Senor Ricardo Montefiori, the governor of the State of Durango and co-owner of El Placio de Plaser de Esmeralda. A very small man, dressed in a tan coat and pants, a matching cravat and a stockman's hat, he strode straight up to McKillian.

"I've warned Senorita McKillian repeatedly about her violence and her insane outbursts here in Durango and most specifically in my establishment. Now I've had it. As governor of the State of Durango, I'm ordering this officer here to place her under arrest. Officer, she is to be remanded into custody with no bail."

Major Manuel Hernández of the Durango constabulary appeared at his side in a tan police uniform. He was flanked by two deputies in matching uniforms. They sported full, closely cropped beards, crisscrossed bandoleers glinting with brass cartridges and had handcuffs and blackjacks under their belts as well as holstered sidearms.

"Majordomo!" McKillian shouted.

A tall, stocky man in a white linen suit with a thick black leather satchel was instantly at McKillian's side.

"Pay him!" McKillian ordered.

Opening the satchel, those nearby could see it was tightly packed with American banknotes.

"How much?" the majordomo asked.

"Give him a handful," McKillian said. "A very big handful."

Her accountant/majordomo took out a massive stack of one-hundred-dollar banknotes over six inches thick, as many as he could hold in his huge hand. The diminutive governor required both of his hands to contain the large stack of bills.

"I see your point, Miss McKillian," the governor said. "There were clearly extenuating circumstances. I am so sorry for the interruption. Senora McKillian, Senorita, Generalissimo Diaz, please have a very enjoyable evening."

Diaz cleared his throat, unable to take his eyes off the satchel full of one-hundred-dollar banknotes.

"Still there are federal statutes, Miss McKillian," Diaz intoned gravely, "which you have most flagrantly flouted and which—"

"Paga este dos veces!" McKillian bellowed. "Dos." Pay this one twice.

Her accountant/majordomo reached into the bag, pulled out one handful of banknotes, then another.

Diaz glanced over his shoulder at his own personal assistant and said softly, "Hermano, por favor."

Diaz's uniformed adjutant strode up to McKillian's majordomo. Accepting the two tremendous piles of banknotes, he placed them in Diaz's valise, which he kept and carried, chained to his wrist.

"On reexamination, Miss McKillian, you are completely correct," Diaz said. "How our officer corps ever commissioned that despicable piece of filth is a national scandal, which I will most assuredly look into. If he caused you any inconvenience or unpleasantness, I shall personally see to it that our government makes it up to you. El capitan was a disgrace to his uniform. He let us all down most deplorably."

Diaz spat on the capitan's still exsanguinating remains.

Then to everyone's surprise, el capitan—abruptly—came back to life. Sitting up, he pointed an accusatory index finger at Judith McKillian, which zeroed in on her like a gun barrel. He exploded at her in a thundering basso profundo:

"Pu-TA!"

McKillian walked up to him. He was now sitting up and glaring at her balefully. She placed the big Dragoon Colt against his forehead and pulled the trigger. The big revolver boomed and bucked in her fist. The sixth and final bullet blew away most of his frontal lobes and the back of his head.

"That shut him up," McKillian said with utter finality.

Her friends were ecstatic over her performance:

"Bravissimo tambien!" Diaz shouted, applauding loudly.

"Encore! Encore!" the Senorita enthused.

"Excelente, your excelentia!" Sutherland bellowed.

"Hear, hear!" General Shelby shouted.

Edwards treated them to a "Yip-yip-yipping-yipping-yip-ping!" rebel yell.

The crowd, assembled around them, cheered as well as clapping and stamping their feet, shouting their encouragement.

"I say, Generalissimo," James Sutherland suddenly said, looking perplexed, "what happened to Outlaw Torn Slater? He was here just a minute ago."

Diaz paused and looked around the big room.

Outlaw Torn Slater was nowhere to be seen.

"He must have slipped past my men during the commotion," Diaz finally said, shaking his head. "How careless of them to let him get away."

"Maybe it's just as well he took off," the Senorita pointed out. "According to my count, Slater killed over twenty of your best men singlehandedly. The only reason any others survived was that they immediately...*fled.*"

"No telling how many more he'd have killed," Judith McKillian said with a truly transcendent sneer, "had they stuck around."

"He certainly made his intentions toward us known," Diaz said.

"He was...*pel-luc-id-ly clear*," the Senorita said.

"He objected most strenuously to our newest business venture," Sutherland pointed out, "that one in the American Southwest. So I wonder why Slater didn't kill us?"

"Because he ran out of bullets, you imbecile," Judith McKillian said irritably.

"I suppose you'll have to deal with Slater as well as Arizona's territorial government," the Senorita said to Frank James.

"And Outlaw Torn Slater is in no way an insignificant problem," Frank said. "He's the best man I ever saw with a belt gun—either hand."

"He was no slouch with that sawed-off 8 gauger either," Edwards said.

"Or a Big Fifty Sharps," Frank observed. "I've seen him do things with those I didn't think possible."

"And what does that gun do... *exactly?*" Judith McKillian asked.

"It shoots today and kills tomorrow," Frank said. "At least, that's what the Apache and the Comanche tell us."

"Then Torn Slater must be a very good shot indeed," McKillian said, nodding appreciatively.

"That he is, girl," Frank James said, shaking his head in dismay and apprehension. "Unfortunately, for us, that he is."

CHAPTER 14

Otto von Bismarck and Friedrich Nietzsche were now less than a dozen feet from Diaz and his associates. Having just watched the violence erupting around their table, Bismarck considered returning to his room, but then Sutherland made eye contact with him. The German government had had business dealings with Sutherland, and Sutherland quickly recognized the chancellor. Bismarck nudged the younger man with his elbow.

"Sutherland's spotted me. We have to talk to them."

They approached Porfirio Diaz and his friends.

"Presidente Diaz," Sutherland said in a stertorous voice. "Let me introduce you to your most prominent guest—the chancellor of Germany, Otto von Bismarck. Chancellor, meet El Generalissimo José de la Cruz Porfirio Diaz."

In his white linen suit and a matching Panama hat—which he'd removed and held over his chest for the introduction—Bismarck looked and felt more like a tourist than a statesman. But then, considering all the carnage in front of him—Diaz and his friends were seated around Slater's knifed victim, el capitan's naked whip-disfigured corpse and the bloody jumble of wreckage his murder had precipitated—Bismarck felt lucky to still be alive. Furthermore, those seated around el capitan's barely dead body were all splattered with his gore.

Diaz was now up on his feet, as were the gentlemen and the two women seated at his table.

The man, who'd just introduced them, then said:

"James Sutherland, at your service. Now let me introduce the two ladies, who are also close friends to us all, Judith McKillian and la Senorita Dolorosa, who is also la gobernadora of the states of Chihuahua and Sonora."

Bismarck shook hands with el presidente and then with his three friends.

"El presidente," the chancellor said, "I know you as the man who brought law and order to this rebellious land, and I know your friends by the fame and their very impressive...*wealth.* In the world's most august financial circles, you three are viewed with respect and admiration."

With terror and trembling, Nietzsche thought. He knew of the trio's notoriety, and, like Diaz, he knew them to be very much feared and universally reviled.

"And we know of your reputation tambien," the Senorita said. She spoke with a pronounced American accent. "El chancellor de sangre y hierro, as we say in our own Méjicano tongue. Un Mann von Blut und Eisen, as you might say auf Deutsch. Or blood and iron is how Senora McKillian and Senor Sutherland would describe your career in their English tongue."

"And I so admire men with iron in their backbone and brimstone in their blood!" Diaz said emphatically. "Such as you evinced when you trounced those Frenchies at Sedan and united all those eternally warring German states."

"Jolly good show," Sutherland enthused. "We gentleman of 'this earth, this realm, this England' also appreciate a man who knows how to get things...*done.*"

"Speaking of men with iron in their bones," Bismarck said, "that gentleman who was here a minute ago and did for your entire retinue of bodyguards, he was no slouch either in that 'blood and iron' category."

Bismarck decided not to mention McKillian's execution of el capitan for the simple reason that he feared she was a violent lunatic and capable of shooting him next.

"A most regrettable incident," the Senorita Dolorosa said, "and, yes, he is a most deplorably uncouth man."

"I believe he was the desperado they call 'Outlaw Torn Slater,'" Nietzsche said.

"And you recognize him...*because?*" Sutherland asked. His smile was a half sneer, half leer, something between a grin and a grimace. The maniacal glimmer in his eyes set Nietzsche's teeth on edge.

"I ran into him earlier in the day," Nietzsche said.

"And he saw you?" McKillian asked.

"Yes."

"And you lived to tell the tale?" Sutherland asked.

"I'm here."

"For which we are all most pleased," the Senorita said cordially. "And your name is, my good man?"

For the first time, someone wanted to know who he was. Nietzsche did not take that as a good sign. He had hoped to pass through the evening unnoticed and unidentified.

"Friedrich Nietzsche. I assist Chancellor Bismarck."

"Who is remarkably unattended," Diaz said. "The rest of your entourage is where?"

"We just learned that they died from dysentery," Nietzsche said.

"Most Europeans have trouble with our agua and our cuisine," the Senorita said. "But again, Herr Nietzsche, you say you met Torn Slater earlier. How?"

"Slater had killed six men because they were abducting six of your women here. I heard the shots. I am a skilled hospital worker and went to see if anyone needed medical care."

"And he did not kill you because?" the Senorita asked.

"The women were too busy thanking Slater," Nietzsche said, "for him to pay much attention to me."

"'Thanking him'?" Sutherland was nonplussed. "In what way?"

"They were having sex with him—simultaneously."

"All six?"

"I counted seven women," Nietzsche said. "The mistress of this establishment was in bed with him too."

"Let me get this straight," Porfirio Diaz said. "Slater killed six puta-thieving pimps, then bedded down all seven of the mujers he'd just saved?"

"Si," Nietzsche said.

Diaz nodded appreciatively. "As much as I loathe this outlaw—after having had so many unfortunate dealings with him in the past—as much as his depredations have cost my country fortunes in gold and silver, still, I cannot deny that he is mucho hombre y muy macho." Rising to his feet, Diaz thundered, "A compliment on his machismo!"

He then tossed back a glassful of Napoleon brandy.

"He is muy hombre!" the Senorita shouted, standing and raising her glass as well.

They all joined in his toast, except for James Sutherland, who, instead, took off his charro hat. A portion of his pate was slick with gleaming, bone-white scar tissue.

"While you applaud Slater for his skills in murder and fornication," Sutherland said, "let me remind you what he did to me. The ruffian relieved me of half my scalp, then hung me by the hocks over a slow-burning cook-fire. At the time, he described that little tête-à-tête as 'doing me a favor.'"

"How on God's good earth could such savagery ever be construed as doing a man of your decorum and distinction 'a favor'?" Judith McKillian asked indignantly.

"He explained that infelicitous turn of phrase a few moments later," Sutherland said. "As Slater rode off, leaving me there, hanging upside down, my pate smoking and broiling over that hellish fire, he shouted over his shoulder, 'Don't think too badly of me. After all, I'm cauterizing that head wound for you.'"

"'Thank you...*very much,*' I yelled back—in between groans and sobs."

"And what do you think Slater meant by that remark?" Diaz asked, puzzled.

"I believe," Sutherland said, "that remark was the brigand's idea of 'wit.'"

Putting a hand over her mouth, the Senorita could not refrain from chuckling—first softly, then a little more loudly, then raucously and uproariously, until, in the end, she was throwing her head back and blasting them all with deranged gales of lurid, licentious laughter.

"You have to admit," she finally said, gasping for breath and wiping her eyes, "that the comment is fairly fucking...*funny.*"

"I never knew," Diaz said, as soon as his own considerable laughter died away, "Slater had a sense of humor."

"You'll forgive me," Sutherland said, "if I don't share your reverence for Slater's alleged manhood or your admiration for his soi-disant 'wit.'"

"Of course, you are so right," Diaz said, forcing his face into a severe frown.

"But you have to admit," Judith McKillian sniffed, "that you did provoke Mr. Slater most atrociously."

"In what way?" the Senorita asked, leaning toward McKillian.

"I thought you all knew," McKillian said. "There was a reason for Slater's...*pique.* James, here, had rounded up a gang of murderous bounty hunters as well as a tracker, mule-packer, a cook, a guide, of course, myself, and then led us on an expedition deep into the Great Sonoran Desert's scorchingly hot canyonlands. We were to hunt Slater down and corner him, at which point Jimmy was to impale him with his composite bow and one of his trusty tri-bladed steel broadheads. He planned to decapitate Slater, then store his head in a crock of formaldehyde and tour the globe, reenacting his little escapade for millions."

"I gather it didn't turn out that way," the Senorita said with an arrogant stare of withering impertinence.

"It should have!" Sutherland shouted, rising angrily to his feet. "We'd have been bigger than Halley's Comet, richer than the Golconda and more famous than...*God!*"

"Except," McKillian said evenly, "that Mr. Slater had plans of his own. He turned the tables on you, dear James, killing virtually your entire posse—allowing only I and our guide, John Henry Deacon, to escape. He would have killed you too except that Deacon cut you down after Slater rode off, after having left you hanging inverted, with your cranium hovering over that fire, Slater...*frying it to a crisp.*"

"But you must admit, my dear," Diaz said, patting Sutherland's arm in commiseration and shaking an irate finger at the Senorita. "Outlaw Torn Slater was just a little bit out of line there. I mean scalping and charbroiling a man's head? Then making a joke about it and riding off? Really? There are somethings people just...*don't do.*"

"I agree," the Senorita said, fixing Judith McKillian with an admonishing stare. "It isn't...*done.*"

"It was utterly...uncalled for," Diaz said.

"I mean, dear Judith," the Senorita said, shaking her head in disappointment, "I don't care how provoked Mr. Slater was. Barbequing a man's... *brain?* Really?"

The Senorita's voice was stern but there was a hint of mean mockery in her deceptively twinkling eyes.

"Which doesn't stop you, Generalissimo, from ranting and raving about Slater's so-called machismo," Sutherland fumed.

"Point taken," Diaz said. "However, a prudent respect for our adversary's lethality is not the same as a high regard for his character. When it comes to the outlaw's moral fiber, I have nothing but contempt."

"Agreed," Judith McKillian finally said, patting Sutherland's arm in sympathy. "I'm sorry if I spoke out of line."

"Well said," the Senorita said—but her eyes were still smiling and devious.

Turning to Bismarck, Diaz then said, "Other than this last unfortunate contretemps with Senor Slater and his bandito compatriots up on the balcony, how do you like our land of eternal joy so far—our Lord's final fortress, our own Enchanted Eden, our Garden of a Thousand Delights, our little spot of heaven on earth...*madre Méjico?*"

But Bismarck—arguably the greatest orator in German history and, at the time, the supreme master of the language, Bismarck, who had never in his entire life been at a loss for words—could only stare back at his hosts, blank-faced, dumbstruck, abjectly embarrassed, paralyzed with shock.

He found he could say...*nothing.*

At the same time, he had to struggle assiduously to keep his eyes fixed on his hosts and not on the naked remains of Slater's knifed captain of the guard and Judith McKillian's bloody, whip-welted capitan, both men still exsanguinating before them, on the floor.

CHAPTER 15

Back in the chancellor's room, Friedrich Nietzsche sat with Bismarck and kept him company. He was exhausted, but the older man was suffering from insomnia and needed someone to talk to. Diaz had finally located a bottle of acceptable cognac for the chancellor, and he and Nietzsche had been working at it conscientiously.

Even so, Bismarck still couldn't sleep.

"As I told you, I read your reports on Méjico's forced labor program," the chancellor said, "and while I find that system personally appalling, I don't see how or why we should sabotage the emperor's and Alfred Krupp's arms orders because of our personal feelings. The internal affairs of other countries are of no concern to Germany—as long as those nations pose no national security threat to us. Were foreign human rights abuses a priority with us, we would not do defense treaties with Russia, whose history of persecuting serfs, its recent anti-Semitic purges and pogroms and its shameful imprisonment of political opponents is as wicked as that of any nation in the history of the world. Yet those Russian treaties have saved our country from attacks on us by France, Austria and even England for the last fifteen years."

"But, Herr Chancellor," Nietzsche argued, "according to my exhaustively researched papers, Diaz has enslaved 90 percent of his people. In some of his haciendas, the life expectancy of the average peon is eight months. We have never seen—or heard of—barbarism on so massive a scale, and the fact is, if we walk away from this deal, it in no way jeopardizes our 'national security.' Nor is Germany struggling financially. We are in the midst of the greatest economic metamorphosis in world history. Under your guidance, we are changing from an agrarian nation to the most heavily industrialized power on the continent. We don't need Diaz's money."

"But, as you know," Bismarck said, "the cash flow from the agreement would bankroll Germany's military budget for the next twenty years. You also know how impossible it is to get revenue for our defense budget out of our tight-fisted Reichstag? And we are surrounded by ferocious enemies on all sides. Those are facts. Now, thanks to Diaz, I could circumvent those fools in the Reichstag, arm the Fatherland, and I can do it all without raising taxes on hard-working Germans. So the deal is in Germany's best national security interest—despite the generalissimo's obvious loathsomeness."

"You're willing to sacrifice the liberty and the lives of millions of Méjicano people," Nietzsche asked, "including those of women and children, on the altar of Germany's military budget?"

"And are you playing Mephistopheles to my Faust?" Bismarck finally asked.

"No, Chancellor. Mephistopheles is, according to his creator, Johann Wolfgang von Goethe, 'der Geist der stets verneint,' [the spirit that always stands in opposition], and I would never play devil's advocate with you."

Bismarck stared at the younger man and for a while said nothing.

"Perhaps I am the real Mephistopheles," Bismarck said, at last, somewhat wistfully, "'der treue Geist der stets verneint.'"

"In that case, am I Faust?" Nietzsche asked.

"Why not?"

"I am the last person in the world you want to play that part," Nietzsche said softly, his voice almost a whisper.

"And I think you're perfect for the part."

"In no way," Nietzsche said. "You have to believe in *something* to be Faust."

"And you don't?"

"You remember the words of Schopenhauer? 'Sleep is good. Death is better. The best is never to have been born at all.'"

"And you think those are words to live by?"

"I feel them every day, every way, with every fiber of my being," Nietzsche said.

"You really believe that there is *nothing* wrong with death?" Bismarck asked.

"I believe there is something terribly wrong with...*life*."

"Do you *really* believe that?" Bismarck asked.

"No," Nietzsche said. "In truth, Reich Chancellor, I believe in... *nothing at all*."

PART IV

The old doc in Yuma Prison had told Slater that, like Odysseus, he was doomed to fight his own ten-year war at Troy, destined to also wander eternally, searching for his Ithaca. Unlike Odysseus, however, Slater had never had an Ithaca. Although he'd faced down cyclopses, sirens and sorceresses, he had never really known an actual...*home.* Let alone a Penelope.

CHAPTER 1

It was late at night, and Frank James was sitting in his train compartment, staring out the window at the passing chaparral, unable to sleep. Dressed in a black frock coat with matching trousers, boots and hat, he looked, by all standards, to be a prosperous gringo businessman and not a world-famous desperado on the run. In the overhead luggage rack, he had two carpetbags filled with underwear, three boxes of Havana cigars and six bottles of French cognac that Diaz had given him. He needed the cognac for this trip. Never in his life had he been dependent on liquor, but he was now.

Nor had his conversation with Diaz and General Shelby the night before done anything to improve his mood. They had told him that he had to return to the US—to Texas, to be specific—and confirm that the final contingent of Confederate veterans was traveling to Nogales to meet up with the rest of the Shelby Brigade.

* * *

"Those men we got there come to us by way of the White Confederate Citizens' Council," Shelby explained to him. "It's one of the successor groups to Nathan Bedford Forrest's Ku Klux Klan, but quite frankly they aren't up to par."

"Are you saying we cannot rely on these men?" Diaz asked Shelby.

"No, the men will do their duty and fight. Colonel Tremain and his senior officers—the directors of the council—aren't up to the job. They have grown soft. Civilian life has corrupted them."

"And Frank will remedy their softness...how?" Diaz asked.

Frank had thought that an excellent question but said nothing.

"He'll look them in the eye," Shelby said, "give them that Frank James stare and let them know that if their men aren't in Nogales in a week's time, nothing on earth will save them from ours and his righteous wrath."

Frank wanted to tell Shelby that the last time he'd felt "righteous wrath" was at Northfield but that watching those Minnesotans shoot the entire James-Younger Gang to pieces in a matter of minutes had, frankly, burned all that fury out of him forever.

"I was hoping, General," Frank said, "that I'd never have to cross that border back into the US, not for a long, long time—if ever again."

"I wouldn't ask you to travel to Texas if it wasn't critical," Shelby said to Frank, giving him an avuncular clap on the back.

* * *

Frank understood why the general wanted him to go to Texas, but he still didn't like it. He didn't like anything about this trip. He didn't like the sweltering, lifeless, waterless wastes—just outside his train's window. He preferred the lush, loamy bottomlands of Missouri—country for farming. He liked having nearby rivers and streams filled with bass, bluegill and trout for fishing and woodlands filled with deer and elk for hunting. This Méjicano desert country wasn't good for anything—unless you found a way to raise, herd and sell scorpions, tarantulas and rattlesnakes. And make money off it.

God, was Frank sick of Méjico. The more he thought of Shelby and his plans to conquer and reclaim the Arizona Territory for Diaz, using retired ex-Confederate veterans turned Klansmen as soldiers, the more preposterous the idea seemed to him. He'd known a lot of them KKK good ole boys over the years. "The South will rise again," they all liked to shout when they were high on moonshine, but Frank had always thought—then and now—that they were full of shit.

They couldn't whip the North when they had massive armies—totaling almost two million men under arms—run by real commanders, living legends, men like Bobby Lee, Jeb Stuart, and his own commander, William Clark Quantrill. Did Shelby and Diaz really think they could whip the North with a gaggle of ragtag, over-the-hill drunks and degenerates, outhouse sweepings and brain-damaged jailbirds?

With the Ku Klux Klan?

There was a poem he'd just discovered by Alfred Lord Tennyson. It was thirty years old but new to him. It was about another brigade in another time in another war sent on a suicidal mission. Tennyson explained the mindset of those men, who rode to their slaughter. It was shockingly similar to his own fatalistic despair. Tennyson wrote:

Theirs not to reason why
Theirs but to do and die.
Into the Valley of Death
Rode the six hundred.

Boy, Tennyson summed it all up in that one sentence. He knew what it was all about. In the end, a soldier just followed orders and did his job.

The way Frank was doing his now.

But that didn't mean he had to like it.

He hoped and prayed that Diaz would come through with those haciendas and all that free peon labor.

CHAPTER 2

Outlaw Torn Slater could pass as a Méjicano. A quarter-breed Apache, he'd spent a third of his life living with them, and since most Méjicanos were mixtures of indio and European blood, Slater looked like they looked. His ebony hair, flat black eyes, and high, angular cheekbones all screamed "Méjicano." Furthermore, his entire life had been spent exposed to the elements, so his naturally swarthy skin was burned dark as any Méjicano's. He spoke Spanish, Nahuatl and all the Méjicano dialects with unaccented fluency. His faded yellow poncho, frayed straw sombrero, scuffed filthy boots and faded, worn-out Levis added to the impression that he was one of Diaz's more impoverished peasants.

Riding atop a long string of boxcars heading north through Durango and Sonora, he fit right in with the packed-to-overflowing mob of soldados and laborers. Nothing in his appearance said "gringo."

As for gear, Slater limited his hardware to two Army Colts in cross-draw holsters—strapped low across his stomach and concealed by the poncho—and a sheathed Arkansas toothpick in his back sheath. On the reverse side of his Levis, long ago, he had paid a tailor to sew hidden pockets—behind his hip pockets and inside his upper thighs. There, he kept hundreds, fifties and twenties—all US greenbacks. Inside the armpits of his worn-out tan work shirt, the tailor had also sewn secret pockets, which Slater had filled with more hundreds and fifties, and his Levis' outer pockets were stuffed with gold double eagles—instant mordida. US currency was highly prized in Méjico—especially gold or silver coinage—and Slater was traveling with a fortune in US mordida. He'd never known a federale yet who'd turn an hombre in after an exorbitant bribe. They were shit-poor themselves, couldn't afford not to take it, and, anyway, they knew that if they didn't accept it, their superiors would. They also knew that their boss, if he was on the take and they weren't, might very well frame them—or even have them killed—out of fear that they would turn the suborned superior in.

The federales lived by the mordida, and where such payoffs were concerned, personal honor was respected only in the breach.

Slater had learned long ago the importance of making friends when traveling in a group. In both the West and in Méjico, trouble could come unexpectedly and in surprising forms. It helped to have amigos covering your back. The best and quickest way to cement such alliances was with a gift of food and drink, so Slater's shoulder bag—fashioned out of a grain sack—contained his concept of culinary mordida: fresh-baked tortillas, five cans of boiled beef, a slab of hard Méjicano cheese—queso cotija—and a bag of Ancho chilis. Beef was hard to come by for most Méjicano peasants, and Slater had never known a Méjicano yet who did not love poblano peppers con tortillas y carne y queso. Most important, he'd also packed three liters of La Antigua Cruz—his favorite tequila in all of Méjico—to go with the spicy food. Traveling atop boxcars in an arid desert was a thirsty business—especially when tequila was also making the trip—so a two-quart canvas waterbag with a chained stopper and a shoulder rope was his road gear's grand finale.

The hardcase stranger with the flat black eyes and rough laconic but not unfriendly manner quickly became the most beloved hombre atop the boxcar. He soon had muchachos utterly devoted to him. When soldados stopped the train at checkpoints and interrogated the travelers, Slater was surrounded by men who swore on their mother's chastity that they had known the outlaw since the day he'd left his mother's womb in the Tampico whorehouse of his birth.

If that did not win Slater safe passage, a twenty-dollar double eagle or two—which was a year or two's wages to the poor federale, secreted in the man's palm—would quickly and quietly close the deal.

CHAPTER 3

Later that night in his room, Nietzsche found that he couldn't sleep.

Mephistopheles or no, he hadn't budged Bismarck one inch off of his plan to sell Diaz all the arms that the mass-murdering, slave-driving strongman could buy. Germany was going to arm that maniac to the teeth, Nietzsche's report on Diaz's atrocities notwithstanding. Despite his moral qualms about the transaction and despite knowing better, Bismarck was going to close the deal.

So be it.

But if Bismarck was going through with his arms deal, Nietzsche wanted him to know firsthand what he and the Méjicano people were getting into. He would show Bismarck the reality behind his hair-raising reports on Méjico's agriculture, mining and industry. He would demonstrate, for the Iron Chancellor, the rapacious reality behind his myriad words. He would see to it that first Bismarck learned the sordid truth of Diaz's savage and sadistic reign over the Méjicano people—in language that the deaf could hear and the blind could see.

But to show Bismarck the real Méjico, he had to get him out of Durango. Bismarck had to witness with his own eyes how Diaz's hacendados presided over the flogging, starving, enslaving and even murdering of 90 percent of the Méjicano people.

That was the only way he could crack Bismarck's shell and let him see that in this instance, morality trumped duty to king, country, the Kaiser and Alfred Krupp.

Before Nietzsche had met Bismarck, his closest friend—as well as his dazzlingly brilliant and distinguished mentor—had been Richard Wagner. He'd fought with the old man, however, over certain unshakable beliefs, to which the great man was inextricably bound: Wagner was now violently anti-Semitic, obsessed with German Kultur's so-called grandeur. Nietzsche denounced Wagner's belief that Germany ought to rule Europe—even the world—as dangerously deluded.

No matter what the cost in blood, lives, agony and treasure.

Nietzsche frankly thought Wagner was mad.

Still, he was the best, most inspiring friend Nietzsche had ever had. He'd given the younger man a faith in himself that he'd never believed possible. Perhaps that was why he could never convince Wagner that his ideas were more than wrong, that they were wicked on an almost apocalyptic scale. He had not convinced Wagner because he'd admired and respected the old man so much that he could never drive his arguments home as brutally as he should have.

Nietzsche would not make that mistake with Bismarck. He would redeem himself for his failure to redeem Wagner.

Bismarck might continue down this terrible path, but it would not be because Nietzsche hadn't opposed him with everything he had.

But in order to do that, first Nietzsche had to talk to Diaz.

CHAPTER 4

Frank James sat alone on his hardwood double seat. He was grateful for the solitude, although it had cost him a pretty penny.

In Méjico, paper pesos weren't worth much more than Confederate currency up north. Double eagles, on the other hand, had more than an ounce of pure-grade gold in them, so when Frank flipped the conductor a couple of them, the man had personally guaranteed him a private seat all the way to Hidalgo County in Texas's Lower Rio Grande Valley.

Frank didn't exactly dislike other people, but he was more used to robbing train passengers than conversing with them. Anyway, he needed to be alone with his thoughts. He was worn out—sick and tired of robbing banks and trains and then hiding out on the high lines, with Union soldiers or badged-up bounty-hungry lawmen dogging his backtrail every step of the way.

He needed Diaz's brandy now to steady his nerves.

Most of his friends were dead. The outlaw trail had taken its toll on all of them—Cole, Bob, Jim and John Younger too, as well as Clell Miller, Charlie Pitts and Bill Chadwell. Even Jess had come to admit they'd led hellish lives. Guns and cards, robbing banks and trains, running from John Law—day and night, night and day—it just wasn't any life for a grown man, and Frank was well past "grown."

He was now pushing forty—Hickok's age when he caught that last fatal round in Deadwood.

He also didn't like the idea of having Outlaw Torn Slater after him. Man, that was a ghost from his past—and a name to conjure with. When Slater materialized in front of him down there in that whorehouse/gambling hell in

Durango, Frank felt as if he was facing the devil himself and staring into his own open grave. Slater was the genuine article, the real thing, one of a kind, an absolute original, the purest quintessence of outlaw. Case-hardened and triple-distilled, Slater was smarter and tougher than all of them—all those James-Younger boys plus Quantrill and Bloody Bill—put together. And he was more relentless. You never wanted to get on Torn Slater's bad side. He wouldn't give up and never backed off. He'd just keep on coming. Frank James decided long ago that he'd rather eat his pistol than have Slater hunting him. In his own way, Slater was a principled man, except that his principles had far more to do with bloody death, total destruction and punishing anyone who pushed him or one of his very few friends too far than they had to do with the Lord's Prayer, the Sermon on the Mount or the Ten Commandments. Once you got on that man's shitlist, he wouldn't stop dogging your trail until you were scratched off. No sir, pissing off Outlaw Torn Slater was not a profit-making proposition. In fact, it was just a very painful way of killing yourself. Look at what Slater had done to Diaz's federales right there in front of God, Diaz and everyone back in that Méjicano casino-whorehouse!

Yet pissing off Slater was precisely what Frank now seemed to have done.

Nor was going after Slater and putting a round or two in his head a viable option. Lots of men had tried that one. Come to think of it, Frank hadn't seen any of them around lately. In fact, nobody had—they just didn't seem to be around anymore, anyway, anyhow.

So Diaz was now Frank's last, best hope—not only for himself but his family. A hacienda down there in the State of Durango complete with free peon labor, rich fertile soil and abundant rivers and streams sounded just fine to him. His wife, Annie, said she never wanted to leave Missouri—that meant abandoning her family and friends—but all that money they'd be pulling in down South of the Border way, well, all that moolah would dissolve a lot of blood ties. It would be a whole new life too, a great life for her, Frank and their son. So Annie would come around. Frank was sure of it. They could invite family and friends to visit. They could stay too, for all Frank cared.

As for Torn Slater, if he had scores to settle and wanted to come around, well, Frank would deal with him down there on his own turf. He would try talking to Slater first. They had a lot of history together—most of it good times, goddamn good times. Maybe Torn Slater would listen to reason.

Stranger things had happened.

CHAPTER 5

Torn Slater lay on his back atop the northbound boxcar, watching the Big Dipper revolve around the North Star, feeling inexplicably relaxed. That didn't happen too often, but sometimes Torn Slater found himself pondering his own life—not a life spent but misspent. His Apache raiding-party youth, Shiloh and the Hornet's Nest, the years with Quantrill, Bloody Bill and then those James-Younger guerillas, though come to think of it, Frank was the only one of that entire crew he even remotely liked. Followed by twenty years on the owlhoot. Was it supposed to be that way? Maybe. It was all Slater knew. Farming? Cowboying? He'd never cared for either. Big bank jobs—brokered by financial executives or train robberies arranged by payroll shipping agents—that was Slater's idea of work. He'd sometimes follow up with blowouts in towns like Denver, Dodge City and San Francisco replete with palatial hotel suites, high-dollar whores, high-quality whiskey—even French champagne and Russian caviar—as well as high-stakes poker games.

It was a good life, if you didn't weaken.

Then there was the downside. How many years had he spent in Yuma and Sonora Prisons? On his back, he bore the broad white stripes of both institutions, and the rest of his body was a labyrinth of thick, long-forgotten keloid knife slashes and knotty, puckered bullet holes. One of his favorites was a long diagonal remembrance—a mean red bitch of one truly nasty bayonet scar diagonally traversing his chest, inflicted on him by a Yankee soldier at the Shiloh Hornet's Nest. At the very last second, he'd turned away a well-aimed thrust but still caught the sweeping tip of the blade—after which he'd forced the soldier onto his stomach, and, with a knee between his shoulder blades and his hands under his chin, had yanked the man's head up and back, toward his own abdomen until, audible above the battle's din, he'd sensed the thudding sickening *crack!* of the neck and felt the body shudder, spasm, convulse until the man's life was wheezing out of him and then the body settled and became deathly still.

How many times had Slater entered a bank or a post office only to find himself staring into the unflattering but thankfully inaccurate likeness of his own face, up there on the wall, adorning a highly unflattering wanted poster.

What was it that those posters had said?

WANTED: OUTLAW TORN SLATER

FOR TRAIN ROBBERY, BANK ROBBERY, HIJACKING OF ARMS AND TROOP SHIPMENTS, ESCAPE FROM YUMA AND SONORA PRISONS AND MANY COUNTS OF MURDER-MOST-FOUL. FAST ACCURATE PISTOL SHOT, RIFLE MARKSMAN AND A NOTORIOUSLY LETHAL KNIFE SPECIALIST. BACK HEAVILY SCARIFIED WITH THE WIDE WHITE STRIPES OF YUMA AND SONORA PRISONS. REST OF BODY—A MAZE OF MULTIPLE BULLET AND KNIFE SCARS, INCLUDING DIAGONAL BAYONET SCAR TRAVERSING TORSO FROM LEFT GROIN TO RIGHT ARMPIT. PUCKERED BULLET HOLE ENTERING BELOW LEFT CLAVICLE, EXITING ABOVE SHOULDER BLADES. KILLS WITHOUT HESITATION OR REMORSE. IS EXTREMELY DANGEROUS.

OUTLAW TORN SLATER:

WANTED IN 13 STATES AND TERRITORIES AS WELL AS IN SONORA AND CHIHUAHUA MEXICO

$20,000 REWARD
WANTED: DEAD

He had seen them all over Méjico in Spanish too.

What was it Ghost Owl—the female Apache war shaman and possibly the only woman Slater had ever loved—had said of him after she had gazed on the poster? She had stared up at him with those large, expressive, utterly unforgettable eyes and said:

"You must be a very great man that the entire *pindah* [white-eyes] nation rises up against you."

He'd answered simply, "Robbin' banks and trains don't make a man great."

"But by printing your name," Ghost Owl had said, "and by putting your face on that poster, they attempt to steal your soul. They must fear you very much."

"It ain't that much," he'd said—and he meant it.

"No, I think you have very great medicine."

Perhaps, but his medicine wasn't great enough to keep Ghost Owl from getting shot to death, because she was with Slater and on the run from the law. Come to think, most of his friends died hard as well—those two women, Medea and Madelina, shot and tortured down in Méjico, dying for *him*: Bill Hickok buying the farm in the Number 10 Deadwood Saloon and Slater not there to help—despite everything Hickok had done for him. Sitting Bull, back on the rez, Cochise, his father-through-choice and Mangas Coloradas—they were gone. Jess shot dead straightening a damn picture frame. And now Cole Younger? He was rotting away in that Minnesota prison doing life without hope of parole.

What had Diaz said to him once when he was imprisoned in that slave-labor mine in Sonora?

"Your friends are not so tough as you, Senor Slater. When I'm finished with them, they aren't tough at all. They are...*dead*."

Throwing back his head, Diaz had then laughed long and hard and joyously at the thought of all the men and women that Slater had loved and that he had tortured and killed.

And how, at the time, had Slater responded to Diaz?

"Maybe I need tougher friends," he'd said.

In truth, Slater had had the best, strongest, bravest, loyalest, and, most of all, toughest friends imaginable.

So what had gone wrong?

They'd had Torn Slater for a friend, and he'd brought them nothing but trouble—and, too often, death.

Being Slater's friend was the problem.

But nothing bad would happen to Katherine Ryan. Slater had no fantasies about her redeeming his lost and sorry excuse for a soul; he just wanted to help Katherine. She was a woman worth helping.

Slater swore that, for once in his life, he would not let a friend down.

CHAPTER 6

Nietzsche was wearing his white planter's suit and a long, flopping black tie with both ends hanging loose, when he met Diaz at the suite of offices in the brothel-casino that the generalissimo was using for business meetings. Diaz was attired in one of his tan dress uniforms.

"Young Nietzsche," Diaz said, "you requested this meeting and said it was urgent. I am happy to assist you in any way I can."

"Generalissimo," Nietzsche began, "I believe in your leadership in Méjico and in your country, and I want this arms agreement to work—for it to satisfy both you and the chancellor. I worry about the chancellor though. The stress of the job has aged him prematurely. Deep down inside, he's far older than he looks. He's aged in ways you may not see—especially during these last several years. He's far too rigid, too set in his ways. In truth, I have been unable to explain to him how truly marvelous Méjico is. The result of my failings is that he does not understand the miracles that you've wrought here, no matter how much I've sung your praises. But I think I know now how to make him understand."

"And in real terms," Diaz asked, "I should care what he thinks of me and of Méjico, why—?" The generalissimo looked bewildered.

"I do not believe," Nietzsche said, "that the chancellor will come up with the kind of armaments that you most assuredly need and deserve. He thinks, however, that your nation is backward, impoverished, insolvent and squalid and that you can't afford such arms. The problem is that he does not truly understand how much your mining operations and plantations are worth. He does not appreciate their inestimable value no matter how strenuously I've argued and explained. He consequently does not think Germany and the Kruppwerk will get anything of value in return for their invaluable ordnance."

"And to convince the chancellor of the incomprehensible profits his nation would reap from our mining and agricultural enterprises," Diaz said, "you want me to do what?"

"Seeing is believing," Nietzsche said. "If the chancellor could visit a few of your most magnificent and remunerative mines, smelting operations and plantations. If you went with him and explained the efficacy of your labor-management techniques, the industriousness and the extreme productivity of your peons, I think that would go a long way toward convincing the chancellor what a gold mine madre Méjico truly is."

"So you want me to arrange for a tour of these businesses, young Nietzsche?" Diaz asked.

"I would like for you to take him on such a tour personally."

"It would be my honor and pleasure. In truth, I love getting out among the real people, my peons, the heart's blood of my country."

"Do you have any mining operations or agricultural haciendas," Nietzsche asked, "that are not too far away and that we could visit?"

"I have several I can think of right now," the generalissimo said, "that are only a short train ride from Durango. I will invite James Sutherland, the Senorita and Judith McKillian to come along. They may wish to invest as well."

"Excellent."

"They are also among the most profitable of all my operations in Méjico," Diaz said. "If he wants, I could lease them to your country for a small consideration."

"I am sure the chancellor would be most grateful."

"It is nothing."

"I would consider it everything."

CHAPTER 7

It was late at night.

Frank James took a long, deep pull on his brandy flask, put it back into his inside coat pocket and stared blankly out the train window at the passing yucca, prickly pear, sagebrush and rock formations. Damn, that Méjicano desert was a rough place to scratch out a living—drier than a nun's cunt and harder than a whore's heart. It was an arid, ruthless land, and it produced mean, brutal people—people like Diaz and the Senorita. Yeah, but so was Missouri. He, Jesse, their mom, old Zerelda, they weren't exactly softies. None of the James-Younger clan were. Méjico wouldn't be getting any cherry, no siree. He'd do just fine south of that border line.

He slipped the hammered-silver pint flask out of his inside coat pocket. Studying his initials AFJ—Alexander Franklin James—lavishly inscribed on both sides in elaborate gothic script, Frank James emitted a deep sigh. Holding his Stetson, he tilted his head back and helped himself to a long healthy draught.

That was seriously good brandy.

Frank James took down a carpetbag. Opening it, he took out a bottle and studied the label.

It read: *1863 Camus Napoleon La Grande Marque Cognac.* That bottled cognac was just turning twenty years old; the cognac itself was pushing sixty years of age.

It was named after one of the greatest generals and outlaws that the world had ever known—Napoleon Bonaparte. Now there was a thief and a killer who put him, Jess and the Youngers to shame. There was a desperado he and his friends could look up to.

And his cognac was goddamned good too.

It was a hell of a lot better than that white whiskey them hard-mean, hard-bone hill boys had distilled way up in them Missouri Ozarks for the flatlanders below, that nasty bottled lightning he, Jess and their cousin, Coleman Younger, had all grown up on.

Diaz had also given him six boxes of Cuban El Roy del Mundo, King of the World, cigars—the finest cigars on the face of the earth. He'd been smoking them ever since he boarded the train.

It was a hell of a lot better than rolling and smoking quirlies—Frank's usual brand of smokes.

Yes, Diaz was doing him right fine.

Quantrill would be proud.

Diaz was all right.

Méjico was going to be great.

Annie would learn to love it—right down to the frijoles y arroz con queso pollo y chilis. Frank had learned to love that Méjicano grub and Annie would too. So would their son. They'd love it just as much as they'd loved Missouri—maybe more.

Frank took another hard hit on his brandy flask and held the burning cognac in his mouth while he sucked hard on his El Roy del Mundo cee-gar. He finally blew the smoke up at the ceiling. It was the best liquor he'd ever drunk and the best smoke he'd ever enjoyed in his wild, rowdy, hell-bent life.

But Méjico?

Méjico?

All he'd ever known was...*Missouri.*

Frank took another drink and stared at the ceiling.

Where all this would end, God only knew.

CHAPTER 8

Slater lay on his back atop the boxcar, as the night train roared through the desert chaparral—and he thought of the friends he'd made, the ones who'd died or were doing time or were left abandoned and alone on his backtrail.

Where was Calamity Jane? Who the hell knew? She was as good a friend as he'd ever had and what had Slater done for her? He'd left her on his backtrail with her heart broken, her throat smokin', and she was one of the few people, he'd actually cared about.

Belle Starr? She was the only woman he probably didn't have to worry about. She had some security—a profitable ranch in the Nations. Furthermore, she was even colder, meaner and more heartless than he was—and that was going some. It didn't hurt her—or anyone else—if she climbed into bed with him. She had fewer feelings about such things than even he did. Of course, she did tell him once that she loved him, but that was when she was sixteen and only because he'd knocked her up. She'd hoped he'd stick around a while.

Good luck with that one.

Instead, he abandoned her just as fast as he knew how and went straight on the owlhoot.

Forced to find a father for her bastard son, she'd seduced Cole Younger and then declared Cole the kid's old man, forcing him to take her hand in marriage. That's where her life had gone bad, she once said, and perhaps she was right. So maybe bedding her down wasn't a great idea, looking back on it. Trying to fight her off didn't seem to work either, so he suspected they were both stuck with each other.

For a while.

He wondered why they were together at all. That he was even friendly with Belle was a mystery he'd never unravel—although he understood that *friendly* might be too strong a word. Friendship was a concept he and Belle didn't have much experience with. Among other things, friends didn't seem to last too long around them.

All of Belle's friends and lovers were dead or doing time.

Same as Slater's.

So he and Belle got along. There was a connection. Maybe they needed each other in some inexplicable way.

Katherine Ryan? Their paths seemed destined to cross. She claimed that when she was sixteen, he'd impregnated her with her son, Richard, who was now a fine young man. That was something to get his head around. He didn't know what to think of it. Among other things, he liked her and Richard both.

If he could only stay out of Katherine's bedroll, maybe he might still be of some use in her life—actually do some good. That was a strange concept: Outlaw Torn Slater doing some good.

Well, stranger things had happened in that long disease of his life. What was that book the old doc at Yuma Prison had given Slater? It was called *Odyssey.* That was it. The only book Slater had ever read, and, to his undying surprise, he'd loved it. The old doc had told Slater that, like Odysseus, he was doomed to fight his own ten-year war at Troy, destined to also wander eternally, searching for his Ithaca. Unlike Odysseus, however, Slater had never had an Ithaca. Although he'd faced down cyclopses, sirens and sorceresses, he had never really known an actual...*home.*

Let alone a Penelope.

None of it seemed likely—regardless of what the old doc had thought.

The women, whom he bedded down and who had loved him, were the ones he had hurt the most.

J.P. Paxton had summed up his life best. How did that song go? The one called "Yuma Jail"?

You're Outlaw Torn Slater, train–robbin's your game,

Though you hit some banks with Frank and Jesse James.
Cole Younger liked to share in your fame,
But there's hell to pay on your backtrail.
Your wanted posters say no hope of bail
In Yuma Jail.

Now you jumped the fence and you're on the run,
After sendin' a guard to Kingdom Come,
For callin' you 'that hillbilly scum.'
Now a floggin' post's awaitin' your tail
And a hard rock pile's on your backtrail
In Yuma Jail.

Don't look back, boy, on the trail back there,
For the women who loved you or them that care.
There's a wailin' whistle, through your soul it's throbbed,
For the men that you killed and the trains that you robbed,
For the banks that you hit and the women that sobbed.

It's followin' you, boy, up your backtrail.
Don't look back, boy, just listen to it wail,
Back in Yuma Jail.

Paxton wrote another poem-song about Slater called "High Line Drifter." It had been a big hit too, Slater was told, and, again, Paxton had him stone-cold. It began:

You go to sleep at night, dream of good times to come,
But your saddle's still your pillow and your life's spent on the run.
A pistol's in your fist, nearby your horse is tied.
You dream of gold and girls, and dream of friends who have died.
Because you're just a high–line drifter, who
sleeps with a price on his head,
Who sleeps with a gun in his fist, and dreams of friends who are dead.

Hickok and Calamity had nicknamed Paxton the professor, and, damn it, Slater had to admit that that little bastard understood something about Slater that the outlaw couldn't completely comprehend. Paxton had him dead to rights. He'd cut Outlaw Torn Slater dead-center.

Problem was, Slater had never wanted anything different—or even better.

Outlaw Torn Slater was doing the only thing he knew how to do.

And he would keep doing it—or die trying.

PART V

"You ask me," Judith McKillian said, "we have far too many peons. In my opinion, the world would be better off if we had quite a few fewer of these utterly repugnant wretches. Getting a day's work out of them is appallingly difficult—so arduous I truly wonder if it is worth the effort we put into them. I can't imagine how impossible they would be if the gods had given them brains instead of endlessly indefatigable...*reproductive organs.*"

CHAPTER 1

Porfirio Diaz sat under a grass-thatched ramada with Sutherland, the Senorita and Judith McKillian. Bismarck and Nietzsche had just joined them. They were all seated on camp stools and dressed casually in Levis and white cotton shirts. It had been a long hike reaching this lookout atop this very high hill, but Diaz loved the view. It showed his largest, most lucrative silver mine off to its very best advantage. Diaz never tired of the view. Nor did Sutherland, the Senorita or Judith McKillian. All three of them gazed on that towering mountain of silver ore as if it were wealth incarnate.

Diaz had known that the climb would be taxing, and so he had insisted that his guests dress comfortably, informally. Now that the climb was over, they sat under the ramada, sipping champagne chilling in ice buckets, which his retinue of porters had so laboriously trundled up the hill before they got there.

"Ah, compadres," Diaz said, waving his arms expansively, as if attempting to embrace that mountain itself, "do you not thrill to this view tambien like myself?"

Nietzsche would not have chosen the verb *thrill* to summarize his feelings about "the view." For one thing, the mountain's base was shrouded in dark, sooty smoke, emanating from the plethora of smelters, stamping plants and grinding mills ringing the mountain.

"You'll notice," Diaz said, as if reading Nietzsche's mind, "that we've constructed our refining operations, including our amalgamating plants, at the base of the mountain."

"Amalgamating plant?" Bismarck asked.

"An operation, in which we separate out the pure element from the ore's impurities," Sutherland explained.

"It's all very sophisticated," the Senorita said.

"I'm quite sure," Bismarck said, "but what are those things doing on those switchback trails leading to the top? From this far away, they look like ants."

"They're peons," the Senorita said.

The sun was glinting in Bismarck's face. He shielded his eyes by putting both hands up against his forehead. Slowly, his vision refocused, and the scene on the slope came into sharp relief. Nietzsche handed him a telescope, and Bismarck quickly saw that the Senorita was right. Thousands upon thousands of half-naked, barefoot, whip-scarred mestizos, dressed only in breechclouts, were trudging up and down the steep, vertiginous trails, bent under five-foot-high burden baskets of inter-thatched maguey. Rawhide tumplines were stretched taut against their foreheads. The angle of their climb was almost sixty degrees. On those upwardly ascending trails, the baskets were filled with shoring timber, mining equipment, supplies and provisions. On the downward switchbacks, the baskets were filled with ore. The chancellor did not see how the men got enough traction to stay on the trail or how their leg muscles had enough strength and leverage to keep propelling them up the slope.

Bismarck also noticed—interspersed among the peons—overseers with cuarta wrist quirts. They flogged stragglers or any other men who slowed or foundered under the massive burdens.

One man did collapse, and two overseers—in white cotton trousers, shirts and straw hats—were unable to scourge the half-comatose man back up onto his feet. Removing the burden basket from his back and shoulders, they picked him up by his arms and legs, then carried him to the edge of the mountain slope. There, without hesitation or preamble, they swung him twice and pitched his now screaming and flailing body off the mountain. His arms and legs beat the air wildly, as if they were bird wings and capable of producing flight. They weren't. Roaring in terror, his unearthly howls reverberated off the sierras, the cliff faces and the barrancas, like the mournful wailing of the damned in hell—although in this case the hell was in the State of Durango, in this slave-labor prison mine and of this earth and in the Afterlife. When, at last, he crashed on the rocks below, his clamoring and caterwauling abruptly ceased, but the echoes continued to bounce eerily off the mountainsides, canyon walls and through the infinite complexes of arroyos, proliferating in all directions, closer to the ground, for a full minute after his precipitous fall.

"Olé! Olé!" the Senorita yelled, as she stood and clapped loudly.

"Muy magnifico!" Diaz howled, standing and cupping his hands around his mouth to better project and amplify his enthusiasm.

"Damned good show!" Judith McKillian roared, rising to her feet and whaling on both boot tops with her riding crop.

"Nicely played!" Sutherland shouted, slapping his thighs with both hands.

Only after the three friends finished their thunderous applause did the echoing screams of the falling man dim, dwindle, fade and die away.

CHAPTER 2

Unable to sleep, Frank James, still sitting up, stared sightlessly at the train compartment's pitch-dark invisible ceiling, his brain swirling and teeming with memories.

Sleep had always come hard for Frank, but after Jess was killed, a good night's rest had become near impossible.

Ironically, Frank didn't blame Bob Ford all that much for shooting Jess in the back. The governor and the railroads had put so much money on his head, Jess had to worry about the people around him shooting him in the back for the reward, even old friends. Consequently, Jess had grown obsessively suspicious of everyone during that last year or two and was capable of killing even friends based on unfounded mistrust and baseless misgivings. Jesse's erratic behavior was one of the reasons Frank had fled to Tennessee. His brother had become a fuse-lit cannon on a rolling deck in a force-8 gale. Bob Ford probably shot him from behind because he feared Jess was planning to do the same thing to his brother, Charlie, and to himself.

And Bob was probably right.

Jess had written him, telling Frank as much.

So in Tennessee, Frank had become a boring, hard-working, sunup to sundown farmer, and for the first time in his life, and to his eternal surprise, he had found employment that he...*loved.*

So where had it all gone wrong? Where had all their friends—their close, loyal, loving friends—gone? Bob and Charlie Ford were the last two real friends Frank and Jess had had. All the others were dead, doing time or had joined forces with the law. Those still alive and not in jail, well, Jess had driven them off.

What was life worth, if it was nothing but dead comrades, imprisoned friends and a life spent on the owlhoot trail, living under aliases and off ill-gotten lucre?

His wife, Annie, said she didn't think she could take it much longer.

Well, Diaz and General Shelby, what they were offering Frank and Annie was more than a new lease on life, it was a whole new world of comfort, wealth, peace and security, a life in which they no longer had to fear Pinkertons and marshals, a life where for the first time in their lives they could live free and in...*peace.*

In Méjico.

Frank knew what people said about Diaz—how he abused and exploited the peons down there. So what? His ma and pa hadn't exactly babied their own slaves, and those slaves were 99.9 percent of his family's savings and total worth. Until the war erupted, those slaves had been a goddamn good investment. Buy yourself a two-year-old male slave for maybe $200, get them up doing chores by age four, and by age eleven real work. They cost nothing to raise, since slaves grew all the food and sewed their own clothes from grain sacks and discarded clothing. By age fifteen, them boys were worth over $1500 each, when sold down the river in the New Orleans markets to plantation owners in the deep, deep, Cotton-Is-King South.

The girls were worth almost as much, but instead of selling them, Ma tended to keep them working for the family and using them for breeding stock. If you kept a few women on hand, your slaves were a self-reproducing resource. You could add new slaves to your herd every year without having to buy them.

Plus, they paid for their keep and then some, planting and harvesting your crops and caring for your livestock.

No, before Lincoln and Grant blew it all up, those antebellum slaves had been a goddamn good investment and provided people, like the James family and the Younger clan, with a hell of a good life.

But, by God, Ma had whipped them darkies bloody.

Jess always pointed out that she'd whipped him and Frank halfway to death as well, and that was certainly true. They had a peach tree in the backyard with a low, overhanging limb. Ma used to cut switches from it, then string the boys and the slaves up by their wrists from that low limb. She whaled on them with those switches until her arm could no longer move. She then sometimes forced one of the slave women to flog them in her place. After a time, the peach tree, the switches and getting strung up by the wrists had become a daily-nightly obsession for his ma.

Their mother, Zerelda, was one mean old girl, all right.

Anymore, Frank's nights were filled with horrendous reveries of Ma—her hate, her rage and her obsession with revenge.

But it was just the way things were—a time and place where husbands ruled the roost and would take a whip to their wives as well as their children. But not in the James family household. Jess and Frank's father and their stepfathers, too, were helpless before Zerelda's wrath. No one could stop her once her blood was up and a peach switch was in her hand.

She'd use it on Samuel if he got in her way.

Which was why Samuel lit out for California to dig for gold.

To get away from his wife.

Frank purely believed that.

So was that where the violence came from?

From Zerelda?

Was that where it all went wrong?

CHAPTER 3

Slater finally reached El Rancho de Cielo. Sitting in Katherine Ryan's dining room, he was about to enjoy his first real meal in a week.

Katherine was sitting opposite him. An attractive woman in faded Levis, a brown work shirt and with long red hair, Katherine had run the ranch since her husband, Frank, had died six months earlier. Her son, Richard, had three months off from the US Cavalry for compassionate leave due to his father's death, and her daughter, Rachel, was home from college in Boston. Katherine was desperate for her to go back and finish school, but Rachel was resisting.

Slater's report that Diaz was raising an army of ex-rebels, who were coming to storm and seize holdings—800,000 acres in all, her ranch, her croplands and mining operations—could not have come at a worse time for Katherine. Slater wasn't thrilled either, but she and her kids were the closest thing to family he'd ever had.

"You think Diaz is serious about using them to attack El Rancho?" Katherine asked. "It sounds insane."

"Bet on it," Slater said.

The dining room table was already set with fried chicken, fried potatoes and corn on the cob. Richard entered the dining room, carrying a fresh pot of Arbuckles' coffee in one hand and a bottle of Jackson's Sour Mash in the other. He was was six feet four and very well built. His sister, Rachel, trailed him. She was carrying a pan of hot biscuits. Place settings were already on the table. Rachel was a foot shorter than Richard but had her mother's flame-red hair and wide, generous mouth. Both were wearing Levis, boots and broadcloth shirts. El Rancho de Cielo was a working ranch.

"Thought Torn might want a little something extra," Richard said, indicating the Sour Mash whiskey.

"Something to get that Arbuckles' up on its feet," Rachel added.

"Richard," Katherine said, "I still don't understand why the army at Fort Apache can't send a company—or at least a platoon—over here to help us out."

"Like I said, Geronimo's jumped the reservation again, and the whole fort is out on his trail. He's heading south toward the border and is raiding every ranch, wagon train, work camp, stage line, village, anything and everyone along the way. The cavalry's undermanned, as usual, and they have to catch him. Also, US troops aren't allowed to take up arms against our fellow Americans—only foreign enemies of the US government—such as foreign armies. And Diaz is hitting us with a proxy American force—with former Confederates, not a federale army."

"Diaz doesn't want to refight Santa Ana's war," Slater said, "using Méjicano troops. He remembers how that one went. He was there."

"So we're on our own," Katherine said.

"Yes, but we're not without resources," Slater said. "They won't be taking us by surprise."

"I can hire more men," Katherine said.

"Yeah," Slater said, "but the farmhands and vaqueros are all you can get around here, and they aren't going to cut it. Frank and Shelby, on the other hand, will have experienced Confederate veterans—some of them ex-guerilla fighters—men who rode by the light of the moon with Bloody Bill and Captain Quantrill. Hit and run specialists, men who flew the Black Flag."

"The Black Flag?" Katherine asked.

"No quarter given," Richard said.

"Men," Slater said, "who will kill and burn anything and anyone—no questions asked."

"You make them sound like terrorists," Rachel said.

"They are terrorists," Slater said, "and you better get used to it. They're going to hit this place like the Ten Plagues of Egypt."

"And we're supposed to—" Katherine started to ask.

Slater cut her off. "You're supposed to get meaner than a hydrophobic dog. You're supposed to hit them first with everything you have. Slow them down, make them bleed, throw them off their game, and drive the fear of God into them. Make them question the wisdom of their plan."

"And the men we need, who can do these things?" Katherine asked.

"To take on Frank and General Shelby," Slater said, "we'll need men who rode the high lines and ate that hard prison biscuit, who can kill unthinkingly. Men who won't spook at the sight and smell of blood or run when the big guns roar. I rode with them James-Youngers, and I fought with rebs at Shiloh. Men like that are a breed apart. And they're the kind of men you'll be up against. We're going to have to fight fire with fire."

Katherine stared at them, mute, shaking her head.

"None of us know the kind of men you say we need," Katherine finally said.

"And we know even less about how to hire them," Rachel said.

Slater poured a large slug of Jackson's Sour Mash into his Arbuckles' mug. Leaning back in his chair, he took a long pull.

"I do," he said simply, his voice toneless, his eyes devoid of emotion or expression.

Richard grabbed the bottle and poured whiskey in his and Rachel's mugs and then into Katherine's.

CHAPTER 4

"I see nothing wrong with our economic system," Diaz said that evening.

Bismarck and Nietzsche sat with Diaz and his friends in a private room at their hotel, enjoying an opulently catered seafood dinner. Wine was flowing freely. Diaz was in a good mood and smiling broadly. He seemed genuinely amused at Bismarck's and Nietzsche's discomfiture. Diaz's nation had ten forced-labor peons for every free citizen, and the extent to which even his so-called free people were truly free was highly problematic. The thought that an entire nation was inextricably dependent on so many millions of slaves perplexed his German guests to no end.

"Why do you pretend to care so much about our peons?" the Senorita asked Bismarck. "Do you think they care anything about you? They don't spend ten seconds a week worrying about Germany and its people's welfare."

"I was raised to believe that poverty was a sin," Bismarck said, "and your slaves are poverty incarnate, condemned to lives of brutal destitution."

"As long as our peons work," the Senorita said, "they receive daily sustenance, a roof over their heads and clothes to wear. Do you honestly believe we owe them something else?"

"What about freedom?" Nietzsche asked.

Their hosts' laughter seemed to go on forever.

"What's so funny?" Nietzsche asked after their booming, throbbing hilarity finally subsided.

"You suggested that we give them...*freedom,*" Sutherland said, wiping tears of mirth from his eyes and blowing his nose.

"Here in madre Méjico," Diaz explained, "that item is long out of stock."

"So long out of stock," Judith McKillian said, "that we all doubt it was ever in stock at all."

"Any rumors that it ever existed here are completely apocryphal," Diaz said. "Believe me, if it had ever existed here in any form, I would have known, and men like me would have stamped it out—ruthlessly, comprehensively."

"But that doesn't mean that your people don't deserve to be free," Bismarck countered.

In Germany, the chancellor was widely regarded as conservative, but here in Méjico the mistreatment of workers was so extreme that he sometimes felt like a wild-eyed radical.

"I, for one," Diaz said, turning to Bismarck and Nietzsche, "believe freedom to be grotesquely overrated."

"It is certainly counterproductive," the Senorita said. "It would interfere most deleteriously with our workers' productivity, which is, of course, why we have never allowed it to flourish."

"We can barely get any work out of our peons as it is now," Sutherland said querulously, "and under the current system, we can force them to do pretty near anything we want. Yet they still procrastinate and malinger."

"Can you imagine how idle and useless they would be," Judith McKillian said, "if they were free to do whatever they wanted? If they were free *not* to work?"

"If they could lay back in their hammocks," Sutherland said, "gorging themselves on tequila, tortillas, chili peppers and beans—and living off the fat of the land."

"Which is precisely what they would do," Judith McKillian said indignantly, "if we let them get up and walk off the job any time they wanted."

"You speak of your peons as if they were subhuman," Nietzsche said.

"What you don't understand," the Senorita said with surprising gentleness, "is that our peons differ from the citizens in your more advanced lands."

"In what way?" Nietzsche asked, skepticism written all over his face.

"The citizens of your country," the Senorita explained, "are blessed with an ability to concentrate. They possess self-discipline and the capacity to work even when unsupervised. They have that bare modicum of intelligence necessary to work on and complete projects without an overseer constantly breaking a whip over their backs. Our peons have none of those qualities or attributes."

"But Thomas Jefferson, the author of America's Declaration of Independence," Nietzsche said, "wrote that all people are born with 'inalienable rights,' including 'life, liberty and the pursuit of happiness.'"

"My friend," Diaz said, "I am so disappointed in you. Have you heard nothing? How many times must I tell you: By Christ's blood and bowels, by his bloody nails, 'life, liberty and the pursuit of happiness' do not apply to my peons. Without my violent intervention, they would once again be choking on human blood, devouring each other's flesh, sacrificing their daughters' vaginas to barbaric priests and pagan gods. Free these people, you say? I do not want them free. I want them branded, shackled and ruled by the whip. I want them laboring in my mines and factories and fields until they drop. And when they can work no more, even then, I do not want them living in this *liberté, egalité, fraternité* you so luminously speak of. I want them...*dead.*"

Diaz's diatribe left them all speechless, but Nietzsche was determined not to be intimidated. He took a deep breath.

"But your peasants must have some special gifts," Nietzsche said, his voice rising. "The Maya-Aztec empires were in existence for thousands of years before Cortez showed up in Veracruz. They built pyramids, created a religion, produced dazzling works of art and literature. They had their own written language."

"They do indeed possess one supremely singular talent," the Senorita said, nodding her head, agreeing with Nietzsche wholeheartedly.

"What is that?" Nietzsche asked.

"They excel," the Senorita said, "at...*reproduction.*"

"Meaning," Judith McKillian explained, "they breed like fucking...*lemmings!*"

Again, her friends, throwing back their heads, exploded in howling, thigh-slapping, gut-busting...*laughter.*

CHAPTER 5

Still Frank couldn't sleep. As the train rumbled through the night desert, Frank James continued helping himself to his capacious store of brandy and lighting up one Havana after another.

More and more, he found himself haunted by his past. Where had all his mother's hate and rage come from? Zerelda was mean enough to kill Jesus. Jess used to say she was angry enough to "kill a stick and eat a brick." And there was no denying that she had passed some of that anger onto her sons. Furthermore, their only real financial stability had come out of the equity they'd accumulated in their six slaves, and, consequently, Lincoln's Emancipation Proclamation had not only liberated those slaves, it had also emancipated the James family from the only real money that they would probably ever have.

But did Lincoln's freeing of the slaves justify all the cold graves and grieving widows Frank and Jess had left on their backtrails?

Frank had to admit that it didn't.

True, the Jameses had been hard-used and much-abused, but they'd always given back far worse than they'd received. His father used to say that Zerelda, misreading the Old Testament, had come to believe that when God had enjoined her to exact "an eye for an eye," He had meant to write "*a head* for an eye."

His father.

Thinking about the old man brought a wistful, bittersweet smile to Frank's face. He'd loved him more than life itself and was always sorry he'd died before Jess could really know him. He'd blessed the family with a sizable library of the great classics and had read to Frank night after night after night, giving his older son a thirst for learning and literature that he'd never lost. In those years, when his father was with them, Frank had been a bookworm, had shirked his chores—as Frank had read Lincoln had also done—in order to read books. He had even dreamed of becoming an educator and teaching children the classics, as his father had taught him. The old man never took a whip to him, not once.

A popular preacher, his father headed the local church. His sermons were much admired, and he was universally revered throughout Clay and Jackson Counties. When he and the family visited Independence or even Kansas City, Missouri, and walked the streets, people all but bowed and scraped before his father. They called him "the Good Reverend James"—even "the Reverend Doctor Robert Sallee James." Everywhere he and his father went, the townspeople lavished toffee, licorice and free bottles of sarsaparilla on the young boy.

"Nothing's too good for the son of Reverend Robert James," they'd say. "Maybe you'll grow up preachin' the Good News like your dad."

Those were the happiest days of Frank's life, his harpy, harridan, switch-swinging mother notwithstanding.

But his mother's temper, her violent rages and eternal grievances, were grinding away at the old man, driving him to distraction. Finally, at the end of his tether, he hit on a scheme to travel west, earn a fortune in the California goldfields. That it was a fool's errand and, at bottom, simply an excuse to get away from Zerelda was a fact that, in later years, would become transparently apparent to Frank. After all, they hadn't needed any of that goldfield money. Thanks to their slave investments, the James family was relatively well off.

In plain truth, Frank came to believe the old man could not stand Zerelda anymore, had bolted for the west coast out of desperation and had sought to get as far away from her as he could. He kept on heading west, chasing that setting sun, until he ran out of land and was only stopped, in the end, by the illimitable Pacific.

He died in those goldfields. Whether he was murdered for his claim, killed by wild beasts, or succumbed to dysentery, no one seemed to know. Frank could never get the straight of it—no matter how hard he tried.

Zerelda, however, quickly figured out the old man's motivation, and when she did, she felt personally betrayed.

Afterward her wrath knew no bounds. That peach tree hosted a mother lode of razor-sharp switches, and it became the bane of Frank and Jesse's existence. To his dying day, Frank could not stand to even look on a peach, let alone bite into one.

But the old man had been a different story. The gods broke the mold and threw it away when they created him. He not only read Shakespeare's plays and Pope's translation of the *Odyssey* to Frank, he told him stories from those books over and over and over again until they were burned deep into his memory and emblazoned on Frank's very soul. The lives and poetry of Hamlet and Macbeth, of Odysseus and Achilles, of Adam, Eve and even Satan in *Paradise Lost* became as real to Frank as his own life and the lives of his friends.

His old man was inordinately fond of Tennyson's poem about Odysseus, *Ulysses*, which was how the Romans had spelled the great warrior-wanderer's name. Frank thought he'd gotten Odysseus just right. In the poem, Tennyson had an aged Odysseus look back on his life and think:

I am become a name;
For always roaming with a hungry heart
Much have I seen and known; cities of men
And manners, climates, councils, governments,
Myself not least, but honour'd of them all;
And drunk delight of battle with my peers,
Far on the ringing plains of windy Troy.
I am a part of all that I have met.

The old man would read to him the grand soliloquies of *Hamlet* and *Macbeth*, the most dramatic scenes, acting out all the parts for Frank, employing different voices and utilizing vividly dramatic gestures. He read to Frank *Paradise Lost,* which Frank could never get enough of. Frank especially loved Satan's speeches. One of his favorites was Beelzebub's speech to Satan and Satan's response:

"If thou beest he,—but oh how fallen! how changed
From him, who, in the happy realms of light,
Clothed with transcendent brightness didst outshine

Myriads though bright!... Now misery hath joined
In equal ruin... into what pit thou seest
From what height fallen... And till then who knew
The force of those dire arms?

He now sometimes wondered if Jess was sharing Satan's fate.

Frank, to this day, trembled at the thought.

His father also read to him depictions of the world into which Satan had been plunged. The words had terrified Frank as a boy, and as a man, he occasionally wondered if, figuratively, God had hurled him howling into the earthly equivalent of Milton's hell. His life, so far, had been one of unrelieved fire, unending blood and unendurable darkness. Frank frequently pondered the poet's description of that hellworld and what it meant to himself, his own life and whatever future dispensation he was doomed to suffer:

A dungeon horrible, on all sides round
As one great furnace flamed, yet from those flames
No light, but rather darkness visible
Served only to discover sights of woe,
Regions of sorrow, doleful shades, where peace
And rest can never dwell, hope never comes
That comes to all; but torture without end
Still urges, and a fiery deluge, fed
With ever–burning sulphur unconsumed:
Such place eternal justice had prepared
For those rebellious, here their prison ordained
In utter darkness, and their portion set
As far removed from God and light of heaven
As from the center thrice to th'utmost pole.

"Hope never comes...but torture without end." That was the fate to which Satan had been sentenced. Increasingly "torture without end" seemed, to Frank, to be his lot—to say nothing of Jess and what had happened to him.

Staring out the train window at the evanescent spectacle of the passing chaparral, he wondered idly when, if ever, his ordeal would end.

CHAPTER 6

"*What?*" Bismarck asked, his voice rising in shock.

He, Nietzsche, Diaz and his associates were still sitting in the brothel-casino's private dining room. They were now imbibing their postprandial cognacs and smoking excellent Havana *Por Larranaga* cigars.

"Let me reiterate," the Senorita said, giving the chancellor her sunniest smile. "Our peasants aren't good for much, but they do have truly exceptional…*gonads.*"

"Which they employ most prolifically," the Senorita chortled, her voice chiming almost as melodiously as a bell.

"Let me concur," James Sutherland said. "I know Méjico's peon class intimately. I've employed these contemptible cretins by the millions. I know our peons better than they know themselves, and while they don't have much upstairs, one thing they have in superabundance is…*offspring.* Méjico's peons may not be very bright or even a little bit industrious, but you can't complain that there aren't enough of them."

"You ask me," Judith McKillian said, "we have far too many of the odious little bastards. In my opinion, the world would be better off if we had quite a few fewer of these utterly repugnant wretches. Getting a day's work out of them is appallingly difficult—so arduous I truly wonder if it is worth the effort we put into them. I can't imagine how impossible they would be if the gods had given them brains instead of their endlessly indefatigable… *reproductive organs?*"

"All of which is irrelevant to the essential iniquity of your entire economic system," Bismarck said stiffly.

"Not at all," Sutherland averred. "Isn't it obvious, Herr Chancellor, that their gonads are obviously the reason we can't get more labor out of them? Instead of working their derrieres off for us, they procreate their loins off. How can you expect them to get any work done? They do proliferate...*incessantly*."

"Still," Diaz said to Sutherland, "you must admit that there is an upside to all that nonstop copulation."

"Yes, Mr. Sutherland," the Senorita said, "there is a serious upside to all these myriad Méjicano progeny, from which you, the divine Senora McKillian and I have all profited most exorbitantly. Should you tell her what it is or should I, Mr. Sutherland?"

"You tell her," Sutherland said.

"Then I say this to our guests as well," the Senorita said. "When you and your nation acquire our mines and croplands, including our ever-lucrative sugarcane fields, you receive in the bargain legions of free laborers, with which to wring an extortionate profit from our benighted land."

"No labor shortages here!" Diaz shouted. "Our people are constantly producing an infinitely fertile, eternally self-renewing supply of...*peons*."

"You mean slaves," Bismarck rasped hoarsely.

"THANK GAWD!" Sutherland roared with his gaudiest English accent.

"We deserve no less!" the Senorita yelled rousingly.

"No union problems either," Judith McKillian said, sniffing daintily. "No strikes, no demands for forty-hour weeks or eight-hour days or medical leave or pensions or free education or guaranteed healthcare or increased...*wages!*"

"In fact, here in Méjico," Sutherland said with a truly spectacular sneer, "we don't pay our employees anything at all."

"Were it up to me," McKillian said, "I would demand that they pay us instead."

"They do in a way, darling," Sutherland said gently.

"And in what way is that?" Judith McKillian asked, bemused at his suggestion.

"We do, after all," Sutherland said, "receive the fruits of their labor—100 percent of their so industriously labored fruits."

"As well we should," McKillian said sharply.

"It was ever thus," Diaz said.

"And ever shall be," the Senorita said.

"It has always been that way in Méjico," Diaz patiently explained.

"Well said!" Sutherland enthused.

"Nicely done," McKillian agreed.

Bismarck and Friedrich Nietzsche stared at each other in blank, uncomprehending astonishment.

CHAPTER 7

Frank James's father had read many books to him. Frank especially loved Odysseus's adventures—particularly, the tale of how Polyphemus, the cyclops, had trapped Odysseus and his men in his cave. The one-eyed giant roasted Odysseus's men on spits and ate them like hunks of barbequed beef. Knowing that time was running out, Odysseus got Polyphemus inebriated on the highly concentrated wine they'd carried inland as a present to whomever ruled that land. While Polyphemus fell drunkenly asleep, Odysseus had burned out the giant's one huge eye with a heated, sharpened pole. He and his men then escaped, while the giant raged and stumbled blindly about his cave.

But when their ships pulled out away from the island, in a moment of hubris and rage, Odysseus had roared at the cyclops:

"Tell them it was Odysseus did this to you!"

Unfortunately, for Odysseus, Polyphemus's father was Poseidon—the god of the sea and of storms. Poseidon had responded to Odysseus's taunt by forcing him to wander the seas another ten long, terrifying years—damned by the pride that always precedes the fall.

Had that hubris been Frank and Jesse's crucial blunder?

Had they too thundered their names at the gods too many times in blind, ignorant, arrogant rage?

Had the gods, thus, cursed them as they had Odysseus?

Frank had once described his concerns to Jess, suggesting that maybe it had all gone wrong when they'd met John Newman Edwards and he'd started writing those newspaper pieces. Frank told Jess that Edwards had shouted their names at Poseidon, the god of storms, just as he and Jess were midway through the voyage of their lives, Edwards braying that Frank and Jess weren't thieves but Southern war heroes and patriots, reviving, refighting and relitigating the South's "War Against Northern Aggression." Edwards had made the two brothers household names not only in Missouri but nationwide—hell, across the entire world. But in doing so, perhaps he'd trumpeted their names at the gods too many goddamned times, forgetting that they were all sinners in the hands of angry gods and that the gods did not suffer hubris gladly.

But when Frank told Jess and Edwards that Edwards should stop writing about them, Jess had laughed in his face, saying he liked old Edwards and loved those news articles. Edwards said the articles were popular as hell and that people everywhere loved them and that they sold newspapers. Jess added that he liked having people know his name, loved them extolling his exploits, buying him drinks and slapping him on the back. Jess said he loved it that newsmen everywhere were asking him for interviews, hanging on his every word, and that he loved the glory and thrilled to the fear that their names and presence instilled in people, reveling in the adulation and the fame. He, furthermore, told Frank that men made their own luck and that blaming their misfortunes on the gods was cowardly and stupid. People like Frank just didn't want to face the consequences of their actions.

Shakespeare's *Julius Caesar* seemed to agree with Jess, and the Bard's words came back to Frank, hitting him now with all the force of an epiphany. Caesar had once explained to his former friend, Brutus:

"The fault, dear Brutus, is not in our stars
But in ourselves. . . ."

So it seemed to Frank that Jess had brought it all on himself. Through Edwards, he had shouted his and Frank's names at the gods far too many times, with too much condescension and with too many decibels. Instead of genuflecting before the gods above and pledging obeisance, they had been insultingly vain. Now those darkly duplicitous deities, tired of reading Edwards's insolent and ungrateful rants, were having their own say—in their own illustrious way—or so it now seemed to Frank.

One thing was beyond doubt or cavil or equivocation: The walls were closing in, Frank was running for his life, and, as for Jess, he wasn't around to debate the ways of God to man with his brother anymore.

Frank was still sitting alone in his train compartment, and, once more, he took down the carpetbag from the overhead rack and placed it on his lap. Retrieving the cognac bottle, he again studied the label. He enjoyed looking at it. It gave him solace—a reprieve from his worries and cares.

The label read: *1863 Camus Napoleon La Grande Marque Cognac*—named after Napoleon himself!

Goddamn, Diaz had done good—goddamned good.

Refilling his brandy flask, Frank raised it to his lips and offered up a toast to Generalissimo José de la Cruz Porfirio Diaz. What was that toast Diaz liked so much?

A la salut y riqueza y cojones.

To health, wealth and balls.

Balls, indeed.

Frank James slowly savored another life-sustaining draught of Napoleon's own inimitable cognac.

Bottled in 1863, and God only knew how old the cask was.

It was older than Frank James, that was for sure.

Goddamn it, life *was* good.

Thanks to good old Porfirio.

He helped himself to another snort. Holding it in his mouth, he lit up another El Roy del Mundo, drawing deeply on the fragrant Havana cigar.

PART VI

"After all," the Senorita said, giving Nietzsche her most glowingly gorgeous smile, "what are a few impecunious peons to anyone more or less?"

CHAPTER 1

Diaz came through for Nietzsche. Setting up tours of several haciendas, the generalissimo arranged for Bismarck to see what Méjico was like with his own eyes. The train trip to the sugar plantation along the Pacific Coast had been, thankfully, uneventful, and they were traveling in style. Nietzsche and Chancellor Bismarck had a double-club car to themselves in Diaz's "El Presidente Tren Expreso Personal." Diaz's personal express train, it was pulled by an eight-wheel Baldwin locomotive with a diamond-shaped smokestack, and Diaz, the Senorita, Sutherland and Judith McKillian kept Bismarck and Nietzsche company in the luxurious club car. The six of them sat on floor-bolted, leather-padded, black-cherry armchairs. Alongside them were bolted-down matching end tables, which were brass-ridged along the edges so glassware could not slide off. Other brass fittings also gleamed brilliantly throughout the club car. On the tables were silver ice buckets, in which bottles of Henriot Brut Souverain and Laurent-Perrier Grand Siècle chilled. Into the tables were cut circular holes, a half inch deep, into which the patrons could place their champagne flutes. Dishes of Persian caviar; Manchego cheese; pâté; jalapeno, habanero and poblano chili peppers; chorizas; jamón-ham; and thin fresh loaves of pan de pais were laid out before them as well as thick, fluffy, fresh-baked tortillas.

Behind the club car were six sleeping cars, in which each guest had a soft bed, chairs and desk, toilet facilities and other amenities. After the sleeping cars came four dozen ventilated stockcars. These were the quarters for their contingent of two hundred heavily armed federales, who traveled everywhere with the generalissimo. Decked out in field uniforms, the side brims of their campaign cavalry hats were pinned up on the right sides, so as not to interfere with the unlimbering of rifles, sidearms and sabers. The soldados had belted pistolas strapped to their waists, rifles slung inverted from their shoulders and across their backs. Bandoleers of shiny cartridges crisscrossed their chests. Their horses, which also traveled beside them in the stock cars, were saddled and ready to mount. Plank platforms could be dropped over the sides of the cars when they were ready to decamp, so they could ride their mounts directly off the stock cars the second the train stopped.

Whenever they stopped for coal, water and to stretch their legs, Diaz and Nietzsche walked down the long line of cars—in part, to observe the train's security detail. The first time Nietzsche pointed them out to Bismarck, he suggested to the chancellor:

"One gets the sense that the generalissimo might not be universally revered in his eternally suffering land."

Still, the trip in the club car had been pleasant. The refreshments were superb, and Diaz and his three associates—as well as the train's waiters and servers—had done their best to be attentive but not overly intrusive. The entertainment featured two guitarists—one classical, the other Andalusian flamenco—and they filled the car with rhapsodic music. Nietzsche recognized many of the melodies—particularly, four haunting songs of farewell, for which Méjico was justly famous and which the musicians performed to perfection: "O Cara Armonia," "Dolea de Arcasu," "Venecia" and "Canco del Lladre." Nietzsche and Bismarck were both pleased to hear Bach's enthralling and energetic baroque melodies as well as the beautiful and enchanting "Una Flor." The flamenco music was especially electrifying, filled with cascading arpeggios, three- and four-note tremolas, slippery glittering glissandos, single-line picados, played alternately with the index and middle fingers, the thumb rapidly gliding over the adjacent strings as well as golpe finger-tapping of the sound board just above or barely below the strings, the music initially sorda, or soft, but then fuerte, or strong, pounding, stirring.

Their version of "Flamenco Malaguena" was so overwhelming Bismarck had to stand and applaud amid shouts of "Excelentíssimo!" and "Grandifico!"

It was not for nothing that in madre Méjico, music was known as "the brandy of the damned."

The train roared over the Méjicano llano country, wound through mountain ranges, and after negotiating the passes and trestles, gradually descended into the marshy coastal regions—filled with swamps and cane fields.

They eventually pulled into the train station for La Hacienda de Dulce, the largest sugar plantation in all of Méjico.

CHAPTER 2

Further north, a night train lumbered on and on and on through the Great Sonoran Desert, while Frank James continued working his way through his store of brandy—flask after flask after flask. Not that he was getting drunk. The liquor seemed to have no more effect on him than a shot glass of his cognac would have on the two-thousand-mile-long Rio Grande River, which the train was just rolling over.

Damn, that Napoleon cognac was going down smooth. Luckily, Frank had almost four more liter bottles in his two bags, and enough double eagles in his money belt to buy himself all the good drinking whiskey a man could hope for when the cognac ran out.

He'd need something to replace it. Anymore, Frank James couldn't sleep—at all. Memories of his past haunted his brain and tormented his soul. He now viewed his life as one protracted mistake.

In truth, he had never wanted to join up with Quantrill and his Confederate irregulars. He would have preferred to fight in the Confederate Army of Missouri, but when he tried to fight for that army, he came down with one of those damned camp diseases—cholera, dysentery, gonorrhea—the doctors were never sure which. He'd simply fallen out ill—so sick he almost died. By then, the Union Army had laid siege to Lexington, won, and then driven all the official Confederate forces out of Missouri. So when Frank recovered and was well enough to rejoin the Confederate forces, well, there weren't any Confederate forces left in the state for him to rejoin—not after that first year of war.

Even worse, while he was heading home, the Union Army caught up with him. They forced him to sign papers renouncing the Confederacy and swearing allegiance to the Union. They told him it was sign those papers or go straight to prison, so for Alexander Franklin James, signing them versus not signing them was no choice at all.

He eventually regained his health, and afterward he tied up with an irregular unit headed up by Fernando Scott. Quantrill was where the action was, however. Frank was young, headstrong, and, very quickly, he was riding alongside him.

In retrospect, joining that band was where it all went wrong—not only for himself but for his thirteen-year-old brother, Jesse, who, idolizing Frank, had sworn to follow him anywhere—into hell, if that's where the war took him. Looking back on it, that's precisely where Frank had gone, dragging his little brother with him—into a life of murder, pillage, mayhem and rapine.

And William Clarke Quantrill.

Who was that murdering bastard, anyway, and what had been his game? Frank should have known the answer to that one. He and Jess had sold their souls to him for pennies on the dollar. They'd done things for Quantrill that guaranteed him and Jess eternities of hellfire and damnation. Quantrill had no principles that Frank had ever been able to ascertain. He'd started out as an abolitionist of all things, backing Jim Lane and his anti-slavery militias. Living hard, Quantrill played even harder, draining bottle after bottle, while playing high-stakes, all-night poker, betting everything he had on the turn of a card and killing men over minor disagreements like there was no tomorrow.

So why had Quantrill created a Confederate militia? Perhaps because he'd learned that there was more money to be made hunting down and returning runaway slaves to their brutal owners than in killing the owners.

In 1861, Quantrill had first joined the Confederacy down in Texas—while Frank was fighting futilely in Missouri's ragtag Confederate Army—serving with a Cherokee half-breed named Joe B. Mayes. During that period, Mayes had convinced Quantrill that conventional tactics against the North's overwhelmingly superior force—superior in troop numbers, ordnance, transportation and materiel—would never prevail. Instead, he taught Quantrill the finer arts of Cherokee guerilla fighting—hit and run, hostage abduction, strategic retreat, camouflage, counter-offensive, the art of the ambush and other forms of sneak attack. Mayes used to say he could sum up their game in one sentence:

"I hold hostage what the Yanks hold dear."

Frank recognized the terrible logic in what Mayes said, and he taught Frank the efficacy of violent terror judiciously applied to the local population, thereby isolating them from the Union forces and frightening them into submission and cooperation.

Quantrill had initially fought under General Sterling Price—both at Wilson's Creek and Lexington—but by Christmas 1861, he had recruited ten men on his own, had an independent militia force and was bringing war, as he'd come to know it, to the Union Army and to anti-slavery sympathizers. He was officially a guerilla fighter, and Frank was with him.

Quantrill's enemies claimed he flew the black flag of anarchy and massacre—no quarter asked and none given—and Frank had learned to live with that.

In Kansas and Missouri, Quantrill's Raiders quickly became infamous:

In September 1862, they overran an undermanned Union outpost at Aubry, Kansas, and sacked the town.

Later that month, Quantrill and 140 followers raided Olathe, Kansas, and forced 125 Union soldiers to surrender to them.

The next month, October, he destroyed Shawneetown, Kansas.

The following month, Quantrill and his men fought the 8th Regiment Missouri Volunteer Cavalry, torching half the town of Lone Jack, Missouri, as they left.

How many of those battles Frank fought he could no longer remember.

But those conflicts weren't the ones that stuck in his mind. There were battles that passed through the fog of his memory like spectral armies of fading ghosts.

What stuck with Frank—what plagued his dreams—was the massacre of Lawrence, Kansas, in which Quantrill had ordered them to kill "every male-thing" in the town.

CHAPTER 3

Diaz, Bismarck and Nietzsche inspected the sugarcane fields on horseback. They rode up a dirt road, running between two vast fields of cane. Each plant contained several heavily segmented stalks, which sprouted long sword-shaped leaves. Each of the stalks was tipped and tasseled with tiny flowers.

A dozen feet behind them rode Sutherland, Judith McKillian and the Senorita. All six of them sat on Méjicano saddles of black leather. Ostentatiously tricked out in ornate silver and turquoise, the saddles also featured that country's traditional "dinner-plate pommels" and high, heavy cantles. The immense weight of all that heavy gear was hard on their horses, but Nietzsche had to admit, the saddles were comfortable. He was an expert horseman, and his cantle was high and broad enough that he could lean back against it, and after adjusting to his horse's rhythm and gait, Nietzsche felt, at times, as if he was being lulled peacefully to sleep in a rocking chair.

All six of them were well mounted. Diaz had picked out a large black stallion for himself—over seventeen hands high so that he towered above the others. The Senorita was on an obsequiously gentle bay, McKillian a feisty gray, which she made even feistier through the studious and unceasing application of the riding crop looped to her wrist. Nietzsche had never seen her without it and now suspected that she slept with it. Bismarck had been given a flamboyantly colored but utterly imperturbable paint, while Nietzsche rode a rambunctious roan. Nietzsche noted that all six were experienced riders. He himself had trained with Prussia's horse cavalry during the Franco-Prussian War and recognized people who could or could not handle horses.

Diaz had, once again, insisted that they wear trail garb. For Bismarck and Nietzsche that meant Levis, work shirts and tan campaign cavalry hats. For the two women, trail garb meant riding outfits that included jodhpurs, riding boots, pale blouses, dark leather vests and light-colored John B. Stetsons of the finest Andalusian felt.

To get his mind off the heat, the sheer depravity of his hosts and the unutterable tedium of the trip, Nietzsche focused what was left of his waning attention on the sugarcane fields and the surrounding terrain. They were near the coast, and the climate here was swelteringly hot and oppressively humid. The fields were surrounded by swamps and marshes on all sides. In short, the soil and climate were perfect for raising cane.

Diaz and the Senorita were holding forth on the theory and practice of farming sugarcane and manufacturing sugar:

"Saccharum villosum is the most pervasively grown sugarcane inMéjico," Diaz was explaining in sonorous tones. "It's a kind of gigantic grass, really, whose stalk—otherwise known as cane—is packed with sucrose. Our workers strip it first of its thin, shooting leaves, then harvest it with hooked knives, just above the base."

"The trick is not to damage the root," the Senorita said. "That way it will regenerate itself next year, and we will get a brand-new crop."

"Ruining the root is very bad business," Diaz said.

"In fact, it's a flogging offense," McKillian said, whipping her boot top furiously, as if for emphasis.

"Yes, most certainly," Sutherland said, "and we have to watch our peons. After they cut the sugarcane, it quickly sours, so they not only have to work carefully, they have to work fast and efficiently at the same time. If they are either slow or sloppy, our overseers have orders to come down on them hard—immediately."

Up the road, Nietzsche spotted several buildings wreathed in thick grayish-black smoke.

"What are those?" Nietzsche asked no one in particular.

"The rolling mill," Diaz said, "the boiling house and the curing station."

"Then there are the distillery and the stable for the work animals," Sutherland said. "There is also the trash house, where we dry the leftover cane, so we can use it as fuel."

"Why so much smoke?" Bismarck asked.

"Those buildings are filled with furnaces, boiling cauldrons, grinding machines and are heated by the fires of hell," the Senorita said amiably.

"The temperature outside is already over a hundred degrees Fahrenheit," Bismarck said.

"And the humidity's topping a hundred," Nietzsche pointed out.

"And those factories look absolutely diabolic," Bismarck said.

"'*Lasciate ogne speranza*,'" [Abandon all hope ye who enter there] Nietzsche said gloomily, quoting from Dante's poem, *Inferno.*

"You don't know the half of it, ducks," McKillian said under her breath, chuckling to herself, ruefully, mockingly.

CHAPTER 4

Frank James had just refilled his brandy flask and relit another Havana. It was a good thing. As the train hammered through the American Southwest's arid and sun-scorched wastes, his memory was rolling nonstop through those Kansas-Missouri border wars—the battles he'd fought, the banks that he'd hit, the trains that he'd robbed, the men that he'd killed and the widows and children who'd sobbed—who had cursed the James brothers' names and then wept even harder.

Frank James now needed lots of 1863 Camus Napoleon La Grande Marque Cognac and plenty of El Roy del Mundos to get him through this dark night of his forever lost and eternally damned soul.

How could he ever forget February 13, 1866, and the robbery of Liberty, Missouri's Clay County Savings Association? That was a landmark heist—a real record-setter: the first daylight, peacetime bank holdup in America, and its timing was fortuitous. Prior to the Civil War, the US was awash in thousands of poorly regulated wildcat banks, authorized to issue their own currency. Inundated by over five thousand different varieties of currency—many of which were utterly uncollateralized—much of the country's paper money was barely worth the paper it was printed on. So many banks had collapsed that Washington had been forced to decree a single currency, then nationalize over a thousand of the country's surviving banks. For the next several years, Washington then had to flood the banking system with enormous shipments of hard currency.

But the program had worked.

Paper money was finally worth one hundred cents on the dollar.

The great age of bank heists and money train robberies had also begun.

At Liberty Missouri's Clay County Savings Association, Frank and Jess celebrated that golden age by riding off with over $58,000 of depositor funds—in those days an astronomical amount of money.

On the way out of town—while still in a celebratory mood—their gang gratuitously gunned down nineteen-year-old George Wymore, an unarmed student at William Jewell College.

Lieutenant Colonel Samuel P. Cox of the Union Army had enticed "Bloody Bill" Anderson—one of their most ferocious guerilla leaders—into an ambush. After hunting him down and killing him, the gang had taken his corpse to nearby Richmond, Missouri, and had it photographed for the national newspapers. The mocking disrespect with which the photo had depicted Bloody Bill's remains rankled Frank and Jess to the bone. Swearing revenge on Cox, he and Frank hit two banks in and around the city of Richmond, where Anderson's killer was reputed to be working as a cashier.

In the Daviess County Savings Association in Gallatin, Missouri, Jess shot and killed the cashier, a Captain John Sheets, mistaking him for Cox.

After sticking up numerous banks—as well as a local fair in Kansas City—they began robbing trains. Wearing Ku Klux Klan masks, they hijacked a Rock Island Line train in Iowa, absconding with $3,000.

Their money train heists were so lucrative that the railroad industry hired Allan Pinkerton's national detective agency to track the James brothers down. Their gang quickly killed three of his agents—one, John Whicher, they tortured first.

Allan Pinkerton swore a personal vendetta against the James brothers. In one of his attacks on the Jameses' farm, his men bombed the family home, blowing off one of the arms of their mother, Zerelda Samuels. Allan Pinkerton denied that the raid's purpose was arson, but later a letter of Pinkerton's was uncovered, stating that he wanted his agents to "burn the house down."

In Missouri, the Jameses were not without their supporters. The state legislature almost passed a bill granting the James brothers amnesty. Recently enfranchised Confederate legislators did pass a bill limiting the size of the rewards that the governor could place on the James brothers' heads. Still, in Missouri, Frank and Jess were hounded, hunted men.

They began looking for cash-rich banks outside of the state.

In retrospect, Frank believed that robbing banks outside of Missouri was their single biggest mistake. No jury in that state would have ever had the nerve to convict him, Jess or one of the Youngers—certainly not in Clay or Jackson Counties. Their clans' vindictiveness was well established and widely feared.

Unfortunately, the rest of the country wasn't intimidated.

CHAPTER 5

Diaz and his guests dismounted near the sugar mill hitchracks and tied up their horses. Everywhere Bismarck looked, he saw mounted uniformed soldados—sent from Diaz's regional vigilante gangs, his much-dreaded "Rurales." They wore tan military caps and were armed with shotguns and side-arms. Most had cartridge-studded bandoleers strapped across their chests and rifles slung diagonally, stock up, across their backs.

In front of the roller mill stood a bearded overseer with cold, lifeless eyes, long jet-black hair, a matching downward-turning mustache and a sweat-stained sombrero. Dressed in a tan cotton shirt and pants, crisscrossed bandoleers and a pistol strapped to his waist, a steeple-crowned military hat and boots, he was running a peon's wrist thongs through a thick eye hook screwed into the top of a tall post. The peon was naked from the waist up. The post was so high and the man yanked up so tight, he was forced to stand on his tiptoes.

Counting his steps carefully, the overseer walked backward, then stopped to study the task before him. Beside him was a bucket in which were several heavy knotted ropes soaking in a solution.

"What's the liquid in the buckets?" Bismarck asked Diaz.

"Brine," he answered. "The flogging will drive the salt deep into the man's wounds. The salt will see to it that the pain is bone-deep and lasts a long time."

The flogging began, and by the eleventh stroke the man was howling insanely, like some miserable, pain-racked creature gone mad with feral suffering.

"It's only a flogging," Diaz said, with a dismissive shrug, "and it will last a long time. Let's visit the mill."

"It will, no doubt, still be going on," Sutherland said, "when you come back outside."

"Aren't you coming with us, James?" the Senorita asked.

"I've had my fill of rolling mills," Sutherland said. "Really, dear, they are just too sweaty, too stifling and too eternally... *boring*."

"James would rather watch the flogging," the Senorita suggested.

"Wouldn't we all," Judith McKillian said.

"Still, we have promised our German guests a tour of these refining facilities," Diaz said, "and I am determined that we shall give it to them."

Approaching the roller mill, Bismarck felt the heat pouring out of the building in gaspingly hot waves.

"Believe it or not," Diaz said, "what keeps most people out of the sugar production business isn't the hard work and the stifling heat. It's the start-up costs, which I can help your investors avoid. Most of that red ink is due to the cost of labor crews. Here, since labor costs us nothing, we can eliminate those expenses."

"Labor here will cost you," Judith McKillian shouted, laughing giddily, gleefully, "... *nada!*"

Bismarck now got a closer look at the half dozen buildings. Through the steam and smoke, he could see that they were arranged in a semicircle, constructed of brown adobe brick. Each one was three stories high and approximately 150 feet long by 100 feet wide. The windows all had bars.

"The owners here must fear sabotage," Bismarck said quietly in Nietzsche's ear, pointing to the window bars.

"Or they're afraid that the workers will escape," the younger man said.

"That too," Bismarck said, after giving Nietzsche a dismayed look.

"The first building," Diaz shouted in a booming voice, interrupting the two men's tête-à-tête, "is the roller mill, where we press and extract the liquid sugar out of the cane. You will note the windmill on each side of the house. Wind helps to power the rollers."

"And when the wind dies down," Bismarck observed, "I don't suppose your workers are given the day off."

"Not at all," McKillian said. "We switch to mule power, and sometimes, if dray beasts aren't available or are too exhausted, peon power."

"The next is the boiling house," Diaz said, "where we steam the water out of the liquid and reduce the liquid to a boiling-hot porridge. The next building is the curing house, where we extract the pure crystalized sugar from the porridge-like syrup that is left over. There's also a trash house where the leftover cane, called bagasse, is dried and turned into fuel, which we feed into the furnaces. Then there are the distilleries that produce our rum. Next to that building are the stables for the animals. They are all out back."

"What's that larger whitewashed building another fifty yards down the road?" Bismarck asked.

"That's the office building," Diaz said, "where the mill's manager, the clerks and accountants tabulate and record our financial records. They calculate the extraordinary profits that the mills and the fields turn out each year."

"Looks like a lot of work," Bismarck said.

"It is," Diaz said.

"We can't process all the cane all at once," the Senorita said. "Production of the actual sugar is too laborious, too hot and too time-consuming."

"We, consequently, lose as many as a third of our peons per year," Diaz said. "They find work simply unbearable."

"We stagger the planting of the sugarcane," the Senorita said, "so that the crop doesn't come up all at once."

"Down here the weather is so propitious," Judith McKillian explained, "we can plant and harvest any time we want. Climate changes aren't an issue."

"Their bodies deteriorate," Diaz said, "and so they fall prey to every disease known to God and man, which causes, among other things, abject exhaustion. The workers lose all strength. They can barely lift a spoon or fork to their mouths."

"On our sugar haciendas," the Senorita said somberly, "yearly deaths far exceed annual births."

"By an embarrassingly wide margin," McKillian said, nodding gravely.

Unfolding a flamboyantly colored Siamese fan—filled with splashes of bright yellow, gaudy green and garish crimson—Judith McKillian began cooling herself.

"What do you do with so many dead and dying bodies?" Bismarck asked, horrified but grimly curious.

"We cart their repugnantly malodorous corpses to the swamps and drag them to the water's edge," the Senorita said.

"And?" Bismarck asked.

"And the crocodiles do the rest," McKillian said, joyfully whipping her boot top and laughing merrily.

"You dispose of desperately ill peons as well as the already dead?" Bismarck asked. "You don't even wait to see if they…*live?*"

"Their only value to us is in their work," Diaz asked, "and they're easily replaced by healthier peons."

"Don't your workers protest?" Bismarck asked. "Our laborers strike all the time in Europe. In 1848, the whole continent went up in revolutionary flames."

"Occasionally, a prisoner or two gets desperate and insane enough to attack a guard," the Senorita said.

"Or attempt an escape," Judith McKillian said.

"What do you do?" Nietzsche asked.

"We tie them to a flogging post in front of the entire work force and flog them to…*death,*" Judith McKillian said.

"We literally flay them whole with our whips," said the Senorita.

"Afterward, I insist that the hacendados put their heads on posts and stakes," Diaz said, "in places our peons frequent regularly and where the severed heads will be conspicuously visible."

"Delightful," Nietzsche said under his breath.

"Anyone want to step into the roller mill?" the Senorita asked, abruptly changing the subject.

Nietzsche and Bismarck both nodded bleakly, and Diaz opened the door. The heat blew out of the building so hard that it whooshed the air out of their lungs and almost drove the two men to their knees.

"Welcome to our world," McKillian said, smiling brightly.

"It will give your phrase '*Süss wie Zucker*' [sweet as sugar] a whole new meaning," the Senorita said.

CHAPTER 6

As the train headed north, the cognac flask remained locked in Frank's fist. One El Roy del Mundo after another was clenched between his teeth, even as the sun rose over the desert chapparal on his right. In his mind's eye, Frank could still see the blood-red ball of the dawn sun rising over Lawrence, Kansas—which he now viewed as the tomb of his life.

Kansas had abolished slavery in 1860, and that Kansas town was notorious among the pro-slavery factions for harboring rredlegs and jayhawkers—most notably, Jim Lane's and Charles "Doc" Dennison's anti-slavery, free-state militia groups. Those two were hell-bent on driving pro-slavery vigilantes out of Kansas and back into the Deep South. Frank and Quantrill were just as determined to drive those Yankee sons of bitches out of the state or to plant them deep under the dense Kansas hardpan.

Quantrill ordered the assault on Lawrence partly because of "General Order No. 10," issued by General Thomas Ewing. That proclamation had mandated the arrest and imprisonment of anyone giving aid and comfort to the anti-Union, slavery-supporting Confederate guerillas. In reality, that order meant rounding up the female relatives of all suspected Confederates and throwing them into Lawrence's recently and crudely constructed women's prison. Militia women had been declared enemies of the state and hostages to the North.

Before Quantrill and his followers invaded Lawrence, Quantrill had told Frank that they were going to do to those Union sympathizers what they'd done to Frank's stepfather and younger brother, and at the time, that sounded goddamned good. Those bloody fiends had tortured Jess and Dr. Samuels horridly and then blown Zerelda's arm off her body. Those atrocities had driven his ma, Zerelda, completely around the bend—so much so she'd almost flogged one of their slaves to death the next day. Frank wanted vengeance against those jayhawking redlegs so bad he could taste, breathe and feel it.

So at the time, when Quantrill brought it up, the prospect of killing every male-thing in Lawrence had sounded good to Frank—the sort of vengeance-is-mine justice he'd heard so much about in church and from his fire-breathing ma.

Any longer, he wasn't so sure, and, whatever the case, Lawrence had been beyond the pale.

He'd never seen so much hate-filled violence and needless, brutal murder in his life—not before and not after Lawrence. He'd been drinking a lot during the massacre—he'd needed the whiskey to keep his hands steady and to stay sane—and, at the time, he'd seemed to float through the slaughter as if it were all a dream. But as the years went by, and as he read of the carnage in the press, heard tales of the mayhem recited in saloons, heard old friends brag about what they'd done, and as the long-suppressed memories of that day came back to him—first one by one, then in waves—it had seemed to him as if he'd been a spectator rather than a participant. But, in truth, he'd killed his share that day—more than his share. Over the years—gradually, inexorably, agonizingly—the reality of what he and his friends had done that day began to sink in. He had been one of the men with the guns, and he'd done a lot of the killing.

His guilt-ravaged soul could only take so much, and, anymore, Frank did not know if he could live with all the bloodshed and suffering that he and his friends had visited on Lawrence that fateful, insane day.

And later at Centralia.

True, he had been furious over what the Union forces had done to his family—to his stepfather, Dr. Reuben Samuels. Hanging him by the neck from a tree until almost dead, then flogging his fifteen-year-old little brother, Jesse, half to death and then costing his mother her arm—the thought of that brutality still boiled his blood and drove him mad with rage.

But those crimes were nothing compared to what he, Quantrill and their raiders had done to the citizens of Lawrence, the overwhelming percentage of whom cared nothing about the border state disputes that had thrown men like Quantrill, Jess and himself into such homicidal frenzies.

And what they'd done to those people that morning in Lawrence was enough to make the gods howl and the stars weep.

CHAPTER 7

Except for the light pouring from the open, barred windows, most of the rolling mill's interior was dark. Still, Bismarck discerned at least a dozen overseers in tan, sweat-soaked uniforms, patrolling the room's perimeter with holstered revolvers and double-barrel shotguns braced on their hips or propped up on their shoulders. All around the mill, Bismarck saw buckets of brine filled with heavy, coiled knotted ropes.

Gigantic wooden rollers dominated the big room. The windmill near the plant provided the power that moved the rollers back and forth via a complicated system of gears. Surveying the room, Bismarck counted thirty of these roller operations, and the room's din was deafening.

A dozen feet across and six feet thick, their surfaces were covered with sheet metal. They rolled back and forth, back and forth endlessly over the cane, pressing the wet unrefined sucrose out of them. The metal pans containing the rolled cane were fastened to the wooden industrial tables. More than fifteen feet wide, they were at least twenty-five feet long. The sides of the pans were nearly two feet high, and the gargantuan pans were filled with the cane's dense, syrupy residue.

Half-naked mestizos of all ages stood bent over the pans, sedulously feeding and prodding the three-foot sections of sugarcane under the rollers. A teenage boy stood beside each table with an axe resting on his shoulder.

"The axman," Judith McKillian shouted over the rollers' roar, "lops off the arm of any worker who gets his hand trapped under a roller."

At one end of the big pans, the juice was piped into huge, heated cauldrons. Lime and ash were added to help boil out the impurities. Partially clothed peons of all ages and genders, known as "stokers," continually fed fuel—which included dried cane as well as kindling—into the fires under the cauldrons.

"The juice will be transferred into each of five heating pans." Even though Diaz yelled, the words could barely be heard. "In each of the pans, the liquid will gradually be boiled away. The leftover syrup will then be poured into wooden barrels and transferred to the curing house. After crystalizing it into pure sugar, we then ship it to Europe or the US, where it can be sold."

"Into some of the barrels," the Senorita shouted, "we will add more water, producing molasses, which we then distill into rum. We make almost as much money selling the rum as we do the crystalized sugar."

"Any leftover syrup," McKillian bellowed, "we sell as molasses, even though that market isn't as lucrative as the one for crystal sugar and rum."

Unable to stand the heat and the noise any longer, Bismarck headed for the door and exited the building. Nietzsche and the rest followed him.

Standing outside the building, doubled over at their waists, they all panted desperately, struggling to get their breath back. The heat of the rolling mill had taken all the wind out of them.

"You ask me," Diaz said seriously, for once, not grinning, "sugar is where the big money is."

"We grow and harvest cocoa beans as well," the Senorita said. "It's bitter, but when we melt it and mix in sugar, the result is positively addictive."

"Sugar is so valuable to us," Sutherland said, "that we call it 'white gold.'"

As he'd told them earlier, he'd avoided entering the roller mill building. Unlike the rest of them, his clothes were not completely drenched with sweat.

"Thanks to the tropical climate," Sutherland continued, "which allows for almost year-round growing seasons and our superabundance of peons, we can produce sugar throughout the entire year with almost no downtime at all."

"Which, as you explained earlier, is why your peons' rate of attrition is so high," Nietzsche pointed out.

Diaz walked up to Nietzsche. Giving him a hard but jovial slap on the back and the most flamboyant of smiles, he said:

"Now you aren't going to turn bleeding-heart, pasty-face, do-gooding liberal peace-creep on us, are you, young friend?"

"After all," the Senorita said, giving Nietzsche her most glowingly gorgeous smile, "what are a few impecunious peons to anyone more or less?"

"Anyway," Judith McKillian said with great sincerity, "you can't really care about them, can you? You don't even *know* any peons, do you?"

CHAPTER 8

The sun was at its zenith, and the train rolled relentlessly through northern Méjico. Frank's face was buried in his handkerchief, and his body was racked with soft, choking sobs. He had images burned into his brain that he could not unsee and sounds he could not unhear—atrocities no person should ever have to witness.

It started with the collapse of Lawrence's ramshackle women's prison. On August 13, 1863, it had caved in, killing four of the ten female inmates. All of the prisoners were under twenty—a number of them mere girls. Several of them were related to Quantrill's brigands. "Bloody Bill" Anderson—the #2 man in Quantrill's organization—had a sister killed and another female relative permanently crippled. All of Quantrill's men were duly incensed, and it was finally time for Lawrence to pay for its abolitionist ways.

Columns of Quantrill's men converged on Lawrence in the predawn hours. Some had been riding day and night. They were now so exhausted that, to stay mounted, they'd had to lash themselves to their saddles' pommels and cantles, and then hook their belts over their saddles' horns. All of them had rifles slung across their backs, barrels down, and they all packed multiple pistols—some holstered to their hips, others in shoulder rigs, and others still shoved into waistbands and saddlebags.

By 5:00 AM, more than 450 raiders had reached Lawrence's outskirts. Several went to the top of Mount Oread to act as sentries and lookouts. The rest entered the town, which was just starting to wake up.

Their first victim was a pastor. A lieutenant in the 2nd Kansas Colored Regiment, Samuel S. Snyder, was outside in the open, milking his cows.

Passing freebooters shot him dead in plain view of his friend and fellow minister, Hugh Fisher. The killers then continued on their way.

The leaders met at the Eldridge House, a big, well-built brick hostelry. There, they set up their command center. The rest of the men spread out into groups, then dispersed throughout the town.

For the next four hours, the men robbed, ransacked and murdered their way through Lawrence, burning all except two of the stores and businesses. Due to the suddenness and the early hour of the attack, the town and its militia were unable to organize a resistance. In fact, most of their victims were unarmed.

The stories of their barbarities later came out:

Tales of the killers forcing men into buildings, which they then set ablaze, slowly burning their victims to death.

Offering amnesty and safety to those who surrendered, the raiders then gunned them down in cold blood.

Men, lying helpless in the sickbeds, were shot like dogs.

Some men and women hid from the killers, where, in fear, loathing and trembling, they watched Quantrill, Frank and their men slaughter their friends and neighbors without guilt or hesitation.

Frank and his fellow raiders carried hit lists in their pockets of Union sympathizers who were known to live in the town. At the top of the list was the anti-slavery militia leader, Jim Lane. He eluded them, however, by fleeing in his nightshirt through a cornfield at the crack of dawn.

Charles L. Robinson, the state's first governor and a well-known opponent of slavery, made the lists, but he also evaded capture or murder. His big stone barn overlooked the town. Hiding high up in a loft, he was able to watch the entire maddening spectacle at a discreet distance.

The chief newspaper owner and editor, John Speer, was a staunch abolitionist, and the raiders wanted him dead. He fled as well, so the plunderers sated their bloodlust on two of his sons.

One of the murders particularly stuck in Frank's craw. He, Bloody Bill and two other raiders were searching houses early that morning, before the town realized what they were up to. They knocked on the door of a particularly attractive two-story clapboard farmhouse with gingerbread trim located on the edge of town. A kindly-looking gray-haired middle-aged woman—with a buttermilk complexion, a pert nose and a welcoming smile—met them at the door. She was attired in a prim, powder-blue, knee-length dress, buttoned to the throat and wore no jewelry except for a solitary wedding band.

The two men asked if her husband was home, and she invited them in.

"Yes," she said, "my husband, John, is in the backyard with our two sons and his father. They're chopping kindling, milking cows, gathering eggs—the usual farm chores. They'll be done in a few minutes. They're set to plow the south forty after breakfast. Perhaps you'd like to stay and join us."

"Thank you, ma'am," Frank said, "but we're in a bit of a hurry. If we could just have a few minutes with them, we'd be on our way."

"But you look like you've been traveling all night."

Frank admitted that they had.

"I'm told," the kindly woman said, "I make the best deep-dish apple pie in all of Lawrence. If you wanted to try some pie and Arbuckles' coffee while our men-folk finish their chores, I can cut you each a slice. I just hand-cranked some good vanilla ice cream to go with it. The pie is still warm. You should really try some."

So Frank and Bill each ate a slice of her pie, big scoops of ice cream, and drank a half a pot of Arbuckles with fresh cream and sugar. Thanking the woman profusely, they finally went into the backyard to meet her men-folk.

Frank killed the two unarmed men. Bloody Bill executed the sons.

They were returning to the back door on their way to their horses, which were hitched out front. Having heard the shots, the woman of the house was at the back door. Her trembling hands were pressed to her face, and she was sobbing uncontrollably. When they reentered her house, she stepped out of their way in terror.

"Ma'am," Bloody Bill said, tipping his black slouch hat and giving her his widest, warmest smile, "your neighbors were right. You make the best goddamned deep-dish apple pie I ever et."

After the massacre, Frank, Quantrill and their comrades wintered in Texas. The fighting then recommenced in the spring. One of their bloodiest assaults took place in Centralia, and it was bad. That was where Jess had first made his mark as a fearful killer. Prior to that battle—it had really been another massacre of the defenseless—Jess had been a joke. At age thirteen, at the beginning of his career as a guerilla, Quantrill had ordered Jesse to infiltrate a whorehouse, as a young aspiring prostitute, disguised in women's clothes. In that capacity, Jesse gathered intelligence by eavesdropping on the conversations of garrulous soldiers and jayhawkers. When Quantrill's men attacked and robbed the brothel, Jess was able to backshoot any Yankees who were resisting Quantrill's men too effectively.

After the raid, men teased Jesse mercilessly, pinning on him the jeering-sneering nickname "Dingus."

At Centralia, only days after his seventeenth birthday, Jesse killed thirteen men, including Major Johnston.

After Centralia, all teasing ceased.

In terms of sheer slaughter, however, Frank, Quantrill and their comrades never again equaled the violence they had visited on Lawrence.

But, finally, they could all read the writing on the wall. The war was coming to an end, and the Confederate Cause was collapsing around them. In 1864, "Bloody Bill" Anderson was shot to death. Quantrill fled to Kentucky, where he continued staging raids. There, he would die under mysterious circumstances from gunshot wounds inflicted by unknown assailants.

As always, Frank had been loyal to Quantrill—right through to the bitter end—and was at his side when he was gunned down.

PART VII

Jesse James could have escaped that bottomless abyss of violence and rage that had been his brother Frank's lot. But Centralia had been Jess's coup de grace—the final nail in the coffin of his hate. After Centralia, his fate was a foregone conclusion—signed, sealed and delivered. Centralia had done to Jess what Lawrence had done to Frank.

CHAPTER 1

Slater sat across from Katherine and her son, Richard, who had come home from his post at Fort Apache for his father's funeral and had been given three months "compassionate leave."

"I've already telegraphed Belle," Slater said. "She's helping us."

"What kind of weaponry will we need?" Richard asked.

"You've been stockpiling ordnance," Slater said, "in case someone mounted a serious assault on your place?"

"There isn't much law enforcement around here and no military presence at all," Katherine said by way of explanation.

"Still, we hadn't reckoned on an all-out armed military assault backed by a foreign power," Richard said.

"But you have some friends at Fort Apache," Slater said. "You're still a commissioned officer. What kind of artillery could you 'requisition'?"

"He couldn't requisition any legally," Katherine said.

Richard shrugged. "It would have to be off the books."

"You might not have a commission left afterward," Rachel said.

"You won't have a Rancho de Cielo left if you don't get some major firepower," Slater said.

"I'll ride over there and see what I can do," Richard said.

"Mountain mortars, Gatlings, grenades, soldiers," Slater said, "and anything else you can get your hands on and haul back. Howitzers would be primo."

"What kind of army will General Shelby raise?" Katherine asked.

"He helped Nathan Bedford Forrest create and build the Klan," Slater said. "He's worked with KKK chapters all over the South. He always saw them as recruitment centers for a new 'South will rise again' Confederate Army. The offer of all that free land and slaves in Méjico will sound damn good to those rednecks of his."

"Those Klansmen are all trained ex-soldiers, combat veterans?" Richard asked.

"Almost all of them," Slater said.

"Then we're going to have our hands full," Katherine said.

Slater stared at them and said nothing.

"Let's work on that equipment list," Katherine said. "Stuff we have, what we don't have and what we'd like but don't know how to obtain. Armament, ammunition, medical supplies, rations for a couple of hundred men. Lumber for shelter. Blankets. Richard, you're military. You know what goes into these operations. Don't forget money. A lot of this stuff, including manpower, will cost cash on the barrelhead, no IOUs."

Slater helped himself to more Arbuckles'. He topped it off with Jackson's Sour Mash and then paused to look at his W. W. Raymond railroad watch.

"You seem in a special hurry," Katherine said.

"I'm heading out at first light," Slater said.

"Where to?" Richard asked.

"The New Mexico Territory to meet up with a couple of old friends."

"Outlaws on the owlhoot?" Richard asked.

"Lawmen, if you really want to know."

"No shit?" Richard said.

"No shit," Slater said.

"Any special reason?" Richard asked.

"Got reason to think they may want to throw in with us," Slater said.

"They must be more desperate than we are," Richard said.

"The John Laws I'm thinking of need us this time," Slater said. "They're on the run and got no place else to go."

"And we think you need...*lawmen?*" Katherine asked.

"The kind of army I'm rounding up," Slater said, "won't be very disciplined. They don't take orders very well. They'll be as much a threat to each other and to us as to Shelby's troops. We need someone to crack the whip over them and tell them what to do. I also know these men. We can count on them."

"You can't handle these new recruits?" Katherine asked.

"You need patience and self-discipline for that line of work," Slater said.

"And?" Katherine asked.

"Patience and self-discipline are not exactly my strong suit," Slater said.

Standing, he started toward his bedroom, then turned.

"Katherine," he said, picking up the whiskey bottle, stuffing the cork back into its neck and taking it with him under his arm, "I'm taking this with me. I might need to do some more thinking."

CHAPTER 2

Diaz and his friends viewed the visit to the sugar plantation as a resounding success. Since they now anticipated a mother lode of German investments in Méjico, Diaz eagerly agreed to continue Bismarck's and Nietzsche's survey of Méjicano investment opportunities. The next day he took them—first by train, then by carriage—to a cotton plantation.

"Being from Europe," Diaz explained to them in the club car, "I doubt you have visited very many cotton haciendas."

"None," Bismarck said.

"Will this hacienda be as much fun as that sugar plantation?" Nietzsche asked unenthusiastically.

"Raising cotton is certainly simpler and more dependable," the Senorita said, ignoring the mockery in Nietzsche's voice, "than growing and processing sugarcane. As with sugarcane, the profits are huge, but you have to refine the syrupy sucrose on the spot immediately after chopping the cane. If you delay, the sucrose spoils. The potential revenues are less with cotton, but you don't have to process it as quickly and turn it into the final product—cotton cloth. For people who want a high, safe, steady return on investment that is simple and straightforward to pull off, raising cotton may be a more stress-free option."

"Sugar did sound a little complicated," Bismarck admitted.

"And labor-intensive," the Senorita said.

"With sugar, you need a lot of workers to plant, weed and fertilize the sugarcane," Diaz said, nodding his head in agreement. "You need a never-ending supply of peons for all the phases of production," Diaz reminded them. "You need them to first prepare the fields—to dig levies, dykes and irrigation ditches. They must press and grind, then boil the juice and then solidify it, finally crystalizing the pure sugar. To accomplish all this, the peons must work—day and night, night and day, around the clock."

"You need forty pounds of excrement per plant," the Senorita said. "Sugar plants require limitless nutrition—cotton not nearly as much. Animal shit is, of course, preferable, but here in Méjico it's so hard to collect and allocate."

"The peons are always stealing it," Judith McKillian said, "for what nefarious purposes, God only knows."

"Maybe they eat it," Sutherland suggested. "Our hacendados feed them so damnably little that they have to get their sustenance somewhere."

"They smell like they bathe with it," Judith McKillian said.

"So how do you fertilize the sugarcane," Bismarck asked, "if you lack the necessary animal excrement?"

"Why, we use the peon's shit," Sutherland said, irate. He glared at Bismarck, as if the chancellor's question had offended him. "What do you think we do? We can't *not* fertilize our crops."

"You were talking about the differences between sugar and cotton production," Nietzsche said, hoping to get their minds out of the scatological pit they'd wandered into. "You did say that despite the difficulties in harvesting and refining sugarcane, it is, if done right, far more profitable than the raising of cotton."

"Yes, it is," Diaz said, "But you know the irony of all this?" He allowed them one of his more engaging and ingratiating smiles.

"Not really," Nietzsche said.

"In plain truth," Diaz said, "the sugar our customers so desperately devour turns around and devours them. Rotting their teeth, it encases them in fat and fouls their blood, all the while addicting them to its sweetness."

"Sugar's addictiveness is why it's so profitable," Judith McKillian said. "You will pay us anything to satisfy your obscene cravings for it."

"In other words, when you buy and consume our sugar," the Senorita said, grinning maliciously, "you're paying *us* to dig your loathsome graves."

At which point, Diaz, Sutherland and the two women threw back their heads and laughed dementedly at Bismarck and Nietzsche.

CHAPTER 3

At dusk, the train had finally crossed into Texas—not that Frank James had noticed. He'd made the entire trip without sleep or food, subsisting solely on Napoleon cognac and Cuban cigars.

And floating on a sea of memories.

Memories of war, of friends killed, of limbs shattered and of lives squandered.

And, most of all, memories of Jess.

Before Lawrence, there had been hope for Frank. After Lawrence, none. Still, Jess had not been a lost cause. His little brother did not have to go down Frank's road—even after the night that those Union sons of bitches had whipped the boy so brutally and strung up their stepfather, pretending to hang him, and then maimed their mother.

Even after all that horror, Jesse James could have escaped that bottomless abyss of violence and rage that had been his brother Frank's lot. But Centralia had been Jess's coup de grace—the final nail in the coffin of his hate. After Centralia, his fate was a foregone conclusion—signed, sealed and delivered. Centralia had done to Jess what Lawrence had done to Frank.

It was all "Bloody Bill" Anderson's fault. He had been Quantrill's second-in-command but the two men had fallen out over "methods and procedures." Anderson had always been the more radical and vengeful of the two, and in 1864, as the South's military position began to seriously deteriorate, Bill had become convinced that the South needed an overwhelming victory if they were to defeat Lincoln in the '64 election. General

George McClellen was running against Lincoln on an anti-war, peace-at-any-price platform. If they could throw the election to McClellen by handing Lincoln a massive battlefield fiasco, the South could win the war of the ballot box.

So early in the morning, on September 27, 1864—disguised as bluebellies in stolen Union Army uniforms—Anderson and eighty raiders entered Centralia. The city was undefended, and they quickly began ravaging and pillaging everything in sight. Shooting men on sight, they then swilled whiskey from their boots.

Intent on severing the North Missouri Railroad Line, Anderson and a group of his men stormed the rail station. An approaching train eased to a halt alongside them. The sight of all those speciously blue-clad soldiers dispelled any hesitation that the engineer and conductor might have otherwise had.

The two men learned the error of their ways too late.

Anderson's freebooters dragged all 125 passengers off the train. They stripped the uniforms off the twenty-four soldiers on board. On leave from Sherman's Battle of Atlanta, the men were unarmed. Anderson's raiders shot them all except a sergeant named Goodman, whom they took prisoner. After removing the corpses' scalps and carving up their remains, they torched the train and sent it blazing toward Sturgeon, Missouri, with the throttle tied down.

Word of their depredations went out, reaching other parts of the state. Major Andrew Johnston of the Union Army rode into Centralia that same day with his 146 men, knowing that Anderson had at least eighty men under his command. When Anderson's smaller force lined up and prepared to attack, Johnston ordered his men to dismount. Forming a battle line, he waited for their charge.

Major Johnston, however, would soon learn to his fatal dismay that the raiders were superlative pistol shots. Armed with several revolvers each, they fired repeatedly at the Union soldiers, while those men struggled painstakingly to ram rounds down their muzzle-loading muskets.

The guerillas killed most of Johnston's men with Jesse James personally shooting the major. At the time, that killing had made Frank inordinately proud. Looking back on it, the event only made Frank sick.

Bill Anderson, Frank and their men had killed 123 out of 147 partisans—with one soldier wounded and one taken prisoner—while losing only three of their own.

They had flagrantly flown the Black Flag.

Setting the train station ablaze, they rode on out of town, festooned with bloody scalps—and with Sergeant Goodman in tow.

Ten days later, late at night, he, thankfully, escaped.

PART VIII

"You live with death circling over you like a bird of prey, Doc. You see death as your spirit animal, your brother-through-choice, your personal god. I believe your deeply divided soul unites itself only in violence and that, in fact, your soul—to the extent that you have a soul—was created by an act of incendiary violence. You see bloody death not as a curse but as a kind of liberation from...*life*. You see death as a gift, a deliverance, and believe it will come to you as a...*grace*."

—Wyatt Earp on Doc Holliday

CHAPTER 1

Belle Starr sat on the porch of her ranch in an oak rocking chair at Younger's Bend in the Nations. She'd dozed off for a minute but was now awake and staring out over the surrounding grasslands. A crimson sun was setting over the rimrock. A hawk, sharply etched against the reddening sky, was winging over the horizon. She heard a coyote yap, and farther away, up in the high rocks, a mountain lion yowled, then roared.

The boy from the telegraph office, who'd brought her the telegram, was riding back toward town, mad that she hadn't given him a tip. He'd given her a frown just to let her know, and she hadn't liked that look. She hadn't taken shit off Coleman Younger when they were married. She wasn't about to start eating it from some damn, wet-behind-the-ears telegraph messenger. She wished now she had given him a taste of her quirt, the little bastard.

Belle stared again at Slater's telegram. He said in it that he needed a crew and was relying on her to help him round them up.

It made sense. Slater didn't know that many people up this way anymore. He'd been down in Méjico, plying his trade and operating mostly on the single-o, robbing banks and trains Méjicano-style from what she'd heard.

She reread the telegram:

Belle, I need a crew of as many owlhooters as you can find—men who've ridden the highlines and aren't afraid of blood. Men we can count on. A couple of hundred of them—at least. This thing could get rough. Got to make a stop in Albuquerque first.

See you in a couple of weeks.

She'd telegrammed him back.

What's the money?

He got back to her instantly—so fast he'd obviously been waiting by the telegraph office. Or knowing that bastard, he might have even cut into a wire and, tapping the message out on a flat, empty tobacco can, was telegraphing her himself. The bastard knew Morse Code and how to do that sort of thing.

At least $500 per man for a week's work—maybe more.
And it's cash on the barrelhead—not dependent on cracking
open a bank vault or derailing an express train.
Belle, I need you to come through for me. A lot depends on it.

Belle put down the telegram. Slater was serious, and he was asking her for her help. That wasn't like him. Slater never asked anybody for anything, and he was the least solicitous person she'd ever known. He didn't plead or argue or explain or complain. He just reached out and took.

With his Colt in their mouths and their nuts in his fist.

Belle knew. She'd seen Slater in action—lots of times.

She went into the house and brought out a whiskey jug, a glass, a pad of paper, a pen and an inkwell.

She had a lot of thinking to do.

She filled her glass to the brim, placed it on a side table and began listing names and making notes.

It would be a long evening and a longer night.

CHAPTER 2

Goddamn it, Doc Holliday was sick of Wyatt Earp's reckless ways. Trouble followed him everywhere he went—just as the Old Testament always said—"like the sparks fly upward." Sitting here in a Las Vegas bar, deep in the New Mexico Territory, Doc could already count eight people who wanted Earp dead. And that was just a random sampling. He really hadn't surveyed everyone in the joint.

What was weird was that Doc didn't recognize half the gents hard-eyeing Earp. Not that long ago, he'd spent a year in the town and knew pretty near everyone in it. The dry air had been good for his consumptive lungs, and he'd felt at home here—to the extent that he was capable of ever feeling at home. The law had somehow never busted him in New Mexico, and since he'd helped a couple of the lawmen out of tight spots, they seemed to like him—which never ever happened.

But tonight was different.

Half the people in the bar were hardcase strangers, men who looked like they'd kill you for your boots—hell, for the heels—men with no names and an understanding so small you could put it in a gnat's asshole and have room left over for two raisins and a sunflower seed. Where, Doc wondered, did all these hard-asses come from?

Even worse, five of Earp's would-be killers were sitting with him right at his octagonal, green baize-covered poker table. One was dressed like a banker. Decked out in a black suit, tie and vest and a matching bowler, he favored muttonchops and a mustache. He hadn't smiled once the entire evening, had the manners of a gentleman but had the eyes of a sheep-killing dog. Then there were the two cowhands in dark-colored, dirt-covered work shirts and shabby, sweat-stained Stetsons. Their collarless shirts could have also stood a wash and their Levis looked worse. They never stopped grinning and laughing.

Doc believed they'd grin those same grins and laugh those same laughs while they were emptying their sidearms into you.

God, he hated grinning killers.

Doc had holed more than his share; still, he'd never viewed killing men as a laughing matter.

But whatever the case, they had money to burn and attitudes to match, which led Doc to believe that the cows they were running weren't exactly legit—what ranch hands called "slow elk," marked with "a running brand," caught by men "swinging a wide loop" with their cattle ropes.

In short, they were rustling cows, counterfeiting brands and selling them to unscrupulous buyers.

The fourth man at their table, whom Doc also did not recognize, was dressed like a young dandy in a white boiled shirt, a red brocade vest, matching bow tie and elbow garters. Hatless, he shuffled and dealt the cards with studied aplomb and practiced flamboyance. He wanted everyone to know he was "a sporting gent," "a midnight rambler" and "a gambling man." He carried a .36-caliber cut-down Navy Colt in a shoulder rig. He probably kept a throwing knife secreted up his sleeve alongside his wrist, and, no doubt, had a derringer in his boot.

Earp's fifth problem wasn't a man at all but a very attractive lady of the night. Flush with filthy lucre, she was decked out in a red silk gown with a plunging neckline. The dress went well with her long lemon-blond hair, azure eyes and blood-red lip rouge.

Doc had also spotted the Sharps pepperbox stashed up her right sleeve.

Still there was no way any ordinary soiled dove would have had the amazing amount of cash that she had in front of her. Maybe, Doc speculated, she'd owned a house of ill-repute and was here on the run. If so, Doc wondered whether there were dodgers out on her. Hopefully, for her sake, the territory was outside the warrants' jurisdiction.

The game was five-card stud with one small change—only the last two cards were dealt face up. As for the players' gambling acumen, Doc had immediately recognized that all five of Earp's opponents were superior card-players, and, even though Earp was very good himself, they were capable of giving Earp a serious run for his money.

But tonight, their skill was of no consequence.

Tonight, Wyatt was uncommonly lucky.

Which wasn't necessarily a good thing. Doc suspected that, in this game, such luck carried a risk. Doc thought of Earp's luck as a runaway freight train, roaring over vertiginously curving mountain tracks and tottering, tremulous trestles at night, loaded with capped-off dynamite. The train's luck couldn't last the evening, and when it jumped the rails, it would not only crash, it would blow sky high.

But, right now, Wyatt couldn't lose.

And the other players were growing increasingly pissed.

Doc knew Wyatt wasn't cheating. After all, Doc was goddamned good at marking cards, dealing seconds, burying aces on the deck's bottom—up his sleeve, crotch, in his boots, hat, ass, anywhere, anytime—then producing one of them at the first fortuitous moment. So Doc knew how the game was played, and he was as adroit at spotting "card sharps" as he was at pulling off the same tricks himself.

No, Earp wasn't cheating. But he was probably the only person in the bar—aside from Doc—who understood that simple fact. No one else believed in his kind of luck. They might have *heard* of luck like Earp's. They had just never... *seen it.* They had never seen luck as outrageous as his was tonight. They'd never seen a man ride the tiger that hot and hard and heavy for four straight hours.

Holliday personally loved it—since it wasn't his money Earp was raking in. From Doc's point of view, Earp's luck was a marvel to behold. The tiger had graced Doc for extended periods a few times, and it was always the thrill of a lifetime—until, that is, the tiger decided to buck you off, devour your innards and the bill came due. The beast would either tap you out in a gambling hall at some godforsaken gaming table or kill you dead and pick your wallet clean—leaving you spread-eagled on the floor, a bullet in your chest, blood in your mouth, your pockets turned inside out.

In gambling hells such as this one, luck could be a vicious, cold and brutally cynical... *bitch.*

William Cosmos Monkhouse had recently written a lyric summing up the plight of all tiger riders everywhere. Doc couldn't get the damn thing out of his head.

There was a young lady from Niger,
Who went for a ride on a tiger.
They returned from the ride
With the lady inside
And a smile on the face of the tiger.

Well, no one could ride that smiling bastard of a tiger forever, and that was going double for Wyatt tonight. If nothing else, the gamblers he'd beaten would see to it. They would, at some point, drag Wyatt off that damn cat—if the beast did not throw him off first—and it would be up to Doc to stop them from killing his friend.

At moments like these—when the blood was hot, the bullets cold, the guns cocked and the smell of violent death so thick in the air you could choke on it—Doc always felt surprisingly *at ease.* Once, when Earp was feeling surprisingly philosophical about Doc's notorious serenity in the face of impending death—what Earp called "Doc's love affair with death"—he'd said to Doc:

"You live with death circling over you like a bird of prey. You see death as your spirit animal, your brother-through-choice, your personal god. I believe your deeply divided soul unites itself only in violence and that, in fact, your soul—to the extent that you have a soul—was created by an act of incendiary violence. You see bloody death not as a curse but as a kind of liberation from...*life.* You see death as a gift, a deliverance, and believe it will come to you as a...*grace.*"

At the time, Doc had laughed, poured another round, and in between his hacking, tubercular coughs, he had said to his friend—the closest friend he would ever have:

"You sure talk a lot of shit, Wyatt."

But he also knew that Earp had cut him dead center. Maybe that was the bond between him and Wyatt. They were both obsessed with the tiger's capricious ride and didn't give a shit about bloody death or violent destruction.

So be it.

But now, somehow, in some way, Doc Holliday had to keep that damnable tiger from gutting Wyatt like a slaughter steer, ripping out his entrails, then curling up, purring and...*smiling.*

CHAPTER 3

Diaz and his group reached the cotton plantation around mid-morning. It was harvest time, and endless rows of ivory-white cotton, several feet apart, stretched in every direction, all the way to the horizon line. Bismarck had never seen a cotton field before and found the sight hauntingly beautiful.

Nietzsche, however, was oblivious to the splendor. Throughout the entire trip, the Senorita and Judith McKillian had mocked him continually, sneering at what Judith McKillian described as his "cretinous credulity."

The Senorita contented herself with denigrating him as "young Nietzsche," which also rankled him to no end. By "young," Nietzsche believed she meant "ignorant." When he'd finally had enough of their combined ridicule, he shouted angrily at the Senorita, "I may be younger than the men here, but I'm not that much younger than you two women."

"I address you as 'young Nietzsche,' because you have, my dear Friedrich, the innocence of a sensitive and unblemished youth," the Senorita explained. She then gave him a disconcertingly affectionate smile.

"A most callow and stupid youth, you ask me," Judith McKillian said, her voice a hiss.

"I find his ingenuousness quite endearing," Diaz said, giving Nietzsche one of his own more amiable smiles.

"He has the ingenuousness of an imbecile, you ask me," Judith McKillian countered, glaring at Nietzsche.

"I also must disagree," the Senorita said. "I find young Nietzsche's naiveté quite...*refreshing*."

The weather, unfortunately, wasn't all that refreshing. In fact, despite his mounting fury, it was too hot for Nietzsche to debate the matter further. The temperature was now over one hundred degrees in the shade, and it was continuing to climb. The group, once again, sank into quiescence.

The peons didn't speak either. They could barely breathe. Each of them had a huge cotton-ball sack strapped around their necks and across their chests. The bags opened up just under their chins. Sweating profusely and panting heavily, they had stripped off most of their clothing.

"As we pointed out," Diaz said, finally breaking the silence, "raising cotton is a lot simpler than growing and processing sugarcane. The only difficult problem is getting the cotton picked quickly enough—at the exact same time that the balls are blossoming and are in full bloom. Only then will you get peak market value."

"The time pressure," the Senorita pointed out, "isn't as great as it is when harvesting sugarcane. In that instance, the sugar can go bad overnight and can't be processed, so the peons have to harvest and refine the sugar as quickly as possible. Still, cotton-picking does require some haste. The peons can't dawdle."

"And our peons, do they hate picking fast," Sutherland said.

"Not only because the hours are long and hot, and they're exhausted," the Senorita said. "The blossoming cotton balls are protected by hard, sharp thorns that tear their fingers to pieces when they pick quickly."

"Which is why we have to incentivize their cotton-picking," Judith McKillian said. "We have to give them a reason to ignore the thorns and work their cotton-picking little brains out."

"I dread to ask what those incentives are," Bismarck said.

"See those overseers with the wrist quirts, manning each row?" Sutherland said. "Their paramount job is to watch for idlers, procrastinators, malingerers, shirkers, lollygaggers, or those who simply get tired and slow down."

"The facile application of their cuarta quirts brings even the most indolent peon around quite smartly," Judith McKillian said.

"And that's only for lazy peons," the Senorita said. "Our overseers are infinitely harder on the careless, clumsy ones."

"What do you mean by 'the careless, clumsy ones'?" Bismarck asked nervously, dreading the answer.

"One such example is the kind of irresponsible peon who breaks the branch as he or she plucks the cotton ball from it," Sutherland explained. "Future cotton balls won't grow on broken branches, and they can be fragile. So the peons have to pick quickly yet with exceeding care."

"That sounds...*difficult,*" Bismarck said.

"Quite so," McKillian said. "To succeed at the art and practice of cotton harvesting, the peon must demonstrate drive, dedication and determination."

"Our peons must be highly motivated," the Senorita said, "and luckily for our investors, Porfirio and I are superlative motivators."

"Fear can work wonders," Nietzsche noted with mounting apprehension.

"Exactamente," Diaz said. "It's amazing how much fear will motivate otherwise intransigent employees. After I instill sufficient fear into our peons, I can make them work wonders and perform miracles—move mountains, walk on water, raise the dead and bottle lightning."

"But it's kind of hard on your peons," Nietzsche said with wry irony, "isn't it?"

"Of course," Diaz said, "but I want them to put pesos in my pockets and into those of my compadres here. I do not believe it is too much to ask."

"And what do your peons get out of it?" Nietzsche asked.

"They not only get to harvest our cotton," Judith McKillian shouted, "afterward, they get to gin and bail it. They get to turn those cranks, till their arms fall off!"

"Which only benefits you," Nietzsche said. "What do your peons get out of all that excruciatingly difficult labor?"

"If they are lucky, we let them live...*another day,*" the Senorita said to Nietzsche, deadly serious, without a hint of irony, looking him straight in the eye.

"Bastardos!" Nietzsche hissed, rising to his feet and pointing angrily at his hosts.

"No," the Senorita said gently, without heat or rancor, "merely Méjicanos."

"A people," Diaz said, "that you will never understand."

"I understand you all perfectly," Nietzsche said.

"No," the Senorita said, "that is impossible. You will never fathom us."

"Why not?" Nietzsche asked.

"Because," Diaz said with immense kindness, "you will never understand...*Méjico*."

CHAPTER 4

Frank James was still in his train compartment and staring out the window at the early morning sky. He was now down to his final flask and last handful of cigars. He would need them. He was looking back on the Northfield raid, and if Lawrence had been the worst day of Frank's life, Northfield had been the second worst. It had hammered Frank and his friends with the force of a Jehovian thunderbolt.

Frank James wondered if Northfield, too, had been due to hubris. They'd certainly acted cocksure. They'd ridden into town on strong, handsome, blooded horses, wearing long gray dusters, under which they each carried multiple firearms. They were all big men, bold of manner, without doubt or equivocation. Their arrogance all but shouted to the townspeople that they meant the community no good. They had attracted stares everywhere they'd gone.

Such behavior had worked in the past. Their belligerence and fearlessness, combined with a few strategically timed pistol shots, had always cowed the populace into cringing submission.

But not in Northfield.

What had gone wrong?

Unlike Missouri, where everyone walked around armed, Minnesota wasn't even gun country. None of the townsfolk carried firearms. None of them felt threatened—which was one reason Frank and his gang had picked Northfield for their bank job.

Frank still remembered that day: September 7, 1876—the year of the first US centennial, an extraordinary year, during which everything seemed to change. On June 4, 1876, the Transcontinental Express had highballed from New York to San Francisco in only eighty-three hours, truly uniting all the disparate American states into a single, rapidly traversable country, at last, transforming the US into One Nation Under God. The year 1876 had even witnessed the last great Indian victory over the US Army, when on June 26, 1876, the Cheyenne War Chief Crazy Horse had—leading an alliance of the Arapaho and the Lakota Sioux—annihilated Colonel George Armstrong Custer and his 7th Cavalry. Finally on August 2, 1876, Jack McCall shot Wild Bill Hickok—the west's greatest soldier/gunfighter/marshal/Indian scout—in the back of the head in Deadwood's Number 10 Deadwood Saloon.

That year had truly marked the end of an era: the Wild West was no more.

But the final nail in that hundred-year, centennial coffin, Frank now believed, had been hammered in in Northfield. Riding into town on that fateful day, everything seemed to be fine. As they cantered in, four abreast, Frank remembered how their stylish clothes, fine horses and arrogant bearing had drawn hostile stares, but he did not care. In his line of work, one had to command respect. One had to intimidate.

At J.G. Jeft's restaurant, they'd treated themselves to a big blowout—large portions of ham, eggs, fried potatoes and biscuits with cream gravy. The outlaws ate four eggs apiece, not knowing when they'd get their next hot meal.

They were finally ready to make their withdrawal from…the First National Bank of Northfield, Minnesota.

When Jess entered, he noticed that three men were working that day behind the counter: E. J. Wilcox, A. E. Bunker and J. L. Heywood, who sat behind the cashier's desk and who was responsible for the vault.

Pulling their pistols out from under their dusters, the men climbed over the counter.

"Throw up your hands," Jess shouted, "for we intend to rob the bank. If you hallo," Jess then added, "we will blow your goddamned brains out."

Then to everyone's surprise, Heywood, the accountant and acting cashier, refused to open the vault. A Civil War veteran of Vicksburg and Arkansas Post, he'd fought under Ulysses Simpson Grant, and he was, once again, determined to stand his ground and not back down.

Putting a knife to Heywood's throat, Jess demanded he open the vault, threatening to cut his throat "from ear to ear."

Nor was Heywood the only employee to resist. Another was shot trying to escape but still managed to get away. That bloody man made it out onto the street and announced to townspeople that a robbery was in progress.

Now the townsfolk were going for the pistols, shotguns, carbines and rifles that they kept in their stores and homes. From windows, storefronts and rooftops, they opened fire on the outlaws, who were waiting outside the bank for Jesse and the other men who were still inside. The outlaws immediately returned fire with revolvers and rifles.

During the next fifteen minutes, the townspeople all but obliterated the James-Younger Gang. Clell Miller and Bill Chadwell lay dead in the street. Cole Younger was shot through the hip. Foundering under a shattered shoulder, Jim Younger could barely stay in the saddle. Bob Younger's bloody, bullet-fractured arm hung limply at his side. Two weeks later, Charlie Pitts was killed. Only Frank and Jess had escaped alive.

For their part, the outlaws killed two people. Both were unarmed and shot down in cold blood. They murdered a Swedish immigrant, who did not understand their order to clear the street, and Jesse James eventually executed J. L. Heywood, the courageous, weaponless cashier, shooting him in the head.

Still furious—long after the massacre was over—Jess wrote a letter to the *Kansas City Times*, denouncing Heywood, who was now in his grave, saying:

"A man who is a d—d enough fool to refuse to open a safe or vault when he is covered with a pistol ought to die."

That a "damned enough fool" had stopped the gang from emptying the Northfield First National Bank's safe was too much for Jesse James to bear. He had to attack him in public print even after he'd put him in the ground.

Yes, Frank had to admit it. Jess had been a fool, but then they'd all been fools. Northfield had proven that. For all intents and purposes, Frank had died there. After Northfield, nothing was ever the same.

The truth was that even though he and Jess had escaped unharmed and made it back to Missouri, Northfield had, nonetheless, torn the heart out of them both. Northfield was the end of their dreams. Afterward, Frank James was no longer young.

Frank wished he'd have died there.

Well, his brandy had sure died. He was now near the end of his flask and smoking his last Havana.

Even as the train was pulling into the station.

Out the window, Frank saw two men in dark suits and no suitcases. He expected they were waiting for him. It would be good to get out and stretch his legs. Maybe have some breakfast.

It had been a long, hard trip.

Frank James wondered what Texas had in store for him.

PART IX

"[W]e ended up inheriting the worst of two worlds, young Nietzsche: the Spaniard's love affair with vindictive violence, his contempt for cowardice—even to the point of scorning death—and the Maya-Aztec's outright worship of death."

—La Senorita Dolorosa

"I call money 'the Second Blood,' as if it powered our species' true circulatory system."

—Alfred Krupp, the nineteenth century's preeminent arms manufacturer

CHAPTER 1

Kaiser Wilhelm I, the emperor of Germany, sat in Alfred Krupp's waiting room. The largest, most powerful arms manufacturer in the world, Krupp was also one of the most ruthlessly arrogant. He viewed all government officials—from emperors, such as Wilhelm, to presidents and prime ministers, from arms ministers, ministers of state and finance ministers down to their lowliest assistants—as nothing more than employees—ignorant, impotent flunkies to do with as he saw fit.

That Alfred Krupp kept Kaiser Wilhelm cooling his heels in his waiting room rankled the emperor to no end.

Since he had time to kill, he studied the interior. Bismarck had told him once that décor said a lot about the owner's character, and Alfred's walls were covered with framed photos of his biggest, gaudiest howitzers and other field pieces. Alfred had also hung a photo of General Gebhard Leberecht von Blucher—the man innumerable Germans, and many reputable historians, held most responsible for defeating Napoleon—far more so than Wellington, the hero of Waterloo. After all, Blucher had so worn Napoleon's army out that by the time it faced Wellington it was a pale shadow of the army Blucher had originally faced. Surrounding Blucher's photograph were a half dozen military maps of his most famous battles.

If décor was a mirror to Alfred Krupp's soul, that soul was unerringly reflected by and just as unfeeling as the weapons that he designed, manufactured, marketed, and which Wilhelm so eagerly deployed.

That Krupp also sold his finest, most advanced weapons to Russia—and even tried to sell them to France—was a point of acrimonious contention between the emperor, Bismarck and the tycoon. Krupp defended his mercenary transactions by pointing out that those countries paid exorbitant prices for their weapons, thus allowing him to sell them to his homeland at a discount and that those foreign sales, thereby, helped to subsidize his sales to the German government.

Bismarck was particularly critical of such Kruppian verbal sleight of hand. Once, when the Kaiser referred to Krupp as "a bastard," Bismarck had replied:

"The more precise epithet would be 'treasonous bastard.'"

That Alfred Krupp cared so little about their opinions of him, viewing them merely as sources of revenue, infuriated Bismarck and almost drove Kaiser Wilhelm out of his mind. Once, when Bismarck was attempting to explain the arms dealer to the emperor, he'd said:

"The thing you must always understand about Alfred is that 'he does not care a whit to whom he sells his weapons as long as their checks cash and that his heart thrills solely to the chiming of the company till.'"

The Kaiser had responded, "Are you saying that he cares more for his corporate finances than his personal riches?"

To which Bismarck had responded icily:

"Emperor, Alfred owns the Kruppwerk in fee simple. He *is* the company. The corporation's assets...*are his assets*."

And there was nothing they could do about it. Krupp always said he could raze the Kruppwerk to the ground in one hour flat. He'd told Wilhelm and Bismarck once when he was in his cups:

"I have systems in place, set to detonate most of its critical infrastructure at a moment's notice. Before I would let anyone seize those structures and take my firm away from me, I would blow the Kruppwerk off the face of the earth and then burn the surviving rubble down the ground, so utterly, so comprehensively that nothing—*nothing!*—would remain. And I will do it all without scruple or remorse before I will allow any government flunkies to dictate to me how to run my company. I shall then decamp to some more hospitable country—France or Russia come to mind—where my work will be respected *and* remunerated. I shall rebuild my facilities and manufacture my weapons systems there...*for them.* I shall sit back and laugh when France and Russia roll into Berlin and take this nation over. I'll watch my former so-called employers swing on the tsar's gallows or lose their heads under a French guillotine."

On one hand, Willhelm believed the threat was an empty boast—at least, the part about blowing up der Kruppwerk—but, on the other hand, he also knew that the self-centered old bastard was mean enough to do what he said, and if he did not actually blow the Kruppwerk up, he'd do something that would incapacitate it. He knew what made the place tick. He could sabotage it quickly and expeditiously. The part about Alfred Krupp resurrecting his business in a foreign land, that Wilhelm completely believed. Krupp's arms sales to Moscow proved how paper-thin his loyalty to Germany truly was. And even worse, the emperor did not believe Germany could survive without the Kruppwerk and their shockingly accurate, devastatingly destructive artillery. And he knew that Alfred would be happy to set his firm up all over again in a foreign land.

Germany was surrounded by irreconcilable enemies on all sides.

The emperor and Germany needed Krupp.

At last, the door opened, and Wilhelm heard the magnate's deep voice summoning him into his sanctum sanctorum.

Entering, Wilhelm announced: "*Das Versteck des KanonenKonigs.*" [The cannon king's lair]

"It is so good to see you, old friend," Kaiser Wilhelm said. "It has been too long."

"Indeed," Krupp sang out. "How are you doing? Do you hear anything from Otto? Has he cabled you from glorious Méjico?"

"Only," the emperor said, "that he'd like to scourge every square inch of it from the face of the earth."

"Understood," Krupp said, "but you must remind him that such hostile actions are off the table until Diaz's money is in my coffers."

"And, unfortunately, Bismarck has yet to close the deal," Wilhelm said.

"Why?" Krupp asked, his eyes suddenly narrowing, his forehead furrowed.

"He has reservations about Diaz and his entourage."

"What kind of reservations?"

"He thinks they are insane."

Krupp was silent a long moment.

"That's a rather broad diagnosis," Krupp said. "Did you ask our chancellor to be a little more specific?"

"I did. He said that Diaz and his backers are violently out-of-control psychopaths and that he and young Nietzsche will be lucky to escape Méjico with their lives."

"Sounds like he's getting cold feet."

"It's fear talking," Kaiser Wilhelm said. "I read genuine terror in that cable—an emotion I had thought our Otto utterly incapable of."

"I thought Bismarck bled liquid nitrogen," Krupp said.

"I wasn't sure he had any blood at all."

"Or a heart.

"Méjico must be one terrifying place."

"At one time," Krupp said, "they amputated men's hearts and draped themselves in their victims' skins as if they were a king's or a queen's royal raiment."

"It was their idea of haute couture."

"Elegant finery, alluring attire."

"They also threw virgins howling into fiery volcanoes," Kaiser Wilhelm said.

"I thought Cortez wiped the Aztecs out."

"He did, but something's gotten to Otto."

"What about young Nietzsche?" Krupp asked.

"He wrote and sent the cable on Otto's behalf."

"In what capacity?"

"We sent him ahead of Otto to research Méjico's solvency," the emperor said. "He's apparently now acting as Otto's amanuensis."

"Wagner told us he was whip smart."

"Let's hope he can talk sense into Otto," Krupp said. "The revenues from that deal would finance German arms orders and bankroll this country's defenses for the rest of the century."

"We would not have to worry about France, Austria-Hungary or Russia again," the Kaiser said in agreement, "for the rest of our lives."

"Or those damnable Brits."

"Them too," the emperor said.

"A disgusting bunch of arrogant snobs."

"They need a good lesson in humility."

"A painful lesson in humility," Krupp said.

"After Otto nails down that arms deal with Porfirio," the emperor said, "we'll be in just the right position to give it to Victoria, Albert and that sonofabitch, Disraeli."

"We'll never have to take scheiss off any of those bastards again."

CHAPTER 2

It never seemed to end for Doc.

Why had he accepted that eighth seat at the poker table after the last player had cashed out?

How and why had he taken on the task, as his life's mission, of keeping Wyatt Earp alive?

He realized now he would never know the answers to such questions. Doc had accepted decades ago that he would never know why he did...*anything.*

Staring around the bar, he watched the men at the poker table grow increasingly enraged at the heartless and coldblooded way Earp dealt and called out the cards, at the superior ghost of a grin that crossed his mouth each time the cards came up in his favor, and the insolent way that he raked in his ever-burgeoning pots. The men were also furious at the crowd of onlookers that had gathered around the game. The men were not only losing badly, they suffered the added humiliation of losing in front of a large, nasty and vociferous audience, which only added to their anger and mortification.

It had long ago stopped being a question of whether they would try to gun Wyatt down but when. They would accuse Wyatt Earp of cheating, all five would empty their pistols into him, and then—

They would divvy up Wyatt's winnings.

They would probably gun Doc as well. He was Earp's friend, a stranger to their table, and he was the only other man at the table who was not going broke.

How many times had he almost gotten killed backing Wyatt Earp's hand?

By his count, he'd saved Earp twice in Texas, three times when Earp was marshaling in Dodge, and at least six times in and around Tombstone. Doc had not only backed Earp's play at the OK Corral, but afterward, when they had tracked down and killed all the surviving Clanton Gang members they could lay their hands on. As soon as Wyatt had them in his gunsights, he sent their sorry souls to hell without so much as a "by your leave" or a "fare thee well"...with Doc at his side, gun out, always killing his share and more.

The clean-shaven dandy in the white shirt, red brocade vest, matching bow tie and elbow garters snapped Doc out of his revery.

"Man," the dandy said to Earp, "I don't see how you keep winning, hand after hand, pot after pot. It ain't...*natural.*"

Earp ignored the query.

"I asked you how you did it," the man reiterated.

"The Good Book," Earp said. "I read it faithfully every day."

"And consult with the Man Upstairs," Doc added.

"What?" the dandy barked, incredulous.

"I also tithe at church every Sunday morning," Earp said.

"You're mocking me."

"No, sir," Earp said. "I tithe ten percent of my week's winnings like clockwork."

"I've seen him," Doc facetiously pretended to confirm, "and he loves doing it. He's happy as a priest with an altar boy when he's making those weekly donations."

"As Paul says," Earp intoned somberly, "the Lord loves a cheerful giver."

"You always have to stay tight with the Man Upstairs," Doc said. "That's the real secret."

"That way," Earp said, "when you're betting on a really big pot, you can ask Him to help you out, tell him you'll give double next Sunday, and the Almighty will come through for you—just sure as shit stinks and buzzards eat carrion."

"Maybe offer Him 20 percent," Doc said.

"If it's a really big pot," Earp said, "I'll go 25 percent."

"I'd go half," Doc said.

"Every time," Earp said.

"Works for me," Doc said.

"You're full of shit," the dandy said, now seriously incensed.

Doc surreptitiously eased a Colt out of his cross-draw holster. Pushing his legs together, he slid it on his lap.

Earp was coincidentally performing the same maneuver.

"Or maybe you aren't tight enough with the Man Upstairs," Earp said to the dandy.

"I'll bet you're not a cheerful giver," Doc said.

"Fuck you!" the man said, growing angrier with every word. "I don't know how you're doing it, but you're drawing to inside straights and full houses, when you're holding squat. If I call you with an ace-high straight, you top me with a flush. Or when I call you with flushes, you beat me with straight flushes. Luck like that, it's not humanly...*possible.* There's no explanation for it. It's something way beyond luck. And it isn't skill. I have skill. It's like you know what the cards are...*going to be.*"

"Only when God tells me up front," Earp said. "Although, I have to admit, he has been blessing me a lot lately."

"God can be very generous," Doc said to the dandy. "He would be that way with you too, if, for once in your life, you'd just swallow your pride, repent your sins and get straight...*with Him.*"

"Read your Bible and fear God," Earp said.

"And don't forget those weekly donations," Doc added.

"All I know is," the man in the red vest shouted, rising to his feet, "I'm not letting you blaspheme God anymore, and I'm not taking your contempt and your thievery either."

He was reaching for his guns when Earp's first round took out his left eyeball, leaving a smoking, bloody, empty socket where it had entered.

By now four other men and the red-clad woman were pulling their pistols. Earp and Doc were thumbing slip-hammered rounds as fast as they could, but there were too many men drawing too many pistols all at once.

Doc knew then with intractable, irrefutable certitude that he and his friend were going to die.

CHAPTER 3

"You are saying that the chancellor and I can never understand Méjico?" Nietzsche asked Diaz and his friends, his voice skeptically irate.

They were back in the club car of Diaz's Imperial Express Train, sipping excellent cognac, the men smoking cigars, the women the smaller, thinner cigarillos.

"Never," the Senorita said with a sardonic smile.

"I think I understand your point," Bismarck said to the Senorita but gesturing toward Nietzsche. "My young friend, however, is a product of our libraries, universities and an aspiring intellectual. Like Faust, he believes that he can, with enough study, understand everything."

"In short, he is naïve," James Sutherland said.

"Very much so," Bismarck said. "He has read much and believes that books are the world but has suffered few of life's more invincible vicissitudes, its more difficult and more stressful realities."

"Perhaps that is why we say," the Senorita said, "that young Friedrich will never understand our Méjico."

"Perhaps," Judith McKillian said, "because his feelings are too easily hurt, and he is too quick to feel patronized."

"Such talk mortally offends him," Bismarck said.

Diaz stared at Nietzsche contemplatively, studying him as if he were a scientific specimen under a slide, perhaps a previously undiscovered bacterium.

"Young Nietzsche," Diaz finally said, "if you truly wish to understand the Méjicano people, you must understand first our Spanish history. Unfortunately, that history is dark. While the rest of that continent was going through the Enlightenment, the Renaissance, the Reformation, the Scientific Revolution and the Democratic Reform Movement, Spain experienced none of these intellectual breakthroughs. They were occupied by the Moors and, following their traditions, came to spurn all intellectual pursuits, scorned great literature, philosophy, history, science, mathematics and engineering. Instead, they enthused in duels and in the conquest of primitive peoples in far-off lands. Spain continued to be obsessed with the medieval code of machismo centuries after the rest of the world had abandoned it. Our Spanish forebears, consequently, waged extortionately expensive wars on our European neighbors over 'religion' and 'national honor.' They bled our nation white in these quixotic macho conflicts until their country was nothing more than an attenuated shadow of its former imperial self."

"Do you understand the concept of machismo?" the Senorita asked.

"Machismo," Nietzsche stated, "refers to the veneration of physical courage above all other virtues."

"It is fearlessness raised to apotheosis," Diaz said.

"Yes," the Senorita said, "for machismo transcends fearlessness. Machismo is not simply a willingness to fight over pointless—often imaginary—affairs of honor, but it is the utter willingness to die for them."

"Machismo implies an eagerness to die over these meaningless slights," Diaz said.

"Uno hombre macho," the Senorita said, "*wants* to die for them."

"It is based," Diaz said, "in the belief that life, without the fantasy of macho honor, has no intrinsic meaning, and so the illusion of macho pride is the most important of all the virtues—at least, for any man consumed with macho honor."

"In other words," Nietzsche said, "dying for macho pride is no sacrifice at all. We are better off dead without it."

"Bravo," the Senorita said.

"Precisely so," Diaz said.

"Spoken like *uno Méjicano verdado*," [a true Mexican], the Senorita said.

"But Spain's contributions to Méjico are only half of our story," Diaz continued. "There is also our indio puro heritage: countless millennia under, first, the Mayan and then the Aztec rule. While the Spaniards, at least, placed a premium on courage, the Mayan/Aztecs felt that courage was pointless and that a good death was everything."

"As you shall see, we have inherited the absolute worst of two worlds," the Senorita said.

"To say that in their doxology," Diaz said, "courage had no meaning and that death—the true God—was everything is in no way hyperbolic."

"In a very real sense," the Senorita said, "our indigenous, aboriginal people worshiped death and despised life."

"In the Maya-Aztec Afterlife, young Nietzsche," Diaz said, "do you know how the suicide was regarded?"

Nietzsche shook his head.

"The suicide," Diaz said, "was valued every bit as highly as the warrior who died in battle protecting his homeland."

"You mean those men who were sacrificed on the pyramids," Bismarck asked, "and whose blood was then purportedly fed to the gods?"

"Yes," the Senorita said, "those men were revered for their sacrifice, but the common, ordinary, run-of-the-mill suicides who killed themselves for no noble cause, who were just tired of life and only wanted to die, they were viewed in the next life as heroes as well."

"Because they hated life?" Nietzsche asked.

"Exactemente," Diaz said.

"Because they despised life with all their heart and soul and mind," the Senorita said, "they told life to go fuck itself, and they backed that commitment up by killing themselves."

"I'm not sure I understand the reasoning behind their hatred of life," Nietzsche said, "and their adulation of death."

"To a people who view all life as wholly contemptible," the Senorita said, "as the ultimate embodiment of evil, then any self-inflicted death is a cause for celebration and the suicide—any suicide—is to be revered."

"Are you saying that the Maya-Aztecs," Bismarck asked, "viewed death as a thing of beauty and a joy forever?"

The Senorita, Sutherland, McKillian and Diaz treated Bismarck to a loud, long round of applause.

"The chancellor too," Sutherland shouted, "is a student of Longfellow."

"He is much admired here in Méjico," Diaz enthused.

"And, yes," the Senorita said, "down here, death is perceived as both ecstatically beautiful and eternally joyful."

But Nietzsche was not distracted by their laughter and gaiety. "You are saying that the Maya-Aztecs exulted in en masse death? Were that true, their civilization would never have survived for as long as it did and achieved so much—for millenia."

"You are right," Diaz said, "and their end was near. Our people were holding orgies of human sacrifice around the clock, struggling mightily to end it all forever. It was on the verge of total collapse when Cortez arrived and introduced Méjico to the Spanish Code of Machismo."

"And that is how and why," the Senorita said, "we ended up inheriting the worst of two worlds, young Nietzsche—the Spaniard's love affair with vindictive violence, his disdain for cowardice—even to the point of scorning death—and the Maya-Aztec's outright worship of annihilation."

"And that is why," Diaz said, "we say that you will never understand us, young Nietzsche. The adoration of violent death is not burned into your brain and bones and blood. It is not the zenith of your being, the supreme essence of your existence, your life's apologia pro vita sua."

"And until you feel Méjico *violento y letal* [violent and lethal] not only in your heart and mind," the Senorita said with a smile that, surprisingly enough, was not condescendingly derisive or gratuitously unkind, "but down in the uttermost pit of your soul's blackest abyss, you can never be... *uno Méjicano puro.*"

"In sum," Diaz said with considerate but firm finality, "young Friedrich, you will always be a stranger in Méjico magnifico and will never understand us at all."

CHAPTER 4

After dinner, the servants brought Alfred Krupp another cable. He and the emperor were sitting in his study. Replete with dark leather and darker wood, elegant, lavishly bound books lined all the walls. Wilhelm personally found such bookish décor garish, but then his idea of exquisite surroundings—according to his wife—had always been the inside of a bivouac tent. He had to admit there was some truth to her raillery. He had won medals and had truly distinguished himself in the Napoleonic wars for his courage under fire.

In point of fact, he loved combat and would have given anything to have returned to the German Army as a frontline officer. He exulted in all the horror that lesser mortals abhorred—the smoke and blood and screams and the cannons' roar.

He *loved* all of it.

"You reported that you needed our chancellor in Méjico to close the deal," Wilhelm finally said to Krupp, "that Diaz would only deal head-of-state to head-of-state."

"Diaz was adamant about that."

"Well," the Kaiser said, "Otto's apparently losing his nerve. Something's happening over there—something, unfortunately, we had not foreseen."

"Maybe the problem is Diaz," Krupp said. "Maybe the cynical bastard thinks we're out to swindle him."

"We are out to swindle him."

"But of course," Krupp said. "Why else would anyone deal with that barbarous bastard? I intend to loot Diaz and that corrupt little country of his—lock, stock with both smoking-hot in my greedy, grasping fists." Krupp thumped his knuckles on the table for emphasis.

"Unfortunately, Diaz understands our intentions all too well."

"Then we need to convince him our intentions are honorable," Krupp said.

"Even though they aren't."

Krupp treated the emperor to a harsh, barking laugh, his face a contorted mask of scorn.

"Diaz wouldn't know honor," Krupp said, "if it bit him in his cojones."

"You're the gun merchant," Wilhelm said. "You have to offer him something he cannot resist—something that makes you seem indispensable—a deal sweetener."

"A what?"

"A bonus of sorts, that will make the deal irresistible," Wilhelm explained. "Do you have other weapons that are not part of the deal, weapons that won't cost you a lot but will look like a military bonanza to Diaz?"

"I was sending some old guns from the Franco-Prussian War to Santiago, Chile," Krupp said. "I was hoping the gift would inspire their rulers to purchase something more substantial and to sell us more potassium nitrate from their mines for our gunpowder manufacturing firms. The ship captain is to cable us before he hands them the present—in case we have further instructions. I could instruct him by return cable to steam farther north and hand them over to old Porfirio. That dolt will think they're God's engines of the apocalypse."

But Wilhelm remained querulously sullen. "You aren't giving him anything really first-rate, I hope?"

"God, no," Krupp said, indignant. "Do you think I'm verrückt?" Crazy. "I'm sending him a few ancient howitzers and a couple of rapid-fire field pieces."

"Ausgezeichnet." Excellent.

"And he's getting more than he and his blighted land deserve," Krupp said. "One generation ago, his parents were sacrificing their daughters' vaginas to their blood-soaked, Aztec gods. He wouldn't know first-rate artillery if it was given to him by the Almighty Himself and field-tested in hell. I'm only giving him a taste of what he might get down the road if he plays his cards right—just enough to seduce him into buying bigger, better, more powerful guns."

"Extortionately expensive guns."

"But I am sending him models of the very guns we used to steamroll over France in our 1870 war with them," Krupp reminded the Kaiser, "the very guns that allowed you and me to unite our divided and often inimical German states into a single, cohesive state."

"Into what is now the most potent military force on the continent."

"Perhaps in the world."

"And a global industrial power, par excellence," Wilhelm said, "and we owe much—if not all—of that transformation to you."

"You are too kind," Krupp said.

"But accurate," the emperor said.

They were quiet a long minute.

"Still, I'm concerned about your business dealings with Porfirio Diaz," the emperor finally said, giving Krupp a worried look.

"He is no different than any other national leader."

"Bismarck thinks he's a hound of hell."

"His money will spend," Krupp said.

"Money drenched in his peons' blood."

"As I've often explained," Krupp said, "I couldn't care a gnat's ass where my revenue comes from."

"So you've told me a thousand times."

"Or what others do with it after I spend it," Krupp said, reiterating his much-repeated refrain.

"You call it 'the iron law of financial circulation.'"

"I call money 'the Second Blood,' as if it powered our species' true circulatory system."

"Bismarck says Diaz is different," the emperor said.

"Diaz is just another impudent insect from another squalid, fourth-rate, scheiss-stinking outhouse of a country," Krupp argued.

"Bismarck says," the emperor pointed out, "that Diaz has low animal cunning, is devoid of fear or scruples and shouldn't be underestimated."

"Bismarck, Bismarck, Bismarck."

"Germany owes him much."

"He has a poor opinion of me."

"He thinks you have the business ethics of a feral rat," Wilhelm said. "And I naturally have no sympathy for such warped opinions."

"You know how Nietzsche once defined sympathy to me?"

"How?"

"It's a word in the dictionary between scheiss and syphilis."

The two men laughed hard and long.

CHAPTER 5

Doc, Earp and Bat Masterson stood on the plank train platform in the Southern Pacific Railroad Station. It was located on the edge of Las Vegas, New Mexico. The three men wore dark suits, white boiled shirts and cravats. Doc and Earp wore bowler hats, Masterson a Stetson. They each had traveling bags resting on the platform beside them. They were about to catch a westbound train.

With good reason.

The night before, just as six hardcases were about to murder Wyatt Earp in cold blood for his poker winnings, Torn Slater and Bat Masterson had shouldered their way through the batwings, surveyed the situation and thrown down on the six killers, guns blazing.

Doc and Earp were saved, but they were no longer welcome in the entirety of the New Mexico Territory. Nor was Masterson. As for Slater, he'd slipped out the door immediately after the killings and was now nowhere to be found. Not that anyone was looking too hard. Very few men wanted to go gun-to-gun with Outlaw Torn Slater.

Still the town's lawmen were willing to look the other way when it came to the saloon killings the night before. The men that the three of them had gunned that night had prices on their heads—which the constables were only too happy to claim credit for and collect—to do so they had to claim they had killed them, not Doc and Earp, Slater and Bat.

The fact that Earp, Bat and Doc had been well-known marshals also made the town sheriff and his deputies sympathetic to their problems with the law.

But the three men were no longer welcome in Las Vegas, New Mexico Territory.

Which was too bad.

It had been the only town in North America where Doc Holliday had previously been welcome.

And he'd liked it there.

Now, just as they boarded the train, Slater joined them.

"I feel like I ought to thank you, Torn," Earp said uneasily.

"You did thank me," Slater said. "You agreed to go to El Rancho and help out me and Katherine."

"But you're hiring us as well," Bat said. "You're paying us well."

"Yeah," Slater said, "but you don't have to do it, and it'll get dicey in Arizona. Lord only knows what Diaz and Shelby will throw at us."

"It's dicey for us here too," Earp said.

"Case you haven't heard," Doc said, "Wyatt and I have warrants out on us as well. We're all wanted men."

"I didn't know about any dodgers on you," Slater said, "but I did hear about your shootout in Tombstone. It's all over the papers."

"They're calling it," Bat said, "'the Gunfight at the OK Corral.' The newspaper people can't seem to write about anything else."

"Hell," Doc said, "it wasn't even at the OK Corral."

"It was just out on a damn street," Earp said.

"Which is only a way of saying," Doc said, "that we'll be glad to hide out at Katherine's Rancho de Cielo for a while. Give us a chance to clear our heads and let the passions in Tombstone subside a little."

"Give us time to figure out what we need to do," Earp said.

"And I'm glad for the money," Bat said.

"Doc and I can use that cash too," Earp said.

"For lawyers, I'll bet," Bat said.

"Torn," Earp said, "Doc and I are basically trying to say thanks."

Slater said nothing.

"Goddamn it, Torn," Earp said, "why is it so goddamn hard for you to accept a simple thank-you?"

"Wyatt and I want you to know we appreciate the way you and Bat came into that bar and saved our bacon," Doc said.

"Bacon, your ass, Doc," Bat said. "What Torn saved was all our...*asses.* I never saw anyone shoot like that in my life."

Slater still said nothing.

Doc couldn't have agreed with Earp more. Neither of them had ever felt as outmanned, outgunned and overmatched as they'd been in that damn bar—not in their entire lives. They were one second away from going down in a hail of bullets.

Until Outlaw Torn Slater shouldered his way into the saloon.

Doc had never seen a man look so big and imposing and awful and menacing—not in his life, not...*ever.*

Slater must have watched them from the window or doorway, because he entered that bar with both guns already blazing—pistols jumping in his fists with each shot, men falling, cascading into one another like dominoes, dropping all over the saloon, women in red screaming, the piano man leaping behind the piano for cover, the barkeep diving to the floor, customers crouching behind upturned tables.

Doc, Earp and Bat had been gunning men down as well, but Doc would later say that he'd never seen anyone work a Colt as fast, as furiously, or with as much precision as Slater.

"Torn, I heard you're hell on wheels with a Big Fifty Sharps," Bat said.

But if Masterson expected an answer, he wasn't about to get one.

Slater just kept staring up the track, silent.

Then the train was pulling in. The three friends reached down for their carpetbags with one hand, then turned to shake hands with Slater with the other.

But they were too late.

Slater was already walking away toward the exit and the hitchrack.

He had ground to cover.

Outlaw Torn Slater was heading due north, not west.

He was on his way to the Nations.

PART X

"I've done an astounding amount of business with your European business magnates, including your munitions moguls. I have represented countless countries, whom your political leaders, quite frankly, view as morally unsuitable to acquire, possess and employ your more advanced weapons systems. Now no one under you is ignorant of my true role in these transactions. They know I am a front man for these fiends from hell, whom they so desperately despise. Furthermore, they understand with a vivid intimacy precisely how these weapons work and the cataclysmic effects they visit upon civilian populations when they are deployed and discharged. I certainly do. My employees teach these tyrants how to deploy and discharge said weapons, but your friends know all that. I can assure you, Chancellor Bismarck, from firsthand experience, that when it comes to creation and distribution of these engines of mass death and destruction, when it comes to inflicting violence on a global scale, your arms manufacturers, generals and politicians surpass Satan himself in their sheer destructiveness. They, most assuredly, outstrip my feeble machinations. You love to talk about your enlightened ethics and scientific advancement—all of which you lump together under the ludicrous rubric of 'progress'—but your real advances are in your instruments of en masse slaughter. Your real 'elan vital,' your most definitive 'life force' is gauged by the metrics of the apocalyptic annihilation that your weapons systems so blithely visit on humankind."

—James Sutherland, International Arms Magnate

"What are your greatest literary works after all but... *your tragedies?*" The Senorita vigorously shook a finger at Bismarck and Nietzsche. "What are your tragedies—your transcendent works of art, in which every character is monstrously murdered in the end of the tale—if not paeans to nihilism and despair? The life force that rules your democratic world is generated and renewed not by 'Life' but by your love of... '*Death.*' You and your leaders are not that much different from the men here in madre Méjico, not when it comes to the worship of *madre muerta*." [mother death]

—La Senorita Dolorosa

CHAPTER 1

Sitting with Diaz and his associates in the club car of the El Presidente Tren Expreso Personal, Bismarck and Nietzsche appreciated the unstinting hospitality that Diaz was extending to them.

But the generalissimo's savage—often murderous—treatment of his peons also sickened them.

"You've told us all about Méjico's bloody history," Bismarck said to Diaz and his three friends, "but none of that excuses or justifies your love affair with violent death. I will never grasp your glorification of slavery. The American colonists rebelled against tyranny in 1776 and the French against their monarchy in 1789. In 1848, democratic revolutions blazed like wildfire across the length and breadth of Europe. Tyranny and despotism are things of the past, dogs whose days are long done, yet you four exult in them and in forced servitude as if they all were the Second Coming of Christ."

"Oh my God," the Senorita said to Diaz, "they really don't get it, do they?"

"Don't get what?" Nietzsche asked.

The Senorita treated the two men to her sincerest smile. "You do not understand that we're different from you."

"We lack your bourgeois sentimentality," Judith McKillian said.

"Your middle-class morality," James Sutherland said.

Bismarck and Nietzsche stared at their interlocutors, dumbstruck.

"You, no doubt, view Christ's beatitudes as holy writ, correct," the Senorita patiently explained.

"As divine precepts," Diaz said.

"As words to live by," James Sutherland said with a mocking smile.

"Naturlich," Bismarck said soberly. Of course.

"That is because you live in a world consumed by bourgeois sentimentality," Judith McKillian said, "and overrun by middle-class morality."

"But you are abjuring Christ's profoundest teachings," Nietzsche argued.

"Young Friedrich," the Senorita said, staring deeply into Nietzsche's eyes, "I keep telling you that you do not understand how things are in madre Méjico. In your world, the poor inherit the earth and peacemakers are divinely blessed, correct?"

"Is there something wrong with...*that?*" Nietzsche asked, stammering.

"It is not the way of the world," Diaz blustered, angrily shaking his head. "It is not the way things are. Christ does not teach us—what your Immanuel Kant calls—der ding an sich, the thing in itself. Christ teaches us a ludicrous, laughable fairy-tale fantasy, and in doing so he defies...*the natural order of things.*"

"Which is?" Nietzsche asked.

"In our world," Judith McKillian said, "we work our peons to within an inch of their lives—on both our plantations and in our silver mines."

"With our overseers flogging their lazy asses every inch of the way," James Sutherland said.

"Which is the only way we can get any productive work out of them," Judith McKillian said with a truly splendid smile.

"Because that's the way it's supposed to be," the Senorita said.

"Will you never understand?" Diaz said. "Here in Méjico, we do not want our peons enjoying an affluent retirement, sitting back happily, counting their pesos, dandling their grandchildren on their knees, eating their tortillas and swilling tequila. We don't want them luxuriating off the fat of the land."

"You see, young Friedrich," the Senorita said, leaning toward him, her smile now almost ethereally serene, "we don't want our peons to have pensions, healthcare programs, free schools and education. We want them laboring for us, like the loathsome beasts of burden that they truly are, ad aeternum, ad infinitum."

"But what of Isaiah's Peaceable Kingdom?" Bismarck asked. "You surely can't object to that too—where the wolf lies down with the lamb and the child sleeps at the hole of the asp, where humanity at last lives in peace."

"I don't object to Isaiah's Peaceable Kingdom at all," Diaz said. "In Méjico, we love peacemakers. The peaceful never fight back. We can flog and work them like dogs without any resistance at all."

"They are too busy 'making peace' to put up a struggle," the Senorita said, throwing her head back and laughing melodically.

"So you work them to death as well," Bismarck said sarcastically.

"Yes," Sutherland said, suddenly serious, "but unfortunately, not everyone is a peacemaker. There are some who never learn and who will always resist."

"There are always those," Diaz concurred, clapping Sutherland on the shoulder, signifying his assent, "who refuse to understand the way things are, the ding an sich, the natural order of things, the way things work here in Méjico glorioso."

"No matter how many times we flog them," Sutherland said, "or how often we starve them, they just don't get the message and get with the program."

Diaz and Sutherland shook their heads in bitter disappointment.

"What do you do with them?" Nietzsche asked.

"Those insufferable ingrates," Diaz said, giving the two Germans a melancholic, palms-up shrug, "we drag their sorry remains out of our mines and throw them off the edge of a cliff or we deposit their decrepit carcasses in our crocodile swamps and let the crocs finish them off."

"You don't accept that none of us is an island," Nietzsche said, "that everyone is part of the main, that every person's death diminishes each of us because we are all involved in humankind? You don't accept that we are all equal under the eyes of God?"

"How does any of that put pesos in my pocket and wrap putas around the truly awesome, splendiferous immensity of my...*garrocha?*" [pole], Diaz asked, giving Nietzsche his most appealing smile and another one of his eloquently unassuming, infinitely unprepossessing...*shrugs.*

"When you speak like that," Nietzsche shouted furiously at them all, "the angels weep!"

"Oh no," the Senorita said, feigning mock innocence. "He does not know? Oh dear," she said to her associates, shaking her head in dismay. "Young Nietzsche has not been informed." Turning back to him, she said:

"Friedrich dear, there are no angels anymore. We no longer have those heavenly sprites to whine and snivel and to reprimand us, every time we turn around, for our truly reprehensible misdeeds. They've all gone away."

Nietzsche's face was flushed with angry incredulity.

Touching his cheek gently, the Senorita said softly:

"You see, young Friedrich, the angels aren't around anymore, because they're all...*in hell.*"

"What?" Nietzsche said.

"God sent them there, because He said He was"—and here the Senorita quoted with meticulous precision—"'sick and tired of their idiocy and ineptitude,' saying that 'they just couldn't hack it anymore.' Unfortunately, dear Friedrich," the Senorita continued, "we were too clever for them, too tough and too remorseless. We appealed to the angels' greed, pandered to their lust, drowned them in our sin and then engorged them with all our violence and our blood. In short, we remade them in our own wicked image."

"But don't feel bad," Judith McKillian said, chuckling merrily, "I hear they're happier in hell. They now confess that, after their time with us, they found all that heavenly virtue just too fucking...*boring.*"

CHAPTER 2

Slater was standing alongside his mount—already saddled and bridled—in the ventilated stock car, when his train pulled into the railroad station at Younger's Bend. If trouble was waiting for him, he and the big gray could be on the ramp, off the train and hell-bent for leather even as the train was still coming to a grinding halt.

Belle Starr was waiting for him at the station. Dressed in tight work Levis, horse boots and a work shirt, she had a quirt looped to her belt, right alongside the ivory-handled Colt that was strapped in a cross-draw holster to her right hip. The barrel of a sawed-off twelve-gauge rested casually on her shoulder, her wrist draped loosely over the stock. As usual, her eyes were filled with mischief and cruel merriment.

Slater walked up to her and held out his hand. Brushing it aside, she threw her arms around his neck and kissed him full on the mouth.

"Feisty as ever?" Slater asked, after she let him go.

"Always."

"And never saying 'thank you' or 'please.'"

"Never saw any reason why I should."

"Nice quirt," Slater said, glancing down at her horsewhip. "Still beating that kid of yours halfway to death with it?"

"Naw, he finally got the hint and took off. He's living with a squaw on the Cherokee reservation."

"He'll be back."

"He does, I'll strip some more hide off him. It's all the hard-headed little bastard understands."

"Maybe he takes after his ma," Slater said.

"Maybe."

Slater stared at her a while in silence. "You're a hard woman, Belle," he said, shaking his head.

"Only in the heart."

"Where am I staying?"

"At my place."

"In the bunkhouse?"

"In *my* bunk."

Slater said nothing.

Belle reached back with the quirt, as if to lay open his cheek. She then grabbed his head with both hands, the quirt now looped loosely around her wrist, pulled him tight enough to break his neck and kissed him again, this time hard enough to almost crack his front teeth. It was a game she liked to play with him. When she finished, the people in front of the train station were staring at them, gape jawed.

"You'd think they never saw a man get kissed before," Belle said.

"Not like that, they haven't," Slater said, wiping his mouth, hoping to rub some feeling back into his lips.

"I'm serious about you bunking with me," Belle said. "I'm gonna find out whether Outlaw Torn Slater's still got it where it counts. Or if all those years in jail and on the owlhoot—all them beans he et down in Méjico done turned Slater's manhood into frijoles."

Again, Slater said nothing.

But then, no one ever knew what to say to Belle Starr.

"Ain't that many muchos hombres left anymore," Belle said sadly. "Of the Youngers, only Cole's still alive."

"And he's doing life in prison," Slater pointed out.

"That too," Belle said.

"Jess is dead," Slater noted.

"And brother Frank's on the run someplace in Méjico."

"No more."

"What?"

"I run into Frank down Méjico way. He's now headed back up here and loaded for bear. He's lookin' to resurrect the army of the Confederacy. I don't care nothing about that, but I got friends he's coming after with it. I can't let that happen. Belle, *we* can't let that happen."

"Them Rancho de Cielo people?"

"The same."

"I wondered what this was about—why you suddenly... *wanted me.*"

Slater said nothing.

"I still don't understand what you see in that Katherine Ryan woman."

Slater was still silent.

"Then there it is," Belle said.

"There it is."

CHAPTER 3

"And you," Nietzsche said to the generalissimo, "are, most assuredly, one of those for whom hell was created."

They were still sitting in the club car, the men smoking Havanas and drinking cognac.

"Es verdad?" Diaz asked, turning to Sutherland, the Senorita and Judith McKillian. Is it true?

"I'm afraid so, old chap," Sutherland said. "Jesus most definitely would not approve of your business morals and political proclivities."

"No matter how handsomely we all profit off your largesse," Judith McKillian added with a placating smile, patting Diaz patronizingly on the cheek.

"Then what do you suppose hell will look like?" Diaz asked meditatively.

"Percy Bysshe Shelley believed it was a city rather like London," Sutherland cheerfully observed.

"He was most likely correct," Judith McKillian concurred, unfolding her iridescent Chinese fan and, once more, cooling her face.

"Indubitably correct," Sutherland said, amending her remark.

"Quite so," McKillian said.

"Christopher Marlow believed hell resides solely in the human heart," Sutherland said. "In *Doctor Faustus*, he wrote:

Why, this is hell nor am I out of it....
Hell hath no limits, nor is circumscribed
In one self place, for where we are is hell,

And where hell is must we ever be.

"Are you suggesting, dear James," the Senorita said, "that we're in hell already and not Méjico magnifico?"

"Milton seemed to think so," Sutherland said. "He has Satan say in *Paradise Lost*:

Which way I fly is hell; myself am hell.

"Wherever it is," Judith McKillian said, "I am sure that all the best people are there."

"If so," the Senorita said, "the conversation must be most stimulating."

"I'm not sure about that," Diaz said. "Our priests have always insisted that heaven was far more agreeable."

"I personally believe that heaven," the Senorita said, "has to be the most angelically dull place in all of the firmament."

"The strain of living amid all that stern virtue and self-righteous piety must be utterly...*exhausting*," Sutherland opined.

"You are monsters!" Bismarck thundered.

Diaz and his friends stared back at Bismarck and Nietzsche not only in shock but with genuinely hurt feelings.

"Do you stoop to name-calling," Diaz asked, dismayed, "simply because people disagree with you?"

"After all," the Senorita said, "you and your business colleagues are hardly exemplars of Christian charity."

"We don't enslave people," Bismarck said, "and we don't mock God."

"There are some things men don't do to each other," Nietzsche shouted.

"Really?" Sutherland asked with a self-satisfied smirk. "Porfirio, can you think of anything you wouldn't do if someone offered you enough filthy lucre to make it worth your while?"

Diaz treated them all to his most engaging smile.

"Money is not always required, James. I can think of many other motivators. For example, I've always believed that if a man's stomach was empty enough and his dick hard enough, he would do just about...*anything*."

"Truer words were never spoken," the Senorita said, applauding.

Judith McKillian joined her in the hand clapping.

"Furthermore," Sutherland said, "I've done an astounding amount of business with your European business magnates, including your munitions moguls. I have represented countless countries whom your political leaders, quite frankly, view as morally unsuitable to acquire, possess and employ your more advanced weapons systems. Now no one under you is ignorant of my true role in these transactions. They know I am a front man for these fiends from hell, whom they so desperately despise. Furthermore, they understand with a vivid intimacy precisely how these weapons work and the cataclysmic effects they visit upon civilian populations when they are deployed and discharged. I certainly do. My employees teach these tyrants how to deploy and discharge said weapons, but your friends know all that. I can assure you, Chancellor Bismarck, from first-hand experience, that when it comes to creation and distribution of these engines of mass death and destruction, when it comes to inflicting violence on a global scale, your arms manufacturers, generals and politicians surpass Satan himself in the sheer destructiveness. They, most assuredly, outstrip my feeble machinations. You love to talk about your enlightened ethics and scientific advancement—all of which you lump together under the ludicrous rubric of 'progress'—but your real advances are in your instruments of en masse slaughter. Your real 'elan vital,' your most definitive 'life force,' is gauged by the metrics of the apocalyptic annihilation that your weapons systems so blithely visit on humankind."

"The same," the Senorita said, "holds true in your highest and noblest works of art. What are your greatest literary works after all but…*your tragedies?*" The Senorita vigorously shook a finger at Bismarck and Nietzsche. "What are your tragedies—your transcendent works of art, in which every character is monstrously murdered in the end of the tale—if not paeans to nihilism and despair? The life force that rules your democratic world is generated and renewed not by 'Life' but by your love of…'*Death.*' You and your leaders are not that much different from the men here in madre Méjico, not when it comes to the worship of *madre muerta.*" [mother death]

Bismarck and Nietzsche could only stare at Diaz and his friends in mute horror.

"People condemn us," the Senorita said, "because—here in our primitive land—we still utilize the rack, the strappado and the iron maiden, but who invented those macabre machines? You and your European nations."

"Face it," Diaz said. "If we engage in evil enterprises, it is only because you and your European confreres sold us the tools of our trade and instructed us in their savage implementation."

"And you profit handsomely off of every deplorable...*transaction,*" Sutherland said.

"Don't you see?" the Senorita asked. "You and your friends taught us everything we know."

"Have you never heard of 'Love your neighbor as yourself'?" Nietzsche asked Diaz and his friends, still shaken by their debate.

"Or 'if you've done it unto the least of these, my brethren,'" Bismarck asked, "'you have done it unto me'?"

"Uh-oh," Judith McKillian said, giving them her most supercilious sneer, "here comes middle-class morality again."

"Just rearing back to bite us on the arse," Sutherland said, treating them to the most scornfully imperious sneer that Nietzsche had ever seen—one that put Judith McKillian's to shame.

"Don't you just love it," the Senorita said, "when wealthy Europeans and rich gringos put on moral airs."

"I can't get enough of their pseudo-superiority," James Sutherland said.

"And their pseudo-sophistication," McKillian agreed.

"They have turned self-righteousness," the Senorita said, "into high art."

"So you are saying what?" Nietzsche asked. "That you three are utterly without moral principles of any kind and we are fools for still believing in such things as 'love' and 'virtue'?"

Diaz and his three associates stared at Nietzsche in stunned silence.

"Dear Friedrich," the Senorita said, "you finally understand us. You grasp, at last, the way things are here in Méjico supremo."

"Here in Méjico," Judith McKillian said, "life is hard, and if you choose your friends here based solely on their moral principles, you would be muy solitaria tambien." Very lonely indeed.

"But, Senorita," Bismarck said, "you talk as if virtues such as love don't exist. That such concepts are nothing more than conjectures, fantasies, opinions and preferences. Have you never loved anyone? Not even...*romantically?*"

"You mean as Laura loved the inestimable Petrarch," the Senorita asked, "and Beatrice Dante Alighieri?"

"Yes, exactly," Bismarck said.

The Senorita's derisive smile was a wonder to behold.

"In plain fact," the Senorita continued, "Laura and Beatrice loved neither of those impudent imbeciles any more than I have loved any male in that endless queue of demented dolts and dismal dimwits that have strutted, fretted and paraded themselves before me every day of my life since I was twelve years old."

"The rest of womankind is not so cold," Bismarck said. "I know. From a lifetime of personal experience."

"Oh, yes," the Senorita shouted, "you know what it's like to be a wealthy, all-powerful man, but do you know what it's like to be on the receiving end of your tawdry masculine importunings?"

"What it means to constantly have to feign warm feelings," Judith McKillian roared, cutting in, "to pretend to feel deeply about men and their arrogant opinions and the other manly things they are constantly bombarding you with but which you couldn't care less about? To have to pretend to like—even love—men who are so infernally dull that you could barely stand to be in the same room with them? Do you have any idea what ludicrous fools we women honestly believe you men to be?"

"I suppose you mock the sanctity of marital love as well," Bismarck said stiffly, bristling with outrage.

"Ha!" Judith McKillian exploded. "The most deadly creature on earth is the female of the species when she is hunting a husband. You should see her, stalking the game herds, waiting for her prey to weaken and stumble. Once she has the poor bastard in her sights, nothing will stand in the way of her conquest—the mounting and wall-hanging of her trophy. And she shares its carcass with no one. An anaconda, constricting around the throat and torso of its victim, then swallowing it whole, is no less cruel than a woman in the pursuit of the man she so vehemently and duplicitously proclaims to…*love*."

"When pursuing a wealthy, powerful and desirable mate," the Senorita said, "there is no trick so low, no tactic so devious that we women will not stoop to employ it."

"All bets are off!" Judith McKillian shouted with vindictive vehemence.

"You make women sound like black widow spiders bedding then devouring their mates," Nietzsche said.

"An apt analogy," the Senorita said, "although I am more admiring of female wasps."

"In what way, my dear?" Judith McKillian asked.

"The female wasp hides her stinger in her genitals," the Senorita said. "When the male mounts her, boy, does he get a big surprise!"

"Oh, I like that!" Judith McKillian shouted.

Both women roared with laughter.

"Are you saying," Nietzsche asked, shaking with genuine horror, "that women are lying, homicidal, sexual monsters?"

"In a word, yes," the Senorita said, turning suddenly, seriously sincere and giving the young man her most angelically beatific smile.

"I suppose you think even a woman's most sacred and loving wedding vows are also a lie," Bismarck said.

The Senorita and Judith McKillian howled with hysterical hilarity, doubled over at the waist with their uncontrollable guffaws. After finally catching her breath, McKillian scornfully quoted the marriage vow:

"'I promise to love, honor, cherish and obey, until death do us part'? Is that the moronic maudlinity you put so much stock in?"

Again, their laughter pealed.

"In a word, yes," Nietzsche said, after their raucous ridicule subsided.

"Young Friedrich," the Senorita said, her smile, once more, understanding, even empathetic, "I do not know what I will feel for another human being a week from now, let alone until 'death do us part.' If you were honest, you would confess that you do not know either. So how can anyone swear to love someone in perpetuity? None of us has crystal balls that foretell the future...*forever*."

"Then there is the purely practical matter of what the marriage contract does to the man," Sutherland said.

"Tell young Friedrich what that transaction entails," Diaz said.

"He promises to take care of the woman materially and financially," Sutherland said, "and she promises him occasional sex. It changes him overnight from a man whose whole future lies before him to a man only with a past. In short, it castrates and imprisons him."

"Scheiss," Nietzsche grunted under his breath. Excrement.

"You must understand, dear James," Diaz said to Sutherland, while he gently clapped Nietzsche on the back and threw an arm over the younger man's shoulder, "our compadre, young Friedrich here is a romantic."

"In which way?" Sutherland asked, amused.

"He labors," Diaz said, "under the demented delusion that women somehow...*differ.*"

Diaz and his friends erupted in up-from-the-gut, roll-out-the-barrel, thigh-slapping horse laughter, howling until tears of cruelty and ridicule filled their eyes.

"What is wrong with you people?" Nietzsche shouted at Diaz and his friends. "In your world, is nothing sacred? Is everything heretical? Do you care about...*anything at all?* Does truth mean nothing? Is everything lies and illusions?"

"Oh my," the Senorita said sheepishly, placing a hand over her mouth. "After all our work, after all our blood and sweat, I'd almost given up. But Herr Nietzsche finally gets it. I don't believe it!"

"I'd also given up," Judith McKillian said.

"Me too," Diaz said, astonished, "but he's finally starting to understand us, our...*Méjico.*"

"Understand what about Méjico?" Nietzsche asked, genuinely confused.

"The truth of our world," Judith McKillian said. "You're starting to understand our reality...as it really is."

"And that reality is...*what?*" Nietzsche asked.

"It's a joke," Diaz said simply.

"A very bad joke," Sutherland said, nodding in affirmation.

"Don't you get it?" the Senorita said. "The truth you so dogmatically believe in doesn't exist."

"Not here," Diaz said, "not in madre Méjico."

"Here, everything is a snare and a delusion," Judith McKillian said.

"I see it as more like a confidence game," James Sutherland said.

"That too," Judith McKillian said, nodding her head in assent.

"So the words," Nietzsche asserted, quoting Christ, "'Ye shall know the truth, and the truth shall set ye free'—they mean nothing to you?"

"Less than nothing," Diaz said with an eloquent shrug.

"Pilate didn't think much of Christ's obsession with so-called truthfulness either," the Senorita said, shaking her head most emphatically. "Remember what Pilate said to Christ after your savior lectured him about the veracity of his accusers?"

Nietzsche allowed that he didn't remember.

"Pilate responded," the Senorita said, "'What is truth?' And do you remember Christ's answer?"

"Of course he doesn't," Diaz said.

"Explain it to Herr Nietzsche," Judith McKillian said.

"Because Christ had no answer for Pilate," the Senorita explained. "Know why?"

"BECAUSE THERE IS NO TRUTH!" Diaz thundered at the two men.

Nietzsche and Bismarck could only stare wordlessly at their interlocutors, mute with shock.

"Young Nietzsche," the Senorita said with a polite, even empathetic smile, "you are a student of Plato, who taught us to question everything and who argued that the unexamined life is not worth living. Socrates died for those beliefs, and you subscribe to them too. You long for a world of inviolable, Platonic certitude—of eternal ineluctable verities, rooted in unassailable postulates and derived through irrefutable deductive reasoning. But your logic is and always will be flawed: There are no incontestable postulates and there never will be. They are all subjective fantasies. To topple your moral truths, all I have to do is impeach your assumptions and replace them with premises of my own choosing, which from my point of view are every bit as persuasive as yours."

"And when we change your presuppositions," Diaz said, "we contravene your conclusions."

"And your truths are no longer incontrovertible," Sutherland said.

"Most notably, your so-called moral truths," Judith McKillian said.

"Which," Diaz said, "are empty as the everlasting void and nonsensical as a cretin's demented dreams."

"So, you see," the Senorita said, "here in Méjico, your Aristotelian logic no longer obtains, and your moral precepts are patently preposterous. So here, you play by our rules."

"And our rules," Diaz said, "are relentless."

"Which means," the Senorita said, "that in our world, there are no indisputable moral laws."

"Meaning," Nietzsche asked heatedly, "you invent your morality as you go along and use it to justify whatever nefarious schemes you are engaged in at the time?"

"Bravo, Herr Philosopher!" Diaz roared.

Their four hosts treated Nietzsche and Bismarck to a standing round of rapturous applause.

"I knew you'd finally get it," the Senorita said, genuinely impressed.

"I always believed you'd come around," Diaz said, delighted.

"And what do you call your new moral system?" Nietzsche asked. "The Gospel According to the Antichrist?"

"Hmmm, that's not bad," the Senorita said, rubbing her chin pensively, "but if you must know, I call it 'Perspectivism.' After all, what is morality? Certainly, not a hard, fast, black-ink rule book. I see it more as—oh, how shall I put it?—a shifting kaleidoscope of differing perspectives."

"Which evolve as we evolve," Diaz said.

"According to our ever-changing, ever-lucrative, profit-taking, money-making points of view," Judith McKillian announced.

"I'll drink to that!" the Senorita shouted.

She then treated them to a melodious archipelago of gleefully trilling, joyfully tintinnabulating giggles.

Nietzsche could only stare at them with outraged indignation.

To his undying horror, these monsters had, again, shocked him into speechlessness.

Staring into the Senorita's unfathomable but not entirely unfriendly eyes, he did not honestly know what to say.

PART XI

"[T]he moral superiority of your democratic capitalism is not an objectively proven fact or even a universally held belief but merely subjective conjecture. Furthermore, your maudlin meanderings are irrelevant to the way things are, the way of the world, the ding an sich, the natural order of things. In the real world—where sane people live, work and die—the powerful rule the powerless. The strong survive, the weak perish, and that is life. It was ever thus."

—James Sutherland, International Arms Magnate

CHAPTER 1

"We'll get started tomorrow," Belle Starr said to Slater. "I'll introduce you to some of the men I've rounded up. They can drag a few other violently tortured souls into this godforsaken enterprise. It's a real Land of the Lost back here."

"Anyone and everyone with a price on their heads," Slater said, "seems to end up in the Nations."

"No one comes here because it's a golden land of enchantment," Belle said.

"Except you."

"Except me."

"After the war, men on the run," Slater said, "or fleeing some old burnt-out homestead back in the South would post signs in front of the rubble that said... '*GTT.*'"

"Gone to Texas," Belle said, indicating she knew what the initials meant.

"Or hell," Slater said, finishing the complete epigram.

"Now it's Gone to the Nations," Belle said. "Texas is too damn civilized. They got too many lawmen."

"You got Judge Parker here."

"And Parker's deps are getting too damn smart," Belle said.

"I heard Parker's got a black deputy named Bass Reeves," Slater said, "who can track a man across the fires of hell. I heard he could hunt down Lucifer himself, that Reeves ain't got no quit in him."

"You heard right. But Texas is even worse," Belle said. "Those Rangers down there don't back down, and they don't back off."

Slater nodded his agreement.

"They don't take you to the judge," Belle said with a shudder. "They just ride you under the nearest sycamore and string you up on the spot."

For a while, they said nothing.

"So you'll have your pick of the men out here," Belle said. "No matter how desperate your damn enterprise is, it can't be worse than Parker's deps or them Texas Rangers south of here. At least, that's the way a lot of them will see it."

"But there is a catch, right?" Slater asked.

"Some of the very best men," Belle said, "the ones you really want for this operation, are in a bit of a jam. We might have to help them out of it, before they can help you save your friends."

"We need all the hands we can get. I'll be obliged."

Belle stared at Slater, surprised. "Well, I'll be damned."

"What's wrong?"

"You said you'd 'be obliged.'"

"So?"

"I ain't never heard Outlaw Torn Slater thank anyone before."

Slater said nothing.

"Well, let's get going," Belle finally said. "My horse is tied up at the station hitchrack. Brought one for you too."

CHAPTER 2

"And what exactly is wrong with my peonage system?" Diaz asked irascibly, his brow wrinkling.

They were in the club car of Diaz's presidential express train, sipping cognac and watching the State of Durango's chaparral roll past.

"Nothing's wrong with it, Porfirio," Sutherland said. "Your peon-run operations are so damnably profitable you shouldn't have to justify anything to anyone. M-O-N-E-Y answers any and all niggling little queries."

"We should tell our critics to *chingo a sus madres* [fuck their mothers]," the Senorita said, leaning toward Bismarck, staring fixedly into his eyes, her index finger aggressively tapping his chest.

"Look at it from our point of view," Judith McKillian said. "We wouldn't appreciate our own incalculable wealth if our peons weren't so deplorably poor. We'd have nothing with which to contrast our own good fortune. I understand such poverty is hard on our infernally impertinent peons, but when I look at how well off we are and how deservedly those slothful reprobates are suffering, well, I don't know about you, Porfirio, but it makes me feel...*goddamned good.*"

"My dear," Diaz said, "you should feel ecstatic about your inestimable riches. You deserve every penny of your wealth."

"It's not like you...*earned it,*" Bismarck said.

"Your peons," Nietzsche said, "are the ones sweating under burden baskets, who extracted all those profits from your fields and mines."

"So?" Sutherland asked, indignant. "What's that got to do with...*moi?*"

"Dear Friedrich," the Senorita said. "What is the point of possessing inconceivable wealth, if you have to...*work for it*."

"Do you not understand," Nietzsche said, perplexed, "the most pernicious of all evils, the nadir of all criminality is and always has been...*poverty*."

"And your peonage system exemplifies poverty at its most egregious, most horrendous extremes," Bismarck said.

"True," Diaz said, "our peons are poor, but think of all the pesos they put in...*our pockets*. In other words, they are poor so that their superiors, namely us, can live in luxury—reside in villas, dine on caviar and drink vintage champagne. So it averages out in the end, no?"

"It does for me!" the Senorita bellowed belligerently.

Nietzsche shook his head in emphatic disagreement. "To be poor means to be ignorant, weak, malnourished. It means to vector diseases, to be a breeding ground for criminality and for social unrest. Poverty is the shortest route to prison and to the gallows. It is the ultimate crime, the quintessential wickedness—the atrocity engendering all other atrocities."

"True," Sutherland said, "but doesn't your religion teach you that it is sinful to crave riches, that Christ—whom we should all strive to emulate—lived and died a pauper and that, therefore, poverty is noble, that, in plain fact, it is...*Christlike?*"

"Mr. Sutherland makes a very good point," the Senorita said. "When we pauperize our peons, don't we in fact bring them closer to the sterling example of penurious nobility set for them by their lord and savior, Christ Jesus?"

"But you brutalize your poor," Bismarck said, "and profiteer off their misery. They do not live in noble penury but in abject squalor."

"And what's wrong with that?" Diaz asked, beaming one of his most ingratiating smiles.

"Chancellor Bismarck," the Senorita said, "you have to admit that the return on investment here is...*spectacular*."

Bismarck could only stare at her in utter bewilderment.

"And in Méjico," Sutherland said, "we have no union problems whatsoever. The leaders in your country will appreciate that. You, personally, have had no end of problems with your avaricious labor organizers."

Bismarck had to admit they had him on that point.

"He'd have Krupp on board with that one," Nietzsche whispered acerbically to the chancellor.

Still, Bismarck pulled himself together, and his voice returned.

"Back home," Bismarck said, "I am viewed as a ruthless exploiter of labor unions and the preeminent practitioner of Realpolitik on the European continent. But when it comes to cynical opportunism, I am a naïve socialist compared to you four."

"I humbly accept your compliment," Diaz said with a polite bow.

"But you do not appreciate the violent upheaval that your governance will indubitably provoke in Méjico," Nietzsche said. "I am a classicist by profession and know whereof I speak. I have studied the fall of ancient Greece and Rome in depth and detail. Thucydides in *The History of the Peloponnesian War* told us specifically that greed, financial inequality and the lust for power destroyed Athens. Gibbon tells us gross exploitation and mounting penury did in Rome, the world's first and greatest republic. Plato taught us that 'extreme poverty and excessive wealth' are both producers of great evil. His pupil Aristotle agreed, saying: 'Poverty is the parent of revolution and crime.'"

"Your people will rise up," Bismarck said simply.

"Our peons can *attempt* to revolt," Diaz said, "if they so choose. I hope they understand, however, that I live by the military doctrine of 'Overwhelming Force.'"

"Explain it to them, Porfirio," Sutherland said.

"No rebellion is feasible," Diaz said, "if the Senorita and I kill all the rebels, all their friends and family and anyone even remotely involved in the insurrection and the preparation for it thereof."

"Which is why we cherish invaluable friends, such as Herr Krupp," the Senorita said.

"And you two, as well, who have been sent here to supply us with 'the Arms of Overwhelming Force,'" Judith McKillian said.

"How do you mean?" Nietzsche asked, confused.

"Our close compadre Alfred Krupp," Diaz said, "has sent you two here to sell us the spectacularly lethal weaponry that we will use to kill any and all ungrateful subjects who might foolishly rise up against us."

Diaz flung his arms wide, as if embracing all of Méjico.

Dumbstruck by the brilliant incandescence of Diaz's smile, Nietzsche would, one day, compare its resplendent radiance to that of "a thousand suns."

CHAPTER 3

Frank James sat with John Harwood and Thomas Tremaine at a big circular corner table in the dining room of the Palace Hotel in McAllen, Texas. A huge rectangular room filled with dark wood chairs and tables, the walls were adorned with paintings of longhorn cattle and Comanche on horseback. The hotel was located in the center of Texas cotton country, much of which was located in Hidalgo County. What land wasn't covered with cotton was devoted to cattle-raising. McAllen was that county's biggest city. The hotel dining room was where the county's biggest cotton growers, cattle ranchers and commodity brokers primarily congregated. Famous for its postprandial, high-stakes, all-night, whiskey-and-cigars poker games, vast sums—sometimes a year or more of cotton profits—could change hands on the turn of a card.

Jesse had loved such games. He didn't like paying up when he lost, however, and had become notorious for welching on his I-owe-yous. Toward the end of his life, high-dollar poker players were reluctant to deal him into their big games. The fact that he might not live long enough to pay off his markers—assuming he chose to do so—also factored in the poker players' financial cynicism.

The steak and eggs had been the first real food Frank had eaten in a week, but he hadn't consumed much of it. Mostly he'd smoked hotel-bought cigars and sipped hotel brandy.

And listened to the men sitting with him.

"As you know, Frank," Harwood said, "General Nathan Bedford Forrest formed the White Knights of the Ku Klux Klan right after the war to protect the white population from rampaging negroes and their rank political predations."

"Forrest, though, had a come-to-Jesus moment," Tremaine said, "renounced the Klan and worked with black groups to help integrate them into white Southern society."

"Old Nate turned abolitionist on us," Tremaine said. "It was a bitter blow for Southerners everywhere—especially those who fought for the Cause."

"Some of our members viewed Forrest's actions as nothing less than treasonous," Harwood said, lighting up his own cigar.

"That's the way I view him," Tremaine said.

"Well," Frank said, "the general is gone now—to his punishment or reward—whichever the Lord decides."

"I vote for punishment," Tremaine said.

"I'm positive it's going to be damnation," Harwood said.

"I'm goddamn sure God feels the same way," Tremaine said.

"What do you think, Frank?" Harwood asked.

"I don't know," Frank James said. "The Lord doesn't confide in me much. He plays his cards close to the vest, at least where I'm concerned."

"Bet you'd like it if He slipped you the schedules of a few payroll trains though," Tremaine said, laughing hoarsely.

"And the itineraries of a few of those high-end express company money shipments," Hargrove said, joining in the laughter.

"I've never turned up my nose at cash money," Frank said. "It can be the handiest damn thing in the world at times."

"Irreplaceable," Hargrove said.

"Especially when you don't have it," Tremaine said.

"You got that one right," Frank said, nodding his head, smiling, trying hard to be agreeable.

"Which is something we wanted to talk to you about," Hargrove said.

"I can assure you," Frank said, "that money is not an issue. I met with Diaz personally. You help General Shelby out with this one operation, and we'll all have money to burn. Those Méjicanos hacendados, they make your Texas land barons here look like hardscrabble dirt farmers."

"Sure, Frank," Hargrove said, "and it's an opportunity we can't afford to pass up. This is the first real chance we've had to resurrect the Confederacy. We're with you all the way. We'll join you outside of Nogales."

"How many men can you bring?" Frank asked.

"We got chapters in Memphis, Jackson, Birmingham, Mobile, Louisville, Greenville, Charlottesville and Atlanta."

"We can recruit a couple of thousand men, easy," Tremaine said.

"The Klan's that big?" Frank asked.

"We haven't called it the Klan for over ten years," Tremaine said.

"I knew those federal boys had come down on the White Knights," Frank said. "Wondered why I hadn't heard much about you for a while."

"Grant cracked down on us over a dozen years ago," Hargrove explained, "and we had to go into hiding. Finally, we changed the names of our organizations."

"Sometimes we call ourselves 'the Red Shirts,'" Tremaine said.

"Other times 'the White League,'" Hargrove said.

"Well, whatever you call it," Frank said, "you'll have money and croplands—millions of acres. You'll have plantations bigger than any of your wildest dreams after you throw in with General Shelby. Diaz has even got slavery down there. He's throwing free peon labor in with the deal."

"Oh, we're in, Frank," Hargrove said, "but still, that's money down the road."

"No offense," Tremaine said.

"None taken," Frank said.

Frank could tell Hargrove was struggling to keep his smile friendly.

"But some of us Red Shirts got us a plan to make us some money a little quicker than the general's thinking," Tremaine said.

"Like right at this very moment," Hargrove said.

"This afternoon, in fact," Tremaine said.

"That's pretty fast," Frank had to admit.

"It's got the kind of payoff that us old boys down here in the Rio Grande Valley like to call... *now money,*" Hargrove said.

"Sometimes we call it upfront whip-out," Tremaine said, "meaning, what a man can whip out of his pocket up front."

"I call it 'run money,'" Frank said. "In case you have to take off in a hurry—say, you got the law crawling up your ass—it's the kind of money you can throw into your travelin' bags right there on the spot when you got no time to spare."

Frank poured a slug of brandy into their coffee cups and they toasted "run money."

"But Shelby's operation is different," Frank said. "His money is real, and it's big, and it'll be a whole new life for you boys."

"But now is *now*, Frank," Tremaine said.

Frank realized he couldn't divert them from their scheme.

"All right," Frank said, "how much hard cash you plan on taking off with?"

"One hundred and fifty thousand total."

Frank nodded appreciatively. "That is a tidy sum, I have to admit."

"You want in?" Tremaine asked.

CHAPTER 4

Diaz and his entourage were still in the club car, smoking Havanas and sipping fine cognac.

"The problem with Jesus," Diaz said, "was that he came from a long line of Hebrew prophets who preached to a slave population of fellow Hebrews, all of whom had spent hundreds of years as the oppressed subjects and/or chattels of different conquerors. Consequently, the credo that Christ promoted was one that comforted slaves, that told them that they were superior to their masters, and that their lack of wealth and power was a virtue and not a curse, which is, of course, a laughably ludicrous...*lie*."

"In short," the Senorita said, "their credo came down to a single belief, that no person is good enough to master another human being."

"What's wrong with that?" Nietzsche asked.

"It's palpably, demonstrably, psychotically false!" Sutherland thundered. "That's what's wrong with it."

"Young Friedrich," Judith McKillian said, while at the same time patting Sutherland's arm in an attempt to calm him down, "James is saying that such beliefs are absurd—especially in Méjico. Here, we wield the whip-hand over millions of impotent wretches every day of the year, and they lack the power to seriously resist us."

"And we do this," the Senorita said, "because we ourselves live by an ethic created not by slaves but by their masters. And in our doxology, we, the masters, are morally superior, because we—not gods—make the rules; therefore, whatever advances our ends is ethically just."

"And Christ's Sermon on the Mount, his parable of the Good Samaritan," Nietzsche said, "His Golden Rule, you would dismiss them as what? Sentimental claptrap?"

"As insane delusions," Sutherland said, "almost criminally detached from the hard realities of the actual world—the world that sane people live in."

"The world that *we* run," the Senorita said, her smile genial and joyous...a thing of true beauty.

"So you would do what to Christ's teachings?" Bismarck asked. "Trample them to pieces?"

"As the dirt under our feet," the Senorita said. Her words were harsh, but her smile was still stunning. "In Méjico, we hope to shatter all of religion's idols and icons, replacing them with an ethic that extolls the virtue of the strong and the successful rather than the weak and the...*moronic*."

"It is why I have disenfranchised and, for the most part, dispossessed the Catholic Church," Diaz said.

Nietzsche knew that Diaz was actively expropriating the Church's shockingly lucrative haciendas.

"Why on earth did anyone allow a plague of penurious insects," Sutherland said sharply, "to create this absurd Judeo-Christian code of conduct anyway?"

"It's a code that the entire civilized world lives by," Bismarck said.

"But not us," the Senorita countered.

"We like to go our own way," Judith McKillian said, "and we follow a credo that transcends your tedious ramblings about right and wrong, about the just and the unjust."

"We live in a world," Sutherland said, "in which the strong write their own codes of behavior."

"In a word, young Nietzsche," the Senorita said, "we are beyond your trite and dreary concepts of...*good and evil.* I like to think of us as the embodiment of anti-Christianity—as anti-Christs, if you must know."

"It is only right," Diaz said. "The world should always let the people who are ineluctably successful and indisputably superior to everyone else—people such as ourselves—write the laws, rules and regulations under which their underlings should live."

"In fact, if you wish, we will dictate that new ethic," the Senorita said, "the moral code of el hombre superior"—the superior man—"to you, young Nietzsche, and you can write it down for us. You can do that, can't you? You are a prodigiously gifted author. I have read your last book, *Human, All Too Human,* in translation. You would be perfect for our new endeavor."

"'Hombre superior,'" Sutherland said, scratching his head. "I like that phrase. We need to shorten it though. In English we have the word 'super.' Perhaps if we shortened 'superior' to 'super' that would work."

"Hmmm," the Senorita said meditatively, "the code of the superman, who lives beyond good and evil—by the code of the Antichrist."

"I say," Sutherland enthused, "I *really* like that."

"I do too," Judith McKillian said. Standing, she began to energetically flog her boot top with her riding crop.

"Voted on and approved by acclamation," the Senorita shouted. "Young Friedrich, you will ghostwrite our magnum opus for us, and you can call our new ethical system 'the Philosophy of the Superman.'"

"Why would I wish to codify an ethic that justifies enslaving entire nations against their will," Nietzsche asked, "when such actions are transparently immoral?"

"In your opinion," Sutherland said, "such actions are immoral. But the moral superiority of your democratic capitalism is not an objectively proven fact or even a universally held belief but merely subjective conjecture. Furthermore, your maudlin meanderings are irrelevant to the way things are, the way of the world, the ding an sich, the natural order of things. In the real world—where sane people live, work and die—the powerful rule the powerless. The strong survive, the weak perish, and that is life. It was ever thus."

"'As it was in the beginning,'" the Senorita quoted, "'it is now and ever shall be, world without end, amen, amen.'"

"Your peons will rise up," Bismarck said darkly, prophetically.

"Which is why we pay you so handsomely for all that state-of-the-art weaponry your Alfred Krupp so graciously sells me. Enough of those outrageously apocalyptic death machines, and I can put the entire population of Méjico in the ground, if necessary, before they can loosen my grip on power."

"Or touch one peso of the wealth," the Senorita said, "that Porfirio, our friends and I have so philanthropically invested in Méjico miraculo."

"Though most of it, dear Senorita," Sutherland said, "we do invest in... *ourselves.* I know I certainly do."

"And you will do what with Christ," Nietzsche asked, "when He returns and explains to you the error of your ways?"

"I would have the old fraud busted for all those embarrassing scams he was always perpetrating—such as performing miracles without a license," the Senorita said.

The two women's laughter soared.

"And if He doesn't appreciate our generosity," Judith McKillian said, after finally catching her breath, "I'll flog His ass halfway to death and nail him back onto His cross all over again."

She began savagely thrashing her leather boot top all over again, her eyes blazing like balefire.

"I don't know about you, dear Judith, but I recognize no authority higher than I myself," the Senorita said.

"Indeed," Judith McKillian said.

"Well said," Diaz agreed.

"Exactly so," Sutherland said enthusiastically.

"If Christ returns," the Senorita said, "we will teach Him the consequences of propagating such deranged, degenerate drivel as 'blessed are the peacemakers' and 'the meek shall inherit the earth.'"

"In short, young Friedrich," Judith McKillian said with inexpugnable hauteur, "we will teach that rude rapscallion the error of... *His ways.*"

PART XII

"I prefer to think that we march to a different drummer, one possessed by rousing rhythms and booming cadences, hammering out thunder rolls that reverberate through our souls like Wagnerian Gotterdammerungs. Now you may argue, instead, that we are trudging along to Franz Liszt's 'Death March,' and I wouldn't necessarily disagree."

—La Senorita Dolorosa

CHAPTER 1

Slater and Belle Starr sat behind a cluster of boulders on a ridge overlooking an eight-room, two-story cabin. Constructed out of densely caulked, heavy oak logs, it was approximately six hundred yards away. Through a 15X telescope, Slater studied the two dozen lawmen surrounding it. Crouched behind boulders less than a hundred yards from the building, they were taking a breather. Both sides had thrown a lot of lead at each other for the last half hour to relatively little effect. The outlaws had wounded only a single dep, and Slater had no idea how many men in the cabin had been hit.

Perhaps none.

Slater and Belle were high enough up in the Ozarks that there was a chill in the air. The men in the cabin had fire going in their potbellied stove.

"See the smoke curling up out of the chimney?" Slater said to Belle. It twisted up above the cabin, sooty and dark gray.

Dressed in a peacoat, Belle was still cold and wrapped her arms around her chest for warmth. "Yeah, and I wish I was in there with them. It's a lot warmer inside that cabin."

"That fire could also do them in," Slater said. "That's a stout cabin and highly defensible—except for the chimney."

As if to prove Slater right, the deputies suddenly opened fire, laying down a barrage so heavy that it completely silenced the outlaws and probably forced them down on the floor. They had to wait for a break before they could return to the windows and return some fire of their own. But even as the deputies' fusillade intensified, a lawman with a haversack on his back was racing toward a corner of the building. There, the ends of the logs intersected, forming a crude ladder, which the lawman, as soon as he made it to the cabin's edge, began to scale.

Reaching the roof, he carefully traversed the sloping shake roof. Kneeling in front of the fieldstone chimney in the roof's center, he unlimbered six horse blankets, which, along with a Winchester, had been tightly rolled and tied up. He began quickly forcing them down the chimney.

The dep quickly made his way to the roof's corner just above the crisscrossing ends of the wall logs. He unlimbered the rifle, slung diagonally across his back, and waited there in silence.

It didn't take long for black smoke to start billowing out of the cabin's windows. Convulsive coughing and shouting erupted out of the smoke-choked cabin.

Slowly, one at a time, the outlaws exited the cabin with their hands up.

"I never did like lawmen much," Belle said.

"John Law never good-newsed me all that much either," Slater said.

"Let's give them good old boys a hand," Belle said, shooting Slater a wide smile.

Slater raised his Winchester '76. Specially chambered for .45-90 bullets and with an extra-long thirty-inch barrel, the Winchester company had only made a small number of them. Its tubular magazine held a dozen of the longer rounds. Bigger and heavier than the standard .44 centerfire cartridges and backed by considerably more black powder, it was more accurate and powerful than the normal Winchesters that were rolling off the assembling lines by the thousands each day. Among other things, the rifle's bigger round and heavier powder load increased the bullet's momentum, making it less vulnerable to windage.

And its stopping power was immense. Designed to bring down a two-thousand-pound bull bison with a single, well-placed shot through the beast's thick, dense skull, its stopping power had to be immense.

"You good with that thing at six hundred yards?" Belle asked. "I can't barely even see the cabin from this far away."

Saying nothing, Slater levered a round.

"Torn Slater I knew could knock the balls off a runnin' buck at eight hundred yards," Belle said. "Hitting a man center-mass at six hundred yards wouldn't mean squat to that guy. But maybe he ain't the same man no more. Maybe, after all them years—floggin' his monster on them Yuma and Sonora Prisons' rockpiles and down in them slave-labor mines—maybe after all that, the Outlaw Torn Slater standin' here just can't cut it these days. Maybe he ain't got what it takes—with a Winchester '76 or with a real flesh-and-blood... *woman.*"

Undoing her shirt's top two buttons, she leaned back and stared at Slater searchingly, rubbing her body all over. Moving close to him, she blew hot breath into his ear. When he failed to respond, she began licking it.

Still ignoring Belle, Slater shouldered the big rifle and peered through the scope. Parker's deps were wide-open—their backs and sides totally exposed to him. He started to shoot, hitting them dead center as fast as he could lever fresh rounds into the chamber. After emptying his '76 Winchester, Belle—having, after the first shot, snapped out of her revery—handed him a scoped '73. This one had a twenty-eight-inch barrel. She began reloading the '76.

The deps rose en masse and raced for the edge of the hill. Four of them made it downslope before Slater could kill them. It was just as well. By that time, he was out of ammunition, and Belle was only halfway finished with reloading the other rifle.

CHAPTER 2

"Have you ever heard," Nietzsche asked Diaz and his friends, "of Immanuel Kant's theory of 'the Categorical Imperative'?"

They were still in the club car of Diaz's personal express train and just finishing their tour of several of Méjico's most profitable haciendas.

"Yes," Sutherland said, "I know all about Kant and his moral philosophizing. A lot of rot, you ask me."

"Yes, yes," Judith McKillian said, waving her polychromic Chinese fan furiously in front of her face. "The demented doctrine that says if every person behaved as self-righteously as he does, the human race would prosper beyond all measure, for all time to come."

"What drivel!" the Senorita exploded, enraged at even the thought of it.

"That's not exactly what Kant wrote," Nietzsche said, correcting McKillian—with considerable trepidation.

"Enlighten us, then," the Senorita said.

"Kant's imperative states that if everyone in the world behaved in a certain way and their actions produced a morally optimal outcome, then that act would be categorically... *moral*."

Diaz, Judith McKillian and James Sutherland burst into laughter.

"What's wrong with the Categorical Imperative?" Bismarck asked. "It's the ultimate test of a moral principle, and Kant may well be the greatest philosopher of all time."

"Kant's a categorical moron!" the Senorita shouted.

"The other wrong half of a halfwit!" Judith McKillian shrieked.

"He's assuming," the Senorita said calmly, suddenly reasonable, soft-spoken and smiling cordially, "that everyone is smart enough and disciplined enough to follow the example of someone who lives according to an unimaginably severe and unbending moral code."

"Except that people are too weak, stupid and irresponsible to ever do something like that," Judith McKillian said.

"So Kant," the Senorita said politely, "is living in a dream world."

"No shit," Sutherland said with a jeering sneer. "Can you imagine *me* following that fool's rules?"

"Are you familiar," Bismarck asked, "with Karl Marx's axiom that wealth in the modern world should be distributed 'from each according to his means to each according to their needs'?"

"I know enough about Marx and his friend Engels," the Senorita said, shuddering with revulsion, "to last me ten thousand lifetimes."

"Those two venomous curs," Sutherland said, sharing the Senorita's disgust, "reside, even as we speak, in my own native land…*England.* And that our leaders tolerate their disgusting presence sickens me to my very…*soul.*"

"I am half-English too," Judith McKillian said with barely contained fury, "and I also cannot understand why our parliament doesn't throw those beastly buggers into the middle of the English Channel with anvils chained to their necks, after letting them know that 'la grandeur de la France is…*due east*.'"

"Chain them both to a two-ton anchor," Sutherland said through gritted teeth, "sink them in the Scapa Flow and let them treat all those sunken wrecks down there to their tendentious diatribes about income inequality and the evils of making money."

"On the other hand," Nietzsche pointed out, "those two men are just as cynical about the Judeo-Christian religion as you four are."

"Really?" the Senorita said.

"You don't say?" Judith McKillian said.

"Marx wrote that 'religion is,'" Nietzsche said, "'the heart of a heartless world, and the soul of soulless conditions.'"

"Well said," Sutherland agreed.

"Marx finished by saying that religion 'is the opium of the people,'" Nietzsche said, completing the quote.

"How charming," Judith McKillian said, "none of which expunges or forgives the truly despicable things he has written about people such as ourselves."

"People," Diaz said, "of means."

"I've read," the Senorita said, "that Marx believes that 'all of history is the history of class struggle.'"

He and his friends, once again, howled hilariously.

"What's so funny?" Nietzsche asked.

"The thought of our peons here struggling against...*us,*" Judith McKillian said, barely able to contain her mirth.

"And that is funny, why?" Bismarck asked.

"Oh, they could try," Diaz said, chuckling softly, "but they wouldn't struggle against us...*for long.*"

"Don't you understand," Sutherland said, "we would come down on them like hellfire, apocalypse and Armageddon."

"We would level our peons," Diaz said, "with all those monstrous military machines, which your Alfred Krupp has sold me—"

"Sold to us with your Emperor Wilhelm's blessing," the Senorita interjected.

"—with which we will then pound any and all ungrateful and recalcitrant peons—idiotic enough to rise up—into blood and shit and mud," Judith McKillian said.

"Back into the same blood and shit and mud," Diaz said, "that the Almighty used to create their lazy hides in the first place."

"The original sinful clay of Genesis," the Senorita observed, "out of which they were so disgracefully molded."

Diaz and his friends, again, dissolved into gales of laughter.

After their laughter died away, Diaz asked Nietzsche and Bismarck, "Have you ever heard of Marx's laughable labor theory about 'surplus value'?"

"Yes," Nietzsche said, "and I thought his theory of surplus value makes a lot of sense. It seems obvious that prices are determined by the amount of labor that goes into the production of the item—minus, of course, any other production costs."

"Not in Méjico maravilloso," Diaz said, firmly disagreeing. "Here, our citizens pay us for their frijoles and corn exactly what we order them to pay."

"And if they don't like the prices," Judith McKillian said, smiling smugly, "they are, after all, free to do without and...*starve*."

"The same with healthcare," Diaz said. "If our citizens want medical help, we set the price."

"And if they don't like it," Sutherland said, "they can pay our bitter tariff or...*die*."

"Suppose they simply cut back on their spending," Nietzsche said, "eliminate unnecessary expenses and live more cheaply."

"We can assist them with that lifestyle too," Diaz said.

"They can enjoy free room and board," the Senorita said, "in our forced-labor haciendas and prison mines."

"Living there," Sutherland said, "costs our peons...*nada*."

"Of course," Judith McKillian said, "the work is a little...*onerous*."

Again, their laughter detonated.

"You know what infuriated me most about Engels," the Senorita said, after their merriment subsided.

"What, my dear?" Diaz asked.

"That damnable book of his on conditions of the working poor in England," the Senorita said.

"*The Condition of the Working Poor in England*," Nietzsche said, quoting the book's title.

"The same," the Senorita confirmed. "In it, he blames people like us for their so-called suffering and what he terms 'their pathetically miserable wages.' That book just makes my blood boil."

"A most blackguardly book, indeed, you ask me," Sutherland said.

"Do you know," the Senorita said, "that Engels actually attacks employers who pay their employees...*wages?*"

"I should write a book attacking those employers for their naïve, misguided philanthropy," Sutherland said.

"Here in Méjico," Diaz said, "I would never dream of spoiling our peons with actual remuneration."

"What a disgusting thought," Judith McKillian said.

"Let those pampered English workers spend a year in our plantations and mines," the Senorita said. "We'll whip them into shape in no time."

"They'd find out what the real world is like," McKillian shouted. She recommenced punishing her boot top with her hippopotamus-hide riding crop.

"I'd get Marx and Engels into one of our mines here," Sutherland said, "and watch them stumble and totter under burden baskets brimming with ore until their brains burst and their legs shattered under the strain. Let them feel in their bones and blood what really hard productive labor is like here in madre Méjico. I promise you it's not anything like what their laborers experience in those soft, easy work sites over there in my native land, jolly old England."

"You are evil incarnate," Nietzsche said. He spoke softly, under his breath, but his words were nonetheless audible.

"I prefer to think that we march to a different drummer," the Senorita said, "one possessed by rousing rhythms and booming cadences, hammering out thunder rolls that reverberate through our souls like Wagnerian Gotterdammerungs. Now you may argue, instead, that we are trudging along to Franz Liszt's 'Death March,' and I wouldn't necessarily disagree. But I view the situation from a different perspective, and I believe you do not see the big picture."

"You mean 'the way things are, the way of the world, the ding an sich, the natural order of things,' Nietzsche recited numbly.

"Exactly so," the Senorita concurred. "And as long as we have been talking about your illustrious Friedrich Engels, let me tell you and the chancellor what he has recently written about your beloved Fatherland:

"'The only war left for Prussia-Germany to wage will be a world war, a world war, moreover of an extent to which the violence hitherto will be unimaginable. Eight to ten million soldiers will be at each other's throats on each side, and in the process, they will strip Europe barer than a swarm of locusts. The entire continent will lapse into famine, disease and barbarism unseen in all of history.'"

"And you deserve no less," Diaz said. "After all, it was your people who invented and advertised all those engines of universal annihilation, then wholesaled them to every prospective buyer on every continent and in the world, ourselves included."

"So I think you'll agree," the Senorita said, "you have earned everything that you will soon have coming to you."

"And you predict our fate to be...*what?*" Nietzsche asked.

"Apocalyptic upheavals," the Senorita said, now suddenly stern, unsmiling, as terminally serious as damnation and death. "Your world will be ravaged and racked by convulsive earthquakes, the utter destruction of the mountains and the valleys themselves. All power structures of your old societies, you shall see them explode into unbounded nothingness, vanishing forever, as if they had never been, from the face of the earth, which indeed was always their inevitable destiny, for, after all, every one of them was based on a lie. Young Nietzsche, there will be wars the likes of which have never been previously seen in this world, in the heavenly kingdom or in Lucifer's hell."

"You seem almost aroused by that possibility," Bismarck said. "You talk as if you long for the total destruction of Germany, Europe and of democratic civilizations everywhere."

"Oh, do we ever, bucko," Sutherland said.

"We'll sit here in madre Méjico," Judith McKillian said, "reading about it in the newspapers and loving every gory minute of it."

"And laughing our fucking asses off," Diaz said.

"Your great powers deserve no less," Sutherland said.

"But never fear," the Senorita said, "Marx may have been right when he told you Europeans that your workers would rise up and unite, saying that they had 'nothing to lose but their chains.' After the coming orgy of continentwide slaughter, which the proliferation of your ordnance and your obsession with democratic capitalism are so recklessly provoking, your workers might very well rise up and come after you and all your other war-loving, saber-rattling, rabble-rousing world leaders."

"And guess what?" Diaz said. "Do you want to know what we will do, when your rebellious workers and mutinous armies turn to us and ask us for our assistance in overthrowing their masters?"

"Our haciendas will grow the hemp," the Senorita said, "our spinning mills will fabricate the fibers, and our factories will manufacture the ropes en masse that our merchants will sell to your inflamed citizenry."

"At an exorbitant profit, of course," Sutherland said.

"After which," Diaz said, "your workers—sick of also fighting in your endless wars—will hang you and your friends by your aristocratic necks from your cities' lampposts and telegraph poles until you are most assuredly, most definitively and most deservedly…*dead*."

"They will execute you just as decisively and expeditiously as the French masses guillotined their own royal rulers only a hundred years ago," the Senorita said.

"But your peons will never rise up?" Nietzsche asked Diaz.

The generalissimo gave Nietzsche and the chancellor his most sublime palms-up shrug and then resurrected his sweetest, most placating smile.

"They can try," he said cheerfully.

PART XIII

"[W]e are entering the last days of the last men, of people without a driving dream, a destiny. People who don't want to think for themselves, who fear progress because they loathe change, who are scared half to death, who want to stay the same at all costs, who demand comfort, convenience and insist on remaining unchanged—no matter how high the cost, who live lives of grievance and resentment and can never see that there is a higher path, a more elevated calling."

—La Senorita Dolorosa

CHAPTER 1

Belle had already dragooned forty-five men into ventilated boxcars and shipped them with their horses to Arizona. The fourteen outlaws that she and Slater had rescued from Parker's deps got the total number of their recruits up to around sixty.

But they still didn't have enough.

Standing beside their mounts, Slater studied the makeshift prison just outside of Fort Smith. A brown adobe building, it was big as a warehouse, dotted with barred windows, and surrounded by stands of cottonwoods.

"How many men did you say Parker has locked up in that jail?" Slater asked.

"Last count, it was almost a hundred," Belle said.

"That would get us over a hundred fifty recruits—total," Slater said.

"And why did you say you wanted an army of a hundred fifty hunted, wanted, hardcore, hard-trade desperadoes?" Belle asked, her eyes and tone skeptical.

"To hold off Lord only knows how many soldados Joe Shelby and Diaz will throw at us," Slater said.

"How many can those two recruit and conscript?" Belle asked.

"Nathan Bedford Forrest organized thousands of ex-Confederates, after they were mustered out of the military," Slater said. "They were created exactly for this kind of mission, so Shelby has access to thousands of paramilitary troops."

"Do they hate America enough to join Diaz's cause?" Belle asked.

"If he offers them Méjicano plantations along with thousands upon thousands of free peon slave laborers plus pesos in their pockets," Slater said, "they'll pimp out their daughters and mamacitas if Diaz asks them to."

"You used to fight alongside some of them good old boys," Belle pointed out.

"One of my bigger mistakes," Slater said.

"You didn't like the War of Yankee Belligerence?"

"Don't like killin' people for no good reason," Slater said, "and I was getting paid jack shit for my trouble."

"You think that's what that war was about?"

"Those men we killed at Shiloh never did nothing to us," Slater said, "nor had we bothered them in any way. It was just rich men, who lacked the balls to fight their own battles, getting poor men killed on their behalf out of pure meanness, blind spite and sick greed."

"Well, looks like, at best, we're going to mount a hundred fifty desperados against Shelby and Diaz's army of thousands," Belle said.

Slater stared at her, silent, and then looked away.

"Sounds like Katherine Ryan's going to have Rome's barbaric hordes hammerin' on her gates," Belle said.

Slater still said nothing.

"Well, the odds don't sound...*inspirin'*," Belle said.

Slater remained silent.

"That woman at El Rancho de Cielo," Belle asked, "has she got something on you, Torn? Torn Slater I knew didn't extend himself all that much for people and never for causes."

"That's enough, Belle," Slater said softly.

"Slater I knew, he hated to use a horse hard or a woman easy," Belle said, "but now he's riskin' everything and everyone, myself included, for some widow woman in Arizona who's in a war with his former friends and allies."

Slater said nothing and directed his gaze instead toward the far horizon.

"I figure six span of mules and a log chain," Slater finally said, breaking a very long silence, "hooked to those bars on the jail back window ought to rip a hole in that adobe-brick wall big enough for those prisoners to escape through."

"Especially if you was to blast out another hole in the wall just under it," Belle suggested.

"That too," Slater said.

Belle was finished with her tirade.

"And when the deps come around after them?" she asked.

"I figure to close that back door with my '76," Slater said. "At that distance—hell, Belle, you could put them down with that Winchester '73 of yours. You wouldn't even need me."

"But it ain't my fight," Belle said.

Slater knew it wasn't, and he knew she was here because of him.

He wasn't sure what to say about that one, so, again, he said nothing.

"You sure you want to do this?" Belle asked.

"We'll be back tonight around 2:00 AM," Slater said, nodding his head, "with horses, several span of mules and a couple of big double-wagons. The bandits can ride the mules, horses, and in the wagons, which those beasts will also be pulling. Better bring those desperados we liberated from Parker's clutches and a dozen extra horses too. And several boxes of ammunition. We may have a fight on our hands, getting these old boys free of Parker and his marshals."

"This has to go off with split-second timing," Belle said.

"And faster than a rabbit can fuck," Slater said. "At 3:13 AM, we have a westbound train to catch."

"The conductor might not want a hundred-plus desperados crowding the law-abiding passengers out of his train," Belle said, "and scaring them all to death."

"That's why I plan on escorting the conductor to the locomotive," Slater said, "and keeping him there with the engineer for the duration of the trip."

"So we're also commandeering a train?" Belle asked, stunned.

"And cutting every telegraph wire we can get close to."

"Well, I'll be damned. Jess and Frank only robbed the fuckers. We're stealin' the whole damn thing."

"I figure once we're out of the Nations and Parker's jurisdiction ends, we're home free," Slater said.

"Especially," Belle said, "after we cut all them telegraph wires."

"After that," Slater said, "we're high-ballin' it straight through to Rancho de Cielo and the Arizona Territory, which is technically a foreign country."

"Where we'll then fight thousands of battle-hardened soldiers with a hundred fifty or so recently imprisoned robbers and killers," Belle observed.

"You forgot to mention that we're rounding up gallows bait and jailbirds too," Slater said.

"I wish you hadn't reminded me," Belle muttered under her breath.

CHAPTER 2

Frank James poured another shot of brandy into his Arbuckles' mug. He then grabbed the steel coffeepot sitting on the table and filled the mug all the way to the brim.

The waitress was just cleaning up the dishes. The two men with Frank had finished off five eggs apiece, a pound each of sirloin steak, flapjacks, bacon-fried potatoes and a big platter of fluffy, light-as-air buttermilk biscuits with cream gravy and butter on the side. They were on their third pot of coffee.

Frank still lacked an appetite.

"What you boys got planned," Frank asked, "that's going to generate that much cash on the barrelhead?"

The waitress had returned to the dining room. It was late morning, and the cafe was now dead empty.

"You heard of the town of Watersville?" Hargrove asked, keeping his voice low, his head down.

Frank allowed that he hadn't.

"Located maybe twenty miles due east of here, it was pretty much founded and is run by...*ex-slaves*," Tremaine said, spitting out the last word with a painful scowl.

"Those one-time slaves formed some kind of communal business organization," Hargrove said. "They pool a portion of their earnings—from their cotton farms, ranches, stores, companies and restaurants. They invest the proceeds."

"The bastards even got their own bank," Tremaine said, now genuinely upset. "Imagine, a slave bank."

"They also got black doctors, dentists and lawyers. They all chip into the trust," Hargrove said. "That's what they call their organization—'the trust.'"

"A lot of that money," Tremaine said, "they use to buy up any good nearby cropland, which they then farm."

"They have college-educated black lawyers who approve their every deal," Hargrove said.

"These lawyers have contacts back east in New York City," Tremaine said. "A portion of these yearly revenues they've invested in the New York Stock Exchange—nothing but blue-chip companies. They got money in the New York Central Railroad and J. P. Morgan's 'Bank of Morgan.'"

"They went heavy in Carnegie Steel," Hargrove said.

"Even heavier in John D. Rockefeller's Standard Oil," Tremaine said.

"You know Rockefeller now has a damn lock on 80 percent of the oil refineries in the United States," Hargrove said, "and those fool blacks got in on the ground floor. They were investing in it right at the beginning."

"They made a fortune," Tremaine said.

"A bunch of smart, arrogant bastards," Hargrove said, "and there's nothing I hate worse in all this world than a smart Negro."

"Especially, a smart, proud black man," Tremaine said.

"So some of the Red Shirts, Hargrove and me got to thinking a few weeks ago," Hargrove said.

"And drinking," Tremaine said. "Nothing like whiskey to lubricate the brain and improve the flow of thought."

"So the boys and us," Hargrove whispered in low conspiratorial tones, "said to ourselves, 'Why should we let them uppity blacks have all that money? It's White Man's Land. We built this country, not them. Time to take back what is rightfully ours anyway.' It's only right, isn't it, Frank?"

"We didn't fight that war," Tremaine said quietly but furiously, "to let them blacks take what's ours."

"I'm not sure I understand," Frank James said. "They plowed the fields and worked the livestock that generated all that revenue. They earned the money they made, didn't they?"

"So?" Tremaine asked.

"So you do understand that you and your friends had nothing to do with their earning of it, you didn't earn it, and that their money *isn't* yours?"

"Did all that bank and payroll train lucre," Hargrove said, "that you and Jess so rudely absconded with, belong to you two?"

Frank had to admit that Hargrove had a point. He had no immediate answer for him, so he kept his mouth shut.

"Think of it as us refighting the War of Northern Aggression," Tremaine said, "just like that newspaper fellow always wrote that you and Jess had been doing all that time."

"John Newman Edwards," Frank said softly.

"What was that?" Tremaine asked, confused by the name.

"That was the 'newspaper fellow,'" Frank said, "who described Jess and my bank jobs and train robberies as an extension of the War Between the States."

"We're doin' the same thing here," Hargrove said.

Frank had already decided to shut up about Edwards. Frank did not want to tell them that he thought Edwards was full of shit and that even Jess would have admitted in his fewer and fewer lucid moments that only a fool would rob banks and trains for anything other than money. Furthermore, all Edwards's news stories had done for the James brothers was make them famous—which was undoubtedly what got Jess killed—and that fame in Frank's and Jess's line of work was little more than suicide. It put such a gargantuan bull's-eye on your back that even the laziest, most cowardly lawmen could not afford to ignore you—not if they wanted to keep their jobs. A reward of that size could even turn trusted friends into back-shooting bounty hunters.

Frank personally believed that Edwards's newspaper pieces filled Jess's head with lunatic delusions, pumping him up with demented fantasies that he was a hero and a legend instead of an outlaw, which was all he and Frank had ever been.

In the end, Frank believed, Edwards had gotten his brother killed.

And would get Frank dead or imprisoned in the not too distant future.

"So what's your plan?" Frank asked.

"Remember how you raided, sacked and looted Lawrence and Centralia?" Tremaine said eagerly.

Now Frank had a sick, nauseated feeling in the pit of his stomach. He feared he'd throw up what little remnants of the steak and eggs he'd managed to choke down. He wanted to tell them that the Lawrence and Centralia massacres were, along with the slaughter at Northfield, the worst days of his life and the biggest mistakes he and Jess ever made.

He also sincerely hoped they weren't planning on doing what he suspected they were. He prayed that they weren't that stupid.

But, again, he vowed to keep his mouth shut. He needed them for Shelby's attack on El Rancho de Cielo, and he didn't want to piss them off.

"This afternoon around 3:00 PM," Hargrove said, "we're hitting Watersville. We're plucking them black bastards like scalded, neck-wrung pullets."

"Us and the boys are cleaning them out," Tremaine said.

"Every bank, train in the station," Hargrove said, "every merchant's till, every decent-sized house in the city, every single piece of rolling stock."

"It'll be a mighty handsome haul," Tremaine said.

"I'd give anything in the world to be there with you boys," Hargrove said.

"Your old war injury?" Tremaine asked.

"Yes," Hargrove said to Frank. "You see, I caught a round in my chest at Vicksburg. The doctors said it was too close to my heart to cut out. I'm okay, but I can't get bounced around too much. It could come loose."

"That's a damn shame," Tremaine said to Hargrove. "We're gonna have us a field day."

"There's a lot of money to be made in that town," Hargrove agreed, smiling broadly at the thought, "and it was kind of you boys to cut me in even though I can't ride with you and tote a gun."

"We're going to be making more than money in Watersville," Tremaine said ebulliently. "I'm also going to have me a couple of good-looking black gals while I'm at it."

"You ever get any of that slave tail?" Hargrove asked Frank.

"Not really," Frank said.

"Your family didn't own any woman slaves?" Hargrove asked.

"Yes, we did," Frank said. "Jess and I didn't bed them though."

He wanted to say to the two halfwits: *"Jess and I didn't* rape *them. We don't* rape *women."* He decided to hold his tongue, however, reminding himself that he'd promised to raise an army for Diaz and General Shelby by recruiting former Confederate soldiers. He needed Hargrove and Tremaine.

Still, he hoped and prayed that the rest of his soldiers weren't as stupid as these two.

CHAPTER 3

"Your problem, young Nietzsche," the Senorita said, "is that while you care about human individuals, you care nothing about society at large—culture, the sciences, economic advancement of a nation. You care nothing about...*humanity*."

"I have dedicated my life to literature and philosophy—to culture," Nietzsche said, his face grave and sober.

"I believe in them too," Bismarck said. "All enlightened, civilized people do."

"But who advances culture, science, technology and industry?" Judith McKillian asked, her eyes glinting with insolence.

"Certainly not the wretched of the earth, whom you two so slavishly sob and slaver over," James Sutherland said with smug snobbishness.

"Fewer than 1 percent of a civilization," the Senorita said, "write the books, create the art, conjure up the medical cures, produce the machinery, construct the great libraries, universities and laboratories, compose the symphonies, do all the hard work of science and all the grand things that improve our lives and shape our futures. Exceptional individuals drive human progress, not your mewling-puling masses. Yet you two have done nothing except condescend to us about how we should devote ourselves to improving the lives of ignorant, indigent, indolent drudges who, in truth, despise art, science, history, philosophy, music—all the disciplines that you two pretend to love with such impassioned commitment."

"It wouldn't hurt your feelings," Judith McKillian asked, "if I called you two 'a couple of mindless morons,' would it?"

"Because we subscribe to Christ's 'Sermon on the Mount' and 'Love your neighbor as yourself,' I suppose you also mock us," Bismarck shouted, outraged. "Those are God's precepts, you know. Would you also call God 'a mindless moron'?"

Friedrich Nietzsche had finally had enough and was hopping mad. That these people would enslave 90 percent of Méjico's population and torture the rest purely for the sake of uncontrollable greed to him was the ultimate insult to God—the worst sort of heresy. Taking a deep breath, he intoned:

"Did you four ever read the Lord's Prayer? Do you know what Christ says at the end of it, when he sums up everything he was trying to say? Christ asks God to 'forgive us our debts as we forgive our debtors.' That is the original, authentic text—not 'forgive us our transgressions.' He says that if you punish people because they are poor and can't pay their bills, you are asking God to punish you in the exact same way. And He will. He will take it out of your hides.

"Christ warns us that we cannot worship God and the demon Greed," Nietzsche continued, "whom Christ calls Mammon. He tells us that a camel has a better chance of squeezing his bulk through a needle's eye than people like you have of squeezing into heaven. When a man of means seeks to follow Him, Christ tells him, first, to sell all his possessions, then give every cent of his entire net worth to the poor. Saint Paul teaches us that the love of money is the root of all evil. John on Patmos in Revelation explains to us in Chapter 13 that before the End Times, an angel will descend and order humanity to give up their greed or be sent howling into hellfire and brimstone for all eternity. One-third of humanity, like yourselves, choose money over God, and guess what? Those people will, one day, fry in hell...*forever.* We are so addicted to greed that, one day, God will give up on us and send one-third of us to hell. So now you know where you four are headed!"

"I think Herr Nietzsche is suggesting that we're going to go to hell," Judith McKillian said with mock terror.

"And that we're a little...*greedy,*" Diaz said, feigning hurt feelings.

"Young Nietzsche thinks that God is a little pissed at us," the Senorita said, pretending to look contrite.

"You four would take the dimes off dead men's eyes," Bismarck exploded, "and suck blood from bats."

"And God hates greed!" Nietzsche shouted.

"You ask me, God hates a whole lot more than greed!" Sutherland shouted back at Nietzsche.

"For openers, He obviously despises us—humankind," the Senorita said.

"God loves us!" Nietzsche countered forcefully. "He sent us 'His only begotten son' to save us."

"'Whosoever believeth in Him,'" Bismarck fervently quoted, "'shall not perish but have eternal life.'"

"And look at how much good all that godly love did for his poor boy," Sutherland said, laughing.

"So much for God's redemption plan," Judith McKillian said, struggling to hold back her mirth.

"Why *did* God let us flog, starve, crucify and torture his poor boy to death?" Diaz asked, genuinely puzzled. "I never have figured that one out."

"For that matter," the Senorita said, "why on earth did God create this whole wretched, morally reprehensible, godforsaken, terrifying nightmare of a world anyway? We aren't the nicest people on earth, but even *we* didn't deserve this ghastly hellhole God has so infamously foisted on us."

"Why did the Almighty so shamefully and ignominiously dump us onto this snake pit of a planet anyway?" Sutherland asked. "I really want to know."

"After all," the Senorita said, "if He is omnipotent and omniscient, if He did create us, the earth and everything around it, then all our suffering is...*His fault.*"

"What he did to us, what he did to humankind is utterly unforgivable!" Judith McKillian said heatedly, her fists clenched.

"There is no excuse for his mistreatment of us," Sutherland said sharply, shaking a finger at both Nietzsche and Bismarck.

"Oh," the Senorita said, smiling abruptly, suddenly demure, "I'm not so sure about all that criticism, Mr. Sutherland. God has one extremely cogent, utterly incontrovertible excuse."

"And what is that?" Diaz asked with a curious furrowing of his forehead.

"The poor bastard doesn't actually exist," the Senorita said sweetly. "Therefore, all this Sturm und Drang, blood and misery, carnage and violence, isn't...*His fault.*"

"Do you really think that is possible?" Judith McKillian asked.

"It's not only possible," Sutherland said with his most conceited, patrician condescension, "it's...*true.* Or perhaps during your visit to Méjico, you haven't had a chance to read the...*newspapers?*"

"And what is it we've missed?" Bismarck asked.

"I suppose you've been too busy saving God's peacemakers," Sutherland said dryly, "His poor of spirit, the meek, who will ostensibly inherit this earth, and so you haven't heard."

"Heard what?" Nietzsche asked, increasingly irate and impatient.

"God is dead," Sutherland said gravely.

"What?" Bismarck said.

"Verdad," the Senorita said. "God is no more."

"As you would say in your tongue," Judith McKillian snarled, "He is...*kaputt!*"

"What happened?" Nietzsche asked.

"Copernicus killed him," the Senorita explained blithely, "when he proved we were no longer the center of the universe."

"And Galileo also did Him in, when he confirmed Copernicus's calculations and asked God to look through his telescope at Jupiter's moons," Judith McKillian said.

"Johannes Kepler honed the blade and also swung the axe," Diaz said with winsome delight. "His laws of planetary motion were too much for El Supremo to bear!"

"Sir Isaac Newton's theory of gravity tightened the noose and yanked open the trapdoor," the Senorita said brightly.

"When Charles Darwin proved we descended from simian progenitors and not the Divine Everlasting, he drew and quartered the Old Guy," Diaz said.

"Louis Pasteur," the Senorita explained, "is now raising the people off their death beds and performing Christ's miracles for Him, making His hocus-pocus...*irrelevant.*"

"Are you saying we no longer need the Son of God?" Sutherland asked with a stunningly insolent sneer.

"Indeed," Diaz said. "We are, in point of dull, tawdry, utterly irrefutable fact, no longer the center of...*Godworld.*"

"Meaning, Jehovah's been kicked off his throne," Judith McKillian said.

"In truth," the Senorita said, "each of us did the deed—every hombre and mujer on the planet, ourselves included—we all stabbed him in the temple. We are all God's murderers."

"We killed him," Judith McKillian said, "and we are still killing Him—every day in every way."

"In case you haven't guessed," the Senorita said, "the earth has a disease, and the disease is...*us.*"

"Humankind," Diaz thundered.

"Unfortunately, for you, my innocent amigo, God's demise will leave a big, ugly, gaping hole in your benighted life," Judith McKillian said.

"Yours too, Iron Chancellor," the Senorita said, smiling sublimely but with mean mockery dancing in her eyes.

"An abyss, really," Sutherland said.

"In what way?" Nietzsche asked.

"We are a naïve species that demands a grand and glorious purpose for all of our actions," the Senorita said. "We require a higher meaning for...*everything.* Without God, we are stripped of all moorings, all morals and all meanings."

"We can't accept the fact," Diaz said, "that the universe is founded on a void, that a priori moral values are empty as prayer and meaningless as an idiot's dreams and that natural selection is the only law of life."

"God's demise," Judith McKillian said, "has turned the human soul into an arid desert of narcissistic nihilism, a sterile wasteland in which humankind in its madness and despair has been eternally, irrevocably and irredeemably...*staked.*"

"A spiraling abyss," Sutherland said, "in which humanity, like Satan, has now been plunged."

"So we are entering the last days of the last men," the Senorita said, "of people without a driving dream and a transcendent destiny. We are now surrounded by people who don't want to think for themselves, who fear progress because they loathe change, who are scared half to death of anything resembling progress, who want to stay the same at all costs, who demand comfort and convenience, who insist on unassailable stasis—no matter how high the cost, who live lives of grievance and *resentiment* and can never see that there is a higher path, a more elevated calling."

"Power is no longer divinely ordained," Diaz said, "and the right to govern is now universally contested."

"Which is where we come in," the Senorita said. "We—the world's captains of industry in league with our esteemed generalissimo—intend to fill that abyss that God's death and departure has thrust on humankind."

"You seek to rule the world?" Bismarck asked, confused.

"Not at all," Judith McKillian said, "but whoever pretends to govern will, from now on, have to share their duties with…*us*."

"And they will do it gladly," the Senorita said.

"They will delight in our presence," Sutherland said, "then praise and thank us for our largesse."

"Even as the kings of earth and Babylon's whores hand their power over to us," the Senorita said.

"Abdicate their power is more like it," Sutherland said.

"You are so right, James," the Senorita said, nodding enthusiastically.

"And they will do so…*why?*" Bismarck asked.

"Because we shall pay them so…*extravagantly,*" Judith McKillian said.

"Don't you agree, Chancellor Bismarck?" the Senorita asked. "Don't you want to be paid…*extravagantly?*"

"I, for one," Diaz said, agreeing emphatically, "wouldn't have it any other way."

"Face the facts," the Senorita said. "No longer having a Supreme Being to order you around is hard for the great mass of humanity to accept. But the picture isn't all gloom and doom. You have something infinitely better and far more amusing with which to replace Him."

"And that is?" Nietzsche asked, dreading the answer.

"You have…*us,*" the Senorita said.

"You see, young Nietzsche," Diaz patiently explained, "we plan on replacing God in your brave new world."

"You can say, 'Thank you, Senorita,' any time you want," the Senorita said to Nietzsche with a glimmering, glittering smile illuminating her face and eyes like the rainbow's end.

PART XIV

"I have the gift of prophecy, and I can tell you on unimpeachable authority that humanity's lot on this planet, from this day forth, shall be pure hell—more droughts, more hurricanes, more ice storms, more climate-induced disasters of every stripe, more tornadoes, more floods, more wars of every size, shape, quality, quantity, degree and dimension, catastrophes beyond all imagining, and belief in ways hitherto unknown and undreamt of." Slamming her fist on the arm of her chair, the Senorita shouted at the entire room: *"From this day forth, our world will be seriously, inevitably, irrevocably...screwed!"*

—La Senorita Dolorosa

CHAPTER 1

Kaiser Wilhelm I sat across the massive oak desk from Alfred Krupp. The old arms manufacturer and industrial magnate had been rambling insensibly about his son in one breath, then bragging about how powerful he and his new generation of cannons were in the next, then segueing into tirades on how titans of industry and war, such as himself, were ill-appreciated and poorly underestimated.

His grievances were legion.

At the moment, he was hectoring the emperor about money, which, he believed, like himself, was not properly understood.

"People don't understand that money knows no morality," the old man fervently expostulated. "It is a universe unto itself, a phenomenon beyond all paltry concepts of right and wrong. Money is the purest, most concentrated quintessence of all power and influence in today's world. Attempts to restrict or circumscribe its natural circulation and flow are sheer madness, inexorably doomed to failure. What we do with money when it lands in our coffers is all that matters. How it was used before it arrived, or after we have discharged it, is irrelevant to our own affairs and no one's business—except for the currency's current proprietor. Someone else will have their way with it after it is no longer ours, and how they employ or misuse it is their concern, not ours."

"I know, I know," the emperor said. "You've explained that to me a thousand tedious times."

"I call it 'Krupp's Iron Law of Financial Circulation!'" the old man said with a smug, self-satisfied smile.

Wilhelm estimated that he had heard the monotonous diatribe at least ten thousand times over the last forty years. He was so sick of it that when Alfred commenced recycling the lecture, he would now bite his tongue or the inside of his mouth in hopes that the pain would keep from fainting dead away with terminal... *boredom.*

For the moment, he attempted to tune the old man out.

Today, those stratagems did no good. Instead, Alfred simply segued into a panegyric on the preeminence of global cash flow and began railing against the enemies of great wealth everywhere, fiends from hell that confronted him at every turn, specifically those meddlesome politicians who sought to "regulate the arms industry," "unionize the Kruppwerk," and tell the men who built it from the ground up—namely, himself—how to run it.

Wilhelm couldn't take it any longer. If he didn't get Alfred Krupp off the subject and direct him onto the point of his visit, he feared he'd go mad.

The Kaiser asked him a direct question:

"Do you think we should really be selling a man as supremely evil as Porfirio Diaz the most feared, murderous and catastrophically destructive weapons on earth?"

"I kind of like old Porfirio," Krupp said with a suddenly genial smile.

"Your personal feelings aside," the Kaiser said, "you do understand that he may well be the most brutally prolific, infernally evil slave-driving tyrant in human history."

"And you get your information from whom?"

"I've been getting the most amazing cables from the chancellor on the subject. He's been quoting his assistant, Friedrich Nietzsche, to me."

"Friedrich who?"

"Nietzsche," Wilhelm said. "The young man Richard Wagner insisted we send to Méjico to research Diaz, his country and his economy. Nietzsche is especially eloquent on Diaz's enslavement of his peons."

"And it is precisely because of his barbaric depredations that I can charge him such vertiginously high prices," Krupp said, "and why he will willingly—indeed, eagerly—pay any bill I send him."

"He's paying them because he's a slave driver?" Wilhelm asked, unable to grasp the connection between being a slave driver and paying extortionate prices for guns.

"He pays my asking price," Krupp said, "because he has nowhere else to go. No other nation on earth will sell him such ordnance, precisely because he is so odious. He also pays me full price in cold hard cash because forced labor yields profits so obscenely outrageous that he can afford to pay me anything I ask—which is why I shall demand the sun, the moon and the stars. And lastly, his oppression of the peons motivates him to buy my weapons in the first place. He needs my guns to protect himself from his own compatriots."

That last sentence reduced Krupp to gales of obscene, ear-cracking guffaws.

He howled and roared until the Kaiser thought he'd lose his mind.

"So Germany," Wilhelm said, "and the Kruppwerk are the only two entities on the face of the earth that are willing to take this monster's money in exchange for highly advanced, disastrously destructive weapons systems."

The Kaiser was instantly sorry he had mentioned "money." Krupp came back at him like a ball off a wall, saying:

"Which we do because we understand the primacy of financial circulation. We understand that nothing should impede the global disbursement of hard currency any more than arterial clots should block the circulation of our heart's blood in the human body."

"Which is why you sell our abominably advanced military weapons," the emperor said, "to demonically depraved tyrants, who torture, slave-drive and murder their own people by the millions."

Whether Krupp heard the Kaiser's remarks was unclear, because he was onto a new harangue even before Wilhelm could finish his last sentence.

"And which is why I sent my son, Friedrich Krupp," Alfred said, "to Méjico—along with a few teasers, namely samples of some of our most famous weapons."

That last statement stopped Wilhelm cold.

Sending his son to Méjico was a really big deal.

The presence of Bismarck, Nietzsche and Friedrich Krupp meant that the old man was about to consummate this spectacularly massive arms sale.

"You're sending Friedrich Krupp?" Wilhelm asked, wanting to make sure he'd heard the old man correctly. "You're sending your own flesh and blood into what is now apparently one of the most dangerous hellholes on the face of the earth to negotiate a weapons contract with Diaz and his pack of blood-crazed hellhounds?"

"I want to make sure Bismarck and that damnable, dummkopf assistant of his, Friedrich Nietzsche, don't completely bollix up the landmark, record-setting arms package that I so painstakingly worked out with the man whom you have so uncharitably termed a mass-murdering, slave-trafficking maniac."

"I just want you to know whom you're dealing with," Kaiser Wilhelm said. "Lord only knows what blood he'll spill once he gets your howitzers and quick-firing ordnance."

"But you also know the extent to which that transaction will subsidize all future arms sales to Germany," Krupp said with a cruel grin.

"You've told me repeatedly that the deal will bankroll Germany's armament program for the next thirty years," Wilhelm said.

"So you do get the picture, right?" Krupp asked.

"Completely."

"Good," Krupp said, "because sometimes, when we talk, Wilhelm, I get the distinct feeling that you're not really listening to me, your feet, mentally, are pointed toward the door and that you'd rather be somewhere else."

"Me, old friend?" the Kaiser said, giving Krupp his widest, most insincere smile. "Never!"

"You sometimes look... *bored*."

"Herr Krupp, how could any man be bored in your august presence? I find you to be the most fascinating man I've ever known."

At which point the emperor was struck by a wave of nausea so overpowering that he almost vomited on the arms magnate.

CHAPTER 2

"Unfortunately, young Nietzsche," the Senorita said, "what you now have instead of God is a yawning, voracious abyss where you used to have a soul. With God dead, there are no absolutes. Nothing is true, and everything is permitted, so of what possible use is there of...*a soul*."

"'Nothing is true, everything is permitted,'" Judith McKillian repeated, savoring the words. "Oh, I love that concept."

"Young Nietzsche," the Senorita said, "you are left nothing with which you could possibly fill the sucking void your soul's departure left. You have tried to infuse that vast nothingness with art, literature, philosophy, politics and music, but none of your arts, sciences, other transitory delectations and even music will suffice."

"Any more than any of Faust's self-indulgent avocations saved him at the end of his play," Sutherland said.

"The hard truth is," the Senorita said sadly, "those artistic amusements of yours, like Faust's, also lack...*staying power*."

"They can't go the distance," Judith McKillian said.

"Can't cut the mustard," the Senorita said.

"Don't have what it takes," Sutherland said.

"None of those passions and amusements can hold a candle to the omniscient omnipotence that your Divine Everlasting offered you," Diaz said.

"Your erstwhile Divine Everlasting," Sutherland reminded them, "who is now—tragically, painfully, unalterably—no longer...*with us*."

"And he had been eternal as well as infinite," Judith McKillian said, her eyes, as usual, habitually mocking, almost laughably insincere.

"Until...*now,*" Sutherland said.

"And He had been everywhere," the Senorita said, "in everything and everyone."

"But now," Sutherland said, "he has so rudely, so unceremoniously, so hopelessly—"

"—and with so little regard for those underlings who slavishly, abysmally and pathetically relied on him—" McKillian said.

"What they are trying to say, young Nietzsche," the Senorita said, staring deeply into Nietzsche's eyes with spurious concern and faux compassion, all the while pretending to wipe nonexistent tears from her dry, cold, large, completely expressionless eyes, "is that your God has, plainly and unequivocally...*expired.*"

"Your God has—irrevocably, irredeemably, irreversibly—left...the building," Judith McKillian said.

"Hmmmm. I wonder, seriously, who or what will take his place?" Sutherland asked, drumming his fingers on the arm of his chair, pretending to appear nervously perplexed. "I mean, we won't be around forever to take up His slack."

"Oh, that one's easy," Diaz said. "The Grim Reaper, Death, will be happy to fill in. He's done it so many times in the past."

"Explain to our philosopher the ultimate, inevitable, final consequences of the Almighty's demise?" Sutherland said.

"We will see more wars," the Senorita said, "more of the plagues that those wars will engender and more plague-induced famines."

"The Senorita means," Judith McKillian said, "more raining of frogs, more ravaging of locusts, more slaughter of the firstborn, more ten calamities of Egypt."

"Humankind will have more hell on earth to deal with," Sutherland shouted, "than Jehovah gave the Jews!"

"I have the gift of prophecy," the Senorita said joyously, "and I can tell you on my own unimpeachable authority that humanity's lot, from this day forth, will be pure hell—more droughts, more hurricanes, more ice storms, more climate-induced disasters of every stripe, more tornadoes, more floods, more wars of every size, shape, quality, quantity, degree and dimension, catastrophes beyond imagining in ways hitherto unknown and undreamt of." Slamming her fist on the arm of her chair, the Senorita shouted at the entire room: *"From this day forth, our world will be seriously, inevitably, irrevocably...* fucked!"

"How can you be so sure?" Nietzsche asked.

"Because," the Senorita answered, her smile serene, almost ethereal, "I shall see to it personally."

CHAPTER 3

"I'm sure your much-beloved son, Friedrich, will do a superlative job of representing you in that arms sale to Porfirio," Kaiser Wilhelm I said.

"He knows how to sell guns," Alfred Krupp said. "I'll give him that. I've sent him all over North, Central and South America—Méjico included. Even Asia, and he always closes the deal."

"He's a good son," Wilhelm said.

In truth, Wilhelm thought Friedrich Krupp was far more capable than his old man, whom he'd dismissed decades ago as a formerly great cannon manufacturer but who was now far behind the times.

"You don't have to deal with his arrogant upstart opinions on everything under the sun," Alfred said. "Do you know he dares to lecture me on the theory and practice of howitzer designs and on the arms manufacturing process? I invented the goddamn business, and he tells me how I ought to be making my own guns, what kind of steel to use and what kinds of new guns I should be developing."

"What does he say?"

"He says I should stop making bronze cannons."

"You should have stopped thirty years ago."

"Yes, yes, but then he keeps hounding me to develop rapid-fire weapons—you know, like France's Mitrailleuse de Freffye 'Canon a Balles'?"

"Why not do it?" Wilhelm asked.

"The French built and deployed them in their war against us," Krupp said. "You saw how effective they were?"

"Your son told me the French misused them. He said they should be employed defensively and in support of infantry, even cavalry. In our war, the French treated them as if they were artillery, which they aren't."

"And we proved who had the superior cannons," Krupp said.

"But you admit your son was right when he told you to phase out bronze cannons," Wilhelm said.

"A broken clock is right twice a day."

The emperor saw he'd angered Alfred and decided to assuage his feelings.

"You and your big guns won that 1870 war for us," Kaiser Wilhelm said. "That war, that victory, unified the disparate German states. You and your howitzers did that for Germany. Your artillery had twice the range, twice the accuracy and fired twice as many shells in the same amount of time as France's. Do you appreciate what you have done for this nation?"

"You are too kind, Emperor."

"I only speak the truth," Kaiser Wilhelm said sincerely. "Napoleon III told me that when he surrendered."

"It was a magnificent day for all of us," Krupp said.

"But Fritz, your son, says the next war will be far worse. He quotes Friedrich Engels, who predicts that the next big European war will see ten million men on each side pitted against each other. Your son thinks rapid-fire weapons will be decisive just as in the last conflict when your long-range artillery turned the tide of war."

"He quotes the Communist Engels?" Alfred Krupp said. "I told you he was a simpleton. I wonder sometimes if he's even my son. I ought to take a horsewhip to his mother—make her tell me who the real father was."

"Please don't accuse Otto."

"No," Alfred Krupp said ruefully, "like myself, Bismarck never could have fathered him."

"I think your son is as manly as any of us."

"You're such a child, Wilhelm," Alfred Krupp said. "I'm surprised you survived the Napoleonic Wars."

"They were the defining experience of my life," Wilhelm said. "In all honesty, everything afterward was anticlimactic—a letdown."

"You even seemed to enjoy the ugliness of battle—the stench of black powder, the thunder of the guns, the screams of the wounded, the sight and smell of blood, the explosion of body parts, the spectacle of men dying all around you. You know your reaction to that carnage is unhealthy, even unnatural."

"As terrible as it sounds," Wilhelm said, "it was the best time of my life."

"You'll find other wars, Wilhelm. If only I could find another son."

"Try to have a little faith, Alfred. Fritz will do just fine when he runs the company. He won't let you down."

"I won't be alive for him to let me down. Because that's the only way he's getting his hands on the reins of power—for me to die."

"I'm sorry you feel that way."

"Oh, Wilhelm," Alfred Krupp said. "It's not that I haven't tried to talk some manhood into him. I've been dictating my memoir and my business philosophy to him, making him write it all out in longhand. I keep hoping he absorbs my hard-earned, old-school wisdom—even some of my manliness. I've acquired none of it on the cheap. Unlike my son, I started out with nothing. Everything I have, I built myself. It was all—everything I have—hard won."

Inwardly, Wilhelm cringed. Alfred had inherited the foundries and the basic cannon designs from his father. True, Alfred had expanded it, but his father had created the business initially. Alfred hadn't built it from scratch. Also Wilhelm had heard that the megalomaniacal old man was forcing his son to transcribe endless lectures of his so-called 'Gospel According to Alfred Krupp.' This was the first time, however, he'd heard the old man himself confirm it.

His heart bled, and his soul wept for poor Fritz. With a father like Alfred, it was amazing Fritz still walked upright and had come as far as he had. Furthermore, Wilhelm knew Fritz Krupp personally, thought him brilliant and insightful. He respected him and liked him. In truth, he detested the old man.

Wilhelm looked forward to working closely with the son once old Alfred was out of the way. Bismarck echoed his sentiments exactly.

He couldn't wait to talk to Fritz some more about those rapid-fire weapons.

Wilhelm wondered what it was about them Alfred Krupp was missing.

PART XV

I, who have neither pity, love nor fear;
The owl shrieked at my birth: an evil sign.
—Richard III

To reign is worth ambition though in Hell:
Better to reign in Hell, than serve in Heav'n.
—*Paradise Lost*

CHAPTER 1

"So why do you do all this?" Bismarck asked Diaz and his friends, waving an arm around the club car. "Enslaving 90 percent of the Méjicano nation, looking to conquer anything and everyone you can, turning Méjico is one tremendous prison camp of nations? Into a torture chamber and an abattoir? What do you get out of it?"

"Would you believe us if we said 'money'?" Diaz answered, gesturing flamboyantly, smiling broadly.

"You already have money," Nietzsche pointed out.

"The Senorita and Judith are two of the richest people in the western hemisphere," Bismarck said. "James here might be the richest man on earth. They have given you a blank check, Porfirio. Through them, you're richer than God."

"Since God," Judith McKillian interjected, "is dead, dear Porfirio is far richer than the long-ago, long-forgotten...*deity*."

"You want to know what drives us?" the Senorita asked. "Everything we do is out of an uncontrollable desire for...*power*."

She leaned toward Nietzsche and Bismarck, staring at them soberly without a hint of irony.

"And if you two could be honest for one second of your unrelentingly hypocritical lives," Diaz said, "you'd admit that the drive for power motivates every one of your own pathetic actions, twenty-four hours a day, seven days a week."

"Why do you think you sought to be chancellor?" the Senorita asked Bismarck.

"Why do you strive to be the finest writer and the most brilliant thinker in all of Germany?" Judith McKillian asked Nietzsche.

"In all of Europe," he said softly, almost to himself. "In the...*world.*"

"It's the lust to control, to prevail, to rule," the Senorita said.

"But you have made Méjico a hell on earth?" Nietzsche asked. "Why? Even unbounded power can't be worth all the misery and carnage you have provoked."

"Maybe not in Germany," the Senorita said, "but in Méjico, power is...*everything.*"

"And why is Méjico so special?" Bismarck asked.

"Because here," Diaz said, "here, we can reign supreme."

"The Brits won't let me rule...*Britannia,*" Sutherland said bitterly.

"Because you'd make heaven a hell," Nietzsche said.

"And turn hell into a hell of hells," Bismarck said.

"They have a point," the Senorita said to Diaz.

"After all," Sutherland said with a humble shrug, "look what we have done to madre Méjico. It sometimes makes even me shudder."

"In all honesty," the Senorita said, "we have not exactly created Isaiah's Peaceable Kingdom."

"Why *would* anyone want to live here of their own free will?" Judith McKillian asked. "Even I hate being here. Even I hate...*Méjico.*"

"Which is the point," Sutherland said. "No one will bother us here. There's nothing here anyone could possibly want."

"No one, except us, would even consider living in this godawful hell on earth," the Senorita said.

"And to rule Méjico effectively," Diaz said with a sad shrug, "you, unfortunately, do have to live in the damned place."

"Milton summed our plight up rather nicely," Sutherland said. "Remember Satan's explanation for why he rebelled against God in *Paradise Lost*?"

"Could you remind us again?" Diaz asked. "I seem to have forgotten that passage."

Sutherland declaimed in sonorous, histrionic tones:

...Here at least [in hell]
We shall be free. Here we may reign secure, and

To reign is worth ambition though in Hell:
Better to reign in Hell, than serve in Heav'n.

"And you choose to stay and rule Méjico, because here and here alone," Bismarck said, "you can reign without foreign interference?"

"Indeed," Diaz said. "Here and here alone are we...*all-powerful.*"

"And what do you plan to do with all this unconstrained power," Nietzsche asked, "now that you possess it uncontested?"

"And don't say make more money," Bismarck said. "You four already have more money than God."

"You really don't know?" Judith McKillian asked Diaz.

"I haven't the foggiest," Diaz said.

"I, for one, would use this stupendous power to acquire more stupendous power," the Senorita said.

"Bravo!" Sutherland yelled. "What else on earth would anyone want to use it for?"

CHAPTER 2

Frank and Hargrove stood on a hilltop, overlooking Watersville, Texas. Through his telescope, Frank James studied the surrounding countryside. Alabaster cotton fields stretched in all directions, an unending panorama of spotless, dazzlingly bright splendor, from horizon to horizon to horizon, interrupted only by the town below. The spectacle was so blindingly incandescent it hurt his eyes and made him wince. Frank was stunned at the sheer, shimmering magnificence of it.

"Every bit of that cotton belongs to those black sons of bitches down there in that town," Hargrove said, "and I'm saying it isn't right."

"Still a lot of money in cotton?" Frank asked, trying to direct Hargrove away from what had become his endless litany of grievances.

"Hell yes," Hargrove said. "The value dropped after the Civil War, but during the last decade it's come back—way back."

"Good," Frank said.

"Yeah," Hargrove said, "but what's not good is that the war cost us all our slaves. They were worth a goddamn fortune—a hell of a lot more than any cotton crop. I'm talking hard currency, real 'spendin' money.'"

"Worth more than pussy?" Tremaine asked facetiously.

"You ever try *spendin'* pussy?" Hargrove asked.

Both men threw back their heads, slapped their thighs and howled with laughter. After their levity passed, Hargrove took a deep breath and said:

"Slaves were most of our bottom-line equity. They were the only asset we had that was worth anything when we asked for a bank loan."

"When we borrowed money each year in New York to finance our plantin'," Tremaine said, "what do you think we leveraged? Our cotton? The banks already owned our cotton for the next six years."

"And beyond," Hargrove said.

"What about your acreage, your land?" Frank asked.

"We had mortgaged our mother earth so many times," Tremaine said, "that the bankers wouldn't give us anything on it anymore. They told us the land wasn't worth anything to them until we paid off our loans on it. To hear them talk, it was like we didn't...*own our plantations anymore.*"

"What did they say," Frank asked, "when you told them you couldn't keep up the payments?"

"They accused us of being 'degenerate gamblers and profligate spenders,'" Tremaine said bitterly.

"Whatever all those big New York words mean," Hargrove said, spitting out each word with contempt.

"Uppity New York cocksuckers," Tremaine snarled.

"So what did you put up for collateral?" Frank asked.

"Our slaves!" Hargrove shouted. "Those bankers told us that slaves were the only really valuable asset that we could still hock. They said that they were worth their weight in 22-carat gold and 60-carat diamonds."

"One banker claimed," Tremaine said, "that those damn slaves were worth more than all the country's trains, factories and steamship lines put together. Plus, the slaves planted, grew and picked all our cotton. Since the average slave was good for thirty or forty years of hard labor, they represented a hell of a lot of capital."

"So the banks said that they'd let us mortgage them for ten times their actual value—and more," Hargrove said passionately, striking the table with the palm of his hand, rattling their coffeepot, their cups and liquor bottle. "With the slaves backing our loans, we could borrow all the hard cash from those East Coast counting houses that we wanted."

"We could borrow money on those slaves," Hargrove said, "from here to the end of time."

"Till hell froze over," Frank James said with dispirited irony.

"Damn straight," Hargrove enthused. "We could borrow as much of that New York money on our slaves as we wanted."

"And then those northern bastards stole them all," Tremaine said.

"We had it made before that damn war ruined everything for us," Hargrove said, shaken and saddened.

"Slaves were the greatest investment in the world," Tremaine shouted, "for everyone, for all of us, even those northern spinning mills."

"Mills that those northern bastards shut down for four years during that war," Hargrove said.

"Cost them factory owners a fortune," Tremaine said. "Cost the North a fortune."

"But they invaded us anyway," Hargrove said.

"Slavery was a goddamn good deal for everyone," Tremaine said, "including the damn North."

"Except for the slaves," Frank quietly and mostly to himself.

Luckily, Hargrove and Tremaine were so worked up they didn't hear him or notice the irony in his remark.

"Those slaves were worth a fortune to the entire country," Hargrove said categorically, conclusively.

"Was owning slaves the same as *now* money?" Frank asked, his tone ironic but subtly acerbic.

"Them slaves were the ultimate *now* money," Hargrove agreed, nodding his head emphatically.

CHAPTER 3

That night, Nietzsche sat with Bismarck in the chancellor's suite. It was lavish by Durango standards but simple and barebones compared to Bismarck's accommodations back in Germany. A long, large corner room, lit with coal-oil lamps and with seven large windows along the walls, it contained three essential living areas—a parlor with leather-upholstered sofas, armchairs and a teak coffee table. The eating area consisted of a teak dining table surrounded by matching straight-back chairs, and the sleeping area at the far end was composed of a large bed with red satin sheets featuring big fluffy blood-red pillows. Flanked by two teakwood bedside tables, three matching chests of drawers stood off to the side along the walls.

Nietzsche feared that Bismarck, who enjoyed a far more opulent lifestyle than the writer, found the suite shabby.

"Do our emperor and Herr Krupp have any idea at all," Nietzsche asked the chancellor, "the kinds of men and women to whom they are selling all their advanced weaponry? Do they have any sense as to the heinous uses to which these people will put these weapons of war? Do Krupp and our emperor even...*care?*"

"Yes," Bismarck shouted, "they care—about their money. Krupp cheerfully sells his best, most terrifying, most destructive artillery to Russia, whose colossal army is deployed along our eastern border, as if they were the barbaric hordes, waiting to break down Rome's gates and sack the city. He also attempts to sell his howitzers to France and Austria-Hungary. Only their distrust of any and all things German stops Alfred from arming France to the teeth and allowing them to link arms with Russia and encircle their eternal enemy, namely us, all of them equipped with the best, most advanced Krupp-built howitzers in the world."

"Can't our emperor rein Herr Krupp in?" Nietzsche asked.

"If I can't control Alfred," Bismarck said, shaking his head disconsolately, "what chance does Wilhelm have of preventing those sales?"

"What possible rationale does Krupp have for selling his weapons to countries that so gravely threaten us?" Nietzsche asked.

"Oh, I have heard his lectures on 'indispensable free flow of capital,' 'free trade' and 'the iron law of financial circulation' until I'm blue in the face," Bismarck said.

"Krupp is insane," Nietzsche said simply.

"No," Bismarck said, "but he does suffer from uncontrollable greed. The tragedy of his malady is that he no longer needs money. He stopped needing it forty years ago. He could dissolve his weapons business and never miss a meal. But making money to him is like fighting a long, brutal war. Once you start, stopping is no longer a viable option. To stop is to surrender and die; so he soldiers on. Moreover, the Fatherland is surrounded by bloody-minded foes on all sides. We need our Kanonkunig"—cannon king—"if we are to survive. We need him more than he needs us."

"Is that true?" Nietzsche said.

"That is the position of the Reichstag and the emperor," Bismarck said. "So far I have not been able to convince them otherwise."

"You've read my reports on slave labor in Méjico?" Nietzsche asked.

"They are very good, but Krupp and the emperor view Diaz as an ignorant leader of primitive land separated from us by a five-thousand-mile moat, and there are no drawbridges that stretch that far."

"So they don't fear Diaz?"

"They aren't even sure he exists. They see him as a fairy-tale ogre that you and I have conjured up to scare small children."

"So they don't care that Diaz murders and enslaves most of his people?" Nietzsche asked.

"They do not care," Bismarck said, "where their money comes from or how it was previously used."

"Then maybe Diaz and the Senorita were right," Nietzsche said.

"In what way?" Bismarck asked.

"That men like us—even Krupp and the emperor—will never understand madre Méjico," Nietzsche said.

The Iron Chancellor stared at Friedrich Nietzsche in silence, his eyes empty of emotion.

CHAPTER 4

The Senorita and Judith McKillian lay on a big circular bed, reclining on huge silk pillows and sheets. On the bedside tables were bottles of champagne, chilling in ice buckets, and bottles of 1811 "Year of the Comet" cognac. They had been reviewing the strengths and weaknesses of both Bismarck and Friedrich Nietzsche and discussing the best ways to deal with them.

"I say we break them both," the Senorita said.

"Bust them both down to sucking eggs?" McKillian asked.

"Exactly."

"I like that."

"And we don't stop," the Senorita said, "not till they do anything and everything we tell them to do."

"How, specifically, should we deal with the Iron Chancellor?"

"All he understands is overwhelming force."

"So we'll give him a full frontal assault."

"He won't be iron-hard when we're done with him."

"We'll teach him the true meaning of fear," McKillian said.

"Young Friedrich?"

"He's different. We should deal with him on a more personal level."

"He's so infuriatingly innocent," McKillian said. "I can't wait to get my tenacious talons into that one."

"He gets under your skin? Why?"

"Call it my desperado's rage at innocence."

"He once referred to me as his 'Lady Mephistopheles,'" the Senorita said.

"We'll make him pay for that one."

"I'm grateful to him for that nickname."

"It does fit somehow," McKillian said.

"Then let us visit him in his bedroom tonight."

"I was thinking the exact same thing."

"We assigned him a four-poster bed, yes?"

"He and the chancellor both have one."

"Excellent," the Senorita said.

"I somehow suspect that young Friedrich is not all that experienced around the female of the species."

"I think he may be a virgin," the Senorita said.

"Oh, that would be...*exquisite*."

"Don't forget your manacles. They are indispensable."

"I will also bring my...*whip*."

"You never leave home without it, my dear," the Senorita said.

"I am most skillful with it."

"I envy you your talent," the Senorita said.

"My cuarta quirt is universally feared."

"And by some, myself included, revered."

"As well it should be."

"A little chastisement—plus a few other dangerous desires and deleterious delectations—will be good for his soul."

"To say nothing of his much-abused flesh," Judith McKillian said.

"His flesh will be most sorely abused when we're done with him."

"To say nothing of his soon-to-be extremely troubled soul."

"When we are finished, his soul will tremble, teeter and totter over hell's...*abyss*," the Senorita said.

"He may have no soul left to lose."

"We'll give him a night of Méjico exotico y erotico he'll never forget."

"A night of wonder and revelation," McKillian said.

"You mean wonder, thunder, hellfire and fornication."

"Scheherazade could give him all 1,001 nights and still have nothing on us."

"We shall compress every one of her 1,001 divertissments into a single torturous night of his doomed and tormented soul," the Senorita said.

"He'll tremble like a leaf and cry like a little girl before we are finished with him," Judith McKillian said.

"You know, I almost pity him."

"Thou, who hast neither pity, love nor fear?"

"I so love that soliloquy."

Judith McKillian recited the lines that they loved so much from Shakespeare's *Richard III*:

I, who have neither pity, love nor fear.
The owl shrieked at my birth—an evil sign.

"We'll turn young Friedrich inside out and upside down," the Senorita said.

"He won't know whether he's looking down from heaven or up from hell."

"Whether to shit or go blind."

"Or to come again," the Senorita said.

"And again and again and again."

"In between the screams."

"Of agony or ecstasy?"

"Agony in ecstasy," the Senorita said.

"You are amazing."

"He called me his 'Lady Mephistopheles,' remember?" the Senorita said.

"He'll rue the day he conferred that cursed sobriquet on you."

"The stones themselves shall weep."

"And the stars cry out from terror and from truth."

Judith McKillian stared deeply, searchingly, into the Senorita's black, bottomless, utterly unreadable eyes.

"We do think alike, don't we?" she said, leaning toward the Senorita, her face aglow with evil radiance and malicious merriment.

"Yes, we do," the Senorita responded.

CHAPTER 5

A flash of movement from down below caught the men's eyes. Raising his telescope, Frank James stared, downslope, at the town. Several dozen men in white, thigh-length hoods were galloping up the main street on big snorting horses, firing pistols into buildings and up into the air in an attempt to terrify the surrounding citizens. Two of the riders blasted away at the buildings with sawed-off shotguns.

The townspeople, however, instead of panicking, quickly filled the rooftops and windows. Many of them were businessmen in dark coats and ties; others were merchants in white shirts; a few of them wore farmers' coveralls. A half dozen women in long dresses of various colors, cinched at the waists, appeared in windows. Two women in long full white skirts and blouses also appeared alongside the men. At least two of them wore bonnets. They looked like they were dressed for picnics, but instead of wicker hampers, they all carried lever-action repeating rifles, double-barreled shotguns and revolvers so heavy that the women had to use both hands to aim and shoot them.

The townspeople then began shooting at the white-hooded raiders almost in unison—a series of rapid-fire blasts so close together that they sounded like one elongated, echoless roar, like something he might have heard on a battlefield, during which countless weapons were being fired seemingly in unison. Collectively, they seemed to shake the ground beneath Frank's horse.

Through it all, savage flashbacks of the Northfield raid—the one where almost all of his gang was massacred—flooded Frank's brain, unwanted, unbidden but utterly beyond his power to cancel or call back. Once again, he could see in his mind's eye:

Jim, John and Bob Younger plus Clell Miller dead.

Cole Younger, shot to pieces, and destined to spend twenty-eight years serving hard time in a hard-rock Minnesota prison.

He and Jess finally made it back, but their return home was an escape from hell worthy of Xenophon's *Anabasis* and Odysseus's *Odyssey.*

Now, watching the comparable massacre below, Frank was reliving...*everything*. He could see, hear and smell it all once again, the shots ringing out, the bullets ripping through his friends' flesh, and the blood spurting and pulsing, then streaming down their faces and chests. The memories came back to him in bursts and flashes, in shards and segments, and with each one, his hands trembled, his stomach lurched, and his eyes teared.

Frank's vision cleared, and again, he watched the carnage in the street: The hooded raiders were forced to stop firing their weapons, and, instead, focused on restraining their rearing, bucking, out-of-control mounts. The men and women on the rooftops and in the windows were still shooting at them—an unending, uninterrupted rolling barrage of deafening gunfire—while a number of the town women continued reloading guns. Whitish clouds of black-powder smoke were enshrouding the windows and rooftops, from which the town's shooters poured forth their relentless volleys of firepower.

"The townspeople have friends providing them with extra weapons," Frank observed in case Hargrove and Tremaine hadn't been able to see the shooters' assistants. "The women are reloading their empty guns and handing them new ones. This is a goddamn massacre—just like Northfield."

Frank finally put down his telescope, unable to observe the bloody debacle below any longer.

"Goddamn them black bastards to hell," Hargrove said heatedly, shaking with blind rage, "every damn one of them."

"Those women down there are damn fine shots," Frank James said respectfully. "I wish we'd have had some of them on our side at Northfield. We could have used their help."

"Damn them to hell too," Hargrove said.

"I believe in giving credit where credit is due," Frank said in disagreement, shaking his head.

Frank returned the telescope to his right eye just in time to see a black woman in a light, floral-print, calico dress fire both barrels of a twelve-gauge Greener simultaneously. The blast almost exploded a man's head completely off his shoulders.

The man next to him was blown out of his saddle by three near-simultaneous gunshots to the chest. One of his big Laredo rowels got hooked under the saddle's latigo on the way down. His horse, a big gray, reared up hysterically. His eyes walling, he bolted in utter panic, dragging the dying man, face down, in the dry, dirty, gunfire street. Massive maelstroms of crimson dust were billowing up behind him, as the gray made his escape from the hell engulfing the town behind him.

Hargrove howled in rage.

"Yes siree," Frank James said, lowering his telescope, nodding his head in appreciation, "I always believe in giving credit where credit is due. Them blacks is damn fine shots, their womenfolk included."

Tremaine and Hargrove could only shake in fury.

PART XVI

"[E]verything is an expression of power—lust, passion, even affection and always pain."

—Judith McKillian, International Financier

"The pinnacle of all great passion is never far from...*death*."

—La Senorita Dolorosa

CHAPTER 1

When Friedrich Nietzsche came to, he was stark naked. His wrists and ankles were red, raw and sore. He was lying on his left side near the bedside table. A Good Samaritan had left a bottle of cognac and a glass on it.

He needed some of that.

In fact, he needed a lot of it.

Friedrich Nietzsche had never been much of a liquor drinker. In college, he'd joined a beer-drinking club, and for a time had enjoyed the beer halls and beer gardens of Germany. Back then, he'd gone home tipsy many a night.

But then he'd gotten serious about his studies, and his drinking days were done.

Until he came to Méjico.

He was told on the ship that in Méjico the water was pure poison, and if you drank it straight, you'd defecate yourself to death. To survive, you had to mix it fifty-fifty with brandy or whiskey. Gin and vodka were nonexistent South of the Border, so if you couldn't find brandy or whiskey, you were told to cut the water with the strongest mezcal or tequila you could find.

Leaning up on an elbow, he grabbed the liter cognac bottle, set it up on the bed, and pulled out the cork. He then filled the glass to the brim and placed the bottle back on the table.

Fuck mixing it with water. He needed cognac straight, and he needed it bad.

He slowly began to remember the night before, and the many malevolent ministrations of Judith McKillian and the Senorita. They might be beautiful as angels, but they were the devil incarnate in bed…

* * *

…Friedrich Nietzsche remembered them coming into his room with a bottle of cognac, two bottles of champagne, an ice bucket and platters of cheese, sausages and chili peppers. They were both tastefully attired in evening gowns and full of bonhomie.

"Young Friedrich," the Senorita had said, "we have been most disagreeable hosts thus far but now would like to show you some true Méjicana hospitality."

They proceeded to ply him with drink, ask him questions about his homeland and the books he was working on. They asked him what he really thought of "madre Méjico" and if he had suggestions on how to expand the economy and the different ways they could improve the living conditions of the people, particularly their peons, assuring him that they were not the "heartless brujas" [witches] that they sometimes seemed to be. All the while, they filled, refilled, refilled and refilled his cognac snifter and champagne flute.

The two women were so heart-stoppingly beautiful, their smiles so enticing and engaging, their eyes so friendly, so sincere he felt himself merging into their bottomless depths. He felt as if the entire universe might be encompassed in their eyes, and as he peered more and more deeply into their immeasurable vastness, he felt himself falling, falling, falling.

Until he came to with a start.

He was then on his side, his arms crossed above his head, each wrist chained to a bedpost, his crossed legs likewise chained by the ankles to bedposts and the bed's foot. The Senorita's face was hovering above his hips, her face smiling, almost beatifically serene.

The evening gown was gone, and she was dressed in a black corset with matching net stockings and high-heeled riding boots heeled with sterling silver rowels. Her face was garishly made up, her lip rouge ruby red, and she was doing things to him that were so exquisitely ecstatic, so surreal yet sensuous he could not believe he was awake and that this was happening to him.

It had to be a dream.

But Judith McKillian was hell-bent on bringing him back to reality. She stood astride his chest, wearing a crimson corset, blood-red riding boots and spurs, her long tresses a deep auburn, her lips and fingernails purest vermillion. Bending her brown hippopotamus-hide riding crop with both hands into a perfect circle, she let go of the tip. It straightened in a flash, humming and vibrating furiously.

"Young Nietzsche," McKillian said, waving her crop like a symphony conductor, "do you think I look good in red?"

"I think you look like a scarlet harlot," Nietzsche muttered, immediately regretting the rashness of his remark.

"Oh, that was so witty, my dear friend," Judith McKillian said. "Senorita, do you find young Nietzsche... witty?"

"I find him droll, and I do detest drollery in young men," the Senorita said. "It suggests that they do not know their place."

"Well, sister-friend, you know what the English say to droll young men who do not know their place?"

"And which bot mot is that, my dear?"

The sin ye do, by two and two,
Ye must pay for one by one

"Exactly," the Senorita said. "While young Nietzsche here does not currently know his... place, tonight he shall learn it."

"I shall teach it to him personally," Judith McKillian said, shaking her thrumming whip in Nietzsche's face. "I shall see to it that you pay for your singular witticisms... most dearly.*"*

Meanwhile, the Senorita was taking the young man to places he'd never imagined—into a concupiscent abyss that knew no limit or satiety. She teased and tantalized his most exquisitely sensitive zones—exuberantly, excruciatingly—always bringing him to the brink of consummation but then pulling him fiercely back.

Not only was his body on fire for the Senorita, she had snared his soul: His mind was hers too. She owned him in toto in a way he'd never imagined possible.

He could not really contemplate anything else, not even the blindingly beautiful and almost demonically desirable Judith McKillian, even when she raised the thrumming quirt high overhead and brought it down with a whistling hiss across his naked bottom, where it cracked like a pistol shot.

Friedrich Nietzsche was brought back to reality with startling clarity. The slashing, lacerating pain was like nothing he'd ever felt. It was seared into his derriere almost supernaturally.

He instantly looked up and found himself staring into Judith McKillian's twinkling eyes. He did not think he'd ever seen a happier human being. His own eyes were flooding with tears and sobs were tearing out of his lungs, but his suffering only seemed to inflame her elation.

But any joy she felt was alarmingly evanescent.

Her eyes quickly became hooded, and her lips were now no longer smiling but were muttering unspeakably foul obscenities, even as her whip strokes increased in power, frequency, and velocity. His agony soon became unendurable.

The decibel level of the whipcracks—now joltingly, jarringly, startlingly sharp—even woke the Senorita from her trancelike state, during which she'd been performing a series of elaborately erogenous undulations on his now unbearably tender extremities.

She too was gazing, not unfondly, into the young man's blinking, soulful, tragically tearful eyes.

"Try not to fight it," the Senorita said. "There is really nothing you can do."

He looked up at Judith McKillian again, ready to beg her to stop, hoping and praying that she would not hit him with that hateful quirt.

But, once again, she was smiling at him sublimely—which unnerved Nietzsche more than the ugliness of her earlier sneering obscenities—all the while fondling the whip, bending it back and forth, back and forth.

"Ah, young Friedrich," Judith McKillian said with immense gentleness, "we shall have such times together, you and I."

He again looked down at the Senorita, hoping for a reprieve, a rescue, anything.

*"Face it, mi amigo, you are all…*ours,*" the Senorita said pleasantly.*

"But what is happening?" Nietzsche asked, confused.

"You are trapped in a combat zone between hate and fear, a world," the Senorita said, "in which lust turns on terror and is just one more weapon in power's arsenal."

*"Doesn't sex have something to do with pleasure?" Nietzsche asked. "Don't passion and affection play a part in love-making? Is everything…*pain?*"*

"My young amigo," Judith McKillian said, "in Méjico everything is an expression of power—pleasure, passion, lust, even affection and always pain."

"Especially lust," the Senorita said.

"And love," Judith McKillian said.

"Which, like all human emotions, is only one more of power's innumerable instruments," the Senorita said.

"But why are you doing this?" Nietzsche asked.

"We are here to teach you the error of your ways," the Senorita said, "and to show you where your cynical arrogance and nihilistic naivete ultimately, inevitably lead."

"And to delineate for you," McKillian said, "your most forbidden impulses and darkest, most devious desires."

"In short," the Senorita said, "we are here to instruct you in the inexhaustible eroticism of unbounded power."

"You see," Judith McKillian said, casually slapping her boot top with her crop, "transcendent ecstasy is power's grandest summit—an unsurpassed, heaven-challenging peak that is never far from... pain. *Or from the voluptuous vicissitudes of all-consuming violence," the Senorita said.*

"Let's put the pistols on the table," the Senorita said. "Let's call a spade a dirty, rotten, bloody shovel. The pinnacle of all great passion is never far from... death. *In short, young Nietzsche, you are in the hands of something...* godlike*."*

"Suppose I said that I don't want to learn these things," Nietzsche said, "that I don't want to visit these places and that I do not wish to play your games."

"But you came to us," Judith McKillian said. "You entered our house."

*"You chose to visit," the Senorita said somberly, "...*Méjico*."*

"A fact that I now most truly and deeply regret," Nietzsche said with absolute conviction.

"I know, young friend," the Senorita said, stroking his cheek, "but it is too late for second-guessing and for heartfelt recriminations. Your die has been irretrievably cast, your Rubicon irrevocably crossed."

"Perhaps years from now," McKillian said, again bending her quirt into a perfect parabola, "when you look back on the lessons you're about to so assiduously and painstakingly learn, you will find consolation in the fact that you never had... a choice*."*

With that, McKillian recommenced with the quirt, while the Senorita returned to her own maddeningly methodical circumvolutions.

*Friedrich Nietzsche was now locked into a never-ending cycle of amorous annihilation countered by criminally carnal cravings, always on the brink of bursting his seams, blowing his boilers and smashing his mind, but with never, ever any vestige of relief. Throughout it all, McKillian's soul-piercing torment was punctuated by blinding flashes of lurid lasciviousness without any discharge or catharsis, only one riotous, unending ordeal, an eternally protracted agony of...*desire. *Any time his body ventured anywhere near the brink of release, the Senorita would pull him back or McKillian would block his deliverance with a crack of her whip.*

Toward the end, he could feel himself going insane—his mind breaking free from his body and shooting above the bed, finally fixing itself in a ceiling corner. From that vantage point, he watched the two vivacious vixens first torture, then titillate his body like crazed harpies from the lewdest, rudest recesses of hell. He listened to their evil laughter harmonize discordantly with his own wolfish wails.

Most horrifying of all, the two sadistic strumpets would not stop, at last, convincing him that his agony in ecstasy would never cease. Their pain-racking predations and libidinous brigandage continued on and on and on through the night, into the relativities of time, into the vilest vortex of hell's inescapable abyss, in the end, spiraling forever and ever out of control into the gaping infinitude of that inexhaustible night without end...

* * *

At last, the sun was coming up, and the two women were done. Unlocking his wrist and ankle manacles, they freed him. Propping him up against pillows, they took turns sitting on his lap, kissing him long and hard, then gazed—fondly, gigglingly, leeringly—into his wet, blinking, red-rimmed eyes. After patting him on the cheek, they were...*gone.*

Friedrich Nietzsche slowly pulled himself back together. His buttocks—now a garish labyrinth of scarlet whip welts—blazed like all the hell furnaces in Dante's *Inferno* with their doors flung wide-open, while his gonads felt as if they'd been flattened by a dropforge, then blasted to pieces with an 88mm cannon. Every orifice of his body felt violated, sore, hard-used. His body and hands convulsed uncontrollably, even as his vision blurred.

Who were these women?

What kind of monsters were Diaz and that degenerate limey, Sutherland?

What kind of a place was...*Méjico?*

God, he loathed this country and everything in it. And, oh, how he hated Richard Wagner for talking him into this trip. He'd settle with that Scheisskopf if it took him a hundred thousand lifetimes.

Damn, his bottom hurt. Staring at his bedside bottle of cognac, he poured an entire tumbler and downed it in a series of enormous gulps. Before he came to Méjico, he barely touched alcohol.

And now...now...now?

Again, he grabbed the bottle off the bedside table and popped the cork. Drinking straight out of the bottle's neck, he did not put it back on the table until his throat burned, his breath was coming in rattling gasps, and his vision scintillated with a trillion glimmering-glittering stars.

CHAPTER 2

Otto von Bismarck put down the cable. The emperor and Alfred Krupp had signed it jointly. They said that a shipment of three rapid-fire .50-caliber Mitrailleuse de Reffye, or 'Canon a Balles,' as well as three C61 and C65 88mm howitzers were about to arrive. The ordnance was heading up the Pacific Coast to where Diaz was to have it picked up. They wrote:

Consider this weapons shipment a signing bonus, a sweetener to our arms deal with Diaz. We cannot stress enough how important to Germany and to the Kruppwerk this business agreement with the generalissimo is. Germany's military and financial security depends on this transaction. You must complete the sale no matter what. Do not return to the Fatherland until you have the contract signed and trunks filled with gold bullion or 100-Reichsmark notes. With men like Diaz, we get everything up front and in cash—no checks or credit.

Bismarck was furious with Wilhelm. He'd written Krupp off decades ago as a mercenary old fool, but he'd thought the emperor had something remotely resembling a moral compass. Now he had to conclude that Kaiser Wilhelm was an even bigger dullard than he'd previously imagined—and he'd always thought of him as inconceivably, incomprehensibly...*stupid.*

Moreover, he wasn't sure that he had a choice in the matter, even if the two men hadn't sent him that blasted cable. Those two fiends from the Underworld, the infamous Senorita Dolorosa and her internationally feared terrorist-financier friend, Judith McKillian, along with their English colleague—that viciously twisted deviant, James Sutherland—had put Bismarck in a trick bag, and he didn't see any way out of it. He would have to give them what they wanted.

What had happened earlier sealed that diabolic deal forever.

* * *

Two nights before, the women had materialized in his doorway. Decked out in evening gowns, they had appeared not as mere women but as mortal goddesses. He could not remember ever having seen two more ethereally radiant women in his entire life.

Oh, how deceiving looks could be.

Behind them, servants in red livery were pushing a cart laden with Napoleon 1811 "Year of the Comet" cognac and vintage champagne as well as plates of caviar, Camembert, pâté de foie gras and beignets. He hadn't had a decent glass of cognac or champagne or quality pâté since leaving Germany, and he was sincerely, unreservedly grateful. He also had to admit he did not mind spending time with two such irresistible ladies.

Maybe they could find subjects to discuss other than money, violence, murder most foul, torture most vile, blood-drenched military conquests and the financial advantages of slave labor.

So the two women had joined him at his sitting table for snifters of Napoleon cognac backed up by flutes of chilled Chateau-Lafite and Clos Vougeot. The chancellor nibbled continuously on Camembert and pâté de foie gras, but he had to admit that the alcohol was going to his head with startling swiftness. True, he hadn't eaten anything all day, but he was a man who could hold his liquor. In fact, his detractors accused him of drinking to excess, so his tolerance for alcohol was more than ample. Never once had he had a problem with drunkenness. Still the food and drink were so exemplary and the two enchanting ladies so inexpressibly divine that the chancellor could not restrain himself indulging in the delicacies.

And, of course, the women filled and refilled and refilled his glasses to the brim, all the while laughing at his jokes and flirting with him outrageously.

Unfortunately, he soon found himself becoming increasingly, inexplicably, incontrovertibly…intoxicated.

* * *

Bismarck could not believe what happened to him next. Looking back on the events that were to transpire, he felt nausea deep in the pit of his stomach. His cheeks flamed with guilt and shame. Self-hate was sweeping over himself in waves. He could not believe that he'd allowed those two demented doxies to play him like a mark.

But he had.

* * *

When Otto von Bismarck came to, he found himself lying supine on the big bed, stripped naked, his wrists and ankles chained to the four bedposts. Six young—shockingly young—delectable Méjicana putas were abasing and degrading every square inch of his—

The Iron Chancellor was at a loss for words.

Their devious degeneracies were so obscene as to be indescribable.

They were abusing his person in ways that it had never been abused before: gyrating, auscultating, horripilating, fellating and flagellating the most vulnerable areas of his anatomy, as if they were—, were—, were—

Vampires.

It was the only term Bismarck could come up with that came even remotely close to describing their actions.

Not that their prurient palpations weren't pleasurable in a certain perverse way, but still he desperately sought—with every ounce of his willpower and moral resolve—to fight off their merciless degradations. Unfortunately, his nervous system had a will of its own, and he could not stop it from weakening, yielding, conceding and, at last, capitulating to the six hell-hot harlots and their relentless ravishments.

In fact, their despoilments were so overpowering that his whole body was now convulsing, rocking with almost seismic force uncontrollably, rocked, then shook with seismic force, while explosions of blindingly white light blazed before his eyes.

Actually, they weren't as much lights as pans of flash powder—held and ignited above four big ungainly cameras, which were set up in each of the room's corners, where men snapped photographs of his writhing body, of his face now hideously contorted by his monstrous cravings and by the six young trollops trans-

gressing every square millimeter of his person without any respect for his rank, reputation or accomplishments.

Even worse, his body no longer showed any signs of resisting. Against his will, he was succumbing to the six witches' multitudinous ministrations, his mouth gaping and groaning, his tongue lolling out of it at the side, his eyes rolling into the back of his head.

Still the endless waves of violent paroxysms would not cease.

And the flash pans continued to blaze, the camera shutters continued to click, and the Senorita and Judith McKillian, who were both sedulously orchestrating the photographic shoot, issued instruction after instruction, order after order, sometimes demanding a close-up here, a high-angle shot there, as well as their continual demands for more and more photographic plates.

Through it all, Bismarck's sobbing howls soared through the night, punctuated only by the two women's dementedly delirious laughter.

* * *

No, the Iron Chancellor had to admit that the two women had him just where they wanted him. As long as they possessed those countless photographs of him fornicating with six amazingly young but astonishingly accomplished courtesans, he would give the Senorita and Judith McKillian anything they wanted. Krupp's most advanced weapons systems were theirs for the asking, as far as Bismarck was concerned.

Young Nietzsche would never understand. He would just assume that the Iron Chancellor had no moral code, no spine, no desire to do the right thing. Nor could Bismarck ever tell him the reason for his betrayal of all that was ethical or holy. Bismarck would have to keep his mouth shut and tell no one no matter how demeaning his silence was.

And what was most embarrassing of all was the shameful, shuddering, crawling delight that he still felt when he recalled those six impossibly seductive sluts and the insuperable assault that they had waged so unrelentingly on his helpless, shackled hulk.

Even more mortifying was the fervent, incessant and utterly humiliating hope that dogged him like a recurring nightmare from another world—one from which he could not awaken: Against every fiber of both his mortal and moral being, part of him desperately wanted the Senorita and Judith McKillian to order those six stupendously lecherous ladies to return to his room tonight—this very evening—and shackle him to the bed and subject him...*to another rapacious round of shamelessly salacious abuse.*

PART XVII

"The French nicknamed the big gun the 'moulin a café—or, the coffee grinder—because it grinds up men like they were coffee beans. Our Prussian soldiers refer to it as 'der Hollenmaschine,' or, the hell machine."

—Friedrich "Fritz" Krupp, scion to the Krupp Arms Manufacturing Dynasty

CHAPTER 1

Frank James, Tremaine and Hargrove shared a compartment on the Texas Southern Pacific Railroad. Since 1881, that line had stretched all the way from the Lone Star State to Los Angeles, California. Frank and his friends, while heading west, would not be entering California. They'd be getting off in southern Arizona, where after a short ride on horseback, they would connect with General Joe Shelby and the rest of his newfound army. Porfirio Diaz had also told Frank before he'd left for Texas that he intended to be in Arizona for the first battle in his war to reclaim Méjico's stolen territory.

"Watersville was a goddamned disaster," Hargrove said angrily, interrupting Frank's thoughts.

"I haven't seen so many shot-to-pieces bodies since Sharpsburg," Tremaine said, shaking with rage.

"Most people call it 'Antietam' now," Frank pointed out.

"Treasonous, Yankee-sucking, sissy sons of bitches call it that," Hargrove said.

Frank stared at him, forcing himself to appear impassive but inwardly desperate to be free of these fools. When they got off the train, he swore to himself he would never speak to either of them again. Fantasizing briefly about putting a couple of rounds into their thick heads, he quickly purged himself of such thoughts. Those days, he wished and prayed, were behind him. Anyway, Jess was the one who loved that life, and his death, Frank fervently hoped, would close that chapter of Frank's life forever.

It appeared now he had one more war to fight.

Then he would retreat into madre Méjico for his new life as a wealthy, respected hacendado.

"I felt like I was in a hurricane of bullets," Tremaine said, describing the Watersville massacre.

"That's how it was at Northfield," Frank said, trying to sound sympathetic. General Shelby needed the troops these two fools were assembling for him. He had to make himself seem friendly. Frank leaned forward and softly slapped Tremaine on the shoulder.

"I swear a half dozen rounds whipped right past each of my ears," Tremaine said. "It was the eeriest, highest-pitched whine I ever heard."

"Press your ear against a telegraph wire," Frank said, "and you can hear the same screech."

"Really?" Tremaine asked.

"Yep," Frank said, "that's why the Comanche and the Sioux called telegraph lines 'the singing wires.'"

"But the telegrams coming out of Watersville were death notices," Hargrove observed, lowering his head between his knees.

"So were those coming out of Northfield," Frank James said, trying to sound philosophical.

"Well, one thing's for sure," Hargrove said, "those Watersville blacks rocked us all on our heels. It'll be a while before we can reorganize."

"The *New York Times* reported," Tremaine said, "that Washington is sending a whole army of federal agents to Texas to investigate."

"I read the *Times*' big front-page article on the raid," Hargrove noted. Picking up his copy of the paper, he read from it aloud: "It says here that 'the citizenry was defending the town against several dozen hooded Red Shirts.'"

"The survivors of that raid and a whole lot of our boys could end up in prison," Tremaine said.

"The *Times* describes the raid as 'aiding and abetting in the furtherance of a criminal conspiracy,'" Hargrove read.

"Frank, you've probably had experience dealing with that particular statute," Tremaine said, chuckling.

"That, I have," Frank said softly.

Hargrove and Tremaine had to laugh at that one.

"Maybe that's why so many of our men volunteered for this operation down in Méjico," Hargrove said. "They figured they'd need a getaway—some place to hide out a while."

"Diaz and General Shelby gave them the financial means to escape Texas," Tremaine said in agreement, "and flee from that invading army of federal agents."

"Every former Klansman in the South and in the border states has signed up for our little adventure," Hargrove said. "We even got chapters from Indiana joining us."

"You and I," Tremaine said to Hargrove, "are availing ourselves of the same auspicious opportunity."

"Neither of us has a burning desire to talk to those federal agents about Watersville either," Hargrove said.

"Frank, I'll bet you're looking forward to that day that you cross that border line into Nogales," Tremaine said, "and leave US law enforcement on your backtrail forever."

Frank nodded his head. "I look forward to it about as much as I look forward to 100-proof whiskey, 200-proof women and 22-carat gold."

"I imagine, Frank," Hargrove said, "that you've had about as much of the American judicial system as you can stand."

"As had your brother, Jess," Tremaine said.

"Poor taste," Hargrove said to Tremaine.

"Perfectly all right," Frank said. "We're friends."

Frank took his hammered silver pint flask out of the inside pocket of his black frock coat. His three initials, AFJ—for Alexander Franklin James—were lavishly etched on each side in gothic script.

"To Jess," he said, unscrewing the cap and holding up the flask. He then took a large pull out of the flask. He held it in his mouth a long time before swallowing. "We shall not look upon his like again," he said, quoting *Hamlet*.

Taking the flask from Frank, Tremaine repeated: "To Jess." He then drank deeply. He stared thoughtfully at the flask before passing it on to Hargrove. "That's damn fine brandy, Frank," he said admiringly.

"The best I could find in Texas," Frank said.

Hargrove took a drink, then said: "Let's make those goddamn Yankee bastards pay for Jess, for Watersville, for the war, for every goddamned thing under the sun."

"Let's start by returning the Arizona Territory to Diaz," Frank James said, "and then claiming those millions of acres of primo Méjicano farmland the generalissimo will be gifting us and our amigos."

"I be you witness there," Tremaine said.

"Amen to that," Hargrove said.

The three men stared at each other and then at the floor of their train compartment in cold, unforgiving silence.

CHAPTER 2

Wagon upon wagon upon wagon was arriving in Durango—all filled with heavy-duty ordnance, and, at last, Diaz and his generals were ready to take Krupp's weapons out to the range and field-test them. Bismarck, Nietzsche and Diaz's civilian friends were invited to attend.

Entering Bismarck's dressing room, Friedrich Nietzsche waited while the chancellor put on white cotton pants and a matching shirt and suitcoat, followed by black riding boots. Catching a glimpse of himself in a wall mirror, Nietzsche noted that he was dressed similarly. White attire reflected sunlight more effectively than darker colors and was far cooler. Among men and women both, it was much the vogue in these hot climes.

Bismarck, however, also noticed that the younger man's countenance was grave.

"You do not seem overjoyed to be attending this morning's artillery tests."

"I'm horrified that Alfred Krupp is donating some very deadly weapons to such an ignoble cause," Nietzsche said.

"The old man did more than that," Bismarck said. "He sent his son Fritz along with the shipment, to show Diaz and his associates how to load and fire the guns. He will be joining us any moment now."

"Now," Nietzsche said, "I'm even more depressed."

A visitor knocked on the door. Bismarck opened it and announced, "Fritz Krupp, welcome to Méjico."

"My friends call me Fritz," Krupp said with a brief bow.

Krupp entered. Smartly decked out in a Prussian officer's uniform, his dark jacket was lined with double rows of vertical metal buttons, and the shoulders were covered with braids and epaulets, the front of the coat with campaign medals. Nietzsche understood that the uniform and medals might not mean anything at all. For wealthy aristocrats such as Krupp—who came from, arguably, the richest manufacturing family on the continent—military service was often honorary. It was quite conceivable that the man had not spent a day of service on a military base, let alone faced enemy fire on a battlefield, and yet he was entitled to wear his nation's uniform and adorn it with garish decorations. Privilege had its perquisites. Bismarck, for example, had spent next to no time at all undergoing military training and had yet to experience combat or service of any kind in the field, yet often, at home, he wore a general's uniform, on the front of which he flaunted an ostentatious array of military citations.

Still, Nietzsche was aware that the emperor and Bismarck had both survived multiple assassination attempts. Bismarck alone had had five of the would-be killers' bullets dug out of him. German politics could be, at times, a blood sport.

Bismarck shook hands with the Kruppwerk's heir and introduced Nietzsche to the fledgling industrial titan.

"I hear you will be demonstrating the guns later today," Bismarck said.

Fritz Krupp shrugged self-deprecatingly. "It's what my father wishes."

"Our friend Nietzsche here," Bismarck said, "is skeptical of our hosts' motives and intentions."

"In what way?" the younger Krupp asked.

"If you hold with the basic principles of tenth-century feudalism and believe that most human beings are property to be owned, worked and slaughtered like livestock and that your chattels deserve nothing more than brutal labor and the most unjust beatings imaginable when they become tired, famished and slow down, I suppose our hosts are just fine."

"So you don't trust Porfirio Diaz with our most advanced weaponry?" Fritz Krupp asked.

"I wouldn't trust him to carry a dozen eggs across Kurfürstendamm Boulevard in Berlin," Nietzsche said. Kurfürstendamm was one of the most famous thoroughfares in all of Europe.

"Then we shall get along fabulously, Herr Nietzsche," Fritz Krupp said. "I have traveled the length and breadth of Central and South America and have met despots so despicable that the gods themselves howl at their misdeeds. Yet even among that rogues' gallery of tyrants and barbarians, Porfirio and his friends stand apart. He is a monster's monster, and his friends are devils. Unfortunately, my father cares only that Porfirio's purloined lucre...*spends*."

"Your father has regaled me many times," Bismarck said, "with his 'iron law of financial circulation.' He cites it when attempting to justify his business dealings with mass-murdering slave drivers."

"He has depressed me, day and night, night and day," Fritz Krupp said, "with that same hateful theory since I was old enough to talk and walk."

"So you disagree?" Nietzsche asked.

"From the bottom of my soul," Fritz Krupp said.

A knock on the door caused them to turn. Nietzsche opened it, and another man in another white linen suit stood before them. He was a good six feet tall, had sharp features and looked to be part Méjicano. He presented them with an ingratiating smile.

"Let me introduce you to Immanuel Carpenter," Fritz Krupp said. "An American, he is also in the arms business—a middleman of sorts."

"My detractors—and they are numberless—call me 'a gunrunner,'" Carpenter explained.

"Carpenter shares our skepticism toward Diaz and his cronies," Fritz said, "but he's an honest weapons broker, utterly fearless and widely respected, even by Diaz and his allies."

"Despite the fact that I have been arming his enemies for two decades," Carpenter said.

"Then why does he tolerate you?" Nietzsche asked.

"That does not sound like our Porfirio," Bismarck said.

"I sell guns to him as well," Carpenter said. "Being an arms merchant by trade, I must do a great deal of business with people whose ethical standards I disapprove of."

"Which is why all of us are here, young Nietzsche included," Bismarck said to Nietzsche. "We are all of us, for the time being, gunrunners—yourself included, young Nietzsche. After all, if you did not wish to help us sell Diaz arms, you could have stayed behind back in Germany."

"Back in Germany," Nietzsche said, "I did not know Diaz and his allies were fiends from hell who somehow cloaked themselves in human flesh."

"But you came here to assess Diaz's and Méjico's financial assets," Krupp said. "Thanks to your assessments, we know that Diaz can afford our weapons. Thanks to you, Herr Nietzsche, the arms sale has gone through. So you are not as pure as you pretend."

Nietzsche did not know how to respond.

A large pot of coffee sat on the drawing room table, and Bismarck poured cups for the four men.

"How lethal are the weapons you have brought Diaz?" Nietzsche asked Krupp.

"They are the same howitzers that leveled Paris," Fritz Krupp said, "during the Franco-Prussian War, plus rapid-fire artillery that even the German Army did not possess during that conflict. My father is arming Diaz with what he refers to as 'the gods of war.'"

"I've heard that those quick-firing weapons aren't that effective," Bismarck said.

"Only because the French employed them as howitzers," Krupp said. "They should be used to defend emplacements or to support infantry, even cavalry."

"Does Diaz understand this?" Nietzsche asked.

"No one does—yet," Krupp said.

"Not even the American army?" Nietzsche asked.

"The American army refused to order rapid-fire Gatlings in quantity during their Civil War, and they still do not fathom their true worth."

"Will you explain all that to Diaz?" Nietzsche asked.

"I will arm the bastard, but not instruct him in the theory and the practice of mass slaughter," Krupp said.

"Nor will I," Carpenter said.

Nietzsche stared at Carpenter a long, hard moment.

"Why do you run guns," Nietzsche asked, "which most people believe to be a dishonorable profession?"

"Unfortunately, I have very unusual avocations—not the least of which is exotically erotic women."

"I'm not sure I understand," Nietzsche said.

"I am drawn to the kinds of women who can make horses prance, mountains dance, eagles soar and volcanoes roar," Carpenter said. He then added quietly: "And corpses come."

"And I gather this hobby has a downside," Nietzsche said.

"It is...*prohibitively expensive*," Carpenter said with a shy smile.

"In that case," Bismarck said, "you must adore the Senorita and Judith McKillian."

"They are death incarnate," Carpenter said, shaking his head.

"Bloody death," Krupp added.

"So you two know them," Nietzsche asked.

"As the fly knows the spider," Carpenter said.

"And the turkey the ax," Krupp said.

"Meaning?" Nietzsche asked.

"To know them is to loathe them," Krupp said.

"Is Sutherland here too?" Carpenter asked.

"Unfortunately," Krupp said.

"So tell us about the guns you two are gifting to these hounds of hell," Bismarck said. "Why did Krupp senior send them here?"

"As a bonus against future arms deals," Carpenter said.

"So I was told," Bismarck said. "Your father called it 'a sweetener.'"

"I can't wait to see them on the firing range," Nietzsche said.

"They are special," Carpenter said.

"Indeed," Krupp agreed. "This time my avaricious progenitor has outdone himself."

CHAPTER 3

Slater sat on the floor of the locomotive, one of his .44 Army Colts in his lap. Belle sat next to him. The conductor sat next to her. He wasn't pleased that Slater and Belle had forced him to spend the entire trip in the smelly, filthy, thunderously loud locomotive. It had been hot and sooty for all of them, traveling in the engine compartment, but by keeping the train's primary staff within eyeshot, Slater had been able to prevent the train from making stops that Slater did not personally authorize and keep the conductor and engineer from informing law enforcement about the hijacking.

The train was slowing now. Sticking his head out the side, Slater saw that they were pulling into the station outside of El Rancho de Cielo. More of a no-horse whistle stop than an actual town, it consisted simply of a cistern water tank, coal and kindling bins and a one-room ticket house.

Slater had wired Katherine Ryan at the last stop, and she was standing beside the tracks, dressed in Levis, a collarless brown men's shirt and a sweat-stained working Stetson. An Army Colt was strapped to her right hip. Further down the track, she had three dozen cowhands and gunfighters backing her up.

She wasn't taking any chances on getting ambushed by the opposition.

Good.

Slater felt like he hadn't slept in a week—mostly because he hadn't. The last eight days had been hard as hell on both himself and Belle...

* * *

...Breaking sixty men out of Parker's makeshift jail also hadn't been easy. The livestock was the problem. Getting his team of twelve mules—six pairs in full harness with chest aprons—had taken a lot of work. Slater was knowledgeable and adept at working mules, but he'd never encountered jacks as cantankerous as these twelve. Twice, he'd had to take the shot-loaded butt-end of his mule whip to their recalcitrant, dim-witted skulls.

Still, he finally got them lined up in back of the jail with two log chains secured to the eight thick steel bars that were driven deep into the whitewashed adobe-brick walls. Slater was convinced that when the mules ripped them out through the bricks, the yank would tear out a wall hole big enough for the inmates to escape through.

Laying his whip over the backs of the lead mules, Slater shouted:

"Hit it!"

All twelve beasts hit their chest straps and collars as hard as they knew how but the bars refused to budge. Slater wasn't completely surprised. In fact, he had developed a backup plan. Earlier, Slater had reamed out three one-inch-diameter holes with a hand drill and filled them with black powder. He'd then inserted both caps and a short thirty-second fuse.

It was time to blow out some bars.

Striking a lucifer on his pant leg, he lit the fuses.

The first explosion ignited the other blasting caps through sympathetic detonation, and at the same time, Slater had again laid the whip across the lead mules' rumps.

The sound of the blast and the crack of Slater's lash inspired the mules to a feat of almost supernatural power. They hit their chest aprons and collars, as if they were possessed.

The bars went flying after the mules, half the brick wall collapsing in their wake.

Amid clouds of brick dust and whitish, black-powder smoke, over one hundred prisoners coughed and stumbled through the newly opened orifice.

Belle quickly organized them, getting the ones she knew and trusted the most into the wagon, which Slater had quickly hitched the mules back up to.

As they raced off for the train, which was stopping outside of town, four deputies opened fire on them.

Slater's Winchester quickly silenced that opposition.

El Rancho's defending forces would soon number almost 160. Slater doubted it was enough, but it was the best he could do.

* * *

The train finally braked to a hard, jolting stop. Slater and Belle climbed down from the locomotive without saying a word of farewell or offering a thank you to the engineer and conductor. They clearly weren't afraid of the two men going to the law. After a week of riding in the engine room with Slater and Belle, the engineer and conductor knew what to expect if they crossed them. They also understood that they had not been harmed.

In fact, Belle had brought a bag of goodies, which she'd shared: ham sandwiches on good sourdough bread, a half wheel of cheddar cheese, oatmeal cookies and five quarts of Jackson's Sour Mash—the best whiskey either man had ever drunk. Furthermore, Slater had given them each a sack full of gold double eagles—more money than they typically made in a year.

So when the two men shouted their goodbyes at the departing desperadoes, they weren't all that upset. All told, they'd made out goddamn well on this trip.

They also knew that if they alerted the authorities, they'd have to hand over their bribes.

Slater doubted they were that principled.

CHAPTER 4

Early that afternoon, Nietzsche and Bismarck joined Diaz and his entourage—Fritz Krupp included—at the firing range. The generalissimo had laid out a small banquet of cheese, sausage, chili peppers, whipped avocados, frijoles, pâté, caviar and fresh-baked bread and tortillas. Vintage French wines—mostly Bordeaux and champagne chilling in ice buckets—along with crystal balloon snifters and bottles of Napoleon cognac adorned the two tables as well.

Before them—and as far as the eye could see—stretched the test range.

An arid plain of rocks, snakes and chaparral, it was dotted by large, white, six-foot-high man-size targets that were erected at two-hundred-yard intervals for over two thousand yards. The yardage was printed on signs posted beside the targets. Nietzsche needed a telescope to discern the last dozen targets and signs.

Krupp stood near several field guns. The closest one was a medium-size howitzer mounted on a caisson with large heavy wheels.

"The testing will begin shortly," Krupp said. "We are currently looking at the C61 and C65 steel breech-loaded cannons. Since they fire an 88mm shell, soldiers universally refer to them as '88s.' You notice I emphasized 'steel breech-loaded.' The French and most of the world had manufactured muzzle-loading bronze-barreled cannons right up until our 1870–1871 war with France. The power, accuracy and rate of fire of our steel artillery soon instructed those countries on the error of their ways."

"What was the rate of fire?" Bismarck asked.

"An experienced crew could take out ten targets per minute from over thirty-five hundred yards," Krupp said. "To achieve that degree of skill, however, takes a six-man team years of coordinate practice."

"What kind of range could a semi-trained team hope for?"

"At twelve hundred yards, the gunner could aim the howitzers just above the tops of the targets and level anything in sight," Krupp said. "Nothing could stand up to its high-powered, high-explosive rounds."

"What is the artillery piece beside it?" Nietzsche asked.

"It's French," Krupp said, "a Mitrailleuse de Reffye 'Canon a Balles,' and we are giving Méjico two of them. We confiscated them from the defeated French army after the Battle of Sedan. A rapid-fire weapon, it nonetheless looks like a cannon and the French used it as such in their war with us. It was no match for our big siege guns."

It looked like a howitzer, but on closer inspection, Nietzsche noted that the barrel contained twenty-five smaller barrels, each one a half inch in diameter.

"It looks heavy," Nietzsche said.

"With its carriage," Krupp said, "it weighs almost a ton. A twenty-five-barrel volley gun, each barrel fires elongated shotgun-type shells, containing a 770-grain, center-fire patched bullet—backed by 185 grains of tightly compressed black powder. A single steel loading plate houses the twenty-five shells. That's twenty-five densely configured rounds in each single blast. Its effective range is thirty-seven hundred yards. The loading plates are held in place by a single manually operated closing lever and are locked against the breech before each volley. A rotating crank triggers these twenty-five rounds in rapid succession. A good crew can lock in place and fire four loading plates a minute. That's a sustainable rate of fire of one hundred rounds per minute. Because the gun is so heavy, a good crew doesn't have to resight it after each volley. They just lock in the new plates and turn the crank. The French nicknamed the big gun the 'moulin a café'—or, the coffee grinder, because it grinds up men like they were coffee beans. Our Prussian soldiers refer to it as 'der Hollenmaschine,' or, the hell machine."

"How did you get these guns?" Bismarck asked.

"We captured lots of them during our war with France," Krupp said.

"How do you aim the Mitrailleuse?" Nietzsche asked.

"An elevation screw is twisted relative to the distance of the target. Also the barrel can be turned sideways while firing in order to achieve lateral sweeping bursts. Such lateral sweeps only work at enormous distances though."

"How does it work at close range?" Bismarck asked.

"You can load it with shells, each of which contains twenty lead or steel balls," Krupp said.

"Like shotgun shells?" Bismarck asked.

"Precisely," Krupp said. "Each loading plate holds five hundred rapidly spreading rounds. Four plates a minute equals two thousand rounds a minute. Multiplied times two guns equals four thousand rounds per minute."

Bismarck and Nietzsche stared at Krupp in stunned silence.

"And your father does not understand the weapon's value?" Bismarck asked Krupp.

"He's rooted in the past and obsessed with the previous triumphs of our howitzers," Krupp said.

"Which took place in the Franco-Prussian war," Bismarck observed.

"Which was a dozen years ago," Nietzsche reminded them.

"Indeed," Krupp said.

"I heard that the French used these weapons to execute Communards in the Bois de Boulogne after the fall of the Paris Commune," Carpenter said.

"I've heard that too," Krupp said. "We believe it to be true."

"They really didn't understand how to use them," Bismarck said, "did they?"

"They didn't," Krupp said. "Neither does my father."

"Or America," Carpenter said.

"That is true," Krupp said.

"We have a few of those," Diaz said, "and have used them in our war against the Yaquis in northern Méjico ever since 1874. We have found them most efficacious. I would buy as many as you can ship."

"Since the French, not ourselves, manufacture them," Krupp said, "that would not be a simple proposition. But you can have these free and gratis with our blessing. Of course, we assume you'll be wanting additional howitzers."

"But of course," Diaz said.

"What is in those boxes?" Sutherland asked, pointing to two or three dozen large wooden crates stacked behind the big guns.

"We've brought you five hundred Mauser rifles," Krupp said, "and twenty thousand rounds of ammunition. Bolt-action and clip-fed, you can fire scores of rounds per minute at effective distances of over a thousand yards. The Mauser is far superior to America's feeble Winchesters."

"If only our peon soldiers were trained marksmen," Diaz said.

"Shelby's troops are," Judith McKillian said.

"Magnifico!" Diaz shouted.

His grin was also magnifico.

PART XVIII

"We'll kick their sorry asses all the way back across the Rio Grande, our victory-sated troops howling for their cowardly gringo hides every step of the way."

—La Senorita Dolorosa

CHAPTER 1

At last, all the unindicted co-conspirators had arrived safely at El Rancho de Cielo and were assembled in Katherine Ryan's parlor. Seated there were Wyatt Earp, Doc Holliday, Bat Masterson, Belle Starr and Outlaw Torn Slater—all of them drinking whiskey and talking about old times. Katherine was there, too, with her daughter, Rachel, and son, Richard—a first lieutenant in the United States Cavalry—who was on compassionate leave from the military due to his father's recent death. They'd just put away a sumptuous dinner of roast pork, yams, corn on the cob, baked beans and sweet potato pie. Ordinarily, Katherine frowned on smoking in her house, but tonight she relented, and half the men smoked cigars.

That she had capitulated to their smoking habit was a clear sign that Katherine needed the men's help badly. Flexibility was not one of Katherine Ryan's strengths.

Richard was wearing his army uniform, brass chest buttons gleaming. He had left his medals and decorations in a drawer. The rest of the men wore trail garb—collarless dark shirts, Levis and riding boots. They had removed their hats and spurs out of respect for Katherine.

They sat in the parlor on Queen Anne chairs, the two sofas and on a half dozen straight-back dining room chairs that had been brought in for the overflow.

"Well," Katherine said, "we put the hundred fifty or so men you rounded up sleeping in tents. The weather is warm, dry, and they shouldn't be too uncomfortable."

Katherine couldn't help but note Belle's derisive snort.

"You have a question, Belle?" Katherine asked.

"Those good old boys in those tents," Belles said, "are used to livin' on the high lines. They're lucky if they get tree limbs over their heads and leaves mixed with twigs to lay their bedrolls on. I heard you got army cots for half of them. They've never had it so good."

"They're so happy with the accommodations here," Holliday said, "they may never leave."

"I'm glad they're happy," Richard said. "We just got a telegram from army intelligence in Nogales. The Shelby Brigade has pitched its tents outside of town on the Méjicano side of the border. Our sources estimated that they're already fifteen hundred strong with new recruits riding in every day."

"How did he get so many men?" Earp asked.

"Shelby has dragged them in from every KKK-type vigilance group in the American South and even some from above the Mason-Dixon Line."

"Apparently," Katherine said, "the offer of hard cash combined with fertile Méjicano acreage plus free peon labor acts on those unreconstructed rebels like catnip on a cat."

"Has anyone reported on their firepower?" Slater asked.

"We have an informant in their army," Richard said. "He's German—an aspiring writer-philosopher named Friedrich Nietzsche—who had been sneaking dispatches to one of our agents in Nogales."

"You and your sister read one of his books and bent my ears back telling me about it," Katherine said.

"Well, he's in Méjico," Richard said. "Are you familiar with Alfred Krupp?"

"The German arms manufacturer," Katherine said.

"The same," Richard said. "He's somehow coerced Nietzsche, Germany's chancellor—none other than Otto von Bismarck—and his own son, Fritz Krupp, into supplying arms for this operation."

"What does that mean?" Earp asked.

"Krupp is equipping them with some of his bigger field pieces," Richard said.

"Alfred Krupp is running guns for Diaz?" Katherine asked in horror.

"He's furnished Shelby with German 88s, among other things," Richard said.

"What are those?" Rachel asked.

"They're breech-loading, 88mm Kanones—C61s and C64s," Richard explained. "They're the same guns that the German army deployed in the Franco-Prussian war, when they obliterated Metz and Paris and when they flattened the French army at Sedan."

"How many does he have?" Slater asked.

"Three of each," Richard said. "Also at least five hundred Mauser rifles along with ammunition. All of these presents are leftover ordnance from the Franco-Prussian War, but they're said to be in excellent working condition."

"In case you think those weapons don't sound like much," Katherine added, "let me remind you that those guns drove the entire French army—the premier fighting force on the continent—to its knees, forcing them into total, abject, humiliating submission."

"Paris was the biggest, grandest, most heavily fortified city in Europe," Rachel said dismally. "Those guns leveled it, and Rancho de Cielo is just a collection of brick buildings encircled by an adobe wall."

"What's their guns' range?" Slater asked. "I saw firsthand what Sherman's artillery did to our Confederate forces at Shiloh, and those howitzers pre-dated the ones that Shelby will be using here. Even so, Sherman's guns would have wiped this place off the face of the earth."

"Shelby's guns have an effective range of four miles," Richard said.

"With those guns," Katherine said gloomily, "Shelby's men don't even have to attack. The general and his troops can just lay back and let those cannons blow this place to hell and gone."

"And we won't have anything that can touch them," Rachel said.

"Those estimates," Richard said, "are on the high side. Shelby's men aren't seasoned artillery specialists who know how to aim and fire their howitzers under combat conditions."

"But he'll have ex-Confederate soldiers," Earp said. "Some of them will, undoubtedly, be former gunnery sergeants and howitzer officers."

"Perhaps," Richard said, "but they won't know European armaments. It'll be a whole different ballgame."

"Also," Slater said, "since the South had no cannon foundries, our artillery was no good. It blew up and killed more of our gunners than the damn Yankees ever did."

"So what do you estimate will be their effective range?" Katherine asked Richard.

"I'd say under fifteen hundred yards," Richard said. "That's close enough that you can sight the howitzers in under forty-five degrees. It's not point-blank line of sight but it's what we call 'low angle' and it's easy to pull off. Just aim the howitzers a few feet above the buildings and blast away. You don't have to compute trajectories."

"If that's low angle," Katherine asked, "what's 'high angle'?"

"Anything above a forty-five-degree elevation. Those trajectories have a longer flight time, a higher vertex and a steeper angle of descent. They are much trickier to calculate."

"So their big guns," Katherine said, shaking her head sadly, "can pulverize Rancho de Cielo even with inexperienced gunners."

"For a good howitzer," Slater said, "hitting a target at twelve hundred yards isn't as simple as making a pistol shot at point-blank range, but it almost is."

CHAPTER 2

Diaz sat in his hotel suite with the Senorita, James Sutherland and Judith McKillian. He poured them each another snifter of cognac. They had been toasting the devastating effect that Friedrich Krupp's ordnance had had on the generalissimo's targets out on the firing range.

* * *

"Fire at nine hundred yards," the gunnery sergeant shouted.

"Fire!" came the thunderous reply.

The big 88mm cannon bucked on its chassis with indescribable force, and, up range, the target vanished into a blazing explosion of splinters and sawdust, of dirt and fire.

"Fifteen hundred yards!"

The same.

"Two thousand yards."

More of the same.

"Thirty-five hundred yards."

Krupp was personally turning the elevation screws on his three Mitrailleuses—each of whose firing plates contained twenty-five 770-grain, .50-caliber rounds—sighting in the big guns.

Again, the orders to fire.

Nine hundred yards.

Fifteen hundred yards.

Two thousand yards.

Thirty-five hundred yards.

Krupp blew their targets to smithereens.

At a thousand yards, Krupp's Mauser rifle hit its targets dead center.

The artillery pieces, the rapid-fire guns, even the Mauser bolt-action clip-fed rifles were his to command.

That day, he was the master of the Durango test range.

* * *

Diaz raised his brandy snifter, and his friends lifted theirs in unison.

"To the retaking of the Arizona Territory."

"Hear, hear," Sutherland shouted.

"At last!" the Senorita dramatically declaimed, seconding the generalissimo's salutation.

"To victory!" Judith McKillian enthused.

"So Senor Krupp is finally coming through for us," Diaz said, shaking his head repeatedly, utterly incredulous.

"All these years he's been visiting us on his North and South American sales tours," Sutherland said, "all the hundreds of promises he's made, the weapons systems he's promised us, but we could not arrange the financing for."

"He wanted 'cash on the barrelhead,' he called it," Diaz said, perplexed. "He was adamant that we pay up front. It's as if he didn't trust us."

"I wonder why he was so hesitant?" the Senorita said.

"Maybe thought we'd stiff him on the bill," Judith McKillian sniffed haughtily.

For a long moment, there was dead silence, then all four friends burst into laughter.

"Senor Krupp knows us all too well," Sutherland finally said, wiping the tears of mirth out of his eyes.

"Now," the Senorita said, helping herself to another long, restorative pull on her cognac, "out of the blue that old miser, Alfred Krupp, bestows on us...*free guns*."

"Great big free guns," Judith McKillian said.

"Bestowing on us, gratis," Sutherland said, "six of the very guns that drove those French bastards to their knees at Sedan."

"And forced Louis Napoleon to raise his hands like a little girl," the Senorita said, "and surrender to the Kaiser, white flags flapping merrily in the breeze."

"Not that Louis was all that merry about it," Sutherland said. "If memory serves, he was more than a little put out—getting clapped into irons and all that."

"I'd like to say," the Senorita said, coughing into her fist with false, sheepish modesty, "that Judith and I were more than a little responsible for Fritz Krupp's cooperation."

"You didn't, did you?" Diaz asked, chuckling. "Really?"

"No," McKillian said, "he doesn't favor women such as ourselves."

"But we did find the key to his heart," the Senorita said.

"And other organs of his body," McKillian said, chortling.

The four of them all but collapsed with vituperative laughter.

"Of course," Diaz said, after the hilarity subsided, "our newfound military might will not come cheap. The Krupp family expects us to cough up a king's ransom in gold and silver bullion for all that new, top-of-the-line weaponry that they want to sell us down the road."

"We'll just have to make those damnably lazy peon miners heave to," Sutherland said.

"I'll see to it personally," Judith McKillian said to Diaz, "that those indolent wretches extract that ore for you, dear Porfirio, if I have to flog the work out of them myself."

"Look on the bright side, Porfirio," Sutherland said, slapping Diaz on the knee, "that'll be some damn fine ordnance that you'll be buying. If Santa Ana had had those guns at Chapultapec, it'd have been a whole different story. He'd have annexed half of America."

"Rather than the other way around," the Senorita said with genuine bitterness.

"So I'll gladly purchase them from him," Diaz said, "and all the other armaments he is willing to sell us, and in the meantime we will get ample use out of those weapons that he has so graciously conferred on us as 'a sweetener.'"

"It is as if they were gifts from the gods," Judith McKillian said.

"With those guns," Diaz said, "General Shelby and his regiments will steamroll over the gringos at El Rancho de Cielo."

"Like Moltke crushed the French in 1871," Sutherland said.

"Indeed," Diaz agreed. "We will begin the reconquest of that territory that the gringos so boorishly filched from us, starting with Arizona. At its legendary Rancho de Cielo, we will drink deep and celebrate an overwhelming victory."

"Excelente," the Senorita said. "But make sure you buy any and all of the Krupp cannons that Alfred will sell you. We'll need every bit of that firepower. Those Americano hideputas won't be ignorant for long. One day they may sabe what happened, and when they do, they won't be pleased with us."

"When they finally figure out who was behind the retaking of Arizona," Judith McKillian said, chuckling happily, "they will be very put out indeed."

"Highly put upon," James Sutherland said, joining Judith McKillian in her laughter.

"Especially when they learn who the new owner of Rancho de Cielo really is," Judith McKillian said, refilling her cognac snifter to the brim, then enjoying a hearty gulp. Holding it in her mouth, she savored the taste of the exquisite brandy a long moment.

"You don't want those Americanos coming down here again and taking half of Chihuahua," the Senorita said.

"And then helping themselves to northern Sonora," Sutherland said.

"When the gringos do come after us this next time," Diaz said, "it won't be like the Battle of Chapultapec and the sacking of Cuidad Méjico. This time we'll be ready for them."

"We'll kick their sorry asses all the way back across the Rio Grande and beyond," the Senorita said, "our victory-sated troops howling for their cowardly gringo hides every step of the way."

"With the arms of Krupp fully ablaze!" Sutherland shouted.

The two women instantly raised their cognac snifters, and the men followed, all of them offering toasts to Alfred and Fritz Krupp and to their inestimable Kruppwerk. Drinking, laughing, slapping each other on the backs and thighs, they drank toast after toast to the Krupps and their German Reich long into the night.

CHAPTER 3

"You said that Krupp sent Diaz five hundred Mausers too," Katherine said. "Are they any good?"

She was still seated in her living room with Slater, Belle and the group he'd assembled.

"They're the best rifles on earth," Richard said. "Bolt-action, magazine-fed, with eight .43-caliber rounds apiece, they have muzzle velocities of well over fourteen hundred feet per second and effective ranges of almost a mile. Even worse, every one of Shelby's troops will be highly proficient with any kind of small arms, and they'll be well versed in hand-to-hand."

"So Shelby's forces outnumber us more than ten to one," Earp said, "and he's coming at us with heavy-duty howitzers, rapid-fire field guns and the finest bolt-action rifles on earth. And we have what? Nada?"

"Not exactly nada," Richard said. "We have a few cards up our sleeves, which we hope Shelby doesn't know about."

"Like what?" Doc asked.

"Five Gatling guns and three Mitrailleuses."

"Mit-what?" Masterson asked.

"Mitrailleuses," Richard said. "They're the same as Diaz has: French rapid-fire weapons left over from the Franco-Prussian War. Krupp confiscated them after the German army wiped out the French at Sedan and gave them to Grant as a present. He and Sheridan sent them along with some Gatlings to Fort Apache to use on Geronimo. With the cavalry chasing Geronimo all over hell's creation, no one was watching the store at the fort, so I 'requisitioned' them."

"Meaning, you stole them," Katherine said.

"The army might very well conclude that," Richard said, "when they finally give up on Geronimo and return."

"Doesn't the US Army need these Gatlings?" Katherine finally asked, after the men calmed down.

"The US Army doesn't understand rapid-fire ordnance," Richard said. "The Gatling gun was available in 1863, but the US Army never ordered any to use in the Civil War. And they needed them during the last two years of that war. Some commanders bought a few, using their own funds, but, otherwise, they weren't deployed very much. They used them at the Siege of Petersburg but that was against a fortification. That's not the way to use them. Artillery would have been more effective.

"Custer could have taken Gatlings with him," Richard continued, "when he rode into the Valley of the Little Bighorn but turned them down. And they were there. Had he taken them, Crazy Horse and Sitting Bull would have joined their ancestors in the Shadowland that very day, and President Grant would have made Custer a general the next day."

"What about those French rapid-fire weapons that you have?" Slater asked. "How do they work? I've fired Gatlings but not those French guns."

"They fire twenty-five rounds simultaneously in a single burst," Richard said, "and the French, historically, have used them like howitzers that were loaded with cannister or grapeshot. Unfortunately, for the Mitrailleuses, howitzers loaded with cannister are more effective at long distances, which are the kinds of ranges that the French use them for. They're also tricky. I've never had much luck hitting anything with one."

Richard turned toward Slater. "Torn, I've had some unusual experiences with rapid-fire weapons down in Méjico and have a few ideas about using them in a different way. The US Army doesn't think much of my ideas, but I'd like to discuss them with you."

"Which is a long way of saying," Rachel said, "that the US Army thinks that Richard got lucky down in Méjico, that he was fighting muchos stupidos Méjicanos and that his 'tactical innovations' would never work against real soldiers."

"By real soldiers," Katherine said, "the Army means white men."

"Are you saying," Slater asked, "that the Army thinks Richard is full of shit?"

"In a word," Katherine said, "yes."

Treating Katherine to a rare, if fleeting, smile, Slater said:

"I like Richard's ideas already."

PART XIX

"Tomorrow will be a day that madre Méjico and the heroes of the Confederate States of America will remember for all time to come—the day Porfirio commenced reclaiming those cherished lands that the United States so ignobly stole from his country almost forty years ago. Tomorrow will also mark the Confederacy's new birth of freedom, as it begins its long-awaited drive to vanquish its Northern oppressors and to reclaim its rightful place on the continent."

—General Joseph O. Shelby, Confederate States Army

CHAPTER 1

Friedrich Nietzsche led Bismarck and Krupp into a Nogales cantina, which he'd been frequenting for the last week or two. The three of them were dressed in white suits, matching shirts, black cravats and boots. Diaz had forced three federale guards on them. Armed with holstered pistols, they followed them at a discreet distance.

By Méjicano standards, the cantina was high quality. In the far corner, a band—made up of a half dozen different kinds of guitars, four horns and one very superior violinist—played all the great Méjicano standards. At the moment, at Nietzsche's request, they were performing the plaintive and hauntingly beautiful ballad "La Golondrina." The kitchen boasted a large and varied menu, emphasizing beef, chicken and seafood.

"Their pollo con mole y frijoles is superb," Nietzsche said to his friends. "If you're hungry, that is."

"I'd sooner eat shit," Bismarck said.

"I'll try it," Krupp said. "It has to be safer than that execrable excrement that the hotel serves us."

"I don't trust Diaz and his cronies not to poison us," Nietzsche said.

He waved to their waitress. Dressed in a white skirt, blouse, her shoulders covered by a red rebozo, she responded with a wide smile and rushed over to their table.

"I'll try the pollo con mole con frijoles," Krupp said.

Nietzsche ordered the same.

"I've been coming here for the last week," Nietzsche said. "Rosario and I have become amigos bonos." Good friends.

"Young Nietzsche," Bismarck said, "we're all men of the world and gentlemen of fortune. We understand these things."

Nietzsche shook his head, dismayed. "It's not what you think." He lowered his voice. "She's my contact with the outside world. She's seeing a US Army lieutenant and can forward any messages we might have to him."

Bismarck nodded approvingly. "She could be useful. I, for one, am not eager to see Diaz acquiring anymore territory than he already has—unless it's the six-foot plot they bury him in."

They raised their tequila glasses in a toast and drank.

"That goes double for the Senorita and Judith McKillian," Nietzsche said.

"And James Sutherland," Krupp said.

"I'm tempted to add your father to our list of miscreants," Bismarck said. "He's armed Diaz and his friends with some very effective artillery."

"I don't know about you," Nietzsche said, "but I feel somehow responsible."

"There should have been something that the three of us could have done," Bismarck said, "to stop Diaz and Shelby in this foolishness."

"I *am* responsible," Fritz Krupp said.

"Nonsense," Bismarck said, clapping his friend on the shoulder, "you didn't ship Diaz those big guns. Your father did."

Nietzsche wanted to say "your morally deranged father did," but, for once in his life, he held his tongue.

"Well," Krupp said, "Herr Nietzsche here can smuggle military intelligence to Katherine Ryan through the military. That ought to be worth something."

"And that's not all I can smuggle," Nietzsche said.

The two men stared at their friend.

"If you two want to get out of this place," Nietzsche said, "and break for the border, Rosario and her gringo friends can arrange for that too."

"How?" Krupp asked.

"When we come here tomorrow night," Nietzsche said, "we'll walk out the door to the railhead, while some of her friends distract the guards."

"Why would they do that?" Bismarck asked.

"Why do you think?" Krupp said, instantly understanding the situation. "We'll pay them."

"How will they distract them?" Bismarck said.

"With spring-loaded blackjacks," Nietzsche said. "They will then spirit us quickly into US territory."

"What would we do there?" Bismarck asked.

"I don't know about you two," Nietzsche said, "but I'm a former artillery and cavalry officer. There's nothing I don't know about those big guns or swinging a saber on horseback."

"And you would do...*what?*" Bismarck asked.

"I would offer Katherine Ryan my services in defense of Rancho de Cielo," Nietzsche said.

"You'd be joining a force that will be hopelessly outnumbered," Krupp said.

"And outgunned," Bismarck said.

"I used those—that Diaz has now—guns to obliterate the French," Bismarck said. "I've seen them in action. Katherine Ryan has no idea what she's in for. She'll think she's facing the Apocalypse of Revelation on the Plains of Armageddon."

"Then I say 'Viva la Guerra!'" Nietzsche said, raising his glass. Here's to war. "Viva l'amor!" Here's to love. "Y viva la meurte!" Here's to death.

Nietzsche threw back his drink, while his friends groaned. Bismarck poured each of them another round.

"Count me in," Bismarck said. He drained his glass.

"I can't let you two go to hell alone," Fritz Krupp said—and drained his.

Nietzsche gulped his drink as well.

Friedrich Nietzsche, Fritz Krupp and the Iron Chancellor were going to war.

CHAPTER 2

Slater sat in the kitchen with Richard, Katherine and Rachel. A fire-blackened coffeepot and cups sat on the table between them. Richard poured each of them a cup of Arbuckles'.

"I understand rapid-fire ordnance," Richard said, "even if the US Army doesn't. I used a couple of Gatlings against infantry charges down in Méjico. I saw what they could do to men at close ranges—at less than four hundred yards. Our men laid down intersecting fire, and when the enemy entered those kill zones, those Gatlings turned into murder machines. They cut Diaz's men down like Death's sickle."

"The US Army doesn't understand that?" Slater asked.

"They have artillery on the brain," Richard said.

"What kind of force did you use your Gatlings against?" Slater asked.

"The armies of Chihuahua and Sinoloa," Richard said. "They outnumbered us ten to one."

"Were they seasoned veterans," Slater asked, "disciplined and well trained? Not prone to cut and run?"

"They were tough but raw—recruits, really," Richard said. "Turning and running, though, wasn't a viable option. Diaz armed his officers with multiple revolvers and deployed them directly behind his peon army. They gunned down any soldadoes who did not charge straight at us. Those officers killed far more of their own troops than they did their enemy, namely, us. They drove those conscripts toward our guns like they were cattle. But, yes, those were relentless. Most of them never faltered, and we killed them by the thousands."

"How old were they?" Slater asked.

"Mostly they were young boys and old men," Richard said. "Two weeks earlier, they had been picking cotton, chopping sugarcane or digging ore. Still, no army could have stood up to what we threw at them. We'd even mined the battlefield. They thought they were charging the End Times, and they were."

"Well, we'll be facing some of the most seasoned killers in history," Slater said, "men that fought at Gettysburg, Spotsylvania, Chickamauga, Vicksburg, Cold Harbor, Chancellorsville and the Wilderness. They don't care or quit, and they don't scare. They'll fight you to the last cartridge and to the knives. You better have more than a theory up your sleeve, because when you hear that rebel yell—that *yiiiiippppppppeeeeeee!!!*—and see that crazed glint in their narrowed eyes, it'll freeze you to your marrow. They'll keep coming and coming and coming, and they will not quit until every damn one of them is dead and in the ground. I know. I lived and fought and died with them. Not one of them I ever wanted to see again after that, but if I ever had to go into battle again, those are the kind of men I'd want backing my hand and covering my flank. I hate like hell to be staring into their bloody eyes and blazing gun barrels now."

"Our intel says they're on the march," Richard said. "They should be here in a couple of days."

"Meaning, we don't have time to mine the battlefield," Katherine said.

"Nor do we have enough caps and fuses," Richard said.

"We need layered perimeters," Slater said, "defense in depth, so when one line of defense crumbles, our men can fall back to the next fortified position. But we don't have time for that either. As it stands now, we'll be lucky to dig firing pits and a few trenches, let alone build multiple fortified breastworks. Also we have no way to silence those damned howitzers."

"We can do it, Torn," Richard said evenly. "We can stop those damn rebs, and I got something to silence their howitzers as well."

"Really?" Slater asked. "They'll be deployed half a battlefield away."

"That one's easy," Richard said, smiling. "I'm going to treat those bad old boys to the most terrifying, mortifying weapon ever devised for war or the owlhoot. I'm going to introduce those sons of bitches to...*you*."

CHAPTER 3

Nietzsche, Bismarck and Krupp sat in a closed boxcar, dressed in old frayed clothes—their good clothes stuffed in grain sacks. They were on a train headed north to Rancho de Cielo, surrounded by peasants en route to God only knew. The car was unventilated and hotter than Hades. Nietzsche was uncomfortable, but as a student of the ancient stoics, he had, in times of inexorable distress, learned to adopt an attitude of imperturbable forbearance and indefatigable detachment. That philosophy had allowed him to endure many agonizing crises, most notably his not infrequent medical ailments.

But his companions didn't understand classical stoicism.

They were sweltering, fatigued and depressed—and didn't care who knew it. Bismarck was especially irate. He raved continually about all the joys and pleasures that he was missing out on in Germany, that he was instead forced to endure the tortures of hell on this godforsaken continent, in this squalid joke of a country.

"I could have been on my estate—in Friedrichsruh Castle in the Sachsenwald—riding with my hounds and running down the hares. I could be boating on one of my numerous and beauteous lakes on one of my innumerable yachts. I could have been sitting in a comfortable stuffed chair, drinking Chateau LaFite Rothchild—1882 was one of the great years—listening serenely to the most sublime chamber music imaginable. I could have been transported by Wolfgang Amadeus Mozart's "Gran Partita," or his "Serenade No. 10" with its twelve winds and string bass, the piece that convinced Antonio Salieri that Mozart was, indeed, 'the voice of God.' Instead, I have to suffer all the illimitable indignities that this abysmally abject continent has to offer—afflictions worse than the Fourteen Stations that the Savior had suffered on His cross. If Sutherland, Diaz and those two harpies from hell weren't enough, I'm now in Méjico in a sealed boxcar in 120 degree heat, a hunted man, a price on my head, bouncing and jouncing with every bump, rattling around in this deathtrap of a sweatbox and banging off its sides, like a stone in a tin can, exuding piss, shit, sweat and blood from every pore like, like, like—"

"Like a pork roasting on a spit with an apple in his mouth," Nietzsche said, suggesting an apt simile.

"I prefer baked ham with cloves and pineapple," Krupp said, "and a very cold Riesling."

"You know I was quite a beer drinker in college," Nietzsche said. "I could go for a stein of strong German lager right now with foam drooling over the sides."

"Frosty and icy," Krupp said, "frigid as liquid CO_2, painfully, almost undrinkably...*cold.*"

"And caviar on the side and little toast points," Nietzsche said.

"And you're reminding me how hungry I am!" Bismarck growled.

Suddenly, Nietzsche felt sorry for the older man. The journey—which had been an arduous, nerve-racking ordeal—had been hard on all of them. He was relatively young, however, and Bismarck was up in years. Used to the easy life, their odyssey had, for the Iron Chancellor, been brutal. He'd become in his discomfort so angry that at times he reminded Nietzsche of a gut-shot grizzly bear. Nietzsche had earlier encouraged him to view their odyssey as "a grand adventure," which only inspired Bismarck to even more furiously fulminating heights. Toward the end, he seemed to have confused himself with Odysseus in the *Odyssey* shouting:

"I'm getting blinded by the cyclops!"

Or: "This time Circe's turning *me* into a goddamned pig!"

And finally: "The Sirens are fucking me to death!"

Yes, the trip had been one long dark night of the soul for Otto von Bismarck.

* * *

Their journey had begun the night that they'd returned to the cantina. Even before they could eat their dinner, a contingent of trollops had lured their guards into a side room with enticements of free threesomes. Instead of erotic entanglements, however, the men were met by bearded revolucionarios with crisscrossed bandoleers and wrist quirts, whose buttstocks were weighted with lead shot. A couple of cracks from these makeshift blackjacks and their guards were taking head-throbbing siestas.

Then Rosario's amigos escorted the three friends out a back door and through a labyrinth of alleyways. Halfway down one of the passageways, Rosario hustled them into a cul-de-sac and handed them peasant garb—white cotton shirts, pants with rope belts, straw narrow-brim sombreros and sandals. She let them carry the clothes they had worn—as well as their watches, rings and wallets—in grain sacks. After threading the rest of the alleyway maze, they ended up on the north end of Durango. The men and Rosario had horses waiting for them, and they were kind enough to lead Nietzsche and his friends to the train station.

But to the three men's chagrin, they told them they'd be safer riding with the peons in the boxcars.

"The federales never check our cholos in the animal cars," Rosario explained. "They have no money for the mordida"—for a bribe—"so what's the point? You three, on the other hand, are conspicuous, and they would more than likely catch you. So stay with the peons, and you should reach Nogales on the American border in under two days."

They did, and now the train was pulling into Nogales—on the American side.

* * *

At last, Nietzsche was able to breathe a little easier.

"At the next stop," he said to his friends, "we can jump off, change our clothes and get ourselves a first-class compartment."

"I hope they have food and liquor," Bismarck said grumpily.

"I expect they do," Krupp said. "I expect they do."

CHAPTER 4

A sergeant finally led Sutherland, the Senorita and the McKillian woman to General Shelby's white canvas command tent. As they seated themselves on folding camp stools, they noticed the general in a corner, bent over a map table. A coal-oil lamp provided illumination.

They had made the trip there in an old, uncomfortable, wood-burning train. Traveling incognito, they had dressed plainly. The women wore long skirts with blouses buttoned to the neck. The two men were dressed in old, dark suits. Diaz favored a center-creased, woven-straw Panama hat, while Sutherland was decked out in a black flat-crowned, narrow-brimmed John Bull.

The two woman had complained the entire trip about the shabbiness of their couture.

* * *

"I don't see why we have to dress up like impoverished old... hags,*" Judith McKillian complained at least once every five minutes on the train ride up from Durango.*

"I don't care who knows who I am or what I am doing," the Senorita shouted at Diaz and Sutherland. "I ought to be able to dress however I want. This is an outrage."

Sutherland, however, explained to the irate women:

"Senorita, because in your teens, you were temporarily adopted by an El Paso Texas family, you have dual citizenship in both Méjico and the US. I, too, have acquired passports for both countries, because I do so much business

in America. Porfirio, however, is in a more anomalous situation. True, he has a Méjicano diplomatic passport, but as a foreign leader, he is not supposed to visit another country without notifying the country's department of state. Not only do countries insist on providing security for visiting heads of state, they also make a clandestine attempt to track and keep tabs on them—to make sure that, when they travel around their country, they aren't up to international mischief. It's a mutual understanding that all nations have, honor and respect. What we're doing is a major breach of protocol.

"Furthermore," Sutherland continued, "we are committing an act of war against the United States of America."

"But these clothes," McKillian said, her upper lip curling over her front teeth, "are so disgustingly...common."

"And for what we are about to do up north, we could be lined up against a wall and...shot!" Diaz whispered irascibly.

"So Judith and I have to wear these godawful rags?" the Senorita asked.

"Really," Sutherland said, growing impatient with the women's outbursts, "would it be better if John Philip Sousa and a one-hundred-piece military band followed you around, announcing your presence, every step of the way with stirring march music? Would that appease your obviously insatiable vanity?"

"Don't the words 'They'll shoot you against a wall' mean anything to you?" Diaz asked.

"Oh, really, Porfirio," Judith McKillian said, "shooting men against walls is something that the barbarians in your benighted land do. This is the United States of America. The people here don't do such things."

"Why is that?" Sutherland asked. "Do you suppose that Americans view such acts as...gauche? Or...outré?"

"They don't know the meaning of those words," McKillian said.

"No?" Diaz asked. "What do they do to traitors and spies up there?"

"They hang their miscreants by the neck until dead," Judith McKillian said.

"I thought you knew," the Senorita said to Diaz.

"They do the same in England," Sutherland said dryly. "It is much more civilized."

"After all," the Senorita said, patting the top of Diaz's hand gently, "shooting our enemies against a wall is rather...plebian, isn't it?"

* * *

But, at last, they were with Shelby and his army.

Now it was late dusk. Shelby's executive officer, John Newman Edwards, entered the tent. He also wore a Confederate officer's uniform. Frank James was with him. Wearing a black suit and matching tie, he was taking occasional sips from a liquor flask that he kept in an inside pocket.

Tired from the trip, Diaz and his friends were nonetheless excited by the prospective battle to come. They, too, planned to enjoy watching Shelby's abundantly equipped force of two thousand battle-hardened ex-Confederates overpower, overrun, annihilate and then plunder El Rancho de Cielo. In fact, they all planned on sharing in El Rancho's legendary riches—its sprawling croplands and prodigious mineral reserves.

The general extricated himself from his map work. Pulling up a camp stool, he sat down with his visitors. Edwards unfolded a camp stool and sat next to the general. Shelby then treated them to a wide, confident smile.

"Tomorrow," he said, "will be a day that madre Méjico and the heroes of the Confederate States of America will remember for all time to come—the day Porfirio commenced reclaiming those cherished lands that the United States so ignobly stole from his country almost forty years ago. Tomorrow will also mark the Confederacy's new birth of freedom, as it begins its long-awaited drive to vanquish its Northern oppressors and to reclaim its rightful place on the continent."

With his spine stiff, eyes blazing and baritone voice, Shelby looked and sounded like the embodiment of Southern manhood—not that his gray Confederate uniform was all that prepossessing. Since the battle would begin at dawn, he wore nothing that indicated his rank—no stars, insignia or epaulets of any kind. His poise, bearing and presence, however, spoke volumes. This was a man born to issue orders, who brooked neither doubt nor equivocation from his subordinates to say nothing of defiance.

"So you believe that in the morning the tide of victory will favor us?" Diaz asked.

"Victory will be ours, and it will inundate us with military spoils," the general said.

"Bravo!" Diaz shouted.

Sutherland and the two women joined Diaz in showering Shelby with thanks and congratulations.

PART XX

He would be the true Father of Madre Méjico, not that indio-hideputa whom everyone hero-worshiped and genuflected before as if he were the Son of God and the Aztec's version of Christ Crucified, Quetzalcoatl, rolled up into one: Benito Pablo Juárez.

God, how Diaz loathed that man. Everywhere he went, all he heard was Juarez, Juarez, Juarez. Everyone said that Juarez was the heart and soul of Méjico, all that was good and noble in his country, its founder and progenitor. And if Benito Pablo Juárez was Méjico's soul, Diaz—his detractors said—was its iron boot.

—El Presidente Porfirio Diaz, reflecting on the life of Benito Pablo Juárez

CHAPTER 1

Shortly after midnight, Friedrich Nietzsche, Otto von Bismarck and Fritz Krupp reached El Rancho de Cielo and joined Katherine and her friends in her parlor. It had been a long, hard trip. Still, everyone was up, busy going over their battle plans—especially how to deal with Shelby's impending artillery volleys—which they expected to commence at dawn.

Through an open door, Nietzsche noticed the dining room. On the dining room table, he noticed a roast beef and a baked ham, which were partially sliced, and loaves of bread. Butter dishes were on the table as were bottles of wine and liquor. He also saw three coffeepots were on a kitchen stove. It was a welcome sight. He and his friends had eaten almost nothing during the last few days.

Katherine sensed as much.

"We're ignoring our responsibilities as hosts," she said. "These men have had a hard, long trip. Let's you and I see that these people have something to eat and drink. Would you prefer coffee or alcohol?"

Nietzsche and his friends opted for alcohol and sat down on comfortable, stuffed chairs, where they were quickly served food and drink. Nietzsche then introduced himself, Bismarck and Krupp to those assembled.

"We naturally know who all of you are," Katherine said. "My children have even read Herr Nietzsche's writings—in German no less. They can't stop talking about them. Rachel, what is that book of his you're always quoting?"

"In English the title would translate as *Human, All Too Human*," Rachel said.

"Its sequel," Richard added, "is *The Wanderer and His Shadow*."

"So yes, we know who the three of you are, but what on earth brings you here?" Katherine asked. "You could not have arrived at a more unpropitious time. At dawn, a General Jo Shelby plans to shell us off the face of the earth. Still, you are welcome to bunker down and sit the battle out if you so choose."

"If we can," Nietzsche said, "we'd like to help. We were visiting Méjico, when Shelby and Diaz dreamed up this damn war. We are all appalled at Diaz and how he runs Méjico. His financial backers—Judith McKillian, the Englishman, James Sutherland and that harridan from hell known as La Senorita Dolorosa—are every bit as violent, ruthless and sadistic as Diaz himself. We escaped as soon as we could."

"Remaining in their company and pretending to be their allies," Krupp said, "was no longer a tolerable option. They are far beyond the pale of anything that is even remotely acceptable."

"You don't have to waste your time explaining those people to us," Katherine said. "We've all had considerable ring time with them."

"All of them," Rachel said.

"Then," Bismarck said, "you know that Diaz is arming Shelby's attack on you and your ranch?"

"We had suspected someone was backing his play," Katherine said. "He was too well equipped."

"And it makes sense," Richard said. "Diaz and the Senorita had gazed on the Arizona Territory—and especially on my mother's holdings—with covetous eyes for decades."

"Which is why we are here," Nietzsche said.

"We will do anything to assist," Bismarck said.

"Anything," Krupp said.

"Perhaps you can tell us about their weaponry for starters," Katherine said. "Their range, accuracy, firing rates."

"There is nothing," Krupp said, "about their armaments that I do not know."

"Really?" Katherine asked.

"Why wouldn't he know everything about Diaz's ordnance?" Nietzsche asked. "His family is the biggest arms manufacturer on earth, and his father is the man who gave Diaz all the artillery that he is about to deploy against you."

"Against us," Bismarck reminded Nietzsche. "We're on their side now."

"Technically," Krupp said, "my father did not give Diaz those weapons. He described them in a cable as 'a sweetener' to an even larger possible arms sale."

"And, Kaiser Wilhelm," Bismarck said, "is gracing that deal with his most generous blessing."

"I doubt, however," Nietzsche said, "that they ever imagined Diaz would turn those guns against America."

"But that is what he is doing," Krupp said, "and I can prepare you for what will happen tomorrow. And as they say, 'To be forewarned is to be forearmed.'"

"Then," Bismarck said, taking a long pull on his brandy glass and raising a sandwich with the other hand, "we better get started."

CHAPTER 2

The Senorita, Sutherland and Judith McKillian stood on a grassy hill, slightly to the rear of Shelby, Edwards and Diaz. They were all well positioned—staring down over a rectangular strip of parched grassland nearly a mile and a half in length and a half mile wide.

Before them, on that battleground, knelt Shelby's widely spread-out battalion of nearly two thousand ex-Confederates. Approximately eight hundred yards downfield were deployed Krupp's armaments—a total of three steel, breech-loading C61 and C64 howitzers and two Mitrailleuse de Reffye 'Canon a Balles.'

Since the goal was to keep the attack as anonymous as possible and not to bring the wrath of Washington, DC, and the US Army down on them, their troops were self-clothed, wearing mufti instead of uniforms. They were, however, well armed. Shelby had provided Mausers to those men who lacked repeating rifles.

In the dim distance, a mile and a half away, lay Rancho de Cielo. In front of the corners of its surrounding wall, two Gatling guns were deployed in firing pits. In the center of the field, just in front of the rancho, six Mitrailleuses de Reffyes were similarly positioned. Diaz had told them that his informants told them that they had approximately 150 men hidden along the inside top of the wall, armed with repeating rifles. El generalissimo had dismissed that opposing force as "a contingent of insignificant insects."

"Could you remind me," Judith McKillian asked no one in particular, "why on earth all those troops are assembled on this field? Are they seizing this land for madre Méjico or for the United Confederate States of America?"

"Neither," Sutherland said. "If anyone asked, we are to say that these men are just ranchers who feel that Katherine Ryan had unfairly driven them all off their lands. They are simply reclaiming what was rightfully theirs."

"And we are here...*because?*" McKillian asked.

"Because after the battle, there might be some land acquisition possibilities," the Senorita said. "The Ryan holdings are far too vast, valuable and far-flung for any of the riffraff down there to control and manage. We, on the other hand, own Méjicano haciendas that are millions of acres in size. We have the finances and expertise to run this operation."

"We could do it without breaking a sweat," James Sutherland averred, smiling sweetly.

"How philanthropically generous of us," Diaz said.

Diaz was now turning away from Shelby and Edwards and rejoining his three business associates.

"You may wish to plug your ears," Diaz said, pulling out his pocket watch. "It is now 4:40 AM. In a few minutes, the general will give the signal and the artillery will begin their barrage. They will shell those buildings downfield for at least an hour and a half. Afterward our men shall descend on them like wolves on the fold. They will sweep El Rancho with bullets and bayonets, killing any and all living things that get in their way. The spoils, for all of us, will be...*immense.* Méjico will at last regain all that territory that was so loutishly taken from us almost forty years ago. The first battle in the Second Mexican-American War will have been joined, fought and won."

"And the Second Confederacy will undergo a New Birth of Freedom," Shelby said solemnly.

"And we shall bring the United States of America weeping to its knees!" John Newman Edwards shouted ecstatically.

Shelby turned and commanded his artillery officers at the top of his lungs to:

"FIRE AT WILL!"

The gunnery teams prepared their breech-loading howitzers for the battle to come.

Diaz and everyone else on the hill inserted cotton plugs in their ears.

CHAPTER 3

Torn Slater and Belle Starr were also in a good position to observe the battle to come. The fortlike rancho not only boasted high whitewashed adobe-brick walls, on the corners, facing the battlefield, were mounted vertiginously high watchtowers. Slater's crow's nest was square, eight feet across. Surrounded by wooden railings, he sat on its only stool. Belle was his spotter. Standing next to him, she studied the terrain below. Perched more than a hundred feet over the battleground, they could see everything through their spyglasses and sniper scopes.

Earlier, Slater had carved a groove into the watchtower's front railing, and now his Big Fifty Sharps rifle rested on it. He had an especially good view of Shelby's big guns. Piles of massive shells, gleaming with brass powder casings, were stacked up beside the ordnance.

* * *

Earlier that evening, Fritz Krupp and Bismarck had stood with Slater in his watchtower and had worked out a strategy for confronting Shelby's artillery. Since Krupp's firm had built the guns and Germany had faced the French Mitrailleuses de Reffyes in the Franco-Prussian War, Krupp understood what those guns could do and could not do.

"Yes," Krupp said, "I understand that their effective ranges are well over three thousand yards, but you have to understand that when it comes to artillery, Diaz and his men are amateurs. Their effective range will be less than

twelve hundred yards, which is why you can see those guns moving into place at that range now."

Sure enough, horses were hauling those howitzers, mounted on caissons, toward the front of the troops, the front row of which was positioned less than twelve hundred yards from the rancho's front wall.

"Herr Slater," Krupp said, "Richard Ryan says that he has seen you kill men with a .50-caliber Sharps rifle from more than twelve hundred yards. He also tells me that he has been practicing his marksmanship and can now shoot almost as well at a thousand yards."

Slater said nothing.

"It was provident that he has practiced his marksmanship," Krupp said.

"Are any of your other friends expert shots with a .50-caliber Sharps?" Bismarck asked.

"Bat Masterson was a buffalo hunter," Slater said. "He was bringing down bison from those distances when he was eighteen years old."

"Really?" Bismarck said.

"He was with Billy Dixon at Adobe Walls when Billy killed a Comanche from a mile away with a Big Fifty. Bat paced it off later. A lot of us though thought Bat was the one who made the shot, though he denies it."

"Amazing," Krupp said.

"My old friend, Bill Hickok, killed him a couple of Confederate generals from that distance with a Sharps. What we're doing tomorrow would have been child's play for him."

Bismarck placed a surprisingly congenial hand on Slater's shoulder.

"You know," Bismarck said, "I've always had a special feeling for Americans. My oldest, closest friend, John L. Motley, was an American. Minister to Austria during your Civil War, he convinced me that the North was on the right side of that conflict. He and I worked to keep Europe neutral during that conflict. I liked to think John and I helped Lincoln win that war."

"I fought with the rebs," Slater said.

"I can't say I'm sorry things didn't work out for you," Bismarck said.

"Fighting in that damn war," Slater said, "wasn't maybe the dumbest thing I ever done, but it was up there."

"One reason I agreed to come to this hellish place," Bismarck said, "I'd hoped to travel to your country and visit John's grave."

Neither Krupp nor Slater knew what to say to that one, so both men looked away and said nothing.

Clearing his throat, Krupp said, "Now about those Mitrailleuse de Reffye: There is something you have to understand...."

* * *

"Torn," Belle said, staring up-field through her telescope and shaking Slater out of his revery. "Shelby's howitzer crew—the one to our far left—is swinging into action. They're starting to focus on that pile of shells. One of them is bending over one, and he's picking it up and—"

CHAPTER 4

Diaz, Shelby and their friends stood on the hill staring through spyglasses at the enormous army that Shelby—with the help of Frank James—had so meticulously assembled. They were particularly focused on the firing crews surrounding their big guns. Those artillery bombardments were expected to soften up—in fact, level—Rancho de Cielo in anticipation of the infantry assault.

One man was already lifting the first howitzer shell from the huge shell pile to the gun's rear. He was about to carry it to the breech-loader and insert it into the firing chamber. He was just turning around toward the howitzer, the big shell cradled in his arms.

When, at that precise moment, the first rifle shot from El Rancho de Cielo rang out.

Whitish smoke immediately blossomed in a high, impossibly distant watchtower overlooking El Rancho de Cielo and the battlefield—a watchtower situated almost two-thirds of a mile from the howitzers.

The man's head exploded, blasting gray matter all over the shell pile and the men surrounding him.

"Only one man I knew could shoot like that," Frank James announced to Diaz and his friends.

He then helped himself to his brandy flask.

"Outlaw Torn Slater," Sutherland said sadly, knowingly.

"I, too, have witnessed his prowess with that repugnant rifle," Judith McKillian hissed bitterly.

But then other shots were now cracking, and more whitish smoke clouds were filling then enshrouding the Rancho's two other watchtowers.

Downfield, men in the firing teams, manning the big guns, were instantly going down, dropping like clownish marionettes, their taut strings brusquely, briskly and unexpectedly...*cut.*

"Now those impudent devils have deployed two other Torn Slaters, who are picking off our artillery crews," Sutherland said indignantly.

"What are we supposed to do?" the Senorita said. "We're fighting an army festooned with Outlaw Torn Slaters."

More members of the artillery teams were dropping, more men, more men— And then—

Suddenly, a shot rang out and another artillery team—this time a team on their right—was hit, not the man carrying the shell, who had pivoted toward the ranch, exposing the casing's flat percussive end to the sniper. No, the howitzer shell itself exploded in a blinding, deafening, earth-shaking roar.

With it, the entire pile of artillery shells ignited en masse through sympathetic detonation. The blast from each individual round combining in a single, massive, soul-shattering Gotterdammerung of a thundercrack.

When Frank James's hearing finally returned, his only conscious, coherent thought was that the world was coming to an end.

CHAPTER 5

"Hey, Torn, over...*there*."

Up in the crow's nest, a hundred feet above the battlefield below, Belle Starr was pointing to les Mitrailleuses de Reffyes and shouting at Slater. The din from the exploded artillery shell pile—even at two-thirds of a mile away—was still ringing in their ears. Slater, seated on the stool, was bent over his Sharps rifle and surveying the scene below through his sniper scope. Catching Belle's gesture out of the corner of his eye, he pivoted the rifle in its rail-groove, then paused to study the big twenty-five-barrel guns, each round 770 grains of pre-packaged, unadulterated, readymade...*death*. Those guns were fourteen hundred yards away—two hundred yards farther than the three howitzers—and earlier the two other shooters had elected Slater to take out those men.

As Richard had told him earlier, "It's way too far for me, Torn."

Masterson had echoed that sentiment, saying, "Torn, you're the only man I know outside Billy Dixon who could make that shot."

So Slater now focused his scope on the teams loading and firing les Mitrailleuses de Reffyes. Their sergeant was just lifting a firing plate, containing twenty-five .50-caliber shells, off the pile near the big gun. At fourteen hundred yards, it was a tough shot, but he'd gotten his range at twelve hundred yards with the other two shots. That would help him gauge the difference.

Slater took a deep breath and held it.

Come on, he said to himself. *Your first look is your best look. Don't burn up that target picture.*

Letting the breath out slowly, he squeezed the trigger. The big Sharps bucked against his shoulder and jumped in his fists. His ears dinned with the roar, and the crow's nest filled with more whitish black-powder smoke.

Belle waved the smoke away from his eyes. The man had dropped the shell, was now flat on his back, his brains blown across the ground near what had once been his cranium.

The soldiers from his crew were fleeing the field as fast as their legs could carry them.

Pivoting the rifle in its groove, he studied the men alongside the next Mitrailleuse. They stood paralyzed, their eyes big as silver dollars, their jaws gaped, terrified beyond all reason. So Slater eared the hammer back. Shoving the trigger guard forward, he ejected the spent round from the chamber. Replacing it, he slammed the trigger guard back against the bottom of the breech.

"Belle," Slater said, "could you get me that whiskey flask in my coat pocket. I've been up all night drinking coffee and could use a snort—help me steady my nerves."

"Steady your nerves, hell," Belle said. "A man who shoots other men from fourteen hundred yards like he was shooting rats at the town dump don't need no snort to steady his gun hand."

"I need something," Slater said.

"The Torn Slater I know," Belle said, "he always hated to use a horse hard or a woman easy."

"Sounds like a hell of a man," Slater said—knowing he should have kept his mouth shut, that it was never wise to provoke Belle.

"He used to brag," Belle said, "that he was going to rob every train, hit every bank, kill every lawin' son of a bitch and fuck every woman that got in his way."

"That man could still use that snort. Fourteen hundred yards is one long shot."

Belle handed him the flask, and Slater took a long, deep pull.

"Maybe this will also steady your nerves," Belle said.

Kneeling between Slater's legs, she slowly began unbuttoning his fly.

With a shrug, Slater looked back into the scope's eyepiece. Allowing for windage and taking a deep breath, he slowly, slowly let it out, and squeezed the trigger.

The big rifle kicked, Slater's ears went deaf from the roar, and smoke filled the nest.

"Yes, sir, Mr. Slater," Belle said, "I know a better way to take the edge off your distraught nerves. In fact, I just found the source of your distress. Here we go—oh my. I'd forgotten how *tremendous* your distress can get. Let me see if I can relax you just a little. Consider it a reward for your very excellent marksmanship."

Ignoring her, Slater stayed focused on a new soldier, who was attempting to man one of the Mitrailleuses de Reffyes. He was picking up an artillery shell and lugging it toward the open smoking breech. Slater's crosshairs converged on the man, and as the Big Fifty Sharps exploded, the artillery sergeant did too.

A few seconds later, Slater convulsed…*as well.*

But it only shook him for a moment.

He quickly eared back the hammer, slammed the lever forward and ejected a shell. Shoving a new round into the chamber, he yanked the lever back and sighted in on another unreconstructed rebel.

As he gently squeezed the trigger, he noticed—absently, almost without thinking—that he did feel more relaxed.

CHAPTER 6

Diaz and his friends were struck dumb. All the firing teams manning their big guns were either lying on the ground, headless, or with holes in their chests as big as beer barrels. Their troops, now marching toward the gunnery crews, had witnessed the whole debacle and looked ready to flee, themselves.

Being a battle-hardened—albeit retired—general, Diaz knew he had to do something fast if they were to maintain discipline. Among other things, he had inordinately well-paid informants in all the American army bases near the Méjicano-Americano border. He knew what weaponry they had loaned out to Rancho de Cielo. He'd been told that her son Richard had half borrowed, half absconded with two Gatlings and six Mitrailleuses de Reffyes. He had earlier discounted both weapons as grossly inaccurate and inadequate, but he was less sure now. For one thing, his howitzers, without gunnery crews, were as useless as tits on a stud bull, but their failure would be of no consequence. Shelby had two thousand trained, experienced veterans with blood in their eyes. Just get them moving, and their old lust for revenge would return. Their years of service in the War of Northern Aggression would come back to them in a single, blinding flash of revelation and they would know exactly what to do.

They'd fly the black flag, war to the knife, no quarter asked and none given. They'd shoot the wounded and take no prisoners. The South would rise again, and madre Méjico would redeem her rightful God-given inheritance. Polk had stolen half of Méjico magnifico, and Diaz was here to take it all back.

He would be the true Father of Madre Méjico, not that indio-hideputa whom everyone hero-worshiped and genuflected before as if he were the Son of God and the Aztec's version of Christ Crucified, Quetzalcoatl, rolled up into one: Benito Pablo Juárez.

God, how Diaz loathed that man. Everywhere he went, all he heard was Juarez, Juarez, Juarez. Everyone said that Juarez was the heart and soul of Méjico, all that was good and noble in his country, its founder and progenitor. And if Benito Pablo Juárez was Méjico's soul, Diaz—his detractors said—was its iron boot.

He was sick to death of the constant ugly contrasts drawn between St. Benito and himself, El Diabolo. Juarez had set an example that Diaz had never been able to live up to, and he, consequently, would go to his grave living in St. Benito's shadow.

Well, Juarez's martyrdom would end now, and Diaz's legend would begin. This was the moment that La Madre Méjico Nueva would be born.

Arching his back, Diaz drew an impossibly deep breath and then thundered in clear plain English with every fiber in his flesh and bones and blood:

"BUGLER, BLOW CHARGE!"

The bugler instantly brought his instrument to his lips, as if he were the Angel Gabriel blaring his trumpet before Jericho's walls, as if he were Armageddon and the Second Coming of Christ all rolled up into one single horn player. He then blew charge like it had never been blown before in the entire history of warfare.

The army took off, as a single man, at a rapid trot. Bayonets were already affixed to their lever-action Winchester and bolt-action Mausers. They held their pieces in front of them as they'd done thousands of times before on innumerable battlefields.

Then their rebel yells—their YIP-YIP-YIP-YIP-YIPPING-ING-ING-ING!—tore through the air and rent the morning stillness, the barbarous cry that had so many years ago frozen so many trembling Yankees to their core and brought victory to so many rage-filled Sons of the South.

Diaz, Shelby and their friends were authentically moved and inspired.

It was going to be all right.

The South and Madre Méjico were rising again... *together*.

CHAPTER 7

The night before, Krupp and Richard had spent over an hour explaining to Nietzsche, who had boasted with some small hyperbole of being "an old-time artillery officer," the deployment and usage of rapid-fire weapons. He had listened to their harangue intently, desperate to get back at Diaz and Sutherland, but most of all, at the Senorita and Judith McKillian. Nietzsche now believed his ultimate revenge would be defeating them on the battlefield. They had taken something from the young man, some essential part of his honor and dignity. If he didn't get it back, he wasn't sure he could live with himself.

So Nietzsche focused fixedly on Krupp's and Richard's analysis of the weapons Richard had purloined from the fort and how they could best be used against Shelby's army.

* * *

"Gatlings and Mitrailleuses de Reffyes should be used with coordinated precision," the younger Krupp said. "I've ordered firing pits dug. Sandbags and logs have also been placed in front of them, creating embrasures. You men will stand behind them, supervising the man who is actually on the gun, turning the crank and firing it. Herr Nietzsche, I will place you in charge of the Gatling on our right-hand corner of the field. Wyatt Earp will supervise the other Gatling on our left. Otto, you will supervise the Mitrailleuses de Reffyes, which will be deployed facing the fort in the middle of the field. You will all have additional hoppers, filled with rounds, and as your guns empty, men will reload them—instantly.

You will see that your gunner fires first on the men on the battlefield's edge, gradually turning his fire toward the field's center, thereby driving and compressing the charging soldiers into the middle of the battlefield. Gentlemen, you are to keep those barrels hot."

"The range on the Gatling is almost a mile," Richard pointed out. "How far should they be when I commence firing."

"Four hundred yards. Our rifles can also take a toll from that close up. They will help you drive the enemy to the center of the field."

"And what will happen when we have them in the field's center, crammed together, but still charging our lines for all they're worth?" Bismarck asked. "What do I do then?"

"Chancellor," Krupp said. "You will supervise the firing of the Mitrailleuses de Reffyes. You will have pre-loaded plates, and as soon as you use those, your men will reload others into your guns. As with the Gatlings, you must keep those barrels smoking. To halt is to die. None of you will stop firing until you are so ordered."

"How far should they be when I commence firing?" Bismarck asked.

"Again, wait until the Gatlings have forced Shelby's men into the center of the field. They should be approximately two hundred yards away from you. They will be shooting at you, but you must wait to fire until the last moment."

"Any reason why?" the Iron Chancellor asked.

"Yes," Krupp said, "the guns fire twenty-five rounds at a time in perfect unison. Now the shells leave the barrel clustered together in a tight pattern and they are each filled with double-ought buckshot. The farther they travel, however, the farther their combined shot pattern will spread out. By the time they traverse two hundred yards, those four thousand balls will be well dispersed and cutting down everything and everyone in their path. The enemy will think they walked into a mowing machine. You will cut them down like tall corn. They will never know what hit them. The psychological impact will be overwhelming."

"Nothing like this fusillade," Richard said, "will have ever hit an army in the entire history of warfare."

"Your Mitrailleuses de Reffyes," Krupp said, "in combination with our Gatlings and our repeating rifles, will do to those ex-Confederates what was done to the Union Army at Fredericksburg and the French forces at Sedan."

"What you're describing is hellfire and apocalypse," Nietzsche said, "visited on mortal flesh for a full quarter of an hour."

"You have Cassandra's curse," Krupp said, "the fatal gift of unwanted prophecy."

"And why is my observation unwelcome?" Nietzsche asked.

"Because you have just described," Krupp said, "the shape of war to come."

* * *

And now all El Rancho's four big guns were deployed. Their four Gatlings on the field's near corners, three Mitrailleuses de Reffyes directly in front of the main house and wall and in the field's center. Nietzsche, Earp and Bismarck—dressed in the ranch clothes that Katherine had given them along with their Stetsons—were in position behind them. They also had holstered Colts.

Nietzsche, for one, was antsy. He wondered when he would have to perform. He'd been up all night, however, and was tired of waiting. He'd seen Slater, Richard and Masterson blow a half dozen men off Shelby's big guns and then drive the other gunners into full rout and send them racing from the field.

But then far, far away, he heard a bugler blow charge, and, miraculously, he saw Shelby's soldiers lift their rifles diagonally across their chests at port arms and charge Rancho de Cielo in unison. At least, initially they ran in formation. Within minutes their formation broke, and they were dogtrotting wildly down the field toward them, rebel yells ripping and yipping out of their lungs like the screams of the damned in hell.

CHAPTER 8

Wyatt Earp stood behind the other Gatling on the opposite side of the field. Lord only knew he'd been in every kind of brawl, shootout and knife fight imaginable.

But he'd never experienced armed combat in a war.

Unlike his brothers Virgil, James and his half brother, Newton, Wyatt had been too young for the Civil War. He'd try to run off and illegally enlist, but would get caught, dragged back, and Pa, who'd fought in Méjico in 1840 and hated all wars, would take the birch switch to him. Still, he couldn't stop Wyatt from running off and trying to join his brothers.

Wyatt still felt bad that he hadn't fought in that war.

That his brothers, who had seen combat, wouldn't talk about it rankled Wyatt to no end. He had prized a few stories out of them. Mostly, however, they were silent about what had happened, saying only that it was stuff you never wanted to remember or think about—let alone describe—ever again.

Well, Wyatt, he said to himself, *you're about to find out what military combat is like now.*

It felt weird to be in a fight and not have Doc Holliday beside him, backing his play. During these last few years, Doc had taken it as his life's work to look after Wyatt, as if he were some kind of guardian angel. First, in Dodge City, Earp noticed that when the going got rough and gunmen were slipping up behind him—as well as facing him down—somehow, someway, Doc would materialize. He always had pistols, cocked, and sometimes a sawed-off.

It happened that way a half dozen times when Earp was marshalling in Dodge, and the saloons got dark and the drunks and killers and cardsharps got tired of dealing with Earp's wrath—and his percentage of their take—and they decided to throw down on Wyatt.

Well, guess what? They found that Doc had dealt himself into the play.

If they wanted Earp, they had to go through Doc Holliday.

How and why men partnered up out west was seldom a matter of admiration or fondness. It was a matter of trust and the loyalty trust engenders.

Earp knew Doc had his back. It was a proven fact. He'd covered Earp's ass too many times. Earp had come to accept that Doc was one of the most truest and most reliable friends he would ever have.

And Wyatt had quickly become Doc's friend too.

Well, Wyatt, he said to himself, this time you're on your own. Doc is downfield, high up in a cottonwood tree in a sniper's nest nearly a half mile away. A good two thousand rebs are about to charge you, and you'll get the war you always pined away for but never experienced, and you'll get to endure the thing your old man so deeply and determinedly...*loathed.*

But you'll be fighting this battle without Doc.

Wyatt wasn't even sure he liked Doc. Dark of heart and cynical to the bone, Doc always saw the bad-news side of everything. Trusting nothing-nobody, he'd never been one of those laugh-filled, good-time guys, who were light about themselves and made everything around them lighter and more fun. Doc was many things, but a barrel of laughs wasn't one of them. Doc was there to tell you that he despaired of the human race, that the world was coming to an end, that humanity was going to hell, but not to worry: Extinction could only improve the species. Death, according to Doc, was simply the gods' way of saying, "Good riddance, sucker." Still, when things got really bad, and everyone else was racing for the exits, Doc was the one you wanted with you. When lives were on the line and your back was to the wall, when the guns roared and the floor was slick with gore, you didn't want the good-time, fun-filled guys at your side. You wanted men like Doc or Masterson or Bill Hickok—men who'd never think twice and push it all the way—you wanted men like them backing your hand.

But mostly, when things were impossible and death was staring you straight in the eye, what you really wanted was...*Outlaw Torn Slater.*

Slater had proved that, once again, in that New Mexico bar.

Whatever the case, Wyatt and Doc, anymore, seemed joined at the hip. It had been only a year ago that Doc had backed Wyatt up at what the newspapers described as "the OK Corral," which hadn't even taken place at the OK Corral. The shootout went down in a vacant lot alongside C. S. Fly's photography studio on Fremont Street. Then afterward, when he, Wyatt, had personally hunted down and killed every Clanton who'd put a round into an Earp, well, Doc had been beside him every step of the way on those occasions too.

And those hadn't even been Doc's fights. It wasn't Doc's brothers that had been shot up and killed.

Well, it was time to get down to business. Wyatt Earp had a Gatling gun to supervise and a war to win. And he was fighting for the Union, for blue bellies, against his brothers' former foe—Johnny Reb.

He just hoped Nietzsche would hold up his end. The man wasn't any older than Earp but he somehow seemed younger, more naïve. That he could spend three months in Méjico with Diaz and his crew and still be an innocent, struck Earp as impossibly improbable, but, nonetheless, Nietzsche did not strike him as wise to the ways of the world.

Still, as long as Nietzsche kept that Gatling firing and smoking and as long as Nietzsche and his men didn't break and fall back, he would be fine in Earp's book.

Anyway, Wyatt wasn't here to build lasting, loving friendships.

He was here to kill rebs and maybe turn an illicit buck in the process.

CHAPTER 9

Bat Masterson sat on a stool in his crow's nest. Perched high above the battlefield, he had a magnificent view. Resting his Sharps rifle on a railing groove he'd carved earlier into it, he zeroed in on the gunnery crew manning the howitzer to his far right.

At twelve hundred yards it was a very long shot, but then, hadn't he studied under Billy Dixon, back when he was a teenage buffalo hunter?

And he'd already just made three of those shots.

Twelve hundred yards?

Billy had taught him to make shots like that, and as for Billy?

Hell, Billy Dixon could have made Bat's last five shots standing on his head, underwater, blind drunk.

* * *

There were a thousand Comanche coming down from the rimrock, the last time he fought alongside Billy. They were charging the buff hunters camp out of the dawn sun. There were fewer than a hundred hide hunters lined up to stop them, but they were armed with Sharps rifles and single-shot Springfields. Most of their guns were scoped-in and those hide men could shoot.

Masterson was barely twenty and was dropping Comanche as quickly as he could squeeze the big Sharps' trigger, slam the trigger guard forward, eject another smoking shell and shove another into the breech, then yank the trigger guard back into place.

For those crack shots, it was what Billy would later describe as "a raggedy-ass barn-shoot."

Toward the end of the battle that had left several hundred dead Comanche strewn across the llano, Bat had heard twenty-four-year-old Billy Dixon, who had stood and shot beside him the whole time, emit a Kiowa war-whoop and then roar:

"I smoked that red devil proper—at sixteen hundred yards!"

Later, Bat paced the distance off himself, personally counting out loud every step. To this day, he could still hear Billy Dixon's thunderous pronouncement:

"I smoked him proper!"

* * *

Bat sat in his crow's nest staring out over the battlefield. Katherine's daughter, Rachel, was serving as his spotter. Dressed in cowhand clothes—Levis, boots, collarless shirt and Stetson—she was polite but clearly well educated and all business. Not at all like the barroom trollops, soiled doves and drunken doxies Bat spent 98 percent of his time with.

Where had it all gone wrong anyway? Why couldn't he have spent a life doing positive, constructive things and lived with a real woman, someone like Rachel Ryan?

His mind drifted back to Dodge City....

* * *

He was twenty-four then and marshaling in Dodge. It was late at night, and he was heading home after rounds. He almost made it when his brother Ed—whom he had dragooned into that filthy law-dog business—came stumbling out of the Lady Gay Saloon, clutching his gut, his mouth flooding with blood.

"Bat...Bat..." were his last words.

Jack Wagner and Alf Walker exited, following him, their guns smoking, turning toward him.

But his sidearm was already cocked and raised, arm extended, hand steady.

Two more scallops were carved on Masterson's Colt.

* * *

And they were merely two of the first men he'd killed. How many more would have to die before some gunsel put him down?

But that was then, and this was now. It was time to focus on the battle at hand. Up in his perch, it was time for Bat to concentrate on the two thousand troops that were about to descend on them, whooping their rebel yells and firing their guns, as if all the damned in hell were inside of them, fighting to get out.

Naw, this wasn't any barroom gunfight or "raggedy-ass Comanche barn-shoot." This was the real deal.

Canadian-born, Masterson was too young for the Civil War and never felt it was his fight in the first place. Still, he'd hated slavery and didn't mind having an opportunity to take a stand against it. And Bat was trained for this kind of work. Lord only knew how Billy Dixon had pounded the fundamentals of long-range marksmanship into him. So it was now time to show off some of those hard-won skills.

Shelby's gunnery teams were loading artillery shells into piles close to the big guns, even as Masterson sighted in on the lead sergeant.

"You'll never know what hit you," Masterson grumbled under his breath.

The scope's crosshairs fixed on the man. Squeezing the trigger, Masterson felt the stock hammer his shoulder. Clearing the smoke, he looked through his scope and surveyed the damage.

The man's head was blown clean off his shoulders.

Billy Dixon would have been proud of his onetime student.

CHAPTER 10

Doc Holliday was up in the fork of a big, thick-boughed cottonwood. Concealed four hundred yards downfield in a heavily camouflaged sniper's nest, he and his scoped '76 Winchester were lashed to the tree and densely shrouded leaves and leafy tree limbs.

With his last round, he'd dropped a dogtrotting enemy soldier and was now methodically inserting fresh rounds into the loading tube. He found it tedious work, but it gave him time to reflect on his life—and whatever future he might still have left.

Doc had never been naïve about how he lived. He knew who he was, what he was and what he could never be. He was trained as a professional man—a dentist—and for a time had been successful at it; but, in his heart of hearts, he'd always been something else: a gambler, a rambler, a drifter and, yes, a killer.

In point of fact, John Henry "Doc" Holliday was no goddamn good.

Wyatt often said he and Doc were cut off the same piece of cloth, and Wyatt had certainly holed more than his share, drunk just as many bottles as Doc and fucked as many saloon whores as well. Wyatt, too, was a professional gambler.

Doc, however, saw something else in Wyatt. He couldn't say precisely what it was, but he felt that the man was born for something better. Doc, on the other hand, was born for an early grave. The consumption would see to that. His mother had been tubercular, and he'd contracted it from her when he was young. He'd lived with it his whole life, and it was still killing him. Every day he was a little weaker and that big, black freight train, Death, would not stop, had never stopped, lumbering down the track toward him—its whistle blowing, throbbing, in him, through him—always, with each passing moment, seeming to move just a little quicker, its whistle shrilling just a little louder, the rumble of the rails a little more portentous.

That son of a bitch was coming, and Doc could do nothing to stop it.

But if he could do nothing to postpone his inevitable expiration, he could do something to keep Wyatt alive a little longer, to help him make it through one more violent day or one more bloody, gunfire night.

Why not?

Wyatt was the only real friend Doc had ever had.

In fact, he already knew what his epitaph would be—at least, what he wanted it to be. He thought those last lines from Thomas Gray's *Elegy Written in a Country Churchyard* summed up his relationship with life and with Wyatt just right:

Here rests his head upon the lap of earth,
A youth to fortune and to fame unknown.
Fair science frowned not on his humble birth,
And melancholy marked him for her own.

Large was his bounty and his soul sincere,
Heaven did a recompense as largely send.
He gave to misery all he had a tear.
He gained from heaven (t'was all he wished) a friend.

Doc planned on being Wyatt Earp's friend for whatever remaining months or weeks or days or hours he had left.

So he felt a little bad that, here he was, lashed to a damn tree, picking off rebels with his '76 scoped Winchester, which, by the way, was one hell of a gun.

Maybe you should get one for yourself.

And do what with it?

Doc doubted he had three good months left in his clap-and-TB-infested body.

Fuck it.

There, the gun was reloaded. Raising it and pressing his right eye against the scope, his right cheek against the upper stock, he took aim. Squeezing the trigger, he saw a reb drop dead in his tracks.

Headshot.

He was pleased he still had the eye.

Levering another round into the chamber, he dropped another reb, then another, then another. It was like shooting mechanical ducks in a penny arcade.

Finally, the Winchester was empty again. Grabbing a fist full of bullets from his waist pouch, he began feeding them into the loading tube.

Then a coughing attack shook him like a hound dog shaking a rabbit by its nape.

Luckily, Doc was secured to his tree fork with a lass rope and his rifle was tied to it as well with a leather thong—otherwise he would have coughed both of them out of the tree. And cough, he did. Bent at the waist, spasm after spasm racked his lungs and body, while he projectile-vomited blood, puke and lung tissue down through the branches and oak leaves, a red-hued volcanic eruption of lurid death, puddling the grass below.

It was as bad as it had ever been, and Doc realized now he had even less time left than he had previously imagined.

Guess there's no point in buying one of those '76 Winchesters now, is there, old friend?

So Doc coughed and puked bloody bits of his throat and lungs. By the time he finished, the ground below looked like a ghastly pond of gore and guts—something scraped up off an abattoir floor.

Where and how the world would end, Doc Holliday did not know, but, for him, he understood with inviolable certitude where it was all headed.

He gave to heaven, t'was all he had, a tear.
He gained from heaven (t'was all he wished) a friend.

Still he had a job to do. Looking weakly across the battlefield, he spotted Earp behind his Gatling. He was just barking out field commands at the Gatling gunner—no doubt ordering him to "pour it on."

Doc still felt like he ought to be with Earp. The poor guy looked so alone, commanding that big Gatling, so exposed. Wyatt needed him. Doc was convinced of it.

Well, as long as Earp did, Doc had a reason to live.

CHAPTER 11

Friedrich Nietzsche stood behind the Gatling gun on the right-hand corner of the battlefield just in front of El Rancho de Cielo. Staring at Shelby's two-thousand-man army thundering toward him and screaming their heads off, he wasn't sure how it was going to work out. There were just too many of them, and they kept on coming—a vast wall of armed killers charging Nietzsche and his intrepid band of barely 150 bandits, renegades and jailbirds. The odds of Nietzsche and his friends surviving the day—let alone defeating Shelby—Nietzsche thought glumly, were...*poor.*

Still, he'd had enough of Diaz, the Senorita, McKillian and Sutherland to last a lifetime. Summoning all the hatred in his heart, Friedrich Wilhelm Nietzsche vowed to stand his ground and, with his Gatling gun, take out as many of the enemy as possible.

Krupp had told them to focus on the stand of trees, up field, which Krupp had said was approximately four hundred yards from El Rancho's main wall and building. When Shelby's first troops were even with that grove, Nietzsche and his friends would open fire. Earp would do the same but from the opposite side of the field.

Krupp had said that all hell would break loose soon thereafter.

Shelby's army was trotting closer, closer, closer. The only men firing at those troops were the sharpshooters in the crow's nests, but they were only killing them one at a time—mere drops in an enormous ocean of men—and the enemy was still too far for the Gatlings. At least, according to Krupp. Wait till they are four hundred yards away and then give it to them with everything you had.

Closer, closer, closer.

Suddenly, they were even with the stand of trees.

"FIRE AT WILL!" Nietzsche roared with everything he had. "FORCE THEM INTO THE CENTER OF THE FIELD!"

Which was what his six-man team was doing. When one hopper emptied, another full one instantly replaced it. And their aim was sure. Foot by foot, on both sides of the field, the stream of Gatling 100-caliber bullets were driving Shelby's troops into the field's middle, into a denser, ever-tightening mass.

But now the charging men were also shooting back. Stopping for a few seconds, they would raise their repeating rifles, shoot at the rapid-fire gunners, then lower their heads, run and then fire some more.

Bullets were singing past Nietzsche's ears, but he was oddly thrilled at being so close to...*death.* He was pleased to note that he was not a coward—not at all—but was fearless under fire. He didn't care what those bastards did to him. He was hell-bent not to let Diaz and his friends take one inch of El Rancho de Cielo, and he was determined to get back at those two evil witches for what they'd done to him.

And then suddenly, unexpectedly, his Gatling gunner's head burst like a melon struck by a sledgehammer.

Nietzsche was covered with gray snaky cranial matter, blood spray and bone fragments. The sheer horror of it rocked him—but only for a second. Dragging the man out of the pit, Nietzsche, almost without thinking, grabbed the Gatling's crank. Turning the handle, he gradually, incrementally, infinitesimally, began pressuring the charging men into an ever-denser mass centered in the field's middle.

CHAPTER 12

Otto von Bismarck, Prussia's esteemed chancellor, stood behind his three Mitrailleuses de Reffyes. He was unclear when to open fire. He'd heard Krupp tell the Gatling gunners to wait until the soldiers were four hundred yards away—even with the up-field stand of trees to their left—but Krupp had had no such advice for Bismarck.

* * *

Instead, Krupp took Bismarck aside and said, "Otto, you have to use your own best judgment. No one knows what will happen in those final minutes. Shelby's army might not cluster in the field's middle. Or they could cluster, say four hundred yards away, or a Gatling gun could become disabled, and they could break apart and spread out. Who knows what will happen? Try to wait until they get as close to you and as tightly packed as possible, and when you think the time is right, let them have it."

"But I'm not sure—" Bismarck started to say.

"You have to use your best judgment," Krupp said firmly. Clapping the chancellor on the shoulder, Krupp said, "Otto, I'm counting on you. It's going to be your call—yours alone."

"But—" Bismarck started to say.

Krupp cut him off.

"Just do it," Krupp barked. "Hey," he then said pleasantly, "they don't call you the Iron Chancellor for nothing, do they? And look at it this way: The next time you want to treat the German people to one of your stirring patriotic tirades

about 'blood and iron,' you won't be trumpeting empty words. You'll know the hard truth of war. You will have learned it on your flesh and in your bones. You'll know it in your heart and soul. You'll be blooded."

* * *

The men were in the middle of the field now, packed tight together—growing tighter, ever tighter—and the Gatlings were working perfectly. From the corner of his left eye, Bismarck saw one Gatling gunner's head fly apart, and young Friedrich Nietzsche dragged him out of the pit, then jumped down into the nest and took his place.

Nietzsche was immediately, unhesitatingly, cranking the big gun like he had been born to the job and raised to do nothing else on earth, pouring volley after volley onto the left flank of the tight mass of screaming men. They were now turning to flee but found themselves trapped—logjammed in mid-flight, blocked by the still-charging men behind them—and instead pushed themselves closer and closer into the field's middle in their desperate attempt to escape the firehose of bullets on their flanks. All the while, Nietzsche turned the Gatling's crank, watching the 100-caliber bullets hammering men to bloody pieces, blowing arms and legs apart, smashing heads and tearing them off men's shoulders, ripping holes in their torsos big enough for Caesar to lead his legions through but all the while forcing them tighter and tighter together in the battlefield's center.

Bismarck wondered what Nietzsche was feeling.

But deep inside, he knew what Nietzsche was feeling. He was experiencing the same thing at that very moment. Otto von Bismarck, the Iron Chancellor, felt...*nothing*. Neither pity nor sadness nor guilt nor remorse, only—

Only—

Only—

The exhilaration of raw bloody...*power*.

A feeling he now felt in his soul, and one he intuited that Nietzsche was experiencing and would never forget.

Never.

For the rest of his life.

Of their lives.

A feeling that would change the way they looked at the world forever.

Then Shelby's army was four hundred yards away—and pressed continually into an ever-dense mass.

Then three hundred fifty yards—and even tighter.

Then three hundred.

Then two fifty.

Then two hundred.

They were still densely packed, still charging, their rebel yells rending the air apart like banshee screams from hell.

Then one fifty.

Then one hundred.

Closer.

Closer.

Bismarck didn't even know when or how he'd done it, but suddenly—unbidden, unthinkingly—words were thundering out of him in English, no less, like molten lava exploding out of a volcano:

"FIRE AT WILL! GIVE THEM EVERYTHING YOU HAVE! MAKE THOSE SONS OF BITCHES PAY!"

And then Bismarck's three Mitrailleuses de Reffyes opened up all at once, like the very crack of doom.

The entire middle of Shelby's army seemed, before Bismarck's very eyes, to vanish into a black, vast, boundlessly bloody…*void.*

PART XXI

"Anyone who would go to Méjico for 'natural beauty' would go to hell for the nightlife."

—Judith McKillian, International Financier

CHAPTER 1

Friedrich Nietzsche, Otto von Bismarck and Friedrich Krupp sat with Katherine Ryan and her friends back in her parlor. They'd just consumed a late breakfast of ham, eggs and fried potatoes. None of them had slept in over forty-eight hours, and they'd each put away, what seemed like, a pot of coffee apiece.

They were now sipping Jackson's Sour Mash in order to combat the industrial quantities of caffeine, which they'd ingested throughout the last two days.

"What do you want to do now?" Katherine asked her friends. Nobody said anything, so she asked Belle and Slater, "You two have anything planned?"

"Torn dragged me out here," Belle said. "I figured the least I could do was make him drag me back. We aren't sure it's all that safe for us here anyway. We just got done slaughtering an entire army of God only knows what."

There was no arguing with any of that.

"Chancellor?" Katherine asked Bismarck.

"I don't know about you," Bismarck said, "but Herr Krupp, young Nietzsche and I have to somehow slink on back to Germany."

"Under cover of darkness," Nietzsche suggested.

"That would be wise," Krupp said. "I'm glad we helped you defeat Diaz and Shelby, but we broke about a thousand German and American laws doing so."

"I'm too old for prison," Bismarck said.

"I stole all the US Army ordnance that we used to defeat Shelby and his men," Richard admitted. "According to the military code of justice, that is a capital offense. I have to clean those guns up and get them back to where I found them—before the US Army returns from chasing Geronimo."

"I personally killed over a hundred Americans with one of those Gatlings," Nietzsche said somberly without the slightest hint of bravado or braggadocio. "I don't think I should be hanging around either."

"None of us should," Bismarck said. "I supervised the slaughter of hundreds more when I commanded those Mitrailleuses de Reffyes."

"My father and I donated all those artillery pieces and rapid-fire weapons to Diaz," Krupp said. "I even demonstrated the weapons for him on a Durango firing range."

"Thereby aiding and abetting Diaz in his attempted conquest of American territory," Nietzsche stated numbly, as if by rote.

"The US government would not only hang you for that," Slater said, "they'd hang you *twice* if they could."

"I guess we've all broken a lot of very serious laws," Bismarck said in summation.

"I've told my men here," Katherine said, "to gather up whatever's on that field that the wolves and buzzards haven't devoured. We're going to have one massive funeral pyre over the next few hours."

"Mom and I have decided that it's best for all concerned that we dispose of the corpus delecti," Rachel explained rather indelicately.

"I suggest that we then throw the ashes in the river," Richard said.

"And leave not a trace behind," Nietzsche said.

"A wise decision," Krupp concluded.

For a long moment, they were all silent.

"So you three really want to return to Germany?" Katherine finally asked Bismarck.

"We have to return to Germany," the chancellor said. "Young Nietzsche and I were never supposed to have left in the first place. We weren't supposed to even be here."

"We were on a secret mission," Nietzsche said. "It was all supposed to be undercover, clandestine and incognito."

"Killing almost fifteen hundred people with artillery and rapid-fire weaponry isn't exactly hush-hush and covert," Richard said.

"We were just supposed to be making an arms sale," Krupp said.

"A secret arms sale," Bismarck said.

"But we didn't know we were selling guns to Lucifer in hell," Nietzsche said by way of an explanation.

"So how do you want to head back to Germany?" Katherine asked. "I can help you with money, false identification papers, whatever you need."

"We have fake papers and hard currency," Bismarck said. "But it is your country. You know it better than us. What do you suggest we do, if we want to return home surreptitiously?"

"Los Angeles harbor is a fairly short train ride from here—only a few days," Katherine said, "and you'll be safe once on a boat and out to sea. Also, you three would be less conspicuous in Los Angeles than in the crowded, bustling metropolises of the east. I doubt you'd be recognized out here. Torn, you spent more time on the run than anyone I ever knew. You know Los Angeles?"

"I been drunk there a few times," Slater said.

"What do you think?" Richard asked.

"They'll be fine in Los Angeles," Slater said.

"People there," Belle said, "don't even know what a chancellor is or where Germany is on a map."

"They think it's a town in Texas," Slater said.

"You'd have to round Cape Horn to make it back to Europe," Richard said, "but that might be a plus. No one of any stature will be rounding the Cape. They'd take the train cross-country and catch a boat from an Atlantic port. So your boat won't be crowded. It's unlikely you'd be recognized."

Bismarck slapped both thighs for emphasis. "Then Los Angeles it is, right, men?"

CHAPTER 2

"Well, Porfirio," Sutherland said, "your Second Méjicano-American War didn't work out all that well."

"Verdad," Diaz said.

"That is all you have to say?" the Senorita said. "'Verdad'? You have nothing else to add?"

"Only that I pity poor Méjico," Diaz said.

"What on earth for?" Judith McKillian asked.

"Judith and I certainly don't," Sutherland said.

"Because my people are doomed," Diaz said.

"In what way?" Sutherland asked.

"We are so far from God but so agonizingly close to the United States."

"You have a point, old friend," Judith McKillian said.

"It was ever thus," the Senorita added.

They both clapped the saddened, despairing despot on his shoulder.

Staring out over the field of blood, Diaz shook his head, threw back his shoulders and straightened his posture. Some of his old military bearing returned.

"I have always prided myself on my pragmatism," he announced in deep stertorous tones, "not on my hubris."

"Of which, I must admit," Sutherland said, "we have all exhibited more than our fair share."

"But now," Diaz continued, "I have to confess that the die has been irretrievably cast. The game is irrevocably lost. There is nothing to be gained by remaining here and gazing on this ghastly battleground. In the name of all that is pragmatic, I suggest—I insist—that we all depart at once."

"Where will you go?" General Shelby asked.

"I personally shall return to madre Méjico with all expedition," Diaz announced. "Senorita, I suspect you will wish to accompany me. Senor Sutherland, Miss McKillian, you are, of course, welcome to join us. I have kept our express train fueled, ready, waiting and available at a moment's notice at the station."

"I agree," Sutherland said. "None of us can afford to be identified with this little...*contretemps.*"

"We must put as much distance between ourselves and Rancho de Cielo as is humanly possible," Judith McKillian said adamantly.

"Washington would love to send its soldados back to madre Méjico," the Senorita said, nodding her assent, "shoot our beloved Porfirio and myself against a wall as Porfirio and his compadres did to Maximilian after his loss at Chapultepec."

"Any chance I could tag along?" General Shelby said.

"Me too?" Edwards asked. "Frank, you want to return South of the Border?"

"Not really," Frank James said.

"Nor do I think your return to Méjico is wise," Diaz said. "You don't want to be identified with us for the foreseeable future."

"Is that really necessary?" General Shelby asked.

"My dear friend," the Senorita said, "you have aided and abetted a foreign power in the attempted conquest of sovereign American territory. Do the words *treason* and *war crimes* mean anything to you?"

"How many men did you lead to their slaughter?" Judith McKillian said, waving her arm at the field before them, filled with wounded and slain men. She sat down on a nearby boulder with disgust.

"I suppose that means I can't write about any of this," Edwards said, clearly disappointed.

"You really are a moron," Frank James said to him, shaking his head in disgust.

"After executing our beloved Porfirio and the sublime Senorita," Sutherland said, "they would then seize Sonora and Chihuahua as recompense."

"That is precisely what I'd do, were I them," Judith said.

"So what do you suggest?" Edwards asked.

"As our eternal bard once wrote," Sutherland said, "'Stand not upon the order of your going, but go at once.' Porfirio, I believe we have a train to catch."

"Pronto tambien," Diaz said. Quickly too.

"To madre Méjico!" the Senorita said, pouring her friends each a glass of brandy and shouting her salutation to no one in particular.

"I can't wait for us to return," Diaz said.

"To Durango, yes?" the Senorita asked.

"But of course," Diaz said.

"I love Durango!" the Senorita enthused with a trilling giggle.

"Why on earth would anyone love Durango?" Judith McKillian asked, her upper lip curling with contempt.

"You know what we always say about Méjico and our blessed Durango?" the Senorita asked. "They are words to live by, and they summarize madre Méjico better than anything I have ever heard."

"No," Judith McKillian said, "but I'm afraid I'm about to find out."

Diaz cleared his throat and then orated in sonorous tones:

There is no law in Sinaloa,
No Sunday in Sonora,
No churches in Chihuahua...

The Senorita raised her glass high and thundered the last line of the verse:

And no God in Durango!

"Gawd, I hate Méjico," Judith McKillian muttered under her breath but raised her glass all the same.

"Try to think of the country's natural beauty," Sutherland said quietly with gentle mockery, putting an arm over her shoulder.

"Anyone who would go to Méjico for 'natural beauty,'" McKillian shot back, "would go to hell for the nightlife."

Throwing back her drink, she rose from the boulder on which she'd been seated and hurled her empty glass against it as hard as she could. It smashed dramatically into a thousand pieces.

PART XXII

Don't look back, boy, on the trail back there
For the women who loved you or them that care.
There's a long wailin' whistle, through your soul it's throbbed,
For the men that you killed and the trains that you robbed,
For the banks that you hit and the women who sobbed.
It's followin' you, boy, up your backtrail,
Don't look back, boy, just listen to it wail,
Back in Yuma Jail.
—One of J. P. Paxton's poems to Outlaw Torn Slater, *Yuma Jail*

CHAPTER 1

That night, Katherine Ryan climbed back up to the center bell tower, high over El Rancho—higher even than the snipers' nests on each side of her. Once again, she watched the field through her telescope.

The sky was cloudless, pellucidly clear, and the midnight sky was carpeted with what appeared to be a billion-trillion stars. The broad alabaster swath of the Milky Way was juxtaposed alongside a magisterial full moon—as big as Katherine had ever seen. The night was so brilliantly lit she had enough illumination to read books and newspapers by, but in the clarity of that arid desert air, the field before her now appeared surreal—coming to her almost as a revelation. The battle that had been fought there had saved her ranch and everything she'd worked for. At the same time, however, what she gazed on was unmistakably macabre, difficult to process and shocking to behold.

Her workers and Slater's army of desperados were engaged in a massive all-night undertaking: gathering up the dead, then hauling their bodies to the funeral pyres spread throughout the battlefield. Disposing of so many slain was turning out to be a long, laborious operation. They'd been at it all day, were still at it and would be doing it late into the morning. She still could not believe the sheer immensity of the slaughter that had taken place.

She had been there in her parlor for Krupp's briefing, so she knew how he'd planned to use the three snipers, the Gatlings and the Mitrailleuses de Reffyes. Still, she hadn't been prepared for the sheer barbarism of what she was to witness.

Everything and everyone surprised her—even her son, Richard. She knew he was a superlative marksman and would probably make the shots. Of course, he could always miss, in which case she was there to call out where his bullet had hit and how far off he'd been, so he could correct the next attempt.

But Katherine hadn't anticipated Richard's coldness, his obliviousness to the lives he was snatching with such ruthlessness. Nor had he missed a shot. She'd sat there bearing mute witness through her telescope, staring at the men, the look of shock and horror on their faces, when, suddenly and unexpectedly, a huge, silent, scarlet pit opened up in the middle of their chests—"center mass," Slater had described such shots—even as Richard was already slamming the trigger guard forward, ejecting the shell casing and inserting a fresh cartridge, automatically, reflexively. Yanking the trigger guard back against the breech, he was already sighting in on his next kill.

Nor had Katherine been prepared for the machinelike efficiency of the Gatlings. Krupp had said that in their present form, they were primarily defensive weapons, and she guessed that was true. Still the fury of the Gatlings' bullet bursts was spectacularly...*offensive.* Staring down on the battlefield through her spyglass from her Olympian height, she could see the two Gatlings push the charging soldiers closer and closer to the field's middle, almost like drovers hazing cattle into the open gate of a corral. Then she saw what four Gatlings, three Mitrailleuses de Reffyes and 150 repeating rifles did to over a thousand men packed tightly together into a single dense mass.

She had never seen so much blood in her life.

She hoped and prayed that she never saw anything like that again.

When the Mitrailleuses de Reffyes fired all at once, it was as if hell's doors had swung open wide and that the attacking men were charging into the Inferno's biggest, hottest, most furious furnaces.

Slater had told her that each of the three gun's "firing plates" was the equivalent of twenty-five shotguns discharging their buckshot shells in unison—but backed by far more powder and containing commensurately more stopping power. The three firing plates, combined, would blast fifteen hundred lead balls into Shelby's soldiers—and the big guns could fire six thousand of those balls per minute. To those men on the receiving end, it was simply beyond bearing. Those Mitrailleuses de Reffyes were the coup de grace and the point of no return.

Katherine had watched the survivors turn in their traces and flee the field in blind panic and full rout, dropping their weapons so that they would run away even faster, doing anything and everything to escape the hellfire that they'd just endured.

The battle was over, and the day was…*hers.*

Now, turning to her left, she stared—reflexively, unconsciously—down into what had been Slater's sniper's nest. She'd always felt a strange inexplicable fondness for him even though she had never approved of lawless ways. After all, when she was little more than a fifteen-year-old child and held captive by the Apache, it was Slater—only seventeen himself—who had rescued her from them and also from Geronimo, who was desperate to bed her and make her his wife. No good, decent, church-going, law-abiding gentlemen had come to save her in her moment of unendurable need.

Only Torn Slater had been there for her.

But now she also remembered how early in the battle she had glanced down into Slater's sniper's nest and had seen something so troubling she still couldn't process it.

* * *

Gazing down on the outlaw, she watched as he peered into his sniper scope. Pushing the trigger guard forward, he ejected a spent cartridge, inserted another and snapped the trigger guard back. Squeezing the trigger, the gun bucked, jumped, and the nest filled with more dense milky haze.

Slowly, the smoke dissipated, and Katherine could once again see her friend. He had already ejected the shell casing, had reinserted another and was lining up another shot, when she noticed—

When she noticed—

There was something she couldn't make out. Raising her spyglass and adjusting its magnification, an image finally came into focus. Kneeling at Torn Slater's feet was Belle Starr, her head between his legs, bobbing up and down, up and down, up—

What?

Who were these people?

What were these people?

* * *

Slater hadn't bothered to stop or slow down his loading and firing of the Sharps. He just kept killing the men that were in his crosshairs, utterly oblivious to Belle's libidinous ministrations—reloading, shooting, reloading, shooting, over and over and over again, as casually and nonchalantly as if he'd been calmly plinking empty beer bottles, lined up on a split-rail fence on a country road during a quiet summer day in the middle of nowhere.

Once, after another firefight, Katherine had asked Slater how he'd felt after shooting a man with that Big Fifty Sharps. After a moment of reflection, he'd answered:

"Recoil."

So Katherine Ryan was used to Slater's indifference to death—even violent slaughter—but she hadn't been prepared for what Slater and Belle were doing while he killed those men. Slater was gunning down man after man after man, as efficiently and quickly as he knew how, without pausing or missing a beat, even as Belle was—

Was—?

Was—?

Katherine still couldn't credit what she'd seen.

She sat there for what seemed to be an eternity, staring emptily into silence and nothingness and the void, torn between horror and shock and utter, absolute incontrovertible...*incomprehension.*

She couldn't believe her eyes.

She was no prude, but this was beyond the pale—

This was beyond—

Beyond...

Everything.

She fought to compose herself, to calm herself down.

Come on, girl, pull yourself together, she thought. *You accomplished so much today. Focus on what you achieved, on what's positive. Focus on what you should be thankful for. You have much to be grateful for—your late husband Frank and for so much more, and Richard and Rachel, to those strangers that appeared out of nowhere, one of whom, Fritz Krupp, showed you how to defeat Shelby and his army, and Bismarck and that young man, Nietzsche, all of whom personally battled those marauders at great risk to their lives, and those hundred or so men who also fought to protect your spread.*

And Slater too.

Yes, Slater, no matter what he just did with Belle, yes, always Slater. He had been there when you had nothing, nobody, but there he was, tall and terrible and transcendent, and he threw you on that Indian pony and led you out of that Apache ranchero in the middle of the night and away from Geronimo.

And later it was Slater, not your dear, late, so recently departed Frank, who had fathered her son, Richard.

Yes, Slater, not Frank, gave you Richard.

And then when Richard was imprisoned in that slave-labor mine in Méjico, it was Slater who went down there and broke him out—Slater, always Slater.

Slater gave you your life, your home, your son, your future, and now he'd saved Rancho de Cielo.

No matter how bad or how bleak or how dangerous the situation was, Slater had always been there and would always be there—always.

And he never wanted one damn thing in return.

You owe him everything—no matter what happened.

In his sniper's nest.

In his gun tower.

With Belle.

Hell, face it, you even owe... Belle.

More than Slater, it was Belle who raised that army of... brigands.

In her own way, Belle had had yours and Slater's backs all these years.

You owe Belle too—among so many others, for so many things.

So focus on that.

Focus on that.

Katherine did. Instead of Slater and Belle's dalliance, she also concentrated on the battlefield before her—and what they'd achieved.

The only men left on that field were Shelby's dead and wounded and her own men, who were stacking them like cordwood onto the funeral pyres, then setting them ablaze. Their only company was the gathering hosts of buzzards, wheeling overhead but now descending one at a time to pick at the remains. The near extinction of the great buffalo herds—annihilated by men desperate to starve the country's Indian population into blind submission—had left millions upon millions of bison carcasses to rot on the plains. Death for those herds had been a feast of plenty for vultures, and, in turn, they had proliferated beyond all measure or magnitude.

Now the scavenger birds were everywhere—clearly visible in the moonlight, superabundant, riding the high thermals, observing their eternal vigils, waiting with boundless patience for those who fall. This time they had found a cornucopia to rival the deaths of the great herds, and it did not take long for them to begin their lazy, spiraling, lassitudinous descent. Towering funnel clouds of carrion birds were gyring, spiraling and descending on the devastated remains of Shelby's blasted, bloody and hideously disfigured brigade.

The handful of men—who were still hauling the last few corpses to the pyres—were having to drive the birds off of the remains in order to do their job.

The buzzards weren't happy about it either.

But try as hard as she could, Katherine's mind still drifted back to Slater. What was it that poet-songwriter, J.P. Paxton, had said of him—the one Bill Hickok and Calamity had nicknamed "the Professor"? He'd written a poem about Slater escaping from Yuma Prison. He'd called it *Yuma Jail* and had later set it to music. It had become hugely popular, worldwide. He'd finished the poem by advising Slater:

Don't look back, boy, on the trail back there,
For the women, that loved you or them that cared
There's a wailin' train whistle through your soul it's throbbed
For the men that you killed and the trains that you robbed,
For the banks that you hit and the women that sobbed.
It's followin' you, boy, up your backtrail.
Don't look back, boy, just listen to it wail,
Back in Yuma Jail.

Well, the Professor had warned Slater not to look back, and J. P. was, no doubt, right. Nonetheless, Katherine hoped the outlaw would occasionally remember her and recall their times together with something resembling...*fondness.*

She knew she would never stop thinking about him—not ever, not to her last dying day.

And one thing, she knew, she would never forget. Somewhere in the dim abyss of her brain skulked a last single ineradicable image, which she knew she would never unsee, a vision that was burned into her cranium forever—the memory of Slater and Belle in that gun tower.

But even as she fought to erase that picture, part of her also had to confess that Katherine Julia Ryan was now—and always would be—a little bit in love with…

Outlaw Torn Slater.

EPILOGUE

"We shall have upheavals, a convulsion of earthquakes, a moving of mountains and valleys....[A]ll power structures of the old society will have been exploded—for all of them are based on lies: There will be wars the likes of which have never been seen...."

—Friedrich Nietzsche on the shape of war to come in *Ecce Homo*

CHAPTER 1

Dreams die hard.

For Méjico's Generalissimo Porfirio Diaz and US Confederacy General Joseph O. Shelby, their shared vision of reconquering the United States and reclaiming their lost lands suffered a singularly agonizing demise. The Battle of El Rancho de Cielo was, indeed, the death of dreams.

But at least, it seemed to have purged General Shelby and John Newman Edwards of their lust for revenge against the northern states. Abandoning his dreams of a resurgent Klan and of the South "rising again," Shelby returned to Missouri, resumed farming, and in his later years put on a badge and became, incredibly enough, a...*peace officer.* Edwards went back first to Missouri and then to Kansas, where he worked on newspapers. In 1889, he died at age fifty of alcoholism.

As for Frank James, he also returned to Missouri and, of all things, turned himself in to the governor. He stood trial for two of his train robberies—one in Missouri, the other in Alabama—and for the murder of various personages in the course of the Missouri train hijacking. At his trial, General Shelby testified on his behalf. He was acquitted on all charges. Missouri claimed jurisdiction for all other charges, and he was never tried again. Frank James never spent a day in prison.

Putting away his gun, Frank went straight and worked various legitimate jobs—including shoe salesman, burlesque theater ticket taker, and telegraph operator. Still, he'd always felt "the call," and toward the end of his life went on the speaking circuit, preaching "the Word." Frank liked to say that he used his "misspent life" as his text. Sometimes his cousin—Thomas

Coleman Younger, who'd finally been released from prison after twenty-eight years behind bars—spoke alongside him.

Belle went back to Younger's Bend and never repented her life of violence. She would eventually have seventeen husbands and lovers, most of whom were outlaws and died by violence. Cole Younger, the sole exception, expired peacefully, but only because he'd served three decades in prison. The others either murdered each other in jealous rages or were hanged by Judge Parker or shot by Parker's marshals.

Belle died under a cloud. Riding up a country road, she was mysteriously shot off her horse—cut in two with a shotgun. Burton Rascoe, the New York critic and journalist, traveled to Oklahoma, interviewed friends, relatives and neighbors, and then wrote her definitive biography: *Belle Starr: The Bandit Queen.* Some of her neighbors told Rascoe that Belle had had a sado-masochistic relationship with her son. One night after he came home drunk, Belle, the neighbors said, had savagely quirted him. Rascoe believed that the son had, subsequently, assassinated her.

Doc Holliday's tuberculosis grew increasingly debilitating, and he spent his last years out west, wandering in and out of sanitariums. Arriving in Glen Springs, Colorado, where he hoped the restorative hot springs would improve his condition, his health, unfortunately, deteriorated, perhaps aggravated by the springs' sulfurous fumes. In 1886, he succumbed at age thirty-six.

Bat Masterson left law enforcement to deal faro, run gambling houses, and eventually he became a reporter. One of his fans was Theodore Roosevelt, who was rumored to have hired him as a bodyguard and did appoint him a marshal to the southern district of New York City. He also wrote a column for the *New York World Telegram*. One of his journalistic specialties was sports writing. He became famous for his coverage of boxing matches, most notably those of Jack Dempsey. Attending the 1915 heavyweight championship fight between Jess Willard and Jack Johnson, Masterson served as one of Willard's seconds. He also became famous for his profiles of the Wild West gunfighters he'd known, including Wyatt Earp, Doc Holliday, Ben Thompson and Luke Short. He died at his desk of a massive coronary at age sixty-seven in 1921.

Wyatt Earp lived a peripatetic life, drifting from western town to western town, from goldfield to goldfield, running card games, gambling halls, saloons and mining operations. He traveled as far north as Nome, Alaska, in pursuit of "the big score."

Eventually, settling down in Los Angeles, he became a consultant on silent western films, where he became friends with the film stars W. S. Hart, Tom Mix and Harry Carey and with directors John Ford and Raoul Wash. On the side he sometimes did dangerous, off-the-books assignments for the LAPD, which occasionally resulted in gunplay.

His wife, Josephine, wrote that they were married from 1892 until his death in 1929 at age eighty in Southern California. They were said to have had "a tempestuous marriage" but were, nonetheless, devoted to each other.

Porfirio Diaz spent his remaining years in Méjico plundering that country piecemeal. And he was a spectacularly powerful political leader—so much so that in his time and in the 120 years that followed his death, he was often lauded in the press and even by historians for his thirty-one-year tenure as president. They have tended to dwell inordinately on the thousands of miles of train tracks that he laid and telegraph wires that he strung, the innumerable mines he dug, the millions of acres he cultivated and the monumental amounts of foreign loans that he negotiated for Méjico.

That he did it, however, on the backs of Méjicano peons was usually ignored but it was an inescapable fact. He was credibly estimated to have enslaved 80 to 90 percent of his population, and the barbarity with which these forced laborers were treated was cruel beyond words. He is sometimes called "the George Washington of Mexico." That comparison would be apt if Washington had enslaved 80 to 90 percent of the America population, white citizens included. The descriptions of slavery under Diaz in this book are based on personal testimonies and remembrances of some of the survivors.

Porfirio was not a European oppressor—a Spanish or French grandee who ruthlessly exploited Méjico for financial gain—but native-born mestizo. That he abused his own people on such an epic scale is impossibly painful for many scholars to accept even a full century after his death in Paris; consequently, many historians still have not come to terms with Diaz's atrocities. To ignore his depredations, however, would be like writing about Hitler and Stalin and then ignoring the Holocaust and the Gulag Archipelago. That Diaz's apologists choose to ignore the magnitude and the inhuman cruelty of his enslavements says more about them than it does about Diaz.

Nor did he force his people into peonage to enrich Méjicano oligarchs. He bestowed Méjico's wealth and resources mostly on foreign magnates, who often became absentee hacendados, not even bothering to visit their tremendous holdings. In many respects, these absentee grandees were more brutal than those who resided in Méjico. They never witnessed the violence that their overseers wreaked on their peons in an attempt to wring ever-increasing revenues from that much-abused nation and its people.

Diaz allowed many foreign potentates to exploit his country—as well as the three fictional characters I write about in this book. It was said that by the end of Diaz's reign, he had sold almost the entire country to international plutocrats in the form of decades-long, tax-free leases.

But nothing lasts forever. In 1910, the Méjicano people rose up. For the next ten years, Diaz's predations—and the rage his atrocities provoked—plunged his nation into one of the most violent and bloody revolutions in world history. Driven from power, he spent his declining years living in luxury, in Paris. He died five years later in 1915.

As for Outlaw Torn Slater, Katherine Ryan offered him an easy, even affluent life—an offer, that he chose not to acknowledge, let alone accept. Early one morning, before first light, he rode off—abandoning Belle as well as Katherine. He did care about Katherine, however, and he left her a note, in which he wrote,

> *Katherine, I was born for the high lines, the owlhoot trail. If I didn't rob banks and trains, I wouldn't know who I was when I got up in the morning. It's all I know, it's all I'm good for. As a reclamation project, I guess I'm a bust. I hope I didn't let you down too much.*

Katherine couldn't believe what she had read. Slater had done so much for her—had saved her life and that of Richard in ways she still could not fully credit or comprehend. He'd recruited an army for her, neutralized Shelby's heavy artillery and helped save El Rancho de Cielo from an invading force of two thousand men.

Yet he feared he'd let Katherine down.

Still, it took her a long time to get over that letter.

In some ways she never did.

CHAPTER 2

The months aboard the SS *Bremerhofen* passed uneventfully, and on the voyage around Cape Horn, Krupp, Bismarck and Nietzsche steamed through seas as quiet as prayer and as smooth as polished glass. Krupp and Bismarck spent much of their time sitting in lounge chairs on the deck, wrapped in blankets, smoking cigars, drinking coffee and reflecting on their stay in Méjico.

They spent their evenings—or when the weather was inclement—drinking whiskey in the bar.

Krupp fascinated Bismarck with his knowledge of ordnance, particularly those weapons systems still on the drawing boards. Nietzsche, too, when he left his compartment, would pump Krupp about the new powerful armaments that he, along with Bismarck, increasingly feared would trouble Germany and Europe's future.

Fritz Krupp was not reassuring.

"My father does not understand the murderous potential of our advanced weaponry. His mind is fixated on past iterations of our howitzers and on piling up mountains of money. He views all wars as ending as abruptly his Franco-Prussian War."

"He sees wars as financial opportunities?" Nietzsche asked.

"As profit centers."

Even Bismarck was rendered speechless at that one.

"My father," Fritz Krupp went on to explain, "does not comprehend the increased firepower that smokeless cordite powder will bring to our howitzers and, most devastating of all, rapid-fire weaponry. He does not understand the spectacular new advances that are being made in mechanized weapons systems. He doesn't understand that making obscene amounts of filthy lucre does not justify the unprecedented, unparalleled slaughter to come and our role in facilitating that slaughter."

"You mean the kind of killing we saw in Arizona—what those Gatlings and Mitrailleuses des Reffyes did to Shelby's men?" Bismarck asked.

"Those weapons are nothing," Krupp said. "There is an American named Hiram Stevens Maxim, who has a rapid-fire gun that he could not sell in his own country. My father rejected it out of hand, but the Vickers Company in England is financing its development. One day, we will be forced to produce it as well."

"Is it like the Gatling or the Mitrailleuse?" Bismarck asked.

"Neither," Krupp said. "The force of the recoil on the breechblock ejects each spent cartridge and inserts the next shell mechanically, automatically, without human intervention."

"So it does not rely on a man turning a crank?" Nietzsche asked. "The way I'd had to do?"

"No," Krupp said, "and, one day, I believe it will thereby fire over five hundred rounds per minute."

"Why would anyone want to fire so many rounds so rapidly?" Bismarck asked.

"Because the world has seen what we did to France with a conscript army," Krupp said, "and what Lincoln did to the Confederacy with his draftees. They crushed their enemies with them. All the nations of Europe have or are, therefore, instituting conscription to counteract our Kruppwerk guns and our army's might. The next big war will see million-man armies charging million-man armies. Maxim rapid-fire guns and long-range artillery, powered by overwhelmingly powerful smokeless cordite powder, will blast those fighting forces to bits and pieces. Those guns will then be used against mills, factories and cities as well. We will see violence of unprecedented, unimaginable proportions."

"Why would any nation fight such a war?" Nietzsche asked.

"Why did the Peloponnesian Wars last twenty-eight years?" Bismarck asked.

"Thucydides said that war was driven by 'the desire for power inspired by greed and blind ambition.'"

"So it was ever thus," Bismarck said.

"The nations of Europe will do much worse to each other than Athens and Sparta could have ever done or even conceived of doing," Krupp said. "I've seen designs for airships that will, one day, work. We will arm them as well and bombard nations from the skies."

"But why?" Nietzsche asked again.

"Because men like my father will sell those nations the Arms of Armageddon...*at a profit,*" Krupp said. "Banks will finance those weapons sales... *at a profit.* We will finance politicians to do our bidding...*at a profit.*"

"Is everything done for a profit?" Nietzsche asked.

"Always for a profit," Krupp said.

"You talk as if you're disillusioned with the arms business," Bismarck said to Krupp.

Nietzsche could tell that the chancellor had developed a grudging admiration and a gradual affection for the industrialist.

"My father and his fellow arms manufacturers will not stop," Krupp said, "until they have wrung every last pfennig from the bleeding earth."

"And what will they do after that," Nietzsche asked, "after they have brought about the Battle of the Apocalypse and visited hellfire everlasting upon the entire globe?"

"They will sell their arms in hell," Krupp said.

CHAPTER 3

For the most part, Nietzsche spent his time aboard ship alone in his cabin. He was inordinately troubled by the events of the last several weeks—by what he'd seen and experienced throughout his entire stay in Méjico. He'd been there longer than Bismarck and Krupp.

So during the entire voyage, he'd sat mostly in his cabin, staring listlessly, sightlessly at his notebook. He was finding it difficult to concentrate. He'd been through so much. Nietzsche had journeyed to a nether world utterly devoid of morality and decency, as he had always known it, a world where only violence—and the power to wield and control it—held sway. A world not where might made right but where might was the...*only right.* A world where the strong prevailed and the weak perished. A world where, as the Senorita once told him, "a priori moral values are empty as prayer, meaningless as a sub-mongoloid's dreams and unfathomable as the dark between the stars—a world where natural selection is the only law of life."

He was secretly beginning to question his own moral values. Somewhere in the innermost recesses of his dark and tortured soul, in the dim abyss of his fevered and increasingly frantic brain, the festering worm of doubt had started burrowing into his previously incorruptible faith and intellectually indomitable ideals. A little, niggling, gnawing, nagging voice was whispering to him repeatedly:

*"What if the Senorita and her friends are...*right?"

The thought wouldn't let him rest, wouldn't leave him alone, wouldn't give him one moment's peace. It started with a gentle tapping, then harder and louder, then a rapping, a clanging and banging until it finally boomed in his skull like the thunder of a kettle drum.

What if the Senorita was right? What if the Senorita was right? What if the Senorita was right?

He had to reexamine everything the Senorita had told him during his stay in Méjico, then measure her arguments against his previously held convictions. Struggling to remember her many outrageous theories and tirades, Friedrich Nietzsche opened his notebook and began jotting down every one of her random thoughts and wild philosophical observations.

He wrote like he was possessed, because he was, filling notebook after notebook after notebook late into the night. When the sun rose the next morning and illuminated his porthole, he was still scribbling frenetically, insanely. His journals were filled with her endless, demented ravings about "slave morality," "a religion of pity," "lower-class *ressentiment*," "Superman," "Perspectivism," "Eternal Return" and "Beyond Good and Evil."

And with a deep breath, he began scrawling: *"Will to Power... Will to Power... Will to Power... Will to Power... Will to Power... Will to Power... Will to Power..."*

In the end the words were pouring out of him faster, faster, faster, his heart pounding wildly, his mind increasingly chaotic.

"WilltoPower WilltoPower WilltoPower WilltoPower WilltoPower WilltoPower—"

He was the descendant of many distinguished Lutheran ministers, but his writing was now insanely out of control. The violently heretical words kept coming, kept coming, kept coming, blasphemously belligerent, *DeathofGod DeathofGod DeathofGod DeathofGod DeathofGod DeathofGod DeathofGod DeathofGod DeathofGod DeathofGod DeathofGod DeathofGod DeathofGod DeathofGod DeathofGod DeathofGod DeathofGod DeathofGod DeathofGod DeathofGod—*

CHAPTER 4

The years passed. Nietzsche became increasingly withdrawn and remote. Bismarck and Krupp believed that he never recovered from his time in Méjico and in Arizona, and they worried about him—not only on the boat trip back to Germany but during the years that followed.

The two men stayed in touch with each other—in part because, together, they were charged with arming Germany's military and maintaining the nation's defenses. Fritz Krupp would sometimes tell Bismarck that in Méjico he'd "gazed on the face of pure evil" and was now convinced that the Fatherland had to be protected against people, no matter what the cost. To that end, he moved the Kruppwerk into warship manufacturing, including the construction of U-boats. Building rapid-fire Maxim guns as well as even more powerful howitzers, Krupp soon became, preeminently, the most powerful arms magnate in the world.

He and Bismarck were, of necessity, sworn to secrecy about their clandestine trip to Méjico. From time to time, however, after a long day of weapons discussions, strategizing and negotiations, they would sit back over brandy and cigars and reminisce about what they had experienced. As much as they despised Diaz and his friends, they had to admit that their trip there had changed them in ways that were depressing, perplexing and yet profound.

Among other things, they had glimpsed the shape of war to come. They saw, with each passing year, how conscription was rolling over the nations of Europe like a plague and how multimillion-man armies were the new reality. They also knew what automatic weapons, properly deployed and employed, could do to such armies. They also discovered, to their horror, that Europe's leaders were blindly naïve to the dangers that such weapons posed.

Kaiser Wilhelm listened to their arguments politely and did what he could to avoid future wars. He died in 1887, however, and Wilhelm II was far more bellicose. Infatuated with the great military that Bismarck and Krupp had so painstakingly created, he was convinced that his country would prevail in any continental conflict. That the new weapons systems, in fact, doomed their possessors to bloody, pounding, grinding, intrinsically defensive trench warfare was lost on the young leader, as it was lost on all the leaders of Europe.

As the years passed, as the two men labored on, late at night after dinner, they, increasingly, found themselves, talking about Nietzsche. Since returning from Méjico, he'd begun writing and publishing books at a frenetic pace—electrifying works that were inciting controversies around the world. The two friends read with interest his diatribes against Judeo-Christian "slave morality"; his advocacy of "the will to power," "the eternal return"; his belief in the civilizational importance of "supermen" and "the death of God." They knew exactly where he'd purloined his brilliant theories.

The Senorita.

How many nights had they spent in the company of her, Diaz, Sutherland and that demented McKillian woman, listening to their pathological pronouncements on those subjects.

Particularly, those of...*the Senorita.*

Ironically, those psychopaths had had an ameliorating effect on Bismarck. He had always been hawkish in his attitude toward and treatment of Germany's labor movement. After all, as an upper-class Junker aristocrat, he'd never had any concrete dealings with actual workers. However, when the Senorita and Diaz took him and Nietzsche on that tour of Méjico's haciendas, he witnessed close-up the hardships and indignities that laborers suffered and what he saw touched his previously untouchable heart and cracked his uncaring shell.

When he listened to the arrogant contempt that those grandees in Méjico had heaped on their workers, he recognized some of his own attitudes and those of Germany's aristocratic classes as well. He no longer looked down on any workers. He had a sense of how they lived, what they experienced, and he knew all too well the scornful attitudes of Germany's elites toward them—attitudes which he had once shared.

Now his former prejudices shamed and sickened him.

In private.

In public, Bismarck, Nietzsche and Friedrich Krupp could never divulge to anyone the story of their trip to Méjico, their utterly immoral and unconscionable work on behalf of Alfred Krupp and their completely illegal participation in Diaz's and Joseph Shelby's attempted invasion of the United States. To reveal their experiences there would have mandated criminal prosecution and conviction for all of them, followed by lengthy prison sentences, if not criminal execution.

So while Bismarck had once been militantly anti-labor, after he returned from Méjico, he was changed. Turning in his traces, he coopted Labor's agenda and passed some of the most revolutionarily progressive social welfare legislation in history—laws that would shape all other social welfare statutes for 150 years to come.

In December 1884, he introduced the first large-scale compulsory insurance to establish universal healthcare. For the first time in history, all blue-collar workers were covered by insurance that provided paid sick leave and unrestricted access to doctors and medical treatment. That same year, he also introduced legislation that paid for the medical treatment of fully disabled workers and also remunerated them for up to two-thirds of their salaries in pension benefits.

In 1886, that coverage was expanded to cover agricultural workers.

In 1889, Bismarck pushed through the legislature and saw signed into law Germany's first old-age pension program. Financed equally by employers and workers, it provided workers with a pension annuity for life, and it covered all categories of workers, including agricultural, industrial, servants and tradespeople. Bismarck also insisted that the German government paid for part of the program.

Unfortunately, all the unhinged harangues that Bismarck, Nietzsche and Friedrich Krupp had had to endure in Méjico—particularly, those of the Senorita—seemed to have had a deleterious effect on Nietzsche. At the time, all three of them had regarded the Senorita's deranged rants as the work of a sick mind, but somewhere along the way Nietzsche had had some sort of twisted epiphany. He was writing book after book after book, in which he reproduced her maniacal monologues—often verbatim—and was treating them as if they were holy writ.

With Europe's intelligentsia cheering him on every step of the way.

Bismarck and Krupp were more ambivalent about Nietzsche's books. They understood that his writings on religion and morality represented philosophic breakthroughs, and they believed his warnings about the new apocalyptically destructive wars to come were prescient. Nietzsche, like themselves, had taken part in the Battle of Rancho de Cielo and understood all too well the consequences of Europe's new killing machines—particularly the Maxim guns, which were now in production in England and which Krupp was also starting to manufacture. Some journalist had dubbed the Maxim "the machine gun" and when they were deployed en masse, they were capable of firing thousands of rounds per minute.

Like themselves, Nietzsche could see it all coming. As he wrote in one of his last and greatest works, *Ecce Homo*:

> *We shall have upheavals, a convulsion of earthquakes, a moving of mountains and valleys.... [A]ll power structures of the old society will have been exploded—for all of them are based on lies: There will be wars the likes of which have never been seen....*

That Nietzsche had stolen those words almost verbatim from the Senorita had not bothered Bismarck or Fritz Krupp all that much, and so they had never attempted to expose the sources for so many of his most iconoclastic ideas. Any more than they cared to reveal the wellsprings for Bismarck's new socialist bent. Among other things, they liked Nietzsche and had no desire to rain on his parade and ruin his burgeoning intellectual reputation.

Nor did Nietzsche, Friedrich Krupp and Bismarck ever have the opportunity to chastise Richard Wagner for his role in concocting Krupp's arms deal. That he had hounded and browbeat the vulnerable and impressionable Friedrich Nietzsche, who had previously idolized the composer, into taking the trip, had been particularly galling. While they were in Méjico, however, traversing all nine circles of that Dantesque hell, the legendary composer had had the poor taste to up and...*die*. Their unfinished business with that great, if demented, genius would remain unfinished.

Bismarck found it in his heart to forgive Wagner, but Nietzsche would go to his grave loathing and impugning him, in speech and in print, at every opportunity—not only because of his untimely and infelicitous death but also for his vile nationalistic and fiercely antisemitic writings.

But then Nietzsche had grown increasingly incensed over many things—so much so that even before his last book, the author had withdrawn, become a miserable, misanthropic recluse, and rumors were swirling about Germany that Friedrich Nietzsche—now considered one of the greatest minds of the nineteenth century—had gone...*mad.*

During one of their late-night conversations, Krupp had told Bismarck that ever since the boat ride back to Germany, during which Nietzsche had retreated to his cabin for days on end, he had feared for the young man's sanity. He believed that the Senorita and Judith McKillian had, in fact, abused Nietzsche in some frighteningly macabre way and that memories of that night were what was driving Nietzsche to the brink of lunacy and beyond.

The two men decided that, despite rumors of his extreme psychosis, they would pay Nietzsche a visit in Basil, where he was living in seclusion with his sister. They decided to show up unannounced so that he would not have a chance to forbid their visit.

To their pleasant surprise, Nietzsche was happy to see them and also wanted to talk about their ill-fated trip to Méjico. Fritz Krupp started off their conversation, explaining to the two men what the Senorita and Judith McKillian had done to him during an earlier trip to Méjico—and worried that the women had tried something similar with Nietzsche.

"I had this talk with Otto," Krupp said, "when we first got back from Méjico. I wish I had told you about my experiences with those two harpies, so let me tell you now."

"Please do," Nietzsche said.

"First, the women got me drunk on brandy and champagne, which I believe they laced with narcotics and perhaps hallucinogens. After lashing my limbs to a four-poster bed, they assaulted my body, initially by themselves, then with putas, and then with...*young men.*

"After all the alcohol and drugs, I finally succumbed to their seductions, at which point flash pans began to blaze and camera shutters began to click. Those two hell-bent harlots burned through photographic plate after photographic plate after photographic plate.

"The witches then threatened to send the photographs to my father, but by that time, I was sobering up. Incensed—in fact, in a blind rage—I told them, 'Go ahead! Send the photos and be damned!' I told them that I despised both my old man and his business. I detested him for being a war merchant, for practicing the death trade, and for chatteling me into the whole sorry enterprise. Anyway, I had stored away so much ill-gotten lucre over the last fifteen years, I didn't need the old man's money any longer. Even my mother wanted me out of the 'merchant of death' business, and, bless her heart, she had set up a trust for me in an attempt to encourage my retirement.

"'Let someone else run our family's House of Death,' she had once shouted at me.

"My father knew nothing of my plans, and it would have crushed him had he found out. So I told the Senorita and Judith McKillian what I intended to do and told them to 'stick their photos up their goddamn asses with the rest of their shit.'

"'Oh, and by the way,'" I told them, "'never plan on seeing another weapon again from my father or me or from any of our friends, namely, every significant arms manufacturer in Europe and in the entire United States of America, meaning every major arms manufacturer in the world. After all, if you did this to me, you'll do it to them, and I will let them know every sordid detail.'

"That very night they gave me every photograph plus the plates and negatives.

"I burned them all in the hotel courtyard."

They were silent a long moment.

"Why have you remained in your father's arms business?" Nietzsche finally asked.

"I fear for our Heimat, our homeland. We are surrounded on all sides by feared and hated enemies, who are arming themselves with the most potent weapons money can buy. I could not turn my back on the Fatherland—not after getting to know people like Diaz and the Senorita and learning how much evil truly lurks in the hearts of men. I have always believed that Bismarck and I, working closely together, could stave off war and keep our Fatherland safe—and up to now, we have."

"I understand," Nietzsche said.

"But I don't understand *you*," Bismarck said. "Like everyone else in Germany, I have read your books as they came out, and while I appreciate the profundity of your insights, some of what you write is...*terrifying*."

"Your hatred of the working classes sounds like exactly what Diaz and the Senorita said about their peons," Krupp said.

"Listen to some of what you wrote about people who work for a living in *Beyond Good and Evil*," Bismarck said:

A good and healthy aristocracy must acquiesce, with a good conscience, in the sacrifice of countless individuals, who, for its benefit, must be reduced to slaves and tools. The masses have no right to exist on their own account: Their sole excuse for living lies in their usefulness as a sort of superstructure or scaffolding, upon which a more select race of beings may be elevated.

"In your book *The Antichrist*, you say they must be sent 'to the wall,'" Bismarck said, "something Diaz and the Senorita did routinely, when we were with them back in Méjico, to anyone who disagreed with them. You condemned it unequivocally then, but now you admire such savagery. You wrote:

I preach not contentedness, but more power; not peace, but war; not virtue, but efficiency. The weak must go to the wall: That is the first principle. And we must help them go.

"Christ's faith in compassion for those less fortunate than us, you dismiss," Bismarck said, "as did Diaz, the Senorita, Sutherland and that despicable McKillian woman. You call it 'a credo for cretins,'" Bismarck said. "You even said:

Compassion drains strength...Suffering is made contagious by compassion... Compassion preserves whatever is ripe for destruction...It gives life itself a gloomy and dubious aspect. Humankind has ventured to call compassion a virtue... Compassion is the modus operandi of nihilism. Let me repeat: This depressing and contagious instinct stands against all those instincts which work for the preservation and enhancement of life: In the role of protector of the miserable, compassion is a prime agent of decadence—compassion persuades to extinction...

"Your passages on women," Krupp said, "are particularly disturbing. Look at what you say about women in *Thus Spake Zarathrustra*:

All too long have a slave and a tyrant been concealed in woman. Therefore, woman is not yet capable of friendship... Woman's love involves injustice and blindness against everything she does not love. And even in the knowing love of a woman, there are still assault and lightning and night alongside light. Woman is not yet capable of friendship: Women are still cats and birds. Or at best cows...

"You then go on to say:

Man should be educated for war, and women for the recreation of the warrior; all else is folly...[E]ven the sweetest woman is bitter... You are going to women? Do not forget the whip.

"In your autobiography, *Ecce Homo*, you write:

Thank goodness I am not willing to let myself be torn to pieces! The complete woman tears you to pieces when she loves you... Oh! What a dangerous, creeping, subterranean little beast of prey she is! And so agreeable with it! A little woman pursuing her vengeance would force overtake even Fate itself. Woman is incalculably more wicked than man, she is also cleverer. Goodness in a woman is already a sign of degeneration.

"Then in that same book," Bismarck said, "you dismiss the women's suffrage movement, their quest for basic human rights, including the right to vote, simply as a sick substitute for having children. You imply that women are nothing more than subhuman breeding animals, whose rightful place in life is 'barefoot, pregnant and in the kitchen.' You tell us:

The emancipated [women]...are simply not up to having children... The struggle for equal rights is even a symptom of sickness; every doctor knows this. The more womanly a woman is the more she fights tooth and nail against rights in general: The natural order of things, the eternal war between the sexes in any case puts her in a position of advantage. Have people heard my definition of love? It is the only definition worthy of a philosopher. Love in its means is war: In its foundation it is the mortal hatred of the sexes. Have you heard my reply to the question how a woman can be cured—"saved" in fact? Give her a child!

"You summarize your view of women," Krupp observed, "by saying, 'Woman is by nature a snake...[F]rom woman comes every calamity in the world.'"

"What we want to know," Bismarck said, "is what happened to you in Méjico?"

Nietzsche stared at them and said nothing.

"Otto and I have had conversations in the past," Krupp, at last, said, breaking the silence, "about the unspeakable wickedness of the Senorita and that McKillian woman. Did they do something to you? I'm concerned that what those two did to you may have warped your attitude toward women—and toward life."

Nietzsche looked away and still said nothing.

"I was also concerned," Krupp went on, "that those two had abused our chancellor and sounded him out on it. He admitted that they had. So I told him about my experiences with them. They were also horrific, but I also told him that as long as I am alive, he—and you—will have no problems with any of those people. I can guarantee that no compromising materials of any sort will be made public."

Nietzsche still said nothing.

"Friedrich," Krupp said, leaning toward the young author, "you are a gifted writer and philosopher. Otto is the father of the modern German nation and the finest German prose stylist since Johann Wolfgang von Goethe. Neither of you deserved to be tortured sexually by those two vile and vindictive vixens and then blackmailed. Before we left for Arizona, I had it out with all of them, Diaz and Sutherland, the Senorita and Judith McKillian, and made my feelings clear. I told them that I would soon inherit der Kruppwerk and would own the largest arms manufacturing firm in the world—whether I chose to run it personally or not. I told them that I would, if they continued their malevolent games, cut Méjico off from the world's weapons and financial markets in one single, lightning...*stroke.* Forever. I would set up other contracts for my competition—to compensate them for any losses in revenue—subcontracting my own deals to them if necessary. None of them—or the Kruppwerk—would lose a mark.

"The hard truth is that none of us like Diaz or his friends," Krupp continued, "and they knew I could do it. I said to them: 'Listen, when I want to buy a woman, I go to a puta. When I want to buy a killing, I hire a paid assassin, and when I want to buy a country, I go to a fifth-rate, barbarous, bullshit little hellhole, just like Méjico, and I buy it outright—lock, stock, with both barrels smoking. Now I've bought you four, and you're going to stay bought. Fuck with me,' I told them, 'and I'm nailing your asses to the whorehouse walls you were scraped off of the night you were hatched out. I'm sending the US military back down to your madre Méjico, and they won't stop until they've burned your entire country down to bedrock and sowed its fields with salt. Then I'll arm every peon, bandito, puta, hideputa and revolucionario in Méjico and pay them to rise up against you. I'll then get you blacklisted...*everywhere.* You won't get financing for ordnance of any kind ever again. You'll be thrown out of every major money and arms market in the world. You won't be able to buy a single pistol. Hell, a cap gun, a burnt-out firecracker, a box of wet matches. You won't be able to get laid in a brass-knuckle brothel shack with a stack of thousand-dollar bills sticking out your asses. You'll never get head in Méjico—or anyplace else—ever again. You'll be so broke you won't be able to get jackrolled by a sick, whiny child or laid by a clap-infested shit-stinking whore. There won't be any point to it. You'll be too poor. Then I'll see to it that you are each flogged, buggered, flayed, drawn, quartered, castrated, cremated with stakes driven through your fucking ashes. Understand me now, putas? Read my smoke?'

"So neither of you have anything to fear. Guns and money mean more to those four than their sick, little games. Believe me, these people fear me more than they love tormenting you."

For a long time, the three men were silent. Finally, Bismarck told Nietzsche that, yes, the Senorita and McKillian had framed him with sexual photographs and that he'd feared their release. He thanked Krupp, again, for helping him out of a difficult situation.

Nietzsche then said he was ambivalent about his time in Méjico.

"On one hand," Nietzsche said, "I learned much, experienced more, was blooded in battle. You could say that I crossed the Rubicon intellectually and artistically. In some ways, my time in Méjico made me a writer, but most important...*a man.*"

AFTERWORD

Fritz Krupp,
Friedrich Nietzsche,
Otto von Bismarck

CHAPTER 1

Friedrich "Fritz" Krupp:
God of War

No God in Durango is a work of fiction. Its storyline notwithstanding, Friedrich "Fritz" Krupp, Otto von Bismarck and Friedrich Nietzsche never met in Mexico, nor did they participate in a second Mexican-American War. There was no such war. Bismarck and Nietzsche never stepped foot on the North American continent—or in the western hemisphere for that matter—nor is there any evidence that Nietzsche knew either Bismarck or Fritz Krupp. Nor did the Senorita, Judith McKillian and James Sutherland ever exist except in the author's imagination.

Krupp, Nietzsche and Bismarck, however, were profoundly influential personages in the late nineteenth century, and they each—unlike virtually all the leaders and pundits of their period—predicted the prodigious and utterly unprecedented carnage that World War I would inflict on Europe. I've always viewed them as three of the late nineteenth century's most fascinating and prophetic figures, which is one of the reasons that I wrote *No God in Durango* and featured these three men as major characters.

Fritz Krupp was singularly controversial and his legacy was highly problematic. His impact on German militarism was especially portentous. After inheriting the Kruppwerk from his father in 1887, he became its sole proprietor. It was already an industrial colossus—famous primarily for its steel production but also for its howitzers, which had, in large part, won Bismarck's 1870–71 Franco-Prussian War and helped to create the new unified German state. Fritz's father, however, never fully understood arms manufacturing. He continued to fabricate and promote bronze cannons—long after they'd been proven inferior to high-grade steel howitzers—and he never appreciated the murderous efficacy of rapid-fire weapons. His understanding of chemical propellants was flawed. Fritz grasped all these things and much more. When he took charge, he quickly changed the company's focus, transforming it into the world's preeminent multi-faceted arms manufacturer. During his fourteen-year tenure as the firm's owner, he produced smokeless, high-powered, cordite-based gunpowder, which helped him to turn out high-speed, high-velocity machine guns, capable of firing five hundred rounds per minute with effective ranges of a mile and a half. He introduced nickel steel to Krupp's arms manufacturing, which—due to its external hardness but internal resilience—gave Germany the toughest armor plating and the most powerful howitzers in the world. Krupp's most impressive World War I artillery piece—the 16.5-inch howitzer, nicknamed "Big Bertha," bombarded Paris from a distance of seventy-five miles—and was made possible thanks to Krupp's use of nickel steel and cordite-based, smokeless, high-velocity gunpowder. Krupp also acquired shipyards and pioneered the production of diesel engines, which would eventually propel the firm's U-boats, tanks and warships.

Fritz Krupp's insights into innovative weaponry would revolutionize warfare for all time to come. He also changed Germany—and not necessarily for the better. There were other great arms firms around the world—Schneider, Armstrong, Vickers, Mitsui and later the Skoda Works in Czechoslovakia—but none of them militarized their countries to the extent that Krupp did. In particular, he mesmerized its political-military leaders with his dazzling new weapon systems—so much so that he turned them into genuine war worshipers. His weaponry convinced Kaiser Wilhelm II, the German High Command and its political rulers that the German army was invincible; and—as much as anyone on the continent—Fritz Krupp made World War I inevitable.

Even when his father, Alfred, had run the Kruppwerk, the German High Command had sought to keep the firm at a discreet distance. They had been wary of the old man's power and influence, and they resisted modernization. They would not even visit Krupp's testing sites; consequently, they failed to understand the capabilities of his new weapons. Fritz believed that the German Army had fallen behind the times, and he eventually went to the new emperor with his concerns.

Recently installed, Wilhelm II was obsessed with war, and at Krupp's Meppen firing range, he became enthralled, feeling as if he were experiencing genuine battlefield violence. William Manchester in *The Arms of Krupp* describes the impact that those tests had on the emperor:

> *This was it: actual shells bursting, targets disintegrating, the ground beneath his jackboots trembling with a deep manly rumble. With a little imagination—and he had a lot—one could envisage the real thing. To Wilhelm that was a prospect of indescribable grandeur. The mere thought of battle moved him to tears, not of grief but of pride, and Fritz saw to it that the effect was heightened by Krupp's band blaring out Heil Kaiser Dir ad Was blasen die Trompeten?*

Kaiser Wilhelm II made Fritz a privy councilor and bestowed on him the title, Exzellenz. Enamored of all things military, Wilhelm came to possess over two hundred military uniforms. Wearing them continually, his coat's front was always festooned with medals, and his saber rattled audibly in its scabbard with each step, his spurs jingling.

Emperor Wilhelm forced the German High Command to attend all of Krupp's arms tests and became such a vocal supporter of Fritz's armaments that a hundred years later, historians were still debating whether he had secretly acquired a piece of the Kruppwerk and was clandestinely profiteering off of it.

But Germany wasn't the only country that Krupp was arming. He sold his weaponry to the Fatherland's most implacable enemies, including Russia, Austria and England. He would have sold weapons to France but they were too suspicious of Germany to buy any. Japan, China and Rumania also hired Fritz as their armorer.

Before he was through, Fritz would sell over forty thousand howitzers to the nations of Europe.

Many German politicians, including the emperor, objected to Krupp's foreign arms sales, but Fritz, like his father before him, was nothing if not imperious. He was quick to take affront and point out that his knowledge and personnel were singularly mobile and that many other nations on the continent would be happy to host his Kruppwerk. His firm acted as if it was a nation unto itself, and that business philosophy foreshadowed that of the twentieth and twenty-first centuries' transnational corporations. While it was headquartered in Germany and its primary customer was the German Reich, it demanded the right to sell its engines of death to anyone it so chose. Consequently, when World War I finally broke out, Germany's enemies would hammer the Reich with Krupp's massively destructive weapons.

Fritz's critics argued that he not only profited off these arms sales to Germany's enemies, but in the run-up to World War I, these sales fanned the flames of war hysteria, instilling so much fear in Germany's foes that they began purchasing arms promiscuously. Critics later charged that this war fever made the Great War almost unavoidable. It is certainly true that the more high-tech, high-powered ordnance that he sold to Germany's enemies, the more arms the Reich would need in order to defend itself against those heavily armed—often Krupp-equipped—countries. Germany's increased purchases of Krupp's weaponry likewise terrified Germany's enemies into purchasing more arms for themselves. Fritz's critics argued that in playing Germany and her prospective enemies against each other, Fritz created a business paradigm that all other global arms merchants would follow for the next 120 years.

America's weapons and munitions firms also became adept at playing Krupp's game in the early twentieth century. In 1934, fifteen years after World War I ended—a conflict that left twenty million dead moldering in their unquiet graves—North Dakota Senator Gerald Nye's special "Merchants of Death" senatorial committee took up the question of whether US firms had, like the Kruppwerk, stoked World War I hysteria in Europe. Senator Nye's committee argued and essentially proved that the world's arms companies had done precisely that, concluding that "the grave menace to the peace of the world is due in no small measure to the uncontrolled activities of the manufacturers and merchants of destruction."

Kevin Phillips, in his book *American Dynasty*, reported that George W. Bush's grandfather, Prescott Bush, and great-grandfather, George Herbert Walker, helped to finance many of America's European arms sales prior to World War I and that Prescott later handled the finances in America for Hitler's first, wealthiest and most generous financial benefactor, Fritz Thyssen, the owner of Thyssen Steel. Thyssen had donated money to Hitler, starting with the Beer Hall Putsche in 1923. Prescott managed Thyssen's American money well into 1942, even though the US was at war with Germany. Prescott did not cease working for Thyssen until the US seized the industrialist's American assets on October 20, 1942.

Nor did the machinations of the world's arms firms end after World War I. Matthew Coulter in his book on the Nye hearings, *The Senate Munitions Inquiry of the 1930s: Beyond the Merchants of Death*, reported that "[m]any U.S. munitions firms did substantial business in Germany during the 1930s, and some experienced huge increases in orders after Hitler took power." Nye's committee pointed out that "the scare of a rearmed Germany" allowed arms manufacturers to increase arms sales to other nations.

Eisenhower's January 17, 1961, farewell address became deservedly famous for his warning that "a military-industrial complex" was exerting "unwarranted influence" on US military policy. He went on to speak of "the disastrous rise of its misplaced power." David Eisenhower later said that Senator Nye's "merchant of death" hearings in the 1930s had deeply influenced his grandfather's thinking.

William Manchester described at great length in *The Arms of Krupp* how Fritz's grandson, Alfried became Hitler's premier arms manufacturer. Serving under Albert Speer, Alfried became the Third Reich's "Factory Fuhrer" and helped Speer organize Hitler's arms manufacturing program, which included the conscription of tens of thousands of slave laborers, many of whom died while working for Krupp, due to inhumane working conditions. After Germany conquered eastern European nations, Alfried sometimes organized the industrial looting of those countries. Alfried Krupp served almost six years in prison for his war crimes.

I described in my own book—*The Nuclear Terrorist: His financial backers and political patrons in the US and abroad*—how the George W. Bush administration sent officials to India and Pakistan, both nuclear weapons states and intractable enemies, to promote the sales of American weapons systems, some of which, coincidentally, were capable of delivering nuclear weapons. They effectively played the two nations off against each other in order to increase arms sales—a tactic perfected by Fritz Krupp 120 years earlier.

In the US, American arms manufacturers became so powerful that no one in the three branches of government could stop the funding of their weapons—even when no one in the US government wanted those weapons. US defense contractors controlled—to a shockingly large degree—the Defense Department's arms acquisitions budgets.

Fritz Krupp's life did not end well. For years he'd vacationed on the island of Capri, where he engaged in sexual orgies with young men. At this time in his life, he seemed to have developed delusions of invulnerability, and he allowed his partners to photograph these orgies. When these pictures became public, Fritz was quickly and unmistakably identified. Even worse, some of his partners appeared to be underage.

At least one Italian newspaper published an exposé of Fritz's secret life. German newspapers picked up the story, and while Fritz attempted to silence the press through legal action, the cat was out of the bag. The photographic evidence was irrefutable.

Publicly vilified, Fritz Krupp died—either from a stress-induced coronary or by his own hand.

CHAPTER 2

Friedrich Wilhelm Nietzsche:
The Prophet of Power

In the 1880s, Friedrich Nietzsche wrote eight books in rapid succession: *Thus Spake Zarathustra*, *Beyond Good and Evil*, *The Genealogy of Morals*, *The Case of Wagner*, *Twilight of the Idols*, *The Antichrist*, *Nietzsche Contra Wagner* and *Ecce Homo*, the last of which was written in 1888. They are the works on which his reputation rests. In them, he envisioned a future in which power worshipers would dominate global governments. He argued that the love of power, rather than the Judeo-Christian religion, would motivate these future leaders and that they would view Christ's peaceable vision dismissively, treating God as if He was dead. The public would demand religiosity from their leaders, who would, consequently, not acknowledge their atheism, but they would, nonetheless, rule their countries as if there was no God.

Nietzsche's precepts were also adopted by many corporate leaders. Wealth is one of power's more obvious manifestations, and corporations are legally designed to make money, not promote the social welfare of their employees or the countries in which they sell their goods. Corporations are sometimes compared to sharks, which must relentlessly ply the seas, killing and eating everything in their path. In their doxology, moral considerations are secondary, even tertiary—often irrelevant—to their relentless pursuit of riches. Punishing CEOs personally for moral improprieties—such as environmental degradation or bias in the hiring and treatment of their employees—is relatively rare and legally challenging, but their directors' boards will quickly call them to account for substantive financial losses.

In *Ecce Homo*, Nietzsche wrote: "I am no mere man; I am dynamite," and he was, again, prescient. He accurately foresaw a violent world, run by men who, privately or publicly, spurned the Judeo-Christian God and His Christ-centric moral values—a world where only power ruled. His "new man" would love war. Nietzsche wrote in *Ecce Homo* that he himself was "at heart, a warrior." He wrote that "wisdom loves only warriors." In *Thus Spake Zarathustra*, he said that "man should be educated for war, and women for the recreation of the warrior; all else is folly." In *The Antichrist*, he wrote that he "preached...power, not peace, but war."

He also said in *The Antichrist* that all power worshipers inevitably despise the powerless and that all world leaders owed them was the grave. He wrote that "the weak and defective must go to the wall [to be executed]: that is the first principle...And we must help them go." He argued in *Beyond Good and Evil* that for the good of Nietzsche's new power elite, the mass of humanity must be sacrificed. He wrote that the mass of humanity "must be reduced to slaves and tools. The masses have no right to exist on their own account: Their sole excuse for living lies in their usefulness as a sort of superstructure or scaffolding, upon which a more select race of beings may be elevated."

In his brave new world, Nietzsche argued that compassion for the weak would be a cardinal sin. He wrote in *The Antichrist:*

> *Compassion drains strength...Suffering is made contagious by compassion... Compassion preserves whatever is ripe for destruction...It gives life itself a gloomy and dubious aspect. Humankind has ventured to call compassion a virtue... Compassion is the modus operandi of nihilism. Let me repeat: This depressing and contagious instinct stands against all those instincts which work for the preservation and enhancement of life: In the role of protector of the miserable, compassion is a prime agent of decadence—compassion persuades to extinction...*

In *Beyond Good and Evil,* Nietzsche wrote that philosophers' passion for "truth" and "reality" is intrinsically misguided. Truth and reality, after all, are based on what Euclid called "postulates" and Nietzsche refers to as "premises" or "presuppositions." Alter those assumptions, and you instantly change your reality. Nietzsche argues that Nature supports his position. In the real world, people are surrounded on all sides not by truth but by the appearances of things. On closer inspection these appearances turn out to be illusory. The earth isn't flat, and it isn't at the universe's center, even though common sense dictates the former and astronomical observations convinced people of the latter for thousands of years. The cock's crowing doesn't cause the sun to rise, even though it appears to. For Nietzsche, "untruth" is an essential condition of life, and the inherent worthiness of truth is a moral prejudice, not an irrefutable fact of life.

Calling his theory "Perspectivism," Nietzsche maintained, in *The Will to Power,* that the world of knowledge is dominated not by immutable truths but by differing perspectives.

In today's world, disdain for political truths surrounds us at every turn. We are faced with the rise of authoritarian politicians, and their political disinformation—based on "Big Lies"—is ubiquitously trumpeted on radio, on right-wing television and online. In their world, Plato's dicta to "question everything" and to veraciously and unerringly "examine life" has gone down in resounding defeat, and Nietzsche's more flexible approach to "truth versus lies" triumphantly holds sway.

Nietzsche believes that the quest for power, not the search for truth, defines and drives the human condition nor does he care about people's "moral intentions"—only the consequences of their actions. Creating a better world for Nietzsche's aristocratic class of superior human men—his Ubermenschen—is his primary purpose. In Nietzsche's doxology, power is the only absolute, and homo sapiens are born to conquer. Philosophy's allegiance to so-called "truth" is not even in the running.

Nietzsche wrote that whoever worshipped at power's altar had to despise women, and his descriptions of women are filled with contempt. He said in *Beyond Good and Evil,* "What is truth to a woman? From the very first, nothing has been more alien, repugnant and inimical to a woman than the truth. Her great art is the lie." In *The Will to Power,* Nietzsche wrote that a woman is "typically sick, changeable, inconstant... she needs a religion of weakness that glorifies being weak, loving, and being humble as divine: or better, she makes the strong weak." In *Thus Spake Zarathustra*, he said: "Woman's love involves injustice and blindness against everything that she does not love…Woman is not yet capable of friendship: women are still cats and birds. Or at best cows…"

And, most famously, in *Thus Spake Zarathustra*, Nietzsche wrote: "You are going to women? Do not forget the whip."

Often, while describing the power-worshiping ethos of the new man, whom he dubbed "die Ubermenschen," Nietzsche enthused over it so energetically he appeared to endorse its arrogance and validate even its violence. He often seemed quite mad, but this lunacy was always a risk. Power is nothing, if not intoxicating, and Nietzsche famously warned us that the study of these outrageously revolutionary ideas could drive the student insane. As he wrote in *Beyond Good and Evil,* "Whoever fights monsters should see to it that in the process he does not become a monster. And if you gaze long enough into an abyss, the abyss will gaze back into you."

Nietzsche, tragically, was not immune to the madness of the abyss.

Still Nietzsche had one stubborn, hard-nosed insight into human progress that haunts us to this day. He understood that arts, the sciences, mathematics, technology, philosophy, political-legal-and-economic systems—a nation's so-called "culture"—are not advanced by the general run of its citizenry. The people who excel in these areas tend to be talented, educated, unusually capable individuals, but they represent, in toto, a small percentage of the population. Nietzsche believed that Western democracy did not do enough to promote their advancement. Toynbee took Nietzsche's thesis one step further. He said in his study of over fifteen world civilizations throughout history that each of them was advanced by what Toynbee called "a creative minority." He determined that a crucial sign a civilization was going into terminal decline was when it codified policies that undermined its creative minority. Two troubling examples of a nation currently undermining its creative minority are United States universities and politicians placing college education beyond the financial reach of most American young people and US immigration policies blocking sorely needed foreign experts in science and the IT industries from becoming US citizens. If, in the Afterlife, Nietzsche and Toynbee were forced to analyze and comment on these problems I'm sure they would twirl in their graves.

That Nietzsche did not understand how a nation could promote its creative minority and simultaneously care for its disadvantaged citizens was one of his many blind spots. In Nietzsche's time, however, almost no heads of state knew how to resolve this paradox. As we shall see later, in the 1880s—when Nietzsche was writing his books—Bismarck was the only political leader to successfully accomplish both tasks. He alone seemed to understand that the modern nation-state was powerful enough to achieve both goals and ought to pursue both.

In the end, while it was true that Nietzsche revered man's warrior spirit, he was never naïve about the shape of war to come. He predicted in *Beyond Good and Evil*, "The [twentieth] century will bring with it the struggle for mastery over the entire earth." He warned in *Ecce Homo* that in future wars, humanity would suffer…

> *…upheavals, a convulsion of earthquakes, a moving of mountains and valleys…[A]ll power structures of the old society will have been exploded—for all of them are based on lies: There will be wars the likes of which have never been seen….*

Nietzsche also came to loathe what he viewed as the barbarism and boorishness inherent in the German soul—so much so that he seemed to anticipate the rise of Nazism. He, likewise, came to hate the country's virulent anti-Semitism. He so despised the nation and its non-Jewish citizens that at age twenty-four, he renounced his Prussian citizenship and for the last thirty years of his life lived abroad.

But, like Plato before him, he loathed the democratic system of government from the very bottom of his heart. He believed its obsession with egalitarianism militated against the creation and nurturing of Ubermenschen.

Nietzsche did serve in the German army from 1870–1871—initially in an equine artillery unit, later as a medical orderly. During that time, he witnessed firsthand the appalling horrors of war. While in the army, he contracted dysentery and diphtheria. During his lifetime, multiple doctors diagnosed him as having also contracted syphilis—although blood tests, which would have elicited a definitive diagnosis, were not scientifically available during his lifetime. Walter Kaufman, an acclaimed Nietzsche scholar and translator, believed Nietzsche's madness was due to "an atypical general paresis"—a form of neurosyphilis—and he speculated that Nietzsche might have also contracted that disease during the war, either while working in a hospital or while frequenting a brothel. After Nietzsche's death, some doctors disputed that syphilis diagnosis.

Nietzsche came of age and wrote his books during La Belle Époch—a European era characterized by peace, relative prosperity, colonial expansionism, technological/scientific innovations and, above all, an unshakable faith in the concept of "human progress." Nietzsche's philosophy flew in the face of La Belle Époch and seemed to tell Europeans and Americans that everything they thought they knew was wrong. Denounced as the high priest of nihilism, for most of his life, Nietzsche's views were also generally viewed as unfavorable. He had warned that his books would be misunderstood, and for years, his iconoclastic ideas were not well received. Toward the end of his life, however, at a time when he was almost completely deranged, his books came to be appreciated. When he died in 1900, he was well on his way to becoming world famous.

In 1908, H. L. Mencken began his landmark—though highly personalized—study of Nietzsche. He also translated *The Antichrist* for Alfred A. Knopf in the United States. Mencken's initial books on Nietzsche were not initially well received. Then World War I intervened, and La Belle Époch crashed, broke up and died—perhaps forever—on the shoals of the Great War. By then, respect for Nietzsche's oeuvre was growing rapidly.

Many of the twentieth century's most distinguished intellectuals were increasingly drawn to Nietzsche and his belief in "the death of God," including his insistence that Judeo-Christianity's essential commandments were not ineluctable, epistemologically derived facts but rather fallible conjecture.

But what of the power-driven, anti-democratic religion that Nietzsche so fervently espoused and with which Nietzsche hoped to replace Judeo-Christianity? While the western democracies of Europe and North America may control a disproportionate amount of the planet's wealth and possess immense global influence, for the overwhelming majority of the world's population, western-style democracy is not a way of life. For them, Nietzschean authoritarianism holds sway. In most of Africa, South America and among Asia's billions, his "will to power" reigns, and the Sermon on the Mount is as meaningless and inconsequential to people's lives as the Martian moons. In so much of that world, the meek inherit nada, and peacemakers have never been divinely blessed. The last remain last, and the first are almost always at the head of the line.

Even in the western nations, Nietzschean authoritarians—often professing to be "political populists"—lay siege to democratic institutions and give the lie to humanitarian ideals whenever they have the chance. He is the patron poet of elitists everywhere, and it is quite possible that most of the world's leadership class live more by Nietzsche's self-created religious precepts than by Christ's beatitudes. The patron saint and personal avatar of American authoritarians, Ayn Rand, borrowed her most inflammatory insights from Nietzsche. She, too, raged against what Nietzsche had called Judeo-Christianity's "slave ethic" and she also proposed that superior individuals were answerable to no higher authority than themselves. In one such case, she even called such an individual "a Superman," which was George Bernard Shaw's translation of Ubermensch. She came to believe that democratic capitalism was the economic system most capable of spawning and sustaining Ubermenschen. Nietzsche, on the other hand, did not spend much time discussing that subject. He did, at times, however, denounce statism, and he always loathed democracy. His views of capitalism are murkier.

Ayn Rand still inspires young, aspiring conservatives in the US. It is ironic that while she was a committed atheist and unalterably opposed, like Nietzsche, to the Judeo-Christian ethical system, most of her right-wing American votaries are devout Christians. Rand, ironically, held that Christian conservatism was a major menace—perhaps the paramount threat—to American democracy, and her disdain for it was almost visceral. She said, at one point, that Christian conservatism "subordinates reason to faith, and substitutes theocracy for capitalism."

That so many religious Republicans have genuflected before a woman who despised them is one of the more curious political paradoxes of our time. Rand's philosophy repudiates all of their Christian beliefs—including Christ's teachings.

Still the rightwing flocks to her. Ayn Rand's impassioned GOP admirers have included Donald J. Trump, Ronald Reagan, Barry Goldwater, Rush Limbaugh, Supreme Court Justice Clarence Thomas, Alan Greenspan, former GOP Congressman Ron Paul, GOP Senator Rand Paul, former GOP vice president candidates Jack Kemp and former GOP House Speaker Paul Ryan, Nobel laureate Milton Friedman, former Arizona governor and Libertarian presidential candidate Gary Johnston, Trump CIA Director Mike Pompeo and Trump Secretary of State Rex Tillerson.

Gore Vidal, however, viewed her appeal to America's hard right as apocalyptically portentous, saying:

Ayn Rand's "philosophy" is nearly perfect in its immorality, which makes the size of her audience all the more ominous and symptomatic as we enter a curious new phase in our society. Moral values are in flux. The muddy depths are being stirred by new monsters and witches from the deep. Trolls walk the American night. Caesars are stirring in the Forum. There are storm warnings ahead.

For over a century, Nietzsche's writings have also influenced not only dubious, right-wing zealots but many highly distinguished, world-class intellectuals. His more august international admirers have included Josef Conrad, George Bernard Shaw, James Joyce, Oswald Spengler, Martin Buber, Ludwig Wittgenstein, Karl Jaspers, Henri Bergson, Martin Heidegger, Jean Paul Sartre, Albert Camus, Michel Foucault, Sir Arnold Toynbee, Carl Jung, H. L. Mencken, William Faulkner, Hannah Arendt, Hunter S. Thompson, Henry Miller and many, many other luminaries.

CHAPTER 3

Otto von Bismarck:
Europe's Preeminent Statesman
In *The Struggle for Mastery in Europe: 1848–1918*, A. J. P. Taylor wrote:

In the state of nature, which Hobbes imagined, violence was the only law, and life was 'nasty, brutish and short'. Though individuals never lived in this state of nature, the Great Powers of Europe have always done so....Each individual state in Europe acknowledged no superior and recognized no moral code.... [E]ach state could justify itself only by being able to resist with force the forcible encroachments of others; and, if Hobbes saw true, the history of Europe should be one of uninterrupted war. In fact, Europe has known almost as much peace as war, and it has owed these periods of peace to the Balance of Power.

Taylor's book is, in large part, the study of a seventy-year period during which European leaders struggled to avoid war and at the same time ensure their country's national security. Taylor's grand practitioner of balance-of-power diplomacy was the Prussian leader Otto von Bismarck, who came to power, as chancellor, in 1862 and served in that capacity until 1890. While it is true that, early in his career, he fought three short wars—with Denmark, Austria and France—in order to unite the thirty-nine disparate German states, he was otherwise a firm opponent of war. In fact, the main reason Bismarck fought to unite the German states was that he felt the small individual German states could not survive conflicts with their larger neighbors, while a united Germany could. So he participated in those brief, decisive conflicts in order to avoid larger conflicts. Keeping the peace was, in Bismarck's world view, in Germany's best national interest and was always, therefore, his premier objective. It was no easy task. Germany was surrounded by potential enemies on all sides—most notably the French on her western border. After the Franco-Prussian War, Bismarck fiercely objected to the annexation of Alsace-Lorraine, arguing that France would view that seizure as casus belli for a subsequent war with Germany. He was alone in his opposition. He lost that battle, but he was correct. That theft created a powerful, unyielding enemy to Germany's west.

Taylor marveled at Bismarck's brilliance in forming alliances, the point of which was to prevent wars. Central to his grand strategy was a strong alliance with Russia, which would effectively preclude serious attacks on Germany's eastern flank. Later, after taking power, Kaiser Wilhelm II and Adolph Hitler would each, in their time, abandon that crucial strategic mandate with calamitous results.

Thucydides argued that Athens' enormous power and her coercion of her neighbors provoked the Peloponnesian Wars. Not wanting to follow Athens' example, Bismarck resisted coercing his neighbors, even though he had the military ability to do so. He even fought the German annexation of Alsace-Lorraine. During the twentieth century, Germany no longer had a statesman of Bismarck's caliber who could keep the country on a peaceful path. Like ancient Athens, Germany eventually resorted to coercion. The consequences were horrific.

Bismarck also feared that Europe's obsession with the Balkan states' eternal conflicts would draw the Great Powers into a Balkan War, which would metastasize into a horrendous continental conflict. He argued, correctly, that the Balkans weren't worth the bones of a single German soldier.

In 1914, a Balkan conflict did, of course, ensue, and World War I was the result.

Bismarck showed the world how democracies might survive in the kind of power-driven Hobbsian jungle that Fritz Krupp had helped to create and for which Nietzsche had provided the philosophical—even religious—rationale. When Germany abandoned Bismarck's diplomatic policies, it sowed the wind. When it opted for war, it reaped the whirlwind.

In order to be strong abroad, Bismarck realized that Germany needed to be stable at home and that the German people had to prosper. He understood, like Plato and Aristotle, that extreme economic inequality at home bred civil unrest and undermined a nation's strength and stability. Bismarck, therefore, legislated universal suffrage, mandated nationwide healthcare, pension plans and provided disability pensions for all German workers.

Bismarck studied the art of war and was more knowledgeable in military matters than virtually any other leader of his era, and he, consequently, understood the utterly destructive nature of modern war. He never saw war as a triumphal crusade but as the reductio ad absurdum of sound statecraft; he believed that war constituted utter diplomatic failure. He viewed military conflicts not only as economic debacles but as creating antagonisms that would lead to future ruinous wars.

For Bismarck, national self-interest was everything—his guiding principle—and he knew, implicitly, that, both in the short-term and the long-run, wars were disastrous and utterly contrary to Germany's national self-interest. The cold-blooded way in which Bismarck practiced his diplomatic craft, forged alliances and kept the peace became known as "Realpolitik."

He was so thoroughly versed in the art, science and practice of war that he came to realize, like Nietzsche, that the next major European conflict would be worse than a national catastrophe. It would be irredeemably apocalyptic. His life's work, during his last eighteen years in office, was to prevent that Apocalypse. His successors were too blinded by their own love of war, their obsessive faith in their Krupp-engendered engines of death and their own Nietzschean "will to power" to comprehend the wisdom behind Bismarck's shrewdly calculated Realpolitik.

To quote D. H. Lawrence's judgment on the consequences of World War I, we "live amid its ruins."

Whether the United States—even now, 125 years after his death—is capable of understanding Bismarck's essential strategic insights, let alone embrace his grand but highly complex vision of foreign policy, is an open question. We do know, however, that had Woodrow Wilson studied Bismarck and focused on defending America's self-interest instead of "keeping the world safe for democracy," he might not have plunged the US into World War I. Had he stayed out of that war, there would have been no Hitler, Lenin, Stalin, no atom bomb and arguably no Mao Zedung later on. Had subsequent US leaders studied Bismarck, they might have refrained from invading Vietnam and Iraq.

His insights are still valuable, and it is not too late to learn from "the Iron Chancellor." Past does not always have to be prologue.

Slavery in the Age of Porfirio Diaz

"Why dost thou beat my people to pieces and grind the faces of my poor?"
—Isaiah 3:15

Several writers and editors have asked me whether slavery under Diaz was as horrific as I've portrayed it in my books. The answer is yes. Throughout Diaz's thirty-one-year regime, from 1880 to 1910, Mexico was a true hell on earth. Few serious books—particularly in English—are readily available on Diaz and his three-decade reign of terror. People subsequently don't appreciate how brutally he ran Mexico and the extent to which he built and based its economy on slavery, which is largely why I've written this afterword.

Slavery became illegal in Mexico in 1829, but since the wealthy essentially appointed the law enforcement officials, there were no serious legal objections to the policy and the practice. And it was slavery. As in the American South, Mexican slaveholders effectively owned their workers, and their workers had no rights under the law. Concealing their proprietorship behind euphemisms such as "forced service," "contract labor" and "peonage," the owners often worked their chattels to death. Nor was escape a viable option. Typically if they ran off, the populace informed on them for the substantial price on their heads or out of fear that, if they did not inform, they might be accused later on of having abetted the escape. In that case they'd face imprisonment and enslavement themselves. Furthermore, Mexico was so destitute that living off the land, after escaping, was onerously difficult. Lastly, observers reported at the time that runaway slaves were almost always caught, and upon their return, faced ferocious floggings and starvation rations. Consequently, only the most recklessly brave or desperately foolhardy ever attempted to escape.

Physical chastisement of slaves was universal. Overseers beat them routinely in order to force more labor out of them. Their overseers called their daily whippings "cleanups." They were administered in the morning at roll call, and during the evening roll call, after the workers returned from the fields or the mines. They were also administered during the day. The overseers beat the prisoners with canes and with knotted hemp ropes, soaked in brine.

The owners habitually starved their peons as well. Chronic hunger tended to fatigue the slaves, making them more malleable. The overseers also believed hunger forced their slaves to work harder in the hope of obtaining extra rations—or for fear of having their rations cut. And of course feeding them inadequately padded the owners' bottom line.

In his extraordinary first-person report on the lives of Mexican slaves, *Barbarous Mexico*, John Kenneth Turner argued that the chief difference between US slavery and Mexican slavery under Diaz was that in the antebellum South, individual slaves had significant financial value. In fact, recent studies indicate that the value of an average slave came to $900 per person. Since that was an average figure, healthy slaves in the prime of life would have obviously brought much more. Turner argued that Southern slaveowners, therefore, had a financial incentive to keep their slaves alive—at least long enough for them to breed replacement slaves. No such incentive existed in Diaz's Mexico. There, the potential slave-labor pool was virtually limitless, and the slaves were, consequently, worth almost nothing. Labor agents received as little as $45 for a slave.

Historians have pointed out that the reason Mexico imported so few African slaves—relative to the American South—was that those who sold the Africans forced laborers could not compete in a market where slaveowners could obtain indigent mestizos for next to nothing. Nor did Spain's rulers believe in paying for slaves. It had been their policy in Europe first and then in New Spain to enslave their subjugated peoples.

I don't mean to suggest that slaves in the American South were well treated. Quite the contrary. After 1840, when the British brought their steam-powered spinning mills online and discovered that the American South's domesticated Native American cotton—with its longer, stronger fibers—was especially desirable for mechanized processing, Southern cotton became explosively profitable almost overnight. In fact, between 1840 and 1860, Southern cotton was as financially formidable worldwide as Big Oil would become in the twenty-first century. In 1860, American slaves, in aggregate, were worth more than the combined assets of both the country's manufacturing sector and shipping lines. Consequently, the US cotton plantation owners began buying up every additional slave they could get their hands on and working them brutally. The harder they worked their slaves, the more cotton they harvested for the mechanized mills in England and the North and the more money the planters made. Moreover, the planters' profligate lifestyles exacerbated their obsessive need for constant cash infusions. They were continually borrowing money from the New York banks against future cotton crops in order to finance their prodigal spending and outrageous ostentation. A slave's failure to meet his or her cotton-sack quota at the end of the day could result in savage whippings.

All I'm suggesting is that Diaz's slaveholders found it easier and cheaper to replace their deceased slaves than America's slaveowners did.

Diaz's slaveowners had three different methods for conscripting men, women and children from the general population of impoverished, illiterate mestizos. Since Mexico had no middle class, that disempowered group constituted between 80 to 90 percent of the country, and Mexico's jails contained a bottomless reservoir of potential slaves. Labor agents often paid jailers to consign their prisoners to them. Since most of these inmates had never appeared before a judge, the labor agents could arrange to have the inmates charged with any crime they wanted and sentence them to their mines or plantations for as long as they wanted them to work.

The agents, or their subagents, could also often convince their prospects to sign bogus contracts for allegedly legitimate labor. Since, during the time of this book, virtually all of Mexico's poor were illiterate, bogus bond-labor agreements were easy to fabricate, falsify and enforce.

Lastly, slaves could be conscripted through the age-old tactic of kidnapping. Because slaves were held incommunicado, once a person was in bondage, friends and relatives would discover it was almost impossible to track that person down. And even if they had succeeded in locating their loved one, finding a way to obtain the person's release would inevitably prove to be a lost cause. As we said before, Mexico's judges and officials were for all intents and purposes in the pockets of Diaz's plutocrats.

At one point in *Dead Men Don't Lie*, I incarcerated Richard Ryan in an especially atrocious slave-labor mine, and life for miners during the Portifiata was truly nightmarish. All nineteenth-century mine tunnels were intrinsically dangerous places, but Mexico's were worse. Known as "ratholes," they followed the veins of ore, regardless of how they twisted or corkscrewed, no matter the fragility of the mountain rock through which the tunnels wound. These shafts required meticulous maintenance, which they seldom got. Ore extraction took precedence over everything else. Cave-ins were a constant danger, and since Diaz's mines were torch-, candle- and lamplit, and since dust and flammable gas were everywhere, mine fires were a continual threat. Moreover, the smelters that surrounded the mountains tended to cannibalize the mine's stock of shoring timbers, which were needed to prop up the tunnels. After all, the ore, which the mines produced, had immense value—and therefore the wood used to smelt the ore had value as well. The miners' lives were worth relatively little to the mine owners.

Still, mining requires some work skills—hacienda field labor less so—consequently, a miner was not quite as economically valueless to a mine owner as a plantation slave was to a hacendado. Often, miners received wages, but the expenses deducted from those wages kept the miner perpetually indebted to the mine owners...hence, keeping him perpetually enslaved. He could not quit his job legally, and if he attempted to flee, he was, as usual, informed on, apprehended, returned, then flogged and starved half to death.

On the whole, hacienda slaves probably had it worse than the miners. On some plantations, a slave's average life expectancy was as little as eight months.

The enslavement of entire families was common on the plantations. If the owners held all the family members in bondage, the husbands and fathers were less likely to rebel: They did not want to abandon their wives and children, and even if they did rebel, long-term hunger and frequent floggings soon broke them of their rebelliousness. Diaz even brought the Yaquis to their knees. A relatively sophisticated agrarian people, the men proved themselves to be fierce warriors when they were threatened. In fact, those Yaqui warriors had been so tough, independent and strong-willed that Spain had never brought them to heel. With his advanced military, transportation and communications technology, however, Diaz waged a war of extermination against them, then relocated the survivors to slave-labor plantations in the sweltering Yucatan, which was as far away from their home in northern Mexico as Diaz could productively move them. The overseers typically broke even the bravest of the Yaquis within a week or two through the twin scourges of starvation and the lash. If the slaves did not break, the slaveowners had them publicly flogged to death or simply killed. After all, the deaths cost them relatively little. In the sugar plantations in Mexico's more tropical regions, the owners sometimes threw their remains into their crocodile-infested swamps.

Both the maya-azteca religion and the Christian faith taught fatalism, and Mexican people had come to accept and absorb it implicitly. Turner says in his book that Mexico's slaves endured the unspeakable horror of their existence with incomprehensible fortitude. Still, while they were uncomplaining, he said he had never heard a Mexican slave sing or burst into joyful laughter.

Another factor that made Mexico's slavery unusually pernicious was the foreign ownership of so many of the country's mines and plantations. A significant number of wealthy Mexicans owned such operations, but, under Diaz, countless numbers of these enterprises were sold to foreign businessmen, often to wealthy Americans. While these owners might occasionally visit Mexico, they were mostly concerned with the revenue their overseers could squeeze out of their haciendas, businesses and workers. These plutocrats paid no Mexican taxes on their profits, and if they did not visit their vast holdings or did not look too closely into their day-to-day operations, they could claim ignorance of the ghastly violence that their overseers inflicted on their slaves.

Slave exploitation tended to be worse on the enterprises owned by absentee magnates.

Which brings us to the attitudes of men like Diaz and the attitudes of the owners of his slave-labor enterprises. That particular topic is so ugly that in this novel I employ considerable dark humor in depicting the plutocrats'—and Diaz's—views of the poor in general and Mexico's peons in particular. I am pleased that most readers appreciate the dark humor in these sections. In point of fact, the reality was much more depressing. These people viewed their slaves as dumb engines of human flesh, who existed solely to enrich the avariciously affluent and imperiously powerful, namely themselves. Even the Catholic Church, in the days when it owned so many of Mexico's largest haciendas, argued that peons were so inherently stupid and so intractably childlike that they only responded to and were only improved by the whip and the rod. So I made the slaveowners in my novel personally sadistic and at the same time tried to make their cruelty comical—even though these people could not have been more unfunny.

Brutality in the nineteenth century was common. Slavery existed throughout the American South for much of that period, and the nineteenth-century Western world, on a personal level, was far more vicious than our own. The beating of women, young people and even employees, including child-laborers, was widespread. In more barbaric countries, it was worse. In Russia, according to Dostoevsky's prison memoir, *House of the Dead*, prisoners were sentenced to as many as a thousand lashes in their Siberian camps.

Even in the twentieth century, Henry Ford's "labor pushers" punished "slow" or "insubordinate" workers with nightsticks, and corporal punishment of inmates was an everyday occurrence in many prisons.

Nor in the nineteenth and twentieth centuries were the upper classes immune from institutional sadism. The British public schools, which produced luminaries such as Winston Churchill, Robert Graves, Roald Dahl and David Niven were infamous for the perversity of their punishments. These men later wrote and talked about the harrowing physical abuse that they suffered, including floggings and child rape. Furthermore, the masters of these institutions were torturing the scions of England's elites. One can only imagine what little compunction or restraint they might have felt had they had the opportunity to torture the weak and powerless—the true wretched of the earth.

So, yes, on a personal, day-to-day level, the nineteenth-century world was more violent than our own, but even so, Mexico under Diaz was unique among the Western nations. When it came to physical coercion, Mexico was in a class by itself.

As to the attitudes of mine and plantation owners toward their slaves, again, I would refer the reader to John Kenneth Turner's *Barbarous Mexico*. His descriptions of the slaveowners' comments on the flogging of their chattels are instructive. These men brag and gloat openly over their use of physical violence, saying that their workers are so lazy, stupid and recalcitrant and that to elicit productive labor from them, constant whippings are mandatory. One such owner boasts that his women slaves *want* the owners to whip them at least once a day whether they deserve it or not. Another plantation owner likes to observe his roll call "cleanup" floggings personally, dressed in fine attire, sitting sublimely on his horse. While he watches the men whipped, he smokes a cigar with languid, lordly hauteur, supremely indifferent to the agony of the men being beaten bloody. Only after he tires of his cigar, tosses it to the ground and rides back to his hacienda does the flogging cease. One of the more iniquitous slave-labor procurers promises Turner, who is posing as an American investor, that he can supply Turner's enterprises with as many as twelve thousand child slaves a year and that once Turner takes possession of them, he can do...*anything he wants with them.*

While Diaz's regime was much wickeder than anything that had come before or after it, he did not create the world or the customs into which the Porfiriato came to be. Spain's mistreatment of the Mexican people set the precedent for his monstrous misbehavior. When Cortes landed at what is now Veracruz in 1519, there were approximately twenty-five million indigenes living in Mexico. By 1650, there were 1.2 million. So Spain's rulers were responsible for the extermination of 90 to 98 percent of Mexico's indio population.

The situation actually became even worse in 1565, when Juan de Tolosa made a spectacular silver strike in Zacatecas at La Bufa, and Spain realized that Mexico was one gigantic mountain of silver. The king quickly understood that he could wrest illimitable riches from Mexico's mountains, but to do so the country needed a massive pool of slave labor. At that point, Spain's exploitation of the Mexican people became genocidally aggressive, and they began conscripting slaves in colossal quantities—as rapidly and ruthlessly as they could. They quickly began to focus on their mestizos; after all, they'd killed off most of their indigenous population.

At times, the Holy Church and the Spanish Crown did attempt to intervene on behalf of the beleaguered peons. There was too much money to be made, however, and the mines and plantations were too far away for Spain's royal and religious elites to monitor, let alone police.

Mexico's Spanish governors also caused the institutionalized systematic legal corruption—known today as "the mordida"—that plagued Diaz's Mexico and still haunts the country today. Some historians believe that of all the abominable crimes that Spain committed against the Mexican people, their system of institutional bribery was the most ruinous, incorrigible and long-lasting.

The Spaniards in Mexico were racist to a degree that was not equaled until the Third Reich. A citizen's legal rights were defined by the percentage of "Spanish blood" flowing through their veins. This legal criterion was clearly preposterous, but many of Mexico's vilest laws under Spanish occupation were based on it.

The Spaniards originated the system under which a foreign power—namely Spain—commandeered virtually all of Mexico's annual GDP. Diaz continued that Spanish system by allowing foreign tycoons and companies to profit off the lion's share of Méjico's resources and peon labor.

Under Spanish rule, the Catholic Church had acquired amounts of land so vast as to be almost immeasurable. When the Mexican government, during the administration of President Ignacio Comonfort, finally began confiscating the Church's holdings, some historians estimate that the Church owned a third of all of Mexico's arable acreage. (Some estimates go as high as two-thirds.) When Diaz came to power, he continued this policy of land-expropriation, dispossessing countless peons. He sold the bulk of these vast tracts to large hacienda owners and foreign investors. Some of these plantations, which he sold off, encompassed millions of acres.

Since these landowners wanted to wring as much revenue as possible from their investments, they specialized almost exclusively in high-profit crops, which they could sell abroad. For the most part, they farmed sugarcane, tobacco, coffee, cotton, bananas and sisal for hemp manufacturing and blue agave for the distillation of alcoholic spirits. Since the Anglo-American-European countries were more prosperous than Mexico, the demand for these goods was immense. Also their currencies were worth more than the peso. The profits of these export crops were so exorbitant, and the hacendados were so avaricious they did not bother to produce enough beans and corn for the Mexican people, so Diaz had to import those foodstuffs from America. As a result, his starving peons paid more than their more prosperous American counterparts in the north did for the same quantities of corn and beans.

So as rapacious as Spain's exploitation of Mexico had been, the carnage and the suffering that Diaz unleashed on the Mexican people was infinitely worse than anything the Spanish had ever imagined. Among other things, Diaz possessed recently developed weaponry, railroads and telegraph communications that enabled him to conquer regions, enslave people and seize lands that had been beyond the reach of previous Mexican rulers. His military power was unprecedented.

The epigraph under this afterword's title—"Why dost thou beat my people to pieces and grind the faces of my poor?"—asks, by implication, why Diaz wreaked so much death and destruction on his people. After all, he was not a foreigner—one of the group he so shamelessly and lavishly enriched at the expense of those whom he'd sworn to serve. Diaz was one of the Mexican people. He should have understood and identified with their misery.

An examination of how Diaz rose to power and then maintained his hold over his country might contain the answer. Early in his political career, when Mexico was screaming for justice and more progressive government, Diaz allied himself with two great liberal presidents—first Benito Juarez, then Sebastián Lerdo. He quickly attempted coups against each of them in turn. His coup against Lerdo succeeded, and after taking office, he quickly betrayed Juarez's and Lerdo's liberal ideals, which he'd once agreed to uphold. When he finally ran for the presidency, he campaigned on the platform that he would not seek a second term, a promise he repeatedly abrogated. Once in office, he subjugated Mexico's judiciary and its press. If political rivals posed a serious threat, he imprisoned them. When he sold 80 to 90 percent of Mexico's economy to the ultra-rich, many of them foreigners, he also tightened his hold on power. In order to protect their investments, these tycoons backed Diaz politically and financially. By throwing the peasantry off their land and forcing them into hacienda debt-peonage, Diaz so impoverished them that they lacked the fiscal and physical means to oppose him. He even reduced the size of the army and the power of its generals so they could not defy him. He relied instead on the marauding, corrupt and largely privatized bands of rurales, which he used as his own personal mercenary army. And he lined his own pockets in the process. At the end of his life, he could flee to Paris and retire in luxury.

So why did Diaz "beat his people to pieces and grind the faces of his poor?" He did virtually nothing in his entire career that did not expand his personal and political power; even at the age of eighty he still sought another presidential term. He was willing to embrace almost any and all actions that strengthened his grip on the country—no matter how catastrophic the consequences were to the Mexican people. Power in perpetuity was his sole raison d'etre, his only driving dream.

And the havoc he wreaked was horrendous.

Did Diaz's oppression change the Mexican people in any way—then and today? These are difficult, complicated and perhaps unanswerable questions. Still, it is important to our understanding of Diaz's Mexico to consider how the Porfiriato affected—and to some extent might have forged—the character of today's Mexican people.

A good place to start might be the chapters in which I dramatize Mexico's Fiesta of the Dead. Originally a maya-azteca festival, the Catholic Church had outlawed it because of its heretical nature. During the Porfiriato, however, the Mexican people had become so depressed and beaten down that Diaz reinstated it, believing the people needed a holiday during which they could let off steam. (Diaz's slaves obviously did not participate in these celebrations, which occurred essentially in towns, cities and villages.)

In many respects the maya-azteca religion had been a celebration of death. This life was a hell on earth, and people were better off departing it as quickly as possible. In their Afterlife, a suicide and a noble warrior were, therefore, treated equally. After all, they both inflicted death—albeit on different kinds of victims—thereby hastening that person's departure from this veil of tears. Death was the supreme gift, and suicides and warriors were both dispensers of that lethal largesse. Nonetheless, even for self-murderers and killers, the Afterlife was an ordeal. A heavenly Christian paradise was never in the offing. The gods did not think humanity deserved it. Human beings were born to suffer, sacrifice and serve. The only hope in the Afterlife that the dead could aspire to was to progress through all eight hellworlds to the Ninth Level, in which the dead might conceivably find...*oblivion.*

Historians have also noted that the great dying off of the indigenous Mexicans between 1519 and 1650 further hammered this obsession with death even more deeply into that dark maya-azteca soul. Robert Jay Lifton described the Hiroshima survivors as suffering from "death immersion" and "death in life." The Mexican people experienced 130 years of Hiroshima, the Gulag Archipelago and the Black Death combined. Some people believe that 370 years later, the hell of that apocalypse is still emblazoned in Mexico's collective psyche.

Yet despite serious, critical differences between Christianity and the maya-azteca faith, Mexico's indios quickly and instinctively embraced the Catholic Church—to a degree that genuinely amazed Mexico's Spanish priests at the time—and during the Porfiriato, the Fiesta of the Dead began incorporating Christian rituals into the festival. In Diaz's day, the celebrants often ended the festival with a mock-crucifixion of a Christ figure.

One reason for the Mexican peoples' rapid and sincere conversion to Christianity was their intense identification with Christ's crucifixion. The Mexican people saw stark similarities between Jesus Christ and their own uniquely popular god, Quetzalcoatl, whom they believed, like Christ, had once walked among them and truly cared about them. The other maya-azteca gods were openly hostile to humanity, and to placate these vindictive deities, the Mexican people had to offer up innumerable human sacrifices annually. Some eyewitnesses claim that their priests ripped the hearts out of victims on the top of their pyramids by the tens of thousands each year. But Christ and Quetzalcoatl cared about humankind. So in their own way, Christ's bloody sacrifice was to the indigenous Mexican people intensely maya-azteca, and they commiserated strongly with His suffering. That He sacrificed himself in such an agonizing way in order to save them from a hateful universe's eternal damnation was to the Mexican people profoundly moving. None of their previous gods had ever contemplated such an act, hadn't really liked humanity all that much and so the sacrifice of their Christ/Quetzalcoatl meant a lot to them. The indios and the first mestizos were passionate about Christ's crucifixion in a way that rivalled that of the most devout European Catholics.

So the fiesta was also dedicated to death and featured candies shaped like skulls, bread of the dead, skeletal costumes, posters advertising that all people were ultimately skeletons and food for worms—symbols and images that appeared ubiquitously throughout the pageant. Similarly, the Catholic Church had promoted the *Memento mori,* which admonished Catholics to constantly "Remember death" and to always remind oneself that this life was transitory—that a more important dispensation awaited us later on. The Fiesta of the Dead also promoted that precept. It exhorted the Mexican people to focus on the Afterlife to come and never, ever to fear death—instead to exult in it and to celebrate it. In fact, the festival is filled with immense amounts of black humor, as if Death itself were a joke. The fiesta seems to say that if we do not fear Death, then why should we fear anything at all?

The Spaniards also brought the cult of machismo to Mexico. A code that revered physical courage, swordsmanship, skill with firearms, horsemanship, sexual promiscuity—in some cases even countenancing rape—and an eagerness to engage in duels, that code also disparaged book learning, the study of science, mathematics, engineering, and it disdained hard work. In the end, this intensely Spanish code helped turn Spain from a great power into one of the poorer nations of Europe. While the Enlightenment, the Reformation and the Industrial Revolution were transforming the rest of Europe, Spain sought to turn the clock back to an earlier, almost violently medieval epoch, and waged continual religious war on the modernizing nations of Europe. In the end Spain lost almost everything, including Mexico.

Cortez was an extreme exemplar of Spain's machismo code—particularly in his utter willingness to risk almost certain death and to kill people en masse, as demonstrated by his slaughter of countless thousands of Mexicans.

Diaz, who began his career as a military officer, was another example of the new, intrinsically Mexican machismo: In Diaz, the Spanish code of machismo, that had honored violence, even homicidal violence, was conjoined with the maya-azteca code that had honored...*death*. Violence and death, the killing and enslaving of people nationwide meant nothing to Diaz, and consequently, he represented the worst, most nihilistic aspects of both codes. Mexican lives were worth nothing to Diaz, not when there was money to be made off of them and power to be gained. Unlike Cortez's conquests, there was nothing heroic about Diaz's achievements or his machismo. That he was a castizo—a so-called "mixed blood" and part indio himself—made the plundering, mass-murdering and enslavement of his own people all the more heinous.

As many people have suggested, fatalism was always part of the Mexican people's essential mindset—as it was in both their maya-azteca and Christian worlds—but their forbearance was neither infinite nor eternal. They did rise up, forcing Diaz into his Parisian exile, where he died. Igniting a Revolution that blazed with cataclysmic violence for over ten years, from 1910 to 1920, their rebellion became a fiery purgation for the Mexican people, one of those rare grass-roots conflicts of the dispossessed against the elites—who, in many instances, resided abroad. Two of their most notable revolucionarios, Pancho

Villa and Emiliano Zapata, led genuine people's uprisings as had Father Hidalgo and José Morales before them.

How do historians, in general, view Diaz? During the last hundred years, scholars have written shockingly few serious biographies of him—and almost none are available in English. Diaz seems to be too big, challenging and perhaps embarrassing a subject for professional historians. Most scholars have focused on Diaz's accomplishments: the thousands of miles of train track that he laid, telegraph lines that he strung and countless mines that he dug. They emphasize the millions of dollars of foreign loans and investments that he brought in. Nor were any good biographies written while he was alive, which is understandable. During his successive administrations, Diaz quashed most critical reportage, reputedly jailing, killing and even blinding investigative journalists. Hence, the first, early biographies written during his lifetime tended to be uncritical, even fawning and sycophantic; worse, they sometimes treated the Mexican people with condescension, as if they deserved no better than Diaz, as if it took a tyrant to elicit profitable labor from them.

The dearth of significant books on Diaz is surprising but not the historians' urge to focus on his material accomplishments and to ignore the crimes he perpetrated against his people. After all, history is, in the main, a polemic of power—a story of nations that rise and of the nations around them that fall—and thus, it is a narrative written by the victors. In the histories of World War II, for instance, there may be a chapter or two on the Holocaust or the Stalinist labor camps, but such works are primarily about how the war was won or lost. A. J. P. Taylor thought history was largely a story of how, when the balance of power swung too far in one direction, the country that attained too much power would begin to bully its neighbors and then eventually invade them. Taylor believed, like Thucydides, that love of money and lust for power caused most wars. Moral issues in such histories take up relatively few pages. Toynbee's view of history is a rare exception to this axiom. Consequently, many historians have argued that Mexico, before Diaz, was, in the minds of foreign financiers, a hotbed of violence, banditry and anarchy and that no one would invest money in that country. Only because Diaz had pacified and stabilized that previously lawless and chaotic land did investors finally pump huge sums into that nation's infrastructure—into its mining, agriculture, industry, communications and transportations systems.

Hence, many historians argue that Diaz brought Mexico into the twentieth century and that without his foreign investors, Mexico's economy would have stagnated, even deteriorated. These scholars argue that—Diaz's depredations notwithstanding—Mexico became a better place because of those investments and the infrastructure they created. That the Mexican people never profited from those ventures does not enter into that calculus.

Given the extreme excesses of Diaz's atrocities, however, and the violence of the ten-year revolution that they provoked, such arguments on behalf of Diaz's reign will not have much staying power. Furthermore, there are two simple, fundamental criteria by which history can judge the success of Diaz's thirty-year regime: a) how well did his people eat and b) how much did the population grow during his presidency? The Porfiriato had been relatively stable. He should have been able to at least provide his people with sustenance. After all, the Aztecs, under Montezuma, were well fed—better fed than the European peasants of that period—and back then, Mexico had had a population of approximately twenty-five million people. Some estimates suggest over thirty million. Under Diaz, however, the population never topped fifteen million, and yet, unlike Montezuma, he'd had to import his corn and beans in order to keep his people from starving to death. During Diaz's thirty years in office, Mexico's population grew by 50 percent, and only after Diaz was forced from office did the Mexican population surpass that of the Aztecs. In fact, in the seventy-five-year period following Diaz's presidency, Mexico's population grew by 500 percent—six times faster than it had grown under Diaz—and Mexico was once again able to raise enough food to feed its people.

So, while some historians will always genuflect before the altar of power—descanting about the enemies Diaz defeated and his industrialization of Mexico—history must not overlook the radical evil Diaz engendered. The lands he seized and sold abroad, the peasants he enslaved and killed, the courts he corrupted, the political opponents he jailed and the journalists he suppressed—those crimes against humanity should not be forgotten. The harm he did to his citizenry was almost unfathomable in its sheer hideousness and devastation; it will always be historically unforgivable.

The Mexican people have evolved enormously since the days of Diaz and Villa. In the Mexican community, their sense of family loyalty—particularly extended family loyalty—are marvels to behold. In his extraordinary history of Mexico, *Fire and Blood*, T.R. Fehrenbach suggests that the Mexican peoples' calamitous history created their love of family and of extended families. To survive they needed the support of one another, and the most basic societal unit is the family. Under Diaz, family was the most reliable group that a person could turn to for help and support. Family life was, therefore, integral—often indispensable—to one's own survival.

Also despite the many negative features of the Spanish and Mexican machismo, both of the codes exalted courage as the preeminent virtue. Without the courage to go on, there could be no perseverance or even endurance. Lord knows the Mexican people under Diaz—and during their entire five-hundred-year history—have needed all the courage in the world.

Viktor Frankl in his landmark memoir of his experiences in the Nazi camps, *Man's Search for Meaning*, argued that for those living in extremity, loyalty has survival value. At Auschwitz he wrote that only those who systematically helped the fellow prisoners within their own small personal group were more likely to survive than the more selfish, predator prisoners. Solzhenitsyn in the second volume of *The Gulag Archipelago* in the chapter entitled "The Ascent" made the same observation. James Clavell, the author, survived four years in Japanese POW camps, and he stressed the same point.

Ironically, Diaz's attempts to shatter the Mexican people—in order to enrich a relative handful of financial predators and to consolidate and enlarge his own political power—may have only made his people's sense of family...*stronger.*

People sometimes ask me where my interest in that country came from. Initially, it came out of my interest in Mexico's revolutionary spirit and struggles. Mexico seemed to me a very dramatic place in which to set novels.

Then two other people stimulated my interest in that nation. Gary Jennings, the author of the classic novels *Aztec* and *Aztec Autumn*, had admired my writing, and so I was invited to work on the last five novels in his fictional *Aztec* series, bringing his series up into the nineteenth century. To do that, however, I needed to do a staggering amount of research into Mexico's history, going all the way back through the Aztecs and the Mayans. It was a peregrination worthy of Odysseus's *Odyssey.*

Then, as I was beginning that journey, something else happened. I was close to an old woman who was widowed and living by herself in North Hollywood, California. Her small apartment building allowed pets, but the larger neighboring buildings didn't, and the old woman happened to have a grayish thirty-three-pound cat named Timmy. He looked more like a large lion cub than a cat.

Her neighborhood was almost entirely Mexican, and she was one of the very few Anglos living there. Timmy fascinated the innumerable Mexican children in her neighborhood and drew them to him like a lodestone. Among other things, there were almost no other animals around, and they would stare at him as if he was an exotic animal in a zoo. The old woman loved children as well as animals and let them into her apartment so they could play with and pet her cat. After all, he was the only animal available to them, and he was a true prodigy. The children were so nice that she began baking cookies for them and serving them lemonade.

Their Timmy visits became ritualized so that the kids getting out of school could join the group that played with Timmy. Every afternoon at 3:00 PM, children from all over the barrio poured into her apartment.

When the kids' parents found out, they began sending burritos and enchiladas with their children to give to the old woman. When the parents learned she loved their cooking, they invited her to their apartments for dinner. None of the parents spoke English, and most of them had never had an Anglo break bread with them before. The kids translated, and the dinners were so successful that the neighbors began visiting her, dragging their kids along as translators. The old woman had suddenly become a part of an extended Mexican community consisting of hundreds upon hundreds of people.

Unfortunately, the old woman's memory began to go and a lifelong cigarette habit was destroying her lungs. Alzheimer's and emphysema had taken hold. When her son visited her and realized she could no longer take care of herself, he talked to her neighbors, saying that he was confused about what to do. A very young couple who lived next door to the old woman told him not to worry about his mother, that she was nuestra familia, our family, and that they would look after her, keep her clean and feed her. He asked them what would happen if she walked out of her apartment and wandered the streets. The husband said he'd thought of it. He was a journeyman carpenter, and, with the son's permission, he would install a doorbell that would ring in his apartment if the old woman left hers.

Nursing homes can be miserable places for elderly patients with Alzheimer's, since they are aggravating to take care of and are at the same time utterly defenseless. After all, if they are abused, they can't remember it. Emphysema also compounded the Alzheimer's problem. The son didn't want to send his mother to a home and liked the couple next door. He trusted them. When they refused to accept money for their help—on the grounds that the old woman was nuestra familia—he forced it on them with the threat that if they didn't take it, he'd put the old woman in state home.

The husband worked long hours. For a three-year stretch, he worked 110 hours a week, which also required a three-hour drive. He'd be so tired that he'd fall asleep standing up in the shower, but he made enough money to make the down payment on a large home in the same neighborhood. He and his wife told the son that they wanted his mother to move in with them.

She joined them, bringing Timmy and all her furniture. When the son visited, he would meet all of his mother's new extended family. The new house was constantly filled with relatives and close friends and had the greatest food and joy and love that he'd ever seen in his life. He came to believe that his mother was happier there than she'd ever been. He found a doctor and two nurses who made house calls. They always found his mother cheerful and they never found a bedsore. Given the severity of her ailments, the doctor and nurses had believed a full-service nursing home had been inevitable. They told the son he'd performed a miracle.

"It wasn't me," he said simply.

When his mother finally died, he took the young woman who'd taken care of his mother for seven years out for lunch. Driving her back to her house, he tried to give her an envelope filled with four figures in cash since the young woman was now officially out of work. It was his way of saying thanks.

She threw the cash envelope on the car seat and shouted at him:

"Don't you understand...*anything?* It was never about the money!"

Slamming the car door, she stamped off and entered her house without looking back.

They, nonetheless, stayed close friends. They are still close friends.

In case you haven't guessed, the old woman was my mother. I owe her for many things, but not least of all is for introducing me to so many amazing and marvelous Méjicanas y Méjicanos. Mom, I couldn't have written this book without you. You made it possible. So to you and to our magnificent Méjicanas y Méjicanos compadres this book is dedicated.

Tu hijo y amigo con amor...*tiempre.*

About the Author

Robert Gleason (aka Jackson Cain) is a former Executive Editor at Macmillan Publishers in New York City. He has written eighteen books—six of them on nuclear terrorism. He starred in a History Channel two-hour special, which was devoted largely to nuclear terrorism, has appeared on PBS, NPR, *Coast to Coast* AM with George Noory, the Sean Hannity and Lou Dobbs shows, on hundreds of other shows and has spoken four times at Harvard. Mr. Gleason has also worked with inmates in over 60 prisons, and New York has named a day after him for the work he's done for prison literacy. He also succeeded in getting the anti-nuclear activist nun, Sister Megan Rice, released from prison. Here is a clip from his History Channel special https://www.youtube.com/watch?v=JXrlcf_R1KY and also from a recent *Lou Dobbs Tonight* show http://video.foxbusiness.com/v/1034524792001/?#sp=show-clips

His website is at www.RobertGleasonBooks.com.

Kensington Publishing Corp.
Joyce Kaplan
900 Third Avenue, 26th Floor
US-NY, 10022
US
jkaplan@kensingtonbooks.com
212-407-1515

The authorized representative in the EU for product safety and compliance is

eucomply OÜ
Marko Novkovic
Pärnu mnt 139b-14
ECZ, 11317
EE
https://www.eucompliancepartner.com
hello@eucompliancepartner.com
+372 536 865 02

ISBN: 9781496762436
Release ID: 152578809